THE DUCHESS OF ASHERWOOD

Mary A. Garratt

This guy is one of those
bluster growley soft
hearted guy's. Prideful
too. Its also the book
where the ton thinks to
snub them but they sit
in their carrage and where
the ton. • Imagine 500
pages, and the book is only
a couple of months of their lives.

A DELL BOOK

Published by
Dell Publishing Co., Inc.
1 Dag Hammarskjold Plaza
New York, New York 10017

Dell ® TM 681510, Dell Publishing Co., Inc.

ISBN: 0-440-12157-4

Printed in the United States of America
First printing—May 1981

"I CAME TO ASK YOU TO BE MY DUCHESS."

"Sir, you've flown into the alts!"

The duke, having voiced the terrible question, calmed. "No, madam. I am here to request you to be my duchess, and I so do."

"Your wife?" whispered Lenore.

"No, madam—my duchess."

Lenore stared at the duke as the meaning of the words engulfed her. She dropped her eyes and shook her head in confusion. "But if I become your duchess, we would have to marry."

"Yes, you will be the Duchess of Asherwood, so treated by everyone," the duke spoke coldly.

Everyone—except the man standing before her . . . the man she had missed so achingly . . . the man she had so longed to see. . . .

THE
DUCHESS OF
ASHERWOOD

1

Lenore Marie Carey Lanier, the young widow of Captain Eric Lanier, fallen at Bussaco, knelt to weed her small garden, and to dream happily of growing the showiest flowers in England. Intent on her task, she vaguely noted the rumble of horses' hooves in the distance. As they became more insistent she wondered who would travel at such a romp down the narrow lane beyond the high hedge of Willowood. Sitting back on her heels, she saw the head of the equestrian skim the top of the boxwood and shoot into view at a monstrous pace. Suddenly, to her horror, the horse's head reared above the hedge, the rider rose in the air, then plummeted out of sight—the only sound the clopping of the runaway's retreat.

Dear God! Lenore sprang up and ran through the gate, to be met by a frightening spectacle. Sprawled on his back, a lad of perhaps sixteen years, his leg weirdly twisted, blood flowing from his temple, lay motionless. Lenore threw herself beside the boy, thrust her earth-stained hand under his shirt, and thanked the Lord when she felt a heartbeat. Expertly running her fingers along the bent leg, she concluded it was not broken.

"Abel, Abel, come at once," she shouted. Watching the youth until the huge manservant emerged from the house, Lenore attempted to recall her knowledge of nursing. The boy must be disturbed as little as possible. I'll bathe the wound here. Dare we move him?

"God above!" roared the big man as he towered over the inert figure. "What happened?"

"His horse threw him."

"Devil take it! What'll we do, ma'am?"

"Have Maria bring towels, a bowl of water, and an old sheet. Hurry, Abel!"

Waiting, Lenore took heart when the lad groaned. Maria arrived, gave one shriek, then chanted prayers in rapid Spanish as she wrung out swabs, handing them to Lenore, who bathed away the blood and matted hair from the long gash.

The lad, semiconscious, gave no resistance. Her task done, Lenore commanded Abel, "Slide your arm under his shoulder, then the other under his knees. Maria, run ahead and hold open the doors; he is to have my room." The husky man cradled the youth, carried him into the house and up the stairs, and laid the limp figure gently down onto the bed.

"As quickly as you can, Abel, go to the village and find Doctor Sagout." Lenore never took her gaze from the boy's ashen face. Just once he opened his eyes, blue as periwinkles, and as unseeing.

So handsome, thought Lenore. Dear God, do not let him die. After seeming eons, Lenore heard the footfall of the doctor. Easement mingled with impatience as the old man trod the stairs slowly.

When he had gone over the boy from head to toe, the doctor growled, "No bones broken, but he'll be a rainbow of black and blue in the morning. Don't want him moved—going to be a time mending—must stay here." The doctor peered over his glasses. "Ought to have someone with nursing lore."

"I had some training on the Peninsula, Doctor Sagout," Lenore said hastily.

"Humph!" he said, then pointed at the maid, demanding, "And you, what's your name?"

"Maria Theresa Cortez Brown, sir."

"Eddie Brown's widow, eh?"

"*Sí*, sir."

"Well, you stay with me—may need something. Mrs. Lanier, Abel, go away and stand guard. Don't let anyone—I mean a living soul—into this room until I tip you the nod. Boy's got to have quiet, lots of it."

"He's going to recover, isn't he?" Lenore was anxious.

"Said so, didn't I?" snapped the old man; then, relenting, "He'll be right as a trivet, little lady. The duke can thank you for that."

"The duke?" asked Lenore.

"Hoy, don't you recognize the halfling? Heath Hollingsworth, Marquis of Asherwood, the duke's son and heir."

"Good heavens," Lenore said, appalled. "We must get a message to his father at once. Doctor, may Abel take your tilbury? I have no conveyance."

"If he don't smash it with his hulk," the doctor snarled, then snorted, "Go on, take it, man. Now, out of here, you two, and God have mercy on anyone who disturbs the marquis. Out! Out!"

Lenore again urged Abel to make haste, then went to the chamber of Madame Lanier, Captain Eric Lanier's grandmother, to recount the frights of the past hour.

"Young Heath, eh?" exclaimed the old lady. "Was

acquainted with his mother; an empty-headed beauty if ever there was one—a real dasher."

"He has a splendid countenance, poor boy, very blond with blue eyes."

"Takes after his mother, most like. Hope he has more in his cockloft than she does." Giving Lenore a sly glance, she added, "Well, there's been such excitement, I'm quite faint. I prescribe we have a brandy; I could use two myself."

"Farradiddle!" Lenore said, smiling. "However, I am a trifle overset—we'll have a ratafia."

Over the cordials, the Lanier widows chatted about the wherefores of caring for the young invalid.

2

The Duke of Asherwood sat still in the saddle—his striking pose one any sculptor would have deemed it a privilege to cast in bronze; the tall, straight figure; head held high; buckskin taut over broad shoulders; reins bent lightly by tapering fingers; breeches molded to long legs; top boots gleaming; the proud stain-smooth chestnut at one with its rider. The duke regarded his head groom, who covered the last few steps of approach at a run.

"Your Grace," said the stableman, panting, "you must have come across the fields."

The duke dismounted and tossed the reins to the

elderly man. "I did." He leisurely peeled off his gloves. "Zeus is a sweet-going horse, nary a stumble, flew the fences. You've trained him well, Henderson."

"Wouldn't let you ride him if he weren't," muttered the ancient groom to himself as he led the chestnut down the driveway. For a moment the duke stood admiring the latest addition to his large string of prime blood, then mounted the wide steps of his palace to the portico where his valet awaited him.

"A good ride, Your Grace?" he asked, then added mournfully, "The hair is in disarray, sir."

His Grace, whose sartorial correctness was renowned, nevertheless distressed his valet by refusing to wear a hat while riding.

"Clough," said the duke, giving his head a toss, "you are a one-stringed instrument and twang the same note each day."

"It is a flaw in your other gates perfection, sir," remonstrated the valet, whose daring stemmed from long service.

"I do not seek to be a dandy. The time, Clough?"

"On to five, Your Grace." Clough opened the door and followed His Grace into the palace hall. The walls echoed as the duke strode across the marble tiles to his library to indulge in what was called "His Grace's brooding hour." Had the duke been queried—no one had ever made bold to do so—His Grace would have termed this time of twilight "his pondering hour." If anyone had had the temerity to inquire about his thoughts, the duke would have given the presumptuous upstart a severe setdown.

His Grace's appearance proclaimed generations of noble forebears. Many of his ancestors, being wise, had foregone pulchritude or opulence to marry wellborn ladies of good sense, even intelligence. Some of the Duchesses of Asherwood had possessed beauty as a principal asset, some great fortunes, but few had lacked minds of their own.

The duke was well-favored; a wide brow under thick, curly dark hair; eyes that turned blue or green, depending on the light; a secant nose between high cheekbones; mouth and chin, speaking firmness and strength of character.

Upon meeting His Grace, all were struck by his fine features. Only upon further acquaintance did the perception dawn that the duke's face was of stone, for he neither laughed nor smiled. His usually immobile features changed only to scowl or to frown. For this reason he was titled by his villagers and tenants alike, "the Dour Duke." Being unsocial, he had few friends. However, men who had dealings with him declared him honorable. Despite his being a recluse—he seldom left the grounds of his estate—he was very aware of the outside world. His widespread correspondence with scholars and men of affairs was a source of bewildered speculation as to when the duke found time to read the number of books, magazines, and pamphlets arriving each week from London, abroad, and even from America.

The sole visitor of regularity, besides the tradesmen who rejoiced in the duke's expensive taste, was the Reverend David A. Thomas, Vicar of Asherwood, who gave thanks that the duke considered him worthy not only of lending him books newly published, but often of extending an invitation to the palace for dinner—a magnificent meal, followed, over port, by spirited discussions on topics of interest to both.

At first the Reverend Mr. Thomas had guarded his tongue carefully. However, after a few evenings with His Grace, the vicar found he could not only speak bluntly, but was expected to do so. "Don't talk meekly to me, Vicar—you imply I'm a slowtop," ordered the duke. "Say your thoughts, sir; I intend to." The words, uttered with a fearful glower, encouraged the vicar to express his opinions openly. Many exchanges flew between the two men, the duke often making the vicar extremely cross, and once or twice the vicar so far forgot himself as to call the duke a corkbrain. They fought in perfect harmony, frequently until dawn.

Once the vicar had, with exquisite logic, destroyed a theory His Grace had spent hours propounding. The duke, in a blaze of fury, shouted, "Do not forget, sir, you are in my living!" and immediately wished his words back in his throat, for the vicar paled, rose, and left the room.

The following day, the denizens were agape to see the duke galloping, as if chased by demons, through the village to the vicarage. There he leaped off his horse, tied it to the fence, raced to the door, and rapped loudly.

The vicar's wife, Rachel, mother of seven, was in the kitchen, kneading dough, her lone maid tending the children in the back garden when the loud knocking echoed through the house. Rachel wiped her hands, and went to open the front door. "Young Jamie, it is not necessary to bang down our door." She peered down, expecting to see the small boy, then her eyes traveled upward to meet the duke's—and she froze. Seeing the color drain from her still pretty face, the duke bowed. "Madam, I regret startling you, but may I enter and see your husband?"

Mrs. Thomas, now completely unstrung, began to babble about expecting a pupil of the vicar's—Jamie Piper, who is back in his reading—and would His Grace forgive her—and of course he could see her husband—and would he come in, sir—her husband was in his book room—and she would show him right now where the book room was.

The duke accepted the chatter in silence, patiently waiting until she indicated the way. Mrs. Thomas hoped that His Grace would look neither right nor left, for with seven children and only one maid, no room could be kept neat in the small vicarage. When the flustered lady reached the book room, she tapped on the door. To the vicar's "Come in," she stood aside to allow the duke to enter.

The vicar, who was pacing the floor after a sleepless night, wondered when he saw the duke if his own mind had conjured an apparition, so many hours had his thoughts dwelt upon His Grace.

Striding to the still man across the room, the duke blurted out, "Vicar, you are encountering a fool who passed all bounds last night; my apologies, sir." The vicar, aware of the cost of contrition to a man of the duke's inherent pride, held out his hand. "Let us not refine upon it, Duke." Then, casting about for some further means of consoling his friend, he said, "Come, sit down, and let me pour you some brandy."

Seated, the vicar lifted his glass and smiled at the duke. Sipping his brandy, the duke said, "I have been reading Bentham's *Introduction to the Principles of Morals and Legislation*. I find him queer in the attic."

The vicar, who knew a gauntlet when he heard one fall, said, composedly, "Not in all his works, sir," and they were away in healing argument, the duke scowling fiercely, and the vicar at ease.

No mention was ever again made of the quarrel.

Not many days elapsed before the duke's agent, John Endfield, called on the vicar to inform him that, should he choose to move, the larger house across the square would be ready within the sennight, and—much to the vicar's joy—his living was to be doubled.

Mrs. Thomas, upon learning of the unexpected largess, cried every time she contemplated their good fortune, and vowed to make a Christmas pudding worthy of even the dear duke's exacting palate.

The vicar searched for phrases to express his gratitude. However, when next he dined at the palace, he sensed that a single syllable of thanks would be out of place; during dinner he merely let drop a glancing reference to his Rachel's pleasure and his children's improved behavior in their new surroundings.

3

The duke's vast holdings were under the supervision of John Endfield, who dealt with the tenants and farmers with firm justice, and was highly esteemed throughout the county. The large palace household ran smoothly, overseen by Mr. and Mrs. Clough, persons of extraordinary competence. Mr. Pettibone, the duke's London solicitor, tended the duke's affairs with dry prudence. All were well rewarded.

Though the duke had no penchant for racing or hunting, his string of horses was known far and wide as "a bang-up set of blood and bone." The stables and all entailed therein were ruled by the irascible Mr. Henry Henderson, to whom even the duke spoke softly and tolerated because of his awesome mastery of horses and their care and breeding. The groom loudly proclaimed his fondness for no man or female. The villagers called him 'Orrendous 'Enry and avoided him whenever possible, which suited Henderson perfectly. However, there was a crack in his armor of dislike in the person of the duke's heir, Heath, Marquis of Asherwood.

The day the duke led the small tot of four to the stableyard and ordered him to be taught to ride, the sour groom scrutinized the sturdy tad gazing up at him with a timid smile, and was lost.

Though no one dared to hint at his weakness, everyone soon knew the marquis had 'Orrendous 'Enry wound tight around his tiny thumb. Henderson had chosen a gentle mare for the lad's first adventure on horseback and was seen many hours holding the boy as the animal paced back and forth—his patience endless. It was not long before Heath was riding with good, even hands, and, reaching his teens, was a young whip roaring over the countryside. Nor did Henderson neglect the boy's handling of ribbons. Heath soon drove to the inch.

The duke took little notice of his son's progress, for he had paid slight attention to the boy after the first years of childhood. The villagers, watching the lad grow into a "sweet young gentleman," shook their heads at the duke's aloofness. Not being privy to His Grace's introspection, they did not comprehend that his "brooding hour" was spent in reliving the reason for his disregard.

The duke frequently began his pondering by conceding his own youthful mistake—running off to Gretna Green with a young girl barely out of the schoolroom, and he just turned eighteen—but then he would quickly excuse himself. In London that night at Almack's, when he was presented to Miss Harriet Featherheath, who was so dazzlingly beautiful, his heart had fallen at her feet. Not surprisingly, for the *haut ton* itself had been rocked by her loveliness.

Miss Featherheath was as exquisite as a butterfly. That she was also equipped with the waspiness of a bee, and a head empty as a gourd, the duke did not know. Addled by love, he had swept her off to Gretna Green. Miss Featherheath, to be sure, was the one who had insisted on an elopement; not only was the idea romantic beyond belief, but her parents, though of an old and honored family, were of limited wealth and faced the burden of introducing five other daughters into society, and she knew she could not request of them the kind of wedding the *ton* would expect of the bride of a duke.

The impulsive elopement soon proved a deterrent to the young couple's happiness. London, however, thoroughly enjoyed the nine-day wonder; it made the social season extraordinarily jocund. Delicious tidbits of gossip replaced small talk—everyone had something to say about the affair that was obviously delicious to the listener. Smirks and giggles abounded; titillating comments ran rife, young girls were sent from earshot so their mamas could exchange nuggets of on-dit; but the ranks were closed against the young couple, who had taken residence in the duke's palatial home in Grosvenor Square.

The duke and duchess, in innocence, sent cards for a large reception, but only the family of the duchess, those deeply indebted to the duke, and a few rakes—one even having the boldness to bring his current bit of muslin—came; all left early.

The duchess, in hysterics, had railed at the duke,

who, within the week, moved his household to Asherwood, where the duchess could reign over the county and where her parties were well attended. In this setting no one could afford to offend the duke.

Settling down to her new life of abundance, Miss Featherheath saw that her sisters were amply supplied financially from the duke's coffers. In return for allowing this largess, the duke was permitted the privacy of his own library, where he found refuge from his lady's unending chatter.

Soon after the elopement, in the clear light of closer acquaintance, the duke saw and admitted to himself that he had married what his friend Wrenham had warned—a peahen. That his love for her endured was surely due largely to his freedom to closet himself in the library at will. The hours spent among his books increased the duke's interest not only in the books themselves but also in acquiring a comprehensive grasp of his vast holdings. To his amazement he found, with Mr. Endfield's help, the intricacies of running the estate challenging and rewarding. He developed a flair for making the propitious move at the auspicious moment, and by selling and buying property and investing the profits, he grew, in time, to be enormously wealthy.

When the duchess announced that she was to have a child, the duke, overjoyed, and well able to squander, showered her with jewels and endured her complaining natter with patience.

In brooding over the past, the duke remembered the years subsequent to his son's birth as a time of contentment but also of confusion. The boy, christened Heath Hollingworth, enthralled him. Over the years the hours with first the baby, then the toddler, and finally the small boy, brought him amusement and joy beyond measure.

During this time the duchess, her beauty undiminished, placid and restless by turns—her moods unpredictable—baffled the duke. He longed for another child, as a factor of contentment.

In the meantime Heath was growing fast. On his eighth birthday the duke determined a tutor be introduced into the household to prepare the boy for Eton. On the duchess's suggestion, her father, who had wide acquaintance with men of letters, was consulted. A note to Mr. Featherheath brought a response recommending a Mr. Julian Sanford, not long down from Oxford, who had tutored the Earl of Windham's sons until they reached school age, when his services were no longer required. Enclosed was a letter of commendation from the earl, praising Mr. Sanford in great style. The duke invited him to Asherwood.

Under close questioning, Mr. Sanford appeared remarkably well-equipped to further Heath in his studies. The duke thought Sanford a bit of town tulip, but home to a peg about horses. The duchess admired his address, and when Heath declared Mr. Sanford to his liking, the matter was settled.

Mr. Sanford was soon well entrenched; Heath enjoyed his lively presentation of lessons and his skilled instruction in handling a horse. The duke found him a worthy chess player and a lively conversationalist. The duchess secured in him an excellent listener who responded to her silliest questions with courtesy. She decided to join Heath in the schoolroom and told the duke she had never known the perusal of books to be so entertaining.

The only person unhappy about Mr. Sanford—

whose manner to the servants was pleasantly correct—
was Henderson, who, everyone knew, was jealous of
the tutor's handling of ribbons.

"He's a Bond Street fripple, Your Grace. You listen
to me, he'll do no good to ye; he's a care for nobodies
and wild to a fault, more like than not." The duke
had laughed and agreed the tutor did tend to sport a
figure, but did not Henderson think him a top saw-
yer?

"He's a deep rum touch, and you watch out for his
flimflams, Your Grace." Mr. Henderson spit and mum-
bled about "nodcocks who were easily shumguzzled."

The duke always swore as he recalled what a blind
fool he had been—a bubble-headed gapeseed—then
would relive the infamous day of his return from a
trip to London to find Clough, white-faced and shak-
en, standing on the portico.

"What is it?" shouted the duke as he jumped from
his carriage. The henchman, too frightened to speak,
handed the duke a note. The duke strode to the library, and without removing his greatcoat, tore open
the envelope to read the missive that changed his
life.

It has come at last—true love—and I must follow my heart. Mr. Sanford has inherited a large
fortune from his uncle, so you need not fear for
my well-being.

Being with you, Heath will not suffer, and I
am so happy.

Good-bye . . .

Harriet had signed the note to her husband "Hat,"
his nickname for her, as though it were a casual message on some trivial change of plans. Slowly he re-

moved his coat, then poured himself a deep drink, the first of many. He reread the note twice, then ripped it to shreds and threw it onto the burning logs. He did not leave the library, and proceeded to drink himself into a stupor.

Clough, after hours of straining to hear the master's ring, ventured to the door, opened it a crack, and peered in. The duke, sprawled in his chair, drink in hand, was staring into space.

"Your Grace," Clough murmured.

"Take my coat and get out!"

"Yes, Your Grace, can I bring—"

"Get *out!*" shouted the duke.

Clough fled.

For the next three days the duke shut himself in the library, ringing for a footman when he wanted another bottle. Clough brought food, but it was barely touched; each day followed the same pattern—alternate drinking and insensibility.

At the end of three days, disheveled, sunk in spirit, the duke permitted Clough to restore him to a semblance of his normal elegance. After a solitary dinner, the duke, weary of his library, went to sit by the small fireplace in his bedroom.

At first his thoughts moved in circles, but gradually he accepted the truth—his wife had run away with another man and he would never see her again. The conviction infuriated and saddened him in turn.

That she should abandon their son and forego being the Duchess of Asherwood for a mere tutor, no matter how handsome and rich, caused the duke to swear and pace the floor, only to throw himself in his chair and bury his head in his hands as he realized he could never again smother her chatter with kisses.

A sudden rage shook him. At eighteen I wed her,

sheltered her from the cruelties of London, indulged her whims, and settled into a sedate husband and father—Good God, she fashioned me into an old man! He sprang from his chair, picked up a hand mirror, and studied his reflection. An old man! But I'm not! I'm a young man deprived of my youth—no!—a fool who sacrificed ten years for the love of—a peahen! He peered closely into the glass. Hoy—I'm not an ancient —his eyes narrowed—by the devil, I'm handsomer than Sanford! But she chose him. The Duchess of Asherwood ran off . . . the Duchess of Asherwood—Oh no, Hat, you can't be Sanford's fancy piece and the Duchess of Asherwood. The duke paused—Divorce!—then flinched. But his eyes grew cold—I'll divorce you, Hat!

The duke yanked the bell rope, and when Clough entered, said, "Clough, pack my bags; I'm going to London tomorrow."

"Yes, Your Grace. For how long, sir?"

"I'm not certain, but two changes will do."

"What about Master Heath, Your Grace?"

"Nothing, Clough. Get out." The duke's eyes glittered dangerously.

"But, sir . . . ?"

"*Out!*" The duke flung the mirror at his valet, who retreated hastily. The glass shattered into jagged pieces.

Before dawn the next morning, the duke drove himself to London, saying good-bye to no one. In London, at great cost, the duke obtained a divorce from Harriet Featherheath, Duchess of Asherwood.

When her father, Mr. Featherheath, read the announcement in *The Gazette,* he tried at once to reach the duke, only to learn His Grace had sailed for France.

The duke did not set foot in England for three

years. What little news trickled back from abroad proclaimed that he was living the life of an out-and-out rake, running mad through the capitals of Europe. His carte blanche legion, he was never seen without a light skirt, and more often two, one on each arm. Once again schoolgirls were sent from rooms while their mothers discussed the latest scandal about the duke.

4

During the duke's absence, Mr. Pettibone and Mr. Endfield administered the duke's vast estate—a heavy responsibility, for neither received a direct communication from His Grace.

Wisely they left to Mr. and Mrs. Clough the bringing up of young Heath, who, under their mixture of indulgence and discipline, grew into a lively lad, well-loved by members of the household and villagers alike.

Tales of " 'Ow I dodged that damn young whip's horse tearing through the square—'Orrendous 'Enry's nag on 'is 'eels," bestowed singular prestige on those fortunate to be thus threatened. Old Tom Doone claimed the longest tally, but everyone knew what a liar he was.

When both his mother and father vanished from his life, Heath, unable to sort out the endless chatter about their disappearance, asked if his mother would be coming home. On being firmly told "No, she will not," he assumed her dead, and never spoke of her again. However, answers concerning his father's return by their convolutions gave him hope, though it waxed tenuous as the years passed.

The duke's homecoming proved as abrupt as his departure.

Had not Mrs. Clough by chance spied the curricle and paired grays spanking up the driveway and quickly spread the news throughout the palace, the Duke of Asherwood would have had to knock on his own door.

Heath, responding to the footman's announcement, raced to the portico and lunged at his father in joy. The duke gazed down at his son's eager, upturned face, so like his mother's, then frowned. "Out of my sight, you young cawker!" Brushing the stunned boy aside, he entered the hall and stalked to the library, calling back, "Clough, come with me."

Heath, crushed by the rebuff, burst into tears. Mrs. Clough gathered the boy in her arms to comfort him. Henderson swore softly, then said aloud, "Enow tears, Master Heath. Foxfire needs a run— shall we take him over the fields?"—an invitation well calculated to restore his idol's good temper, for never before had he been allowed to mount the frisky two-year-old.

Although the duke resumed his life as the master of Asherwood, he left his heir to the ministrations of the Cloughs and withdrew into himself, remote and fiery of temper.

He had been in residence only a short time when Clough brought to his attention the desirability of finding another tutor. "Your Grace, Master Heath has shown a fondness for books, reading many taken from your shelves, but now he needs guidance—a teacher."

The duke, angered, roared that never would he have an educator in the palace again, and as far as he was pothered, the boy could be ignorant as a goat.

Clough, who with his wife had been parents to the boy for three years, was ready for this. He announced quietly, "In that case, Mrs. Clough and I will seek positions elsewhere."

Shaken, the duke conceded to reconsider, provided a suitable man be found.

Clough, who had already consulted Mr. Pettibone, suggested the name of the Reverend David A. Thomas, a family man, father of seven, well praised in the next county for his excellent mind and good offices, then added, "The village parish has been without a vicar for two years, Your Grace. Perhaps you might contemplate Mr. Thomas filling both posts."

"Get him," shouted the duke, "and trouble me no more about it."

"As soon as possible, sir." Clough bowed and left.

Over the years Heath neither avoided his father nor sought his company. The duke's few words addressed to him took the form of sneers or scolds. As he grew older Heath came to disregard or laugh at them.

The duke, though seldom in his presence, took note of his heir from afar. As he brooded he often asked himself what there was about the boy that rankled. Once in a while he admitted the truth— Heath had the countenance of his mother. Harriet's features, one by one, were translated into her son's rugged handsomeness. The duke usually greeted this explanation, when it occurred to him, with instant dismissal. His displeasure stemmed from his son's many faults—his too-ready smile, his tendency to ignore advice, his reckless riding over the countryside—a variety of misdeeds. The counting of flaws regularly culminated in the duke's springing up to search out his son to admonish him for some wrong.

What slightly astonished His Grace was the frequency with which Heath would disappear on a distant vital errand, sent by a member of the household just minutes before his inquiry as to the boy's whereabouts.

5

Today the duke had clasped the arms of his chair, preparing to rise, when the library door opened and Clough walked in without knocking—an unheard-of presumption. Never had the duke been interrupted during his pondering hour.

"What the—" started the duke.

"Your Grace"—his voice bespoke his agitation—"a man has just arrived to tell us that Master Heath has been thrown from his horse and lies hurt in Sir Alfred Lanier's house."

The duke's heart jumped. "The devil you say. What has the greenhead done now?"

"Mrs. Clough and I will go to him, sir." Clough turned to leave.

"Come back here!" roared the duke. "Have Henderson bring the coach immediately. You may follow in the tilbury."

"As you say, sir." Then, because he could not help himself, he added, "May God take care of the boy until we get there." Clough skittered from the room.

When the coach was at the door, the duke ordered the ashen groom, who needed no prompting, to hurry. The duke, filled with impatience as Henderson sped down the longest driveway in England, yelled, "Move, you snail, move!"

"Damme, I'm pushing these nags as fast as they can go."

Finally the carriage shot through the massive gates and tore along the country road, jogging the duke up and down as the wheels hit ruts and stones. The mile to Willowood seemed endless. When the horses slowed, the duke leaped from the coach, flung open the gate, and raced up the walk to the front door, which opened before he could bang his upraised fist against it. In front of him loomed a mountain of a man, who immediately stood aside to give entrance.

"Where is he? Where is my son? Take me to him instantly!" thundered the duke.

"Not quite yet, Your Grace," came a voice, cool as summer rain, from the stairway.

The duke, blinded by the sunlight, peered into the darkness of the hall, then stepped forward. "Why the devil not?"

"Your son is in need of absolute quiet."

"I'll be quiet!" shouted the duke. "Now take me to him!"

"No!" The word struck the duke like a thrown

stone. Then he saw Lenore, slim, auburn-haired, her face friendly but firm. He did not notice that she was extraordinarily beautiful.

The duke, who had never in his memory had any one say no to him, grew red in anger. "Madam, the boy upstairs is my son, and I'm damned if I am going to let him die and I not be with him."

"Your son is not going to die"—her tone was soothing—"unless you go against the doctor's orders and overset the lad with your bellows. The doctor is with him now."

"He can't do that; he is my only child," said the duke, throwing logic to the winds.

"Your Grace, come with me. I will explain the circumstances." Lenore took a step toward an open doorway.

"Dammit, madam, my son lies dying and I should be at his side." The duke started for the staircase.

"Abel!" Lenore commanded sharply.

Before the duke could reach the first tread, the huge man blocked his way.

"No, Your Grace." The big man stood like a rock. "Be so good as to join Mrs. Lanier."

The duke glared and stormed, "Dammit, head off, you!"

"Bunky! Come in here!" cackled a high, cracked voice from the morning room.

The duke froze as if run through by a rapier. With a startled glance at Abel, he wheeled and moved stiffly through the doorway, paused, then shut the door. His eyes flew to a crumpled female wrapped in shawls, seated by the fireplace. Mesmerized, he approached and bent and kissed her extended hand.

"Madame, this is a notable surprise," said the duke testily as he straightened.

"Thought I was booked, eh?" snorted Madame Lanier. "Well, I ain't. Now stand back and let me look at you. Hmm, better shaped than your father, but just as stiff and starchy."

"Madame—my son," pleaded the duke.

"Your lad's going to be fit as a fiddle. The doctor told Lenore so. Now sit down."

The duke glowered.

"Do as you're told, Bunky," ordered the old lady fiercely.

Out of sheer habit left over from his childhood, the duke did seat himself in a shabby chair, surprisingly comfortable. He gazed at the old lady in horrible recollection. Since babyhood he had been in awe of the aged one—grandmother of his boyhood playmates Alfred and Eric Lanier. He had not felt afraid of her exactly, for she had done no more than look upon her grandsons and himself with tolerant scorn, but her regal bearing and elegant manner had kept the three boys in a state of wary respect.

Vividly he relived the day when he and her grandsons, hardly old enough to walk, had come to cuffs. A footman had snatched him by the collar just as Madame Lanier rounded the side of the house. Not seeing her, he had struggled to get free and continue the row.

"What is this, William?" the queenly lady asked.

"Nothing serious, madame, a bit of a mill, and this one's still spunky." With a slight shake, the footman set the boy on his feet.

Overjoyed at the new word, he had crowed, "I'm bunky, I'm bunky," strutting in front of his playmates.

"Enough, young Bunky, no more fratching," decreed Madame Lanier. She had called him Bunky ever since. The duke was gratified that she alone used the name. Alfred and Eric had refrained because at first they were barely able to talk. Later, threats of cracking their heads together if they dared use the appellation had held them still.

Staring at the old lady, the duke again lived through the winces he had endured at her fondness for the hated nickname.

Misreading his silence, the old lady spoke. "So, you find me aged and ugly, don't you? Dwindling into the grave."

Pushing memory away, the duke responded, "No, madame, but I am surprised to encounter you here, for you vowed no one would see you away from London this side of heaven."

Madame Lanier snorted, "And you wouldn't if that nose-led Alfred had not allowed his nipsqueeze wife, Martha, to close the town house and oust me here." Mimicking her daughter-in-law's whine, she intoned, "Alfred, Willowood has always been reserved for widows of the family; now that you have two to frank, they should live together there." Reverting to her own voice, she added, "That's Eric's widow you came to points with out there. Cool one, ain't she?"

"Eric's widow? I'd heard he was shot while on the Peninsula, but I had no idea he had wed."

"If you didn't shut yourself up like an oyster, you'd have known he married before going to the Penn," she chortled. "Made Alfred and Martha mad as fire."

"Why? Is she not a lady?"

"Don't be a lobcock. Of course she is—no grandson of mine would be tenanted for life to a female not a lady. She was the daughter of a vicar in Kent—Lawrence Carey, younger son of the Will Careys', an outstanding family, but without a feather to fly with.

Sent his daughter to Lady Letitia Ware's for a season in London. Eric met her at Almack's; threw his handkerchief the instant he saw her. Alfred and Martha were furious—wanted him to dangle after a rich wife—but marry Lenore he did, and they were happy until he was shot, leaving her only a bundle of debts. Eric was a gamester." The old lady giggled. "Took that right from his grandfather. I resided in Dun territory most of my married days. Beau Lanier was a ramshackle court card—winning pence one day, losing pounds the next—and a dapper dog, too. Great one for muslin company. Did I ever tell you what I did to one of his light skirts?"

Before she could embark on what the duke felt sure would be an outrageous story, there came a rap on the door and Lenore entered carrying a tray.

"Don't tell me you have come to put me to bed, missy," snarled the old lady. "I won't go!"

"No, indeed, Mamère, it would be most uncivil, for you have a guest. I've brought brandy. I suspect His Grace needs some and you must join him." She poured a full glass for the duke and filled the other to the half mark.

"Good!" chortled the old lady, "but I'll have it to the top, missy'"

"No," contradicted Lenore in a level tone, "I have no time to spend caring for you through the night."

"Saucebox!" exclaimed Madame Lanier. "Bunky, this is Eric's wife, Lenore Lanier."

The duke, who had risen, bowed and took the proffered glass. "Madam, is there any news concerning my son?"

Lenore smiled. "The doctor says he is resting in comfort, but must be watched for the nonce. The doctor will come down to see you later."

"Thank you, Mrs. Lanier."

"Mamère, you have ten minutes, then I'll return to put you to bed."

"Won't go!" growled the old lady.

"Yes, you will, darling . . ." Lenore said, pausing. "Then maybe the duke and I can have a rubber of piquet while we await Doctor Sagout."

"You're a wicked gel!" proclaimed her grandmother-in-law fondly.

"Indeed so," said Lenore, then with a nod to the duke, she left the room.

"Needle-witted, that one," said Madame Lanier, chuckling. "Now tell me, Bunky, why such a niff-naff man as yourself has buried your bones in Asherwood."

The duke replied in icy tones, "You know my past, madame."

" 'Course! All London heard how you cut a dash all over Europe," she snickered. "A devil of a rake and a complete—"

"Madame," asked the infuriated duke, "must we talk on it?"

"Yes, I want to hear about your orgies. It's a dead bore living here and—"

"Madame," the duke interrupted, "I'd forgotten what a lover of on-dit you are, even dead gossip."

"Quite right, Bunky. What else have I?"

The sad truth of her words broke the duke's wrath. "There is too little time tonight to recount my wickednesses, but some day I will shock you to your delighted toes."

"Famous, Bunky, famous." She fell silent, then began to nod off.

Shortly Lenore entered, accompanied by Abel, who lifted the old lady without waking her and left.

"I will be back," said Lenore as she closed the door.

Alone, the duke, confused and miserable, paced the floor. He welcomed Lenore's return.

"Your Grace, do sit down and allow me to tell you about Heath."

Angered again, the duke said, "Mrs. Lanier, it is an indignity not to permit me to see him."

"Sir, I realize you are undone by the events of this evening, however, the doctor assures me you need not have such deep worry for your beloved son."

Astonished by the words "your beloved son," the duke could think of nothing to say.

"More brandy, Duke?"

"No!" the duke refused shortly.

"Then please let me relate to you what took place."

The duke stood for a moment, then reluctantly seated himself opposite Lenore. She's beautiful, sprang into the duke's mind.

"Heath was riding past Willowood on his way home —I presume—when something frightened his horse, who reared and jumped sidewise, tossing Heath into the grass at the edge of the lane."

"Not holding the reins tight, the young zany," growled the duke.

"Perhaps not, but I surmise it to be the snake Abel later found dead that spooked the horse. Be that as it may, sir, what signifies is that Doctor Sagout is convinced the boy will be well recovered in a short time."

"How long?"

"I can't say for a certainty, but . . ."

The sound of wheels gave her pause.

The duke rose. "That will be Mr. and Mrs. Clough of my household, and, Mrs. Lanier, if you believe me difficult to restrain, you will discover the Cloughs formidable foes."

"Then you square up to them, please, Duke," said Lenore, rising and going into the hall.

The duke followed and undertook the task of calming the overexcited Cloughs—not very successfully—until Abel, with great aplomb, invited the couple to "adjourn to my domain for a light repast." After much fuss, the Cloughs were persuaded, but not before Henderson was beckoned in to join them.

"My apologies, madam, for this onslaught," said the duke when they were again seated in the morning room.

"Understandable, your Grace."

They stared into the fire. Suddenly Lenore broke the silence. "Eric spoke fondly of you when we discussed his childhood; told me how jolly a lad you were."

"I'm sorry, for your sake, the captain died."

"It is sad—he was a brave soldier." Lenore sighed. "It's been one long year since."

"You have been in Willowood all this time?" asked the duke in surprise.

"Oh, no. Upon my return to England, I lived in London for some months until Alfred offered this house for Madame Lanier's and my residence."

"Very generous," commented the duke dryly.

With a faint smile, Lenore said, "Do let us converse about Heath; he is so handsome and appears a fine young man—you must adore him."

The duke scowled at her. "Madam, that is where you are out. 'Adore' my son? I don't even like him."

"Farradiddle," said Lenore, laughing, "you love him dearly."

The duke, so furious that had she been a man he would have called him out, sought phrases to snub her.

"Madame, I have heard there are those who read minds, but I am sure Eric Lanier would not have married such an oddity. He was known far and wide for throwing his handkerchief for ladies of beauty— happily lacking brains."

Lenore giggled. "It won't make a scrap of difference what you say, you love your son deeply. Ha, maybe you are a nodcock who does not admit the truth even to himself."

The enraged duke glared at the smiling Lenore, her words ringing in his ear. Suddenly he blushed, a dark crimson rising from his neckcloth to his brow.

"Stupid," drawled Lenore kindly, then stood up. "Come, we may have a long wait—a rubber of piquet?"

The duke, confused by self-recognition, his temper barely reined, said flatly, "Play piquet with a female— never! Ladies know nothing about the game."

"I do—Eric taught me. We spent many an hour at piquet." Lenore placed the table and cards.

"I never play unless there are wagers." The duke sought to frighten her.

"Naturally not. A game for no stakes would be a dead bore."

"High stakes!" growled the duke.

"What do you suggest?" Lenore shuffled the cards.

The duke named a figure double his usual hazard.

"Quite right. That sum I cannot match, but halve it and you may cut for deal."

The only alternative being to sit and stare at the fire, the duke took his place and picked up the cards.

At first, his thoughts thready, the duke played care-lessly, but shortly became aware he gamed with a lady capable of giving his pride in his ability a smart setdown. By concentration, he retrieved some of his losses and, to his surprise, enjoyed the battle of wits.

Hearing footsteps descending the stairs, the duke sprang to the door to admit Doctor Sagout.

"Ah, Your Grace, this is a most fortunate night for you. The marquis, with care, is going to be plucked up in no time."

"Praise God!" cried Lenore and burst into tears.

The duke stared at her in astonishment—the lady who, cool as ice, had played a master game of piquet, was now crying like a schoolgirl.

"Well, Duke?" said the doctor, scowling upon Lenore's tears in high disapproval.

"Doctor, my thanks, sir. When may I see the boy?"

"Not tonight; he's asleep."

"Then when can I take him home?"

"The day I so inform you, Your Grace," the doctor said impatiently. "Meanwhile have Mrs. Clough come to help nurse him; the Cloughs have been parents to him for years." The doctor gave the duke a reproving frown.

"Mrs. Clough, of course," said Lenore with a slight sob. "The Cloughs are here, Doctor. I'll call them." She left on her errand.

The duke, fearing the doctor might not reveal a serious complication in front of Mrs. Lanier, asked, "Heath is truly all right?"

"Stop nattering," snapped the doctor. "I said so, didn't I? I'm going now. The Jameses may have their twelfth any minute and I've need of sleep. Think females would have something better to do than have babies."

"Take my coach, Doctor; Henderson can follow in your tilbury," offered the duke.

"Drive your cattle? Never! With me, old Sue's more reliable. 'Night, Duke."

They walked into the hall and the doctor looked

around for Lenore. "Say good night to Mrs. Lanier. She's a beauty right and tight—if there wasn't a Mrs. Sagout . . ." The doctor sighed. "But there is. Well, good night again. Oh, yes—might give Mrs. Lanier a nod of thanks, Duke. No question she saved the boy's life."

Closing the door behind the doctor, the duke heard voices and waited for the Cloughs and Henderson as they returned to the hall.

On seeing the duke, Mrs. Clough rushed to him and broke into great sobs. "Oh, Your Grace, I'm so happy. I'll take care of Master Heath as if he were my own." She swung to her husband. "Mr. Clough, you get the basket I brought, then go ride with Mr. Henderson and cozen things at home. Remember, His Grace likes his eggs cooked three minutes—no more, no less—and for nuncheon you make—"

Lenore put her arm around the chattering woman. "Mrs. Clough, it will most undoubtedly be difficult, but I am persuaded His Grace, with the aid of Mr. Clough, will be able to rub along without you in this emergency. Let me show you to your room, and please stop crying. Heath must not see a trace of weeping—he is only used to your beaming smile."

"Oh, yes, yes, yes." Mrs. Clough gave a great gulp.

Addressing the duke, Lenore said, "Your Grace, come my way for nuncheon tomorrow; you'll be a most welcome sight for your beloved Heath." She extended her hand, then, when the duke bowed over it, added, "And bring the gold you owe me."

The duke raised his head and gave her such a ferocious frown that the Cloughs and Henderson caught their breath in expectation of a thunderclap. The three gaped when the duke responded in a calm voice, "Keep watch and ward over my adored son, madam," then turning, said, "Don't stand there at half cock, Clough. Henderson, bestir yourself and drive home slowly. Good night."

In the carriage the duke tried to sort out his thoughts. He had been worried, angry, distraught, harassed, then laughed at—it was outside of enough! Dammit, how dare that female tell him he loved his son? And how dare she be right!?

At the palace he ordered Henderson to have the phaeton ready at all times, and to bring his own carriage midmorning. Clough, going with his master to the library, inquired the duke's preference as to where he would dine.

"A cold supper here," replied the duke.

When Clough arrived bearing a tray of mutton, lobster, savory biscuits, and fruit, he found the duke pacing.

"Your Grace," the valet spoke softly while he placed the tray by the duke's favorite chair, "I feel most convinced Master Heath will recover shortly. He is young and—"

"Go away, Clough—no, wait." The duke scowled as they faced each other.

"Yes, Your Grace?"

"Do you think . . . ?" The duke paused. "Are you under the impression . . . ? Dammit, Clough, do you believe I am—er—fond of my son?"

"Very, Your Grace," riposted Clough.

"What in all that's holy leads you to that fustian?" Clough hesitated.

"Speak up, man!" the duke said, glaring.

"Your Grace, you have given Master Heath every advantage—a splendid education, the best training in the handling of horses, everything required to bring him up the true gentlemen he is."

"Would have done the same for any stray who came under my care." The duke dismissed the whole idea.

"Yes, sir."

"Well, Clough?"

"What you said is true, Your Grace, but you wouldn't have watched the stray's every move."

"I did not!" roared the duke.

Clough let a slow grin spread over his face.

"Yes—well, what I observed, I disapproved," said the duke.

"No, your Grace, you pretended to find him wanting," Clough said, with sudden boldness. "You try to discover every fault you can in the boy, but it does not signify. Your delight in Master Heath, if I may say so, shows through at every turn."

The duke stared at Clough in stupefaction. "Is he aware of this?"

"Yes, Your Grace, he is," Clough said evenly, "and he holds you in topmost esteem and affection."

"Good God!" The duke, his brain in a tumult, went to the window. He had always recognized Heath as polite and respectful, but that his son might have the slightest feeling of regard for him had never seemed possible—too harsh and cold had been his dealings with the boy. He gazed blindly on the garden.

"Your Grace," Clough urged gently, "it is late and you must be hungry; come and have your supper."

The duke wheeled. "Don't speak to me as if I were Heath—get out of here."

Clough backed away hastily. "Good night, sir." The duke was uncertain whether he heard a faint chuckle as his valet closed the door. Going to the tray, the duke lifted the silver cover, started to slam it down, but realized he was hungry, and proceeded to eat unseeing, his thoughts in a whirl. Supper finished, he threw himself on the couch, determined to evaluate the day's happenings. But instead he fell asleep.

Unaware of Clough's coming and covering him, the duke slept the night.

6

Heath, beloved Marquis of Asherwood, lay drifting in and out of consciousness. Once he perceived the figure of Mrs. Clough, which reassured him; more than once he dimly saw an unknown lady; and later thought he beheld a man of great size.

When daylight came, he opened his eyes in total awareness and gazed around the strange yellow and white room. Moving his head, he made out the outlines of Mrs. Clough. As he stared she rose and came to the bedside, then, to his amazement, lifted his hand, pressed it to her lips, and kissed it three times.

"Oh, Master Heath, thank God, you are going to be well and strong." Tears streamed down her face.

Heath, having no recollection of his accident, asked, "Why not?" But speaking triggered a sharp pain in his head, and he closed his eyes.

Mrs. Clough, horrified, cried, "Oh, my poor darling, my poor dear lad. . . ."

Heath managed to whisper, "What happened?"

Vaguely he gathered from Mrs. Clough's stream of chatter that he had been thrown from his horse. This news so dumbfounded him that he fell asleep. Later he woke to see the unknown lady of his fitful dreams regarding him. She said most cheerfully, "Ah, you're better, much better. Your father will be delighted; he is so desperately worried. I'm overjoyed that I can deliver him such good news."

Heath, startled by the idea of his father harboring even a fleeting disquietude, stared at the beautiful lady, who put a soft hand on his cheek and said, "Best sleep now." Heath obeyed.

When next the boy woke, he kept his eyelids lowered and tried to untangle the astonishment of the previous afternoon and night. He had been tossed by Clover, brought to a strange house, Mrs. Clough was here, and he could assume the lady with the soothing voice to be his hostess. The big man's presence puzzled him. It was all so confusing. . . . He slept.

At the same time, at the palace, Clough, carrying a tray, knocked on the library door to be greeted by a howl of rage.

"Get in here, Clough!"

Clough braced himself for the tirade—swift in its coming—and listened quietly as his sins and crimes were enumerated, ranging from why had he not roused the duke the night before so he could go to bed, through a long list of misdeeds—many heard before—to where the hell was the duke's breakfast?

Clough placed the tea tray on the desk and left.

The duke, slightly assuaged by his tea and toast, went to his dressing room to bathe. In the bedchamber, Clough selected neckcloths in a studious manner. Allowing his valet to assist in his dress, the duke refused the first five neckcloths offered. Clough, with patience, presented the sixth—one for which the duke had a special fondness. Feeling his valet had been put down enough, the duke condescended to let Clough tie a perfect Oriental.

The duke stepped onto the portico just as Henderson swung the carriage up the driveway. The duke, now mellowed, asked Clough if he had any messages for Mrs. Clough.

"Tell her, sir, everything goes in the usual manner here," the valet said blandly, then raced on, "and wish Master Heath soon to be plucked up—oh, yes—assure him, sir, he can rest easy about his rabbits."

"Humph," said the duke, deciding to overlook Clough's thrust.

At Willowood's gate Henderson, helping the duke alight, said, "Say to the young whip that after he ended up in the whisendine, his horse had the good sense to gallop home and is stout as she ever was."

"I will, provided I'm allowed to see him," replied the duke darkly.

"Well, have someone else pass my words on then," ordered Henderson tartly.

Abel opened the door. "Welcome, Your Grace. I've great pleasure to report your son is much improved. Mrs. Lanier says you are to go straight upstairs—his room is on the right."

The duke nodded and took the stairs two at a time.

"Father!" called a weak voice from the bed. "It's bang-up good of you to come." The duke surveyed his son's white face, surmounted by a wide head bandage. For a moment, overwhelmed by his relief, he could not speak, but habit was strong and his first words were gruff. "Only a flippery whipster would let a garter snake frighten his mount." The duke heard a gasp behind him, but Heath only grinned. "You're right, sir, it was addlepated. I'm not the complete hand you are, though I intend to be someday."

"Not if you continue to ride bird-witted. Henderson said to tell you Clover is in whole shape; she ran to the stable after giving you the toss."

"Good, I worried about her—she's a sweet goer, even if skittish."

"Clough says your rabbits are being cared for."

Heath, pleased, nodded.

"You are all right, son?" The duke scowled fiercely.

Heath, surprised at his father's concern, replied, "Don't be overset, sir, I'll soon be up and falling all-a-bits again." He gave a soft chuckle.

"Most likely," said the duke.

"Your Grace," said a voice behind him, "I regret to interpose, but Heath must have rest." Lenore had followed the duke into the room.

"Madam," the duke returned, ready to give Mrs. Lanier a proper setdown, but Heath intervened.

"She's right, Father, I do feel slightly wool-headed."

"Shall we go?" prompted Lenore.

In the morning room Lenore faced the duke. "Heath is truly on the mend. He rested quite easily. Mrs. Clough never took her eyes off him, though how she could see him through her tears I do not comprehend. The woman's a fountain."

"Mrs. Clough is like a mother to the boy," quoted the duke stiffly.

"Oh, come, do not be toplofty," said Lenore, seating herself on the sofa. "I mean no offense to Mrs.

Clough—besides, he is not a boy. Do sit down, Your Grace."

"Heath is only sixteen—a boy," the duke averred firmly.

"True, but he may never be a man unless you and the Cloughs permit him to grow up," Lenore said evenly.

"Madam, you come it too strong," growled the affronted duke.

Lenore, gazing up at the man frowning down on her, laughed. "Possibly, Your Grace." She rose. "Well, have you brought me my winnings?"

"Madam!" The duke goggled at her. "You lack—er—er—"

"Delicacy? Quite so, sir, but when the egg woman awaits in the kitchen, and without her eggs we can have no nuncheon, I cannot afford to come the lady." Lenore held out her upturned palm.

The duke, who had never dealt with either tradesmen or egg women closely, slowly drew out his purse and put the sum he owed in Lenore's hand.

"Thank you," said Lenore briskly. "You will excuse me while I see the patient woman paid."

Feeling stifled, the dazed duke walked to the opened window and stared at a well-kept vegetable garden. Suddenly he whirled and studied the morning room. The room, though mellow and warm, unmistakably lacked upkeep; the draperies were faded, even mended; the chairs and sofa showed marks of their many cleanings; the carpet had lost its nap in places, carefully concealed, where possible, by odd tables and stools.

When Lenore returned, the duke, at the window, said, "Madam, yours is a splendid garden."

"All honor goes to Abel; his is a very green thumb. He does the kitchen gardens, working long hours with no complaint." She laughed. "But if I require help in my flower beds, he mutters frightful Moorish words, which I'm sure would even shock Mamère."

"Mamère?"

"Madame Lanier—it is my pet name for her."

The duke fell silent.

"Your Grace, I must speak of Mamère. There'll be no forgiveness if I do not send you to her. She seldom leaves the bedroom and is lonely—a visit from you will put her in high gig."

The duke scowled. "She wants me to relate stories of my outrageous behavior in the past."

Lenore tittered. "What a wicked old vixen she is." Then she saw the duke's glare. "Just make up some wild capers, they will serve."

"And have her pen them to all her friends by the first post?" exclaimed the duke moodily.

"Don't be put about on that score. Mamère cannot write now. I do the letters, and I promise to omit your more colorful tales."

"I do not desire her to repeat even my make-believe frisks to you, madam. Because they're not rare and thick enough to please, she will elaborate to her liking."

"Oh, dear," Lenore mused. "Let me see—ah, you can head off by assuring her you were foxed into insensibility at the time and can't remember what occurred."

"It's true, but it won't do for her," the duke replied gloomily.

"Then weave a Banbury tale and threaten that if she says one word to me, you'll keep your tongue forever."

The duke glared at Lenore. "Females! I will introduce a little low talk and hope it beguiles her."

"Splendid! I'll take you to her now—oh, one thing —whatever you concoct, make it shocking; Manère finds living in the country devilishly slow."

The duke, numbed by the cynical advice, followed Lenore into the hall, where they met Abel.

"Mrs. Lanier," the big man began grimly, "I was coming to you. Madame Lanier ordered a bottle of brandy and flew into such a pet when I tried to argue that I had to—"

"I understand, Abel." Lenore smiled as she and the duke climbed the stairs, and added, "Mamère is the household's tiny tyrant."

Stepping into the bedroom, the duke heard, "So, Bunky, you conceded to call on me after all. I'm surprised you didn't cry off, you're so lofty—I had brandy sent up for us."

The duke kissed the old lady's hand, then picked up the bottle and gave it to Lenore. "Madame, I never drink brandy before nuncheon."

"Jack-pudding! Your father wasn't so niff-naff, and your grandfather—hoy, they were men!"

As it was well established that the duke's grandfather had died from numerous ailments caused by spirits and that, soon after, the duke's father had met his death by falling off a horse while drunk, the duke felt Madame Lanier's giggles misplaced. Staring at her icily, he waited.

Suddenly she stopped her glee and said, "Don't be cross with me, Duke. Come along and sit there." Then turning to Lenore, she ordered, "You, missy, go garden or whatever you do; you're too soon out of the schoolroom to hear what the duke is going to tell me, even if you were smart enough to marry my grandson."

Lenore laughed, made a mock curtsy, and left the room.

"Sassy puss," cackled the old lady. "Now, Bunky?"

Later the duke entered the morning room, sat heavily in a chair, and moaned, "Madam, please ring for some brandy."

Lenore, alarmed at his shaken appearance, asked as she went to the bellpull, "What is it? Is Mamère all—"

"Famous, oh, she's famous; it's I who am undone." The duke stared at Lenore with glazed eyes.

"Some brandy, please, Abel." Lenore seated herself opposite the duke. "What on earth happened?"

The duke gave her an agonized glance. "The minute you were out of earshot, she demanded to hear about my 'orgies' as she called them. I hemmed a bit, then related some details of a party given in Paris, but she soon cut short my tame recital and launched into tales of her father's and brother's low doings. Mrs. Lanier, I was once titled the 'Rake of Europe,' but I vow to you, never in my life did I . . ." he shuddered.

Lenore stared at the distraught duke, then fell to laughing so hard she cried. Using a handkerchief, she fought to control herself. When Abel entered and poured a drink for the duke, she buried her face in a pillow, then, after he closed the door, went into peals again.

In terrible tones the duke said, "Madam, I see nothing to amuse you so highly. Please enlighten me."

"It's that Mamère should pitch even too rum for you," Lenore stammered between giggles.

The duke, uncertain whether he had been insulted or not was, however, fully persuaded he had had enough of females for one day—even if this one was beautiful. This stray observation so surprised him he stared at Lenore, who was wiping her eyes, then admitted to himself—it could not be questioned—Lenore Lanier was strikingly lovely. Completely bemused, the duke rose, bowed, and in a chilly voice said, "Madam, I will leave you now."

Nearly recovered, Lenore said, "Your Grace, you haven't forgotten you were invited for nuncheon, have you? Oh dear, I'm sure Mamère gave you a nasty turn, but please don't put yourself in a pucker—the vicar didn't."

The duke stood stunned. "The devil you say?!"

"Oh, yes," Lenore nodded. "He only chuckled and hoped she wouldn't contaminate me with the vulgar chronicles."

The duke gaped at her.

"Oh, do not fret, she doesn't. It's the reason she finds me so insipid."

"But the vicar is a man of the cloth," said the duke.

"Indeed so, a man of the cloth endowed with a kindly heart—rare enough in these days," Lenore said, then added impatiently, "Do sit down. Mamère's tales of the long dead hurt no one and give her great solace."

The duke paused, then resumed his chair. "Mrs. Lanier, be obliging enough to keep her away from Heath."

"Oh, she would not think of relating her outrages to a young man. She often says to me, 'I like older men who have an air of *à la modalité*—I love to see their faces burn crimson and their eyes grow round, especially if they consider themselves blasé.'"

"She's beyond everything!"

Lenore shook her head. "She's a city-bred lady immured in a backwater, who, missing her friends and London, finds fun where possible. Abel?"

Abel announced nuncheon.

"Thank you, Abel. Duke, you are alert to expect eggs, but Maria's Spanish touch will surprise you."

After the meal, the duke suggested a rubber of piquet as they awaited Doctor Sagout, adding that Lenore need not assume she could win every game, for he did not enjoy losing—or intend to lose—his brass, then proceeded to play so carefully that Lenore lost only a few groats.

After checking his patient, the doctor entered the morning room and grumbled about being late—all due to the James baby boy's resistance to coming into the world. Then he announced that Master Heath was on his way to good health but must be confined for another few days. Adding a spate of complaints on the woes of being a doctor, he took his leave.

Following a brief visit with Heath, the duke met Lenore, who jingled coins. "Your winnings, sir." She let the pieces dribble into his hand.

"Thank you, Mrs. Lanier. I shall look forward to our next game."

"Indeed so!"

"May I come tomorrow?" asked the duke.

"You may run tame in this house as long as Heath remains, Your Grace."

"Very gracious of you. Thank you." The duke bowed and left.

At the palace, the duke pondered the whys of Mrs. Lanier's distraction, for she was unusually quiet during nuncheon and played only a fair game of piquet. On impulse the duke wrote to invite the vicar to dine, handed Clough the note to give to Henderson, and bade him return immediately.

His errand done, Clough found the duke in his chair by the fire.

"Clough, you taste the scandal broth in the village—don't deny it. Now, what does the gossip report on the situation at the household of the widows Lanier? Are they well financed, or do they run thin?"

The valet hesitated, embarrassed.

"Speak up, man!"

"Er—Your Grace, from the little that has come to my ears—by chance, just by chance . . ."

"Yes, yes, Clough, go on."

"Madame Lanier has hung on Sir Alfred's sleeve for many years, and the young Mrs. Lanier is lightly breeched—the captain leaving a tiny pension, but a large number of gaming debts. The lady edges on very low ebb indeed." Clough began to warm to his subject. "It's rumored, sir, that Sir Alfred paid off the captain's debts—to save the good name of the family—but that Mrs. Lanier puts aside small amounts from her income to repay Sir Alfred."

"Dammit, Clough, Lanier has more brass than he knows how to spend; why should he press her?"

"It's his wife, sir—'tis said she came the ugly when Captain Eric married against her wishes."

"And Lanier is too much under the cat's thumb to do anything about it—the pigeon," the duke growled.

"It is said, Your Grace, that Sir Alfred wished someone to care for Madame Lanier, other gates Mrs. Lanier would be without a thatch over her head."

"That nipped is the captain's widow?"

"Yes, Your Grace."

"Clough," the duke spoke severely, "the widows Lanier household cannot afford to feed a growing lad like Heath, and I can't afford to lose at piquet often."

"Sir?!" exclaimed the startled henchman, who bragged of being employed by one of the richest gentlemen in the country.

"I mean, you clodpole, I cannot lose enough blunt to Mrs. Lanier to make a difference. If I do, she'll twig to my plans in a thrice."

"Oh, of course, sir," agreed the valet.

"Clough, go through our larder and select any viands that will keep, fill some baskets, then have Henderson deliver them to Willowood. No vegetables—they have sufficient—but all else, including jellies, spices, and wines."

"Right away, Your Grace." Clough gave a faint smile. "It's a pleasure to serve you, sir."

"Cut your stick," shouted the duke, "and send in Mr. Endfield."

The rest of the day the duke occupied his mind with problems of the estate.

The vicar arrived at the requested hour to find the duke in an austere mood; he barely spoke during dinner. When the port was on the table, he ordered Clough to withdraw. The vicar, in apprehension, tried to tally his misdemeanors of the week past, but could recall none.

"Vicar," the Duke flared suddenly, "I heard shocking news of you today." The vicar blinked. "I learned you permitted Madame Lanier to recite her deplorable stories to you."

The vicar, through nervous relief, laughed. "Yes, Your Grace, I'm afraid I did let the wagfeather have her way."

"You surprise me, sir, you, a man of the Church, listening to such low on-dit."

"Oh, I did not listen," the vicar replied cheerfully.
"What?!"

"Quite so. As soon as I saw—or should I say heard—the direction of her tongue, I stopped attending and, instead, planned my Sunday sermon—a rather strong treatise on the sin of gossip."

The duke scowled, "Very neat, sir, but why would you allow the lady to prattle in such disgraceful vein?"

"Because it makes her content."

"Content?"

"Exactly. Madame Lanier is a lonely old lady who adores scandal, marooned far from her beloved London, bereft of contemporaries, too much of a gentlewoman to gossip with the captain's widow. She yearns for an ear. If it pleases her—and it does—to try and shock me, I'll gladly pretend to hearken."

The duke studied his friend through hooded eyes. "Wrote your sermon, eh? Vicar, you are a great gun or a fool."

"A bit of both, probably, like the rest of us mortals," the cleric said, chuckling. "But I do grant my hair stood on end at some of the language. How a lady would ever hear such words confounds me." He shook his head.

"Her husband, doubtless—a bad one, so I've been told." The duke pushed away from the table. "Come, a rubber of piquet. I want to learn how to lose artfully."

"What?" The vicar stared at the duke.

The vicar, when told the why of the strange request, hastily concurred, and gave the duke some extraordinarily useful tips.

7

The next day Heath, feeling better, greeted his father brightly. After a chat about horses and other doings, the duke, noting Heath's fatigue, left. Downstairs, he knocked on the shut door of the morning room; a frosty voice bade him enter.

"Good morning, Mrs. Lanier."

The lady, standing at the window—her back to him—did not answer. The duke waited. Suddenly she whirled, eyes blazing. "How dare you?!" The duke gaped at her.

"How dare you send over enough food to feed Wellesley's troops for a week?"

Enlightened, the duke replied quickly, "But, madam, Heath eats like Wellesley's troops."

"Sir, every inch of our cupboard space is filled and baskets are strewn about the floor."

"You must have a small kitchen, madam."

"Stop your fustian; you have my meaning. I'm not an alms case."

"Madam, I'm bowled out. How could anyone who has seen your vegetable garden ever image you a case for alms?"

"Humdudgeon! The provisions you sent could last this household a year!"

"Not with Heath bedded here."

"And wines, sir, does Heath drink wine? There's sufficient in the pantry to keep him bosky for six months."

"The wines are for me, madam."

"Hoy! They would hold you foxed for a sennight, even if you drank a bottle an hour." Lenore looked up at him, her arms akimbo, her expression cross.

"Come, madam, don't take sniff at me, 'tis Clough who deserves the scold. I merely proposed that Heath might wish some of his favorite dishes, and you are aware of Clough's fondness for the lad—er—young man."

"Well, Your Grace, you may instruct your groom to take most of Clough's generosity back to the palace."

"You mean ask Henderson?! Lord, I'd never venture to order so—he ripped up mightily having to lug the baskets here. If I merely hinted he freight them back, he would leave my service immediately—it would be a devil of a clunch."

"Oh, go away!" Lenore stamped her foot.

The duke frowned. "Do you insist? I had hoped for a rubber of piquet. The vicar gave me some new tips for play and I'd like to try them."

"Don't roast me, sir. Heath says you're a 'bang-up to the knocker player.'"

"It is the voice of my greatly loved son speaking. Yesterday you lost a groat or two, but today, I intend to beat you to flinders."

The duke scowled so threateningly that Lenore could not suppress a giggle. "Zany! Well, the table's ready, but I give fair warning, I'm still in a tweak; Maria can scarce thread her way through the baskets."

"I will order Heath to eat hardy, madam."

"Oh, fudge—draw for deal."

Neither being given to talk at the table, the games were swiftly played and the duke, with masterly skill, managed to lose a sum that brought sparkle to Lenore's eyes. Prepared, the duke, on parting, dribbled a small stream of gold into Lenore's cupped hands, then vowed dreadful revenge on the morrow.

8

The next forenoon as the duke alighted from his carriage at Willowood, the front door opened and Doctor Sagout emerged and sped down the steps, yelling to the duke, "Deliver me from damn females; may the devil snatch them all!" Hurrying to his tilbury, he climbed in, and slapped the reins on the back of his horse, who took off in fine style.

Eyeing the retreating tilbury, the duke exclaimed, "What on earth?"

"Hoy, plain as a pikestaff," Henderson said, chuckling. "He's had a mill with the ladies and I ain't surprised, Your Grace. Females are queer stirrups for any man."

The duke merely nodded at this explanation and strode up the walk to the door, which opened instantly. Abel stood stern.

"Is Heath all right?" shouted the duke.

"Yes, sir, but you better go right up to see him."

As Abel spoke the doors to the morning room flew open and Lenore said sharply, "So, you saw the quack leaving!"

"Yes, madam; he seemed mad as a wasp."

"And I'm at dagger drawing with him. Do you know what the whopstraw wanted to do?" Her voice rose. "He wanted to bleed your son."

"A usual procedure, madam," said the duke levelly.

"Not while I tend Heath. I watched more young men on the Penn die after some loose screw put leeches to them than I care to number."

The duke, who had read the latest medical journals about the dangers of bleeding, asked, "What did you say to the doctor?"

"I walked into the bedroom and saw the wretch holding a bottle full of those horrid things, and I queried, very politely, if he intended to apply those to Heath. 'Certainly, madam' was his reply. I explained that he was not to bring one of the nasty creatures within a mile of your son. He then proclaimed that he was the doctor and would employ any means he deemed best. I said, 'Not in my house!'; then he said that I was an empty-headed female who hadn't an inkling about doctoring and would I leave the room! I said, no, I would not, and that he was not even to uncork the bottle. He then announced, 'The duke will not approve of your cluntering in.' I replied that you would prefer my interfering to having a dead son. He then ordered me out and started for me. I called Abel, who, by the finest of chance, was standing outside the door, and he ushered the medicaster from the house—and that is when you encountered him."

The duke, who had followed her tale with grave interest, nodded, and headed for the stairs.

Entering the bedchamber, he gaped at the empty bed. "Heath?!"

"Over here. Father," called Heath from the chair by the window.

"What the devil are you doing out of bed?" roared the duke.

"Don't overset yourself, sir. Mrs. Lanier said I could only gain strength if I sat up; I'm here for ten minutes."

"The female's insane—get back to bed this instant! Can you walk, or shall I carry you?"

"I have a minute to go—then you may help me." Heath laughed. "Oh, Father, I wish you could have seen the kickup when Doctor Sagout tried to bleed me. It was famous—Mrs. Lanier dashed well hurled it at him—he got mad as bedlam. For a moment I feared he might plant a facer on her, but she stood strong. May not be a doctor, but she's up to snuff in taking care of me."

"Your minute's up. Come!"

Heath took the duke's arm and limped to bed.

"Father, don't ride grub on Mrs. Lanier—she's good to me—we play chess and talk by the hour. It'd be devilish boring without her."

Peering down at his son's white face, the duke, for the first time in years, smiled.

In astonished joy Heath held out his hand to be clasped, grinned, and said, "Oh, Father, you are a great gun!"

A surge of well-being flooded the duke.

Squeezing his son's hand, he said, "Get some sleep; I'll not blue-devil Mrs. Lanier."

To the duke's surprise Lenore had recovered her calm.

"You saw Heath, sitting up and strong, whereas if Doctor Sagout had had his way, Heath would have been rag limp."

The duke frowned. "Madam, it is far too early for Heath to be out of bed."

"Nonsense! On the Penn, where there were not enough cots for the wounded, the soldiers soonest on their feet I observed to be quickest mended."

"Nevertheless, I forbid you to let him put a foot on the floor for the next few days."

Lenore pursed her lips. "Your Grace, I have no wish to deceive you, but if you push me to it, I must, for I intend to get Heath up each day and the devil himself cannot stop me."

Staring at the defiant lady, the duke felt he could not endure this madhouse any longer. Bowing, he said, "Good day to you, Mrs. Lanier," and started for the door.

"Return tomorrow and see how much improved Heath is." The words echoed in his mind when he entered his carriage.

Henderson, who from Abel had had the story of the doctor's and Mrs. Lanier's quarrel, noted signs of thunder in the duke's face, and held his tongue.

At the palace the duke studied the papers Mr. Endfield had placed on his desk—of enough import to engross his full attention.

Unexpectedly a knock interrupted his work. He was startled to see, in response to his "Come in," the Reverend David Thomas standing in the doorway. "Vicar!" The duke jumped to his feet.

"There is no one in the hall and I am in deep need to talk to you, sir."

"You are always welcome, Vicar. Throw down your hat and coat and permit me to pour you a brandy—it's a cold day."

The cleric brightened and did as bid. Facing each other in chairs at the fire, the vicar spoke. "You must be told, sir, that all in the village rejoice at Heath's returning health—yes, yes, very well indeed—the wishes for the boy. Rachel related to me just this morning how everyone tells her of their good wishes; good wishes abound, Your Grace. One could almost—"

"Vicar, stop your babble; you did not come at this queer hour of the day to list garbled good wishes, so get to the nut of the matter. Drink your brandy, if you require courage."

The vicar took a long draft of the spirits, then said, "Your Grace, I have been approached in a shocking and in delicate manner. It appals me. Last night, while I wrote in my book room, two men came to the window, peered in, then tapped on the pane, giving me a nasty turn."

"I don't wonder at it. What did you do?"

"I confess, I yearned to run from the room, but it occurred to me that Mrs. Thomas and the children might be overset, so I went to the window and shouted for the lurkers to go away. They shook their heads, then held an envelope to the glass, and I read your name in bold letters. The men said—loudly enough for me to hear—to let them in, for they had no plans to hurt or rob me, but that they must consult me. I hesitated, but because of the envelope, I released the latch. I must admit they behaved with civility—they spoke of their sorrow at alarming me—then explained it of the direst import that their visit be kept secret. They said that because I am the only regular visitor you receive, I must bring you the letter—the contents of which you would understand—then not in a threatening, but almost a pleading way, bade me hold my tongue, and said they would return from time to time with further word for you, and left through the window. I did not sleep throughout the night."

The duke frowned. "Vicar, I can understand your initial fear, but if they did not intimidate you, it puzzles me as to why you lost your rest over the task of delivering a letter."

"Because, sir, they were French." The vicar's voice quavered.

Taken aback, the duke exclaimed, "French?!"

"Their use of English was awkward, most awkward." The vicar shook his head.

"French . . ." mused the duke, then said briskly, "Well, Vicar, the letter then."

"Oh, yes, yes." The vicar reached into his inner pocket and placed the heavy cream-white envelope, marked with "The Duke of Asherwood" in large script, in the duke's outstretched palm.

The duke moved to his desk, slit the flap, drew out two sheets, and began to read.

The vicar, never taking his eyes off his friend's face, saw his color drain as he read and reread the pages, leaving the duke ashen.

"Myles, are you all right?" The vicar, in his distress, so far forgot himself as to call the duke by his first name—a usage he had held in his thinking for many months.

The duke replied in strained tones, "Good God, sir, you bring grave news."

"Not treason, Your Grace?" asked the alarmed vicar.

There seemed an endless pause before the duke answered. "No, not treason, but there is danger."

"Dear God!" said the vicar.

"Danger for even the innocent in this affair—no, no, let me assure you, there's no peril for Mrs. Thomas or the children, but I must ask your aid and also swear you to absolute secrecy."

"What do you wish me to do, Your Grace?" the vicar asked simply.

The duke considered his words before he spoke.

"Visit me, as always, and carry such papers I give you to the Frenchmen and, in turn, deliver to me alone the papers they present to you."

"Gladly, Your Grace."

"It is a fearful coil—I cannot inform you of its nature, but I can tell you—it changes my life completely."

"Your Grace!"

"I require your understanding, sir. Soon I will have to make some strange requests of you. However, they affect you only lightly; the important matter is the exchange of documents. As for me, I swear to you, my involvement is not treacherous, but occasioned by a debt long overdue that must now be paid."

"When shall you desire to see me again, Your Grace?" asked the vicar, rising.

"Come tomorrow about noon. If questioned, say you want a book I promised you." The duke went to the vicar and put his hands on the shorter man's shoulders. "My friend, you must also fulfill another command of mine—Sleep! It serves no good to have my vicar heavy-eyed, and there is no reason for you to do other gates."

The men shook hands and as the vicar turned to

go, the duke said softly, "Bless you for calling me Myles, David."

The vicar paused for an instant, then left the room, warmed by the duke's words.

The duke walked slowly to the desk to read again the second page of the fateful letter:

> . . . my enemies will attempt to build great fires. You, *sans* a spouse, would add logs to their flames; therefore it is imperative—if you are to carry out my request—that you marry.
>
> I can see you cringe, dear Duke, a magnificent scowl furrowing your handsome brow—but I am unmoved. There must be a duchess in residence in London to protect all in this concernment— *mais, oui*—especially yourself, *mom ami!* The events cannot be under the auspices of the "Rake of Europe"—*Non!*—an abigail's whisper, a footman's wink, could drive you from England forever.
>
> A duchess, in place, safeguards not only you but everyone; she will lend respectability in the eyes of your household, even though—I stress— even though the lady must never learn of the affair—her innocence itself is a shield.
>
> Myles, I turn to you as an old friend, and I lay this heavy burden, for you are the only man in England in whom I have total trust.
>
>   In deepest gratitude,

A burden indeed, thought the duke, but knew his response to the letter. No man had a better right to call upon him. The duke paced the floor, remembering what little he could of the painful period when he lived the rake throughout Europe—dissolute, drunken, careening through France, Spain, and Italy, bent on destroying himself.

It was N. who at a party had recognized that the duke, reeling, falling, was not drunk—as the other guests justly assumed—but raging with fever. It was N. who ordered his own carriage and, taking the duke into his own home, wakened his own physician to care for the ill man. It was N. who recruited the best nursing care available, and spent as much time as possible from his duties to encourage and amuse his ailing guest. It was N. who urged the duke to forego his determination to die and, instead, to resume his life in England.

Going to his desk, the duke took pen and paper and scrawled one word—"Yes," then spent a sleepless night making plans.

The London house on Grosvenor Square had to be opened—an enormous undertaking, for it had been unused since the duke's flight to Asherwood. Mr. and Mrs. Madcape, whom he maintained as caretakers, occupied only a small set of rooms; the rest of the mansion lay under hollands.

In the morning the duke gave Mr. Endfield directions concerning the requirements in London. An architect and a decorator were to be found to draw plans for refurbishing the house, then they were to be brought to Asherwood to submit the plans. Mr. Endfield, supplied with money and a letter to the Madcapes, took his leave.

The duke then wrote a note to Heath, saying he

could not visit this day, but would tomorrow. Handing the message to Clough, he ordered that he be undisturbed. When alone, he paced for a time and finally threw himself on the divan and sighed, shuddered at the idea of marriage—Nothing worse could befall me! —and fell asleep.

The duke was wrong.

9

Roused by Clough's sharp rap, the duke growled, "Come in." Prepared to snarl, he saw Clough's distraught face and sprang up. "Clough! Is it Heath?"

Clough, white and trembling, whispered, "No, Your Grace, but you'd better come. It's—it's in the drawing room, sir."

Brushing by the stricken man, the duke crossed the hall to enter the great room. There he stopped dead and stared at his solicitor, Mr. Pettibone, who stood— a marble statue—at the fireplace. The duke's glance sped to a large chair where a nun sat, her pale hand smoothing the hair of a little boy who knelt beside her, his head buried in her lap.

"Pettibone! What . . . ?" asked the duke.

Too agitated to present her properly, the solicitor murmured, "Maybe you'd best hearken to the sister."

The duke turned to the nun who gazed at him calmly. "You wish to see me, Sister?"

The nun, her voice gentle and clear, asked, "You are the Duke of Asherwood?" The duke nodded. "This lad, then, is your son." She patted the boy's head.

"Sister!" the duke exploded. "You run mad! What is this caper, Pettibone—blackmail?"

The solicitor shook his head.

"This boy is your son."

The nun leaned over and in a soft tone said, "Stand up, Charles, no one will hurt you."

Slowly the child lifted his head and gradually straightened.

"Oh, my God!" exclaimed the duke, stunned, for in front of him stood himself as a child. Every feature—the hair, the stockiness—every line—his own. No court in the land could deny his parenthood.

Overcome by the silence, the boy hid his head in the nun's shoulder.

Finally Mr. Pettibone spoke. "There is a letter, Your Grace," and thrust a sheet into the duke's hand, wincing at His Grace's bewildered face.

The duke, who had never taken his eyes off the child, slowly lowered his head and read:

Dear Mr. Pettibone,

When you read this letter, I will be dead. I accept now that I have not much time, so while I can, I write to appeal for your services.

The good sisters have promised to take my son Charles to you, and I place with you the responsibility of doing your best for the boy.

You will readily see he is the duke's son, born after I ran away with Mr. Sanford. At the time of Charles's birth, I confess, I believed Mr. Sanford his father; but within two years it became plain he was not.

Mr. Sanford, to his everlasting credit, treated Charles as his own up to the day he drowned. After that tragic event, I discovered I had the dread disease soon to take me, and realized I must make provision for Charles. There is no money left— gone for my illness—I am destitute. Only the blessed mercy of the gentle sisters gives me some peace. Their promise relieves my anguish.

Take the boy to his father, if you think it wise, or make whatever arrangement you deem prudent. May God guide you!

My deepest gratitude,
Harriet Sanford

The duke stood benumbed.

Mr. Pettibone finally spoke. "Your Grace, I felt impelled to come to you."

"You made the correct decision, Pettibone." Then, he asked the nun, "Did my wife suffer at the end?"

"No, Your Grace. After we gave our promise concerning Charles, she died in serenity."

Poor Harriet. Memories of the beautiful, laughing young girl flashed through his mind, but his heart hardened. She had deprived him of the boy's babyhood and permitted another man to take his place as father to his son.

There ensued a long silence while the duke considered his new responsibility. Nodding to the nun, he at last said, "I will bring up the boy. You may leave him with me now." He pulled the bell rope and Clough entered. "Clough, this is my son Charles; take him and prepare a room for him."

"Yes, Your Grace." Clough moved toward the lad,

who, in tears, cringed, then clung to the nun, who spoke. "Your Grace, Charles needs a woman to care for him; he is young and unused to men."

Mr. Pettibone and Clough exchanged glances in fear of the duke's response to such cosseting, but he merely said, "Of course, Sister. Clough, get Mrs. Peablossom. Mrs. Peablossom has nine children of her own." Then the duke, gazing at the boy, said, "Sister, you have gone to a great amount of trouble to restore my son. What is the calling of your order?"

"We care for the sick and the poor, Your Grace."

"Do you have a hospital?"

"No, we are a small order."

"Then, Pettibone, I charge you see a hospital be built and financed for the order."

"Your Grace!" the astonished nun said in a whisper.

"Speak of this to me later, Pettibone . . . Ah, Mrs. Peablossom." The duke addressed the plump, buxom woman who trailed Clough into the room and curtsied. "This is my son Charles—ah, Clough has told you. Please take the boy to the nursery, see that he is fed, stay with him until he is comfortable, and sleep near him. Clough, please serve refreshments to my guests—I will be in the library—and Clough, no word of this is to reach Heath. I will explain to him myself."

"Your Grace, a word with you before you leave." The nun was turning Charles around to face the beaming Mrs. Peablossom, who held out her hand, then, when the boy slowly put out his hand, popped a sweet into it.

Surprised, Charles looked up at her. She leaned over and whispered in his ear, "I've got a hobbyhorse upstairs who told me to tell you his name is Nutmeg, and he wants you to ride him." Charles turned to the nun, who nodded and smiled. "Go along, Charles."

"Charles, my name is Mrs. Peablossom," she said, giggling. "Silly, isn't it? You call me Mrs. P., and now let us hurry, for we mustn't keep Nutmeg waiting."

The boy gazed up at the twinkling face and reached for her hand.

"Good gracious, I found another sweet," said the cheerful voice of Mrs. P. as she led the boy from the room.

The nun broke the silence. "Your Grace, your generosity overwhelms me and will also our order. You will be remembered in our prayers always."

"Thank you," said the duke coldly.

"But it is of Charles I must speak. He has had a very sad life and must have love and tenderness; he is not yet eight and young for his age."

"He will have all the attention required, Sister." His tone was chilly.

"Sir, I am of an order that does not speak unless in the direst necessity. Thus, when I urge you to treat Charles gently, I am trying to convey volumes."

"No one in my household is mistreated, Sister. Pettibone, see to the sister's journey, then, if you can, come for a visit; I have need to talk to you."

"Thank you, sir. I shall arrive tomorrow."

"Good, we will talk then. Thank you both for your trouble." Bowing stiffly, the duke left the room.

Clough immediately appeared with tea and cakes. Mr. Pettibone and the sister left the palace shortly.

10

For two days the duke did not leave the library. He reviewed his past life, his present dilemma, and pondered his uncertain future. On the second evening Clough brought him the news that Heath, now able to come home, desired to be sent for in the morning.

"Impossible! He is not strong enough to be moved; that female may kill him," roared the duke. "I'll go tomorrow and see for myself."

"An excellent idea, sir. May I suggest you have a good dinner and sleep in your own bed this night?" Clough added in a subdued voice. "And perhaps you will allow me to shave you, sir."

The duke glared at his henchman, who awaited the flood of the duke's anger, but he only said, "You're a havey-cavey fellow," and let Clough restore his appearance.

The following morning the duke, entering Willowood, paused, astounded to hear a shout of laughter ring out from the morning room. Going to the open door, he saw his heir, fully clad, seated across from Madame Lanier.

"Father, you're here! Come in." Heath rose and balanced himself on a cane. "Mamère has been telling me the most famous story," then, puzzled by the glower his father directed to the old lady, added hastily, "about how you shot a duck and it landed on your father's head, causing him to fall into the marsh. Did his gun really go off and down two ducks?"

"It did, saving me a well-deserved caning. Where is Mrs. Lanier?" The duke stood prepared to express his feelings—not only about letting his son out of bed, but permitting him to come downstairs.

"She's gone to the village, Father. She asked me to deliver her regrets at not receiving you, but important business necessitated her absence."

A wave of frustration swept over the duke.

The old lady chuckled. "I told you she is no fool, Bunky."

"Are you set to go home now, Son?" the duke asked impatiently.

"Yes. Mamère, I'll come to see you soon." He kissed the lady's cheek. "Father, please wait while I say good-bye to Abel and Maria." He hobbled to the door, saying, "See, Father, I only need a cane, and that not for long," and left.

"Bunky, that is a darling boy you have; makes me wish I were fifteen again—I'd fling my cap over the windmill for such as he."

"Well, madame, that is one misfortune I have been spared."

"Hoy, you're in a tweak because you can't give my smart granddaughter the trimming you planned for her."

"Madame, I do not like females quacking my son."

"Poppycock! You can see for yourself he's more plucked up than if the fool doctor had had his way. You can also realize Lenore's as shrewd as she can hold together. Why, Bunky, if you had an ounce of brains, you'd make an offer for her and let her run your household—Devil take you, what's the matter with you?"

The duke was staring with his mouth open, while a deep pallor spread over his face.

"Oh, don't get into a hubble-bubble—no one is going to bullock you into making an offer for her. Probably wouldn't have you anyway; she should be riveted to someone bang-up to the echo, not a country hide-his-head like you."

"Thank you, madame." The duke's tone was freezing.

"Don't get stuffy with me, Bunky. I remember you from the time you were in leading strings. It's sad— you were as pretty behaved a young man as your lad, Heath, until you met that ninnyhammer wife of yours."

"I have just learned that Harriet is dead," the duke informed her.

"Humph. Too bad for her—too young to die—but it's lucky riddance for you."

The words held the duke still.

"She was a diamond and a flosshead; I cried the day I heard you had eloped with her. Far too far beneath your touch, Bunky." The old lady smiled and held out her hand. "Come, I'm foolish beyond permission. Maybe I prattle on because I loved your mother and father, and would like to see you happy."

The duke gazed at the shrunken figure, then stepped forward and, taking her thin hands in his, kissed each, saying, "Your servant, madame," and left the room.

The hall rang with "good-byes" and "come our ways." Abel helped Henderson, who had come to retrieve the last pieces of baggage. Mrs. Clough bustled about, seeing that nothing was left behind. Even the elusive Maria peeked around the kitchen door to wave farewell. When the party was assembled Heath limped ahead, with Henderson step-in-step to keep his idol from mishap. The duke halted Abel inside the door and gave him a chamois bag, the contents of which delighted him later.

The drive to the palace was quiet, Heath a touch homesick for the household just vacated, the duke's thoughts turbulent, and Mrs. Clough busy making plans to check on what had been overlooked at the palace, so long bereft of her supervision.

Clough welcomed the party, even kissing his wife, much to her confusion. Heath protested going to bed, but, when finally relaxed on his pillow, quickly dozed, then slept.

The sound of footsteps overhead awakened him, then frightened him, for the nursery had been unoccupied since he had outgrown it. He called loudly for Mrs. Clough, who came running from his study.

"Who's in the nursery? I hear footfalls up there."

Mrs. Clough paled. Heath started to rise.

"No, no!" she spoke sharply. "It's all right."

"Well, who?" demanded Heath.

"I cannot tell you," replied the flustered and unhappy Mrs. Clough.

"Why not?" asked the now angered Heath.

"I'll get your father; you stay in bed." She ran from the room.

Heath rose, put on his robe, and seated himself by the fire. More noise stirred his curiosity further.

The duke, dismayed at Mrs. Clough's report, rushed up the stairs, calling back to Clough to bring some brandy.

"Well, young jackstraw, no rest, eh? Are you feeling better?"

"Yes, Father." Bored by questions about his health, Heath went to the heart of the matter. "Who's up in the nursery, chasing back and forth?"

"Clough is bringing—Ah, here he is."

Clough, with a smile for Heath, poured two glasses and left quickly.

"Here, Son, you may want this before I finish—I shall."

"Father, who is upstairs?" Heath demanded impatiently.

The duke winced at the crash of the toppled hobbyhorse. Taking a large swallow of his drink, the duke said, "Four days ago, Mr. Pettibone brought a little boy—he is your brother."

Heath stared at his father. "Impossible—Mother is dead."

The duke nodded. "Yes, but only within the last month."

"She died when I was a child!"

"No, Son, so you believed. But she died just recently."

Stunned, Heath stammered, "Mother has been alive all these years? Where?"

"Your mother ran away with the tutor, Mr. Sanford; I've had no knowledge of their whereabouts until Mr. Pettibone appeared with your brother."

Heath lowered his head and stared at the carpet—his mother—his tutor; scenes of lessons and riding ran in his memory. Raising his eyes to his father's, he asked, "And Mr. Sanford?"

"He drowned some time ago."

Heath looked long and hard at the duke, as if to

learn more from his expression, then whispered, "She did not care enough about me to try and see me." His voice became harsh. "And now she bestows my step-brother for you to bring up—what a poser!"

"No, Son, your own brother."

"My own brother?!" Heath sneered.

"Yes, unbeknown to either of us, your mother carried my child when she left Asherwood."

"Fudge, it's a bobbery," Heath said bitterly.

"No, Heath, no trick. Wait until you see him; there can be no doubt. If I were a child, we would be two halfpennies in a purse."

Emotions raced across Heath's face. He drank a sip of brandy. "Father, how dreadful for you!"

"And you, Son? What of you?" his father asked softly.

"I'm knocked bandy."

The duke shook his head wearily. "I've played ducks and drakes with our lives—I should have told you of your mother long ago."

Heath spoke quietly. "Father, I scarce remember her; I was too young when she disappeared. And now I discover she never wanted to even learn of me. But you—you have been so very good to me over the years."

For this extraordinarily undeserved tribute, the duke had no words. Heath misread his silence.

"Am I hardhearted, Father? Mother had great beauty, but didn't give a groat for me. What happened to her?"

The duke handed Heath her letter.

Reading it through, Heath peered at his father and smiled. "So, I have a younger brother! By Jupiter, it rather excites me."

The duke frowned. "It need not, because you are not going to have anything to do with him."

"What?! My own brother?"

"Quite. I have given thought to the boy. He is to be brought up exactly as you were: the Cloughs and tutors to tend him, then Eton and Oxford, but no more attention from me than you had."

"No!" Heath exploded.

"What?" The duke glowered at his son.

"No! You will not treat Charles as you did me. My bringing up I understand and accept, but Charles is not going to be deprived of a father or a brother."

"He is my son; I decide for him as I see fit."

"No, Father, that's where you're out. We'll receive him as your son and my brother—we will be a family."

"A family? Never!" the duke shouted, then paused. "You may conduct yourself as you please, but I intend to have nothing to do with him. Do you understand?"

"No, sir, I do not. Why must you feel this way?"

The duke took a drink, then said, "Your mother caused me hours of pain and left you to my care. I want no further responsibility of such a nature."

"Then I will see to it!"

"All right, let it be on your head."

The duke and his son glared at each other, then the duke, displeased, whirled and left the room.

Tired by the clash of wills, Heath closed his eyes and listened to the running footsteps overhead.

Suddenly he rose and rang for a footman, instructing that Mrs. Peablossom bring the boy down. Waiting, Heath experienced great sadness for his parents' tangled lives. However, when Mrs. Peablossom entered and curtsied, Heath smiled warmly.

"Mrs. P., how are you?"

Mrs. P., her large apple-colored face shining with pleasure, bobbed another curtsy and said, "It's chirping merry to view you stout, Master Heath."

"Umm. Where is my brother?"

"Here, Master Heath." She reached behind her wide skirts and pushed Charles forward.

Heath gasped at the boy's likeness to their father, then said, "Charles, I'm glad to meet you."

The child would have run out of the room if Mrs. Peablossom had not held him firmly. Heath indicated that she sit down, and watched Charles hide his face in her lap. "Charles, you might—" Mrs. Peablossom started to say, but Heath cut in quickly, "Let him be." Then, to her amazement, he gave her an extravagant wink.

"Mrs. P.," began Heath solemnly, "you heard that I was thrown from my horse."

"Oh, yes, and a ghastly thing it was, sir."

"It was bacon-headed, Mrs. P. Do you know why I was thrown? I will tell you—I should never have been riding alone."

Mrs. Peablossom, well aware that the son of the house, since in nankeens, had ridden many miles alone, started to speak, then stopped.

"I should have had someone with me, for then I would have been warned," proclaimed the finest young whip in the county.

"Yes, sir, quite the thing, sir."

"However, Mrs. P., it is most difficult to find a riding companion. There is Henderson, but he is too busy in the stables to go out with me often."

What a whopper, thought Mrs. P., for she knew Henderson to drop any task to accompany his idol at any moment, but decided to hold her tongue.

Heath continued. "And there seems just no one to ride with me." He sighed.

"Very sad, sir." Mrs. P., not above playing a game, shook her head.

"Yes, Mrs. P., it's very discouraging. I'm blue-deviled—so much so that I would teach a body, if one could be found, who wished to ride with me—even someone who had never been on a horse."

Mrs. P. felt Charles's head move. But she looked at Heath, who though pretending to gaze at her, eyed the boy.

"You don't ride, do you, Mrs. P.?"

She burst into laughter. "Ah, sir, what horse could hold the likes of me?" The absurdity of his question made her shake all over with glee.

"Mrs. P.," Heath sounded stern, "it is no cause for whoops. I desperately need someone to ride with me."

At this, Charles straightened and turned to Heath, saying shyly, "Would I do, sir? I have never been on a horse, but I would try very hard to learn, sir."

Heath gazed at him in astonishment, "You, Charles, you?! You think you could learn to ride a horse?"

"I'd like very much to try, sir, if you—"

"By Jupiter, Mrs. P.!" Heath slapped his leg. "There's my answer! You believe you could manage, eh, Charles?"

"I wish to—" Charles hesitated. "I really want to very much, sir."

"Well, come here then, and let me see your hands." Charles went to Heath and held up his palms. Heath took them in his own and studied each carefully. His heart ached at their white slenderness, but he exclaimed in loud tones, "Mrs. P., he has the hands of a rider!"

"Mind you that!" Mrs. P. beamed.

"Charles"—Heath peered into the clear eyes that gazed so hopefully into his—"the first thing you have to do is study the lines of a horse. Mrs. P., will you be so good as to reach up for the horse on the shelf—ah, thank you Mrs. P.—and now, if you will leave us, we can begin our lesson. I'll ring when I'm through with this budding nonesuch."

"Very well, Master Heath, and Charles . . ."

"Never mind, Mrs. P., Charles is going to be very busy."

Mrs. Peablossom giggled, curtsied, and left.

Charles, whose eyes had never left the model of the horse, asked, "May I touch it, sir?"

"Touch it? Of course you may, for it is yours." Heath put the statuette in Charles's hands. The boy clasped the horse and tears started down his cheeks.

"Charles," asked Heath gently, "have you had a chance to cry since our mother died?" Charles shook his head. "Well, now is the time." Heath gathered the boy in his arms and seated him on his lap. Charles, letting his head fall on Heath's shoulder, wept for a long time. Gradually his tears turned into sobs, then tiny gulps. Heath held him until he was quiet. Suddenly Charles clutched his horse, threw his arms around Heath's neck, and began to cry anew. Surprised, Heath asked, "What now, Charles?"

"These are happy tears, sir; I have a friend and I am not afraid anymore."

Heath laughed. "Then stop being missish and let me show you about your new horse."

Charles unwound himself and posed his tear-stained face so he could study Heath's eyes. "Sir, may I please call you Brother?"

Setting the lad on his feet, Heath responded, "Yes,

little brother, you may call me Brother, for brothers we are, and brothers we will be all our lives. Now go into my dressing room and wash your face, and hurry; we are going to be busy."

Charles thrust the horse at Heath, turned, and ran. When he came back, face shining, Heath, seated at the desk, indicated the chair drawn up beside his own —the bronze horse was within Charles's reach.

The next hour proved the happiest in Charles's short life.

11

The duke, disturbed and angry as he left Heath, headed for the stairs to be met by Clough, who informed him that the vicar awaited him in the library. What now, wondered the duke, and went slowly to the first floor.

One glimpse of the duke's face warned the vicar that a wrong word could incite wrath.

"You bring bad news," growled the duke.

"*Au contraire*," said the vicar, in hopes of lightening his friend's spirits. Once the duke had told him his pronunciation of the French language would throw a Frenchman into spasms.

"Impossible! There is no good news in the world," vowed the duke.

"*Mais, non*. The Frenchman visited me last night and said all goes well."

"That is it—no letter?" asked the duke.

"No, just that all is *très bien*."

"Damme, it may go *très bien* for them, but as for me—I'm in a bumble bath."

"Myles, can I help?"

The duke scrutinized his friend the vicar, then nodded. "Yes, David, you can—you can listen." He moved to the side table and filled two glasses with brandy as the vicar installed himself in his usual chair. Seated, the duke falteringly began to enumerate his woes with the tale of Charles's arrival, but grew more eloquent as he moved to the climax of his story —the opening of his London house and his need to acquire a duchess.

"My dear Duke, you are in a hobble!" whispered the vicar, stunned by the strange twist of events. "A duchess?!"

"Yes, damme, and to be leg-shackled is the last desire I have in this world. I dislike females intensely." The duke shuddered.

"A veritable coil, Myles. And you *must* take a wife?"

The duke nodded gloomily. "Yes. I'm fair capped by it all. Why, I don't even have the acquaintanceship of an acceptable female. I know one Cyprian in London, but I would—No! Impossible!"

The vicar took a deep breath, then spoke very softly. "Duke, I believe you do know one on whom you could fix your interest—a most eligible lady—one of rare qualities, actually—one who lives quite near. . . ."

"Stop!" shouted the duke. "Do not let her name pass your lips. I estimate her unsuitable in every direction!"

"You do? Why?" asked the surprised vicar.

"She and I come to cuffs almost every time we are within earshot."

"How strange. I find her kind and of good sense. Rachel and the children welcome her whenever she comes to call."

"Oh, she is good-hearted; Heath found her so, and Mrs. Clough chirps her praises loudly, but dammit, she goes against my pluck. Despite her pockets to let, she dashed well hurled it at me when I sent the household some baskets of viands to feed Heath—proud to a fault!"

"She is proud, but is that a fault?"

"She crosses me at every turn and possesses a flaming temper. Had a devil of a dustup with Doctor Sagout; sent him flying, and then quacked Heath herself."

"He is better, you tell me." The vicar made a soft thrust.

"Oh, she was in the right—don't believe in bleeding a body myself—but she let him out of bed far too soon. Might have booked him."

The vicar murmured, "She plays an excellent rubber of piquet, and is very pleasing to gaze upon."

Such irreverences acted like a spark to the duke's fury. "Damme, David, you're pitching it too rum—she could be Venus herself and it would not signify." The duke stopped and glared at his friend, then shouted, "Good God! You want me to get riveted to that female!"

"Precise to the pin, Myles; the lady would make you a splendid wife."

"I don't want a wife," wailed the duke.

"And a very superior duchess. She is of the first stare

and in London would be welcomed by the highest sticklers of the *ton*."

The duke leered at his vicar suspiciously. "So, Madame Lanier has been arming you so you can shoot me down."

The vicar broke into laughter. "Looby, no, Myles, not she—far too busy trying to shock me green. No, it is my own sweet wife and the ladies of the county who twitter like birds about how joyous and romantic all would be if the Dour Duke married the darling Widow Lanier."

"Dear God!" exploded the duke.

"Quite so," said the vicar. "I wonder to what the young widow attributes the immediate stop of chatter whenever she joins or passes a group of ladies."

Thoroughly angry now, the duke snorted, "Probably started the on-dit herself."

"Heavens, no, she's bewildered—has asked my Rachel once or twice if she displayed a sartorial solecism."

"And you! You—my supposed friend—propound I assuage the prattleboxes by making an offer for the quarrelsome lady?"

"Yes, my dear Duke. I do; she is truly delightful and—"

"We would mill all the time!" shouted the duke.

"All the better; you will fratch happily for many years to come."

The duke jumped from his chair and blazed down at the vicar. "Go home! Get out of here before I plant you a facer!"

The vicar retreated hastily to the door, then said, "Think on it, Myles. She is a lady of marked good sense," then hurried out.

The duke paced the floor, sometimes banging his

fist on the desk in anger, then rubbing his hands together in despair. He must wed; he must have a duchess; and he knew no female other than the brangling Mrs. Lanier. In the village the silly bleaters were gabbling—the sapskulls. Old Madame Lanier had told him out and out—the grudgeon. Even the vicar! All bullocking him to make an offer for the one female who made him cross as crabs. It's Dead Sea fruit! But I must have a duchess—I'm at a devil of a stand—but I must have a duchess, a duchess, a duchess. Suddenly the duke stopped still and slapped his clenched fist to his forehead.

Ah, yes, I must have a duchess!

12

The lady of "marked good sense" sat at her desk at Willowood, a frown marking perpendicular lines between her brows. A letter lying before her compelled her anxiety. Its message—cold and stiff—informed her that Sir Alfred Lanier would hereafter be unable to deposit further funds to the account of Mrs. Eric Lanier—signed by the solicitor.

How like Alfred, Lenore thought, visualizing the stern man who had disapproved of his younger brother taking a poor girl for his bride.

Eric had described the scene when he had gone to his older brother to proclaim his love for Lenore

Marie Carey, daughter of the Vicar of St. Swithens, near Provinder.

"Eric, you run mad." Lenore could almost hear Alfred's high, sneering voice. "She is but a penniless vicar's child—a good name, granted—but has neither position nor wealth. She brings you nothing. It is past all bounds, dear boy."

"Nevertheless, I love her and will wed her."

"Then expect no help from me," proclaimed the cold gentleman of vast wealth.

"You will come to the wedding, I hope, generous brother of mine."

"Certainly. Martha and I always do the family duties, though why you marry in such an out-of-the-way place as Provinder . . ."

"It is Lenore's home; naturally we marry there. However, if you judge the ride will upset Martha, do assure her we will understand," Eric said coldly.

"We shall see," replied Sir Alfred, nodding in dismissal.

"My brother," Eric reported to Lenore later, "is a toplofty bore."

Lenore silently hoped Lady Martha would choose not to attend the marriage. Lenore remembered when she had met the formidable lady at parties and found her tongue cruel. One night at Almack's Lady Martha had cornered Lenore and questioned her sharply, "This is your first season, is it not?"

"Yes. Lady Leticia Ware kindly sponsored me," responded the young Lenore.

"Oh, Lady Ware." Lady Martha's tone dismissed Lady Leticia as hardly worthy of being in the *ton*. "I believe you have been introduced to my brother-in-law, Captain Eric Lanier," the lady said languidly.

"Oh, yes!" Lenore could not conceal her pleasure at the sound of his name.

"A charming young man," continued the relentless voice, "but not a gentleman of substance. It is his brother's and my hope that he marry a suitable lady who can sustain a proper mode of living for an officer —either by her wealth or being of such rank in the *haut ton* that his career will be furthered."

Lenore, already more than half in love with Captain Eric Lanier, felt as if a glass of cold water had been thrown over her. She said nothing, but a flush crept up from her neck. Fortunately Lady Martha was distracted by another, and Lenore was able to slip away. She tried to avoid Eric the rest of the evening, but he searched until he found her crying in a side alcove.

"What did the miserable Martha say to you?" he demanded harshly. Lenore shook her head. "I saw her chattering at you and attempted to rescue you, but when I could get through the press of dancers, you'd disappeared. What did she say?"

"I can't tell you," cried the stricken Lenore.

"You do not have to—my darling, sweet Martha revealed to you her great desire—that I marry a high-flyer with barrels of blunt."

Lenore gasped at this display of insight and wisdom.

Looking down into her startled and woebegone face, Eric Lanier, younger son, threw back his head and laughed loudly, then he recovered enough breath to speak. "My precious Lenore, I cannot possibly marry a gel with rolls of soft, because I am going to marry you and make myself the happiest man in the world."

Lenore was so astonished at this declaration—opening the gates to her idea of paradise—that she burst into wild sobs of joy.

The captain, with soldierly aplomb, gathered his tearful love into his arms and permitted her to dampen his uniform until he could reach his handkerchief to dry her tears. Soon Lenore turned up a timorously smiling face.

"Now, Lenore, my dearest heart, do not hiccup, for I intend to kiss you, and nothing must interrupt such a pleasure." Eric then carried out his intent, to Lenore's delight.

To everyone's relief the arrogant, critical, and bothersome Lady Martha chose not to attend the nuptials of the "feckless Eric."

The wedding was small, but so happy that even the lofty Alfred broke down and behaved—for him—unusually agreeably. The tiny church blazed with flowers. Eric's fellow officers, in dress uniform, dazzled the young ladies present, two of whom met their future husbands that sunny, gladsome day.

Now seated at her desk at Willowood, Lenore let a tear rise and roll down her cheek.

Leaving a gay party of wedding guests, Lenore and Eric had gone directly to their new home—a house discovered in London, which Lenore had loved on first sight.

Lenore's only sad moment came in bidding farewell to her father, who rallied her spirits by announcing he had so enjoyed her wedding, he might consider having one of his own and that she keep an eye peeled in London for a female who would suit him.

For two years the young Laniers' home teemed with gaiety. The ladies and blades of London agreed that to be friends of the Laniers, to dash in and out of their home, to gather for their parties, to include them in any caper, was the most famous fun. Eric, tall, handsome, and dashing, and Lenore, sweet, smiling, and full of wit were the most popular couple in the city.

Upon Eric's receipt of his orders to go to the Peninsula, Lenore immediately announced she would go with him. Eric tried to persuade her that wives, unwelcome on the Penn, found living there difficult. Lenore merely said, "My dearest love, where thou goest, I will go." Eric reluctantly gave in.

Despite Lenore's plans to travel immediately with Eric, her father died—as he had lived—quietly, in his sleep, so Lenore remained in England two months before she joined her beloved husband.

In Spain Eric welcomed her with the tenderness he had always shown, and was near tears when he led her to the hovel that, perforce, had to be their home. Lenore, dashed by its starkness, nevertheless assured him her delight of reunion overshadowed any discomfort.

Eric kissed her—she was to realize later—a kiss of farewell, for never again would she encounter the Eric she had wed.

An intrepid soldier, Eric, away from the field of battle, sought the company of officers who, like himself, devoted their time to gaming. Lenore grew used to the sight of Eric's batman, Abel, trudging up the steep hill to salute and announce that the captain, detained, would sleep in the barracks. Very soon Lenore, on spying the huge man from her front window, would run to the door and wave her understanding, thus saving him the climb.

When home, Eric, though loving, was restless and

insisted they play piquet for high stakes. If she protested, he called her his little nipsqueeze, and dealt the cards. To preserve the little household monies afforded her, Leonore became an expert player.

One day Lenore, bored, lonely, while passing the hospital tent, on impulse offered to assist the overworked doctors, who accepted gladly any aid extended.

Eric at first demurred but shortly, relieved that his wife seemed more content, relished his freedom.

For two years Lenore tended the wounded and lent willing hands wherever needed. The doctors, noting her dedication, taught her, then learned to rely on the skills she developed in the ways of healing.

The afternoon Eric's senior officer climbed the hill to relate that Eric had been shot from his horse, dying instantly, Lenore wept tears of grief for the Eric she had wed, and relief for her release from the Eric he had become, for she had long realized the bitter truth—Eric loved her, but loved gaming more.

Arrangements were quickly made for her departure from the Peninsula. A note from Lady Leticia Ware, insisting she come to Ware House upon her arrival in England, comforted her. But the journey proved long and wearisome.

Lady Leticia's heart ached when she gathered the thin and begrimed widow into her arms. "To bed with you, my little one," was spoken as she propelled Lenore up the stairs. Tucked in a soft, warm bed, Lenore gladly fell into oblivion.

Two days of sweet care and nurturing food did much to restore the new widow, who, on the second evening, in better spirits, rose for dinner.

A goodly pile of letters awaited her—Lady Leticia had forbidden that any mail disturb Lenore's rest. Most were notes of condolence, but one was a stiff message from Sir Alfred Lanier, announcing he expected her at the office of Eric's and his solicitor the next afternoon.

Lenore remembered Mr. Wodly, the solicitor, as a wedding guest at her marriage. She went early to his office and asked if she might consult him before Sir Alfred arrived. The benevolent man welcomed her warmly and chose with care words to cushion the blow about to befall her. She would remember that Eric, being a younger son, received no income other than his pay as an officer. True, there was a small pension, but it could scarce cover her smallest expenses.

Lenore, not surprised, did not take the report badly, but, noticing Mr. Wodly's harried expression, asked what troubled him.

"Were you aware that Eric was a court card?"

"Indeed so. His gambling disturbed me greatly while we were on the Penn." Mr. Wodly frowned, and Lenore added, "I could not stop him."

"Dear Mrs. Lanier, it never occurred to me to question you could even try, for Eric Lanier was his father's son—gaming in his bones. His grandfather ran down two fortunes—Eric came by it naturally."

Lenore gazed at him. "I never heard Eric mention either his father or his grandfather."

"Both stuck their spoons in the wall before he was three." Mr. Wodly shook his head. "Both wild to a fault!"

"Poor Eric," Lenore said, sighing. "Tell me the whole, Mr. Wodly. What are Eric's debts?"

"My dear, first let me explain that some of his fellow officers have forgiven his notes, but others feel the necessity of having them paid."

"The forgivers are merciful. Appraise me of the total, please."

Mr. Wodly mentioned a sum that caused Lenore to gasp.

"Oh, no, he could scarcely have had the hours to lose so much."

"I'm afraid he was a gapeseed gamester—his senior officer verified the list."

"What am I to do?" wailed Lenore. "I have no money other than the pittance my father left me and the pension."

"Sir Alfred will be here shortly. I think he has some suggestions for you. If you will forgive me, I'll let him propose them."

"Mr. Wodly, this is a terrible coil!" Lenore began to sob.

"Please do not cry, my dear; Sir Alfred hates weepiness."

Surprised at his urgent tone, Lenore asked, "Why?"

"Crying is the way Lady Martha winds him around her thumb," explained Mr. Wodly simply.

The vision of the stiff-faced Martha using tears to get her way so amused Lenore that she burst out laughing—pleasing Mr. Wodly very much.

Mrs. Eric Lanier is a muffin, the solicitor averred to himself.

When Sir Alfred came, he ordered Mr. Wodly from the office, proceeded to read Lenore a lecture on the folly of an Army officer getting riveted too young— Eric was thirty before he wed—and the further evils of marrying a penniless chit of a girl, then pointed out the wickedness of gambling, implying perhaps she too had whiled away her time at the tables.

Lenore listened with patience, awaiting the hammer's fall.

At long last Sir Alfred pronounced in solemn tones that he intended—to save the family honor—to pay his brother's debts; no stain was to besmirch his lineage. However, in return, Lenore must do as he directed.

"Martha and I have had serious chats concerning your future. Aware you are quite rolled up, anything we do is from the goodness of our hearts." Lenore nodded. "Martha and I have decided you may live in Willowood, our home in Somerset, where all the widows of the family have ended their days, with one exception. Until now, my grandmother, Madame Lanier, has refused to leave London. Now, because there will be someone to tend her, she has consented to go, provided you meet with her approval."

Lenore stared at him aghast. "Madame Lanier, Eric's grandmother?"

"The same. A formidable female, I grant, but she favored Eric and will most likely be partial to you."

Lenore, dismayed, tried to remember what Eric had said of his grandmother. "Grandmother has kept the whole family in a bustle for years, with her impolite out-and-out talk and endless gossip. She's a silly lamb, who says whatever pops into her head—true or false. Alfred doesn't like her by half—she always called him the Twiddlepoop, and me the Lobcock."

"What does she call Lady Martha?" Lenore had asked.

"The goosecap dowd," had been Eric's prompt reply.

Lenore had laughed, but now she grew afraid. She realized she must accept Alfred's offer, for, though Lady Leticia urged her to remain as her companion, Lenore sensed the dear lady did not have enough income to support them both.

There was one ray of hope. "Alfred, maybe Madame Lanier will not take to me."

"She will," Alfred said grimly.

Poor lady, thought Lenore, she has no more choice than I do.

"I will arrange a visit to her home, then you will see Martha's and my plans are wise for you both." In a burst of generosity, Sir Alfred added, "If you keep my grandmother content at Willowood, I will place a sum of money in your account each month."

Surveying the rich Alfred, Lenore had a desire to kick him in his leg, so elegantly encased in yellow satin. Rising, she said, "I suppose I'm grateful to you," then walking and opening the door, she added, "but tell me, Alfred, how many tears did Martha squeeze out to persuade you in this sweeping of widows out of London?" Her last glimpse of Alfred showed his mouth fallen open.

Two days later Lenore received a note saying that Sir Alfred's carriage would be at Lady Leticia's door in the early afternoon to deliver Lenore to Madame Lanier's home.

Alighting in front of the dark, gloomy house, Lenore shook with fright. Even the generous, spirited Lady Leticia had murmured of Madame Lanier's forked tongue. To Lenore's surprise, the maid who opened the door dimpled cheerfully and ushered Lenore into a bright morning room, where, almost buried in shawls, the alarming Madame Lanier sat by the fire.

"Come in, come in," growled the old lady as the maid announced Lenore. "Come where I can see what kind of a wet goose you are—marrying a Lanier."

Lenore stepped forward, and the ancient lady raked

her from head to foot. "So, 'twas you who wed the Lobcock, a trifling boy if ever there be one."

Lenore listened to the words carefully, then answered, "Madame, I am the wet goose who married your grandson, whom you and I loved dearly."

The old lady's head shot up and she glared at Lenore. "So, you loved him, eh?"

Lenore sighed. "Yes, madame, very much."

"And you think I did too?" the old lady scowled.

"Yes madame, more than anyone."

"Valiant-tongued, ain't you?"

"My father always demanded I tell the truth, and the truth is that you adored Eric."

"Make him happy, did you?"

Lenore took a deep breath. "Yes, I think I did."

"He was a leg; why didn't you stop him gaming?"

For an instant Lenore hesitated, then peering into the hooded eyes, said, "Madame, is there a lady in the universe who could distract a Lanier from what he wished to do?"

The old lady cackled. "Not any Lanier man. That pudding-hearted Alfred is under the cat's paw, but no Lanier man would be reined by a female. Go pull the bell; I can see you ain't blockish, and if I'm going to have to live with you, I want no featherhead. What did Eric say about me?"

"He told me you were his wicked old grandmother, who called him Lobcock, and that you keep the whole family in an uproar and always have. He informed me of it with great pride."

"Humph, a good one, the Lobcock; not woodenheaded like the Twiddlepoop."

There was a knock on the door and the maid entered.

"Bring some brandy, Daisy."

The young girl shook her head.

"You heard me, saucebox, bring us some brandy."

Daisy stood still.

"Oh, ratafia then; can't even drink your health proper, thanks to that fubsy-faced Martha."

"I prefer ratafia," said Lenore as the maid left.

"Then you're queer in the attic," grumbled Madame Lanier; then, glinting sharply at Lenore, "You ain't a bluestocking, are you?"

"Don't gammon me," said Lenore, giggling. "Eric would never have wed such a one. Please, let us talk of Willowood."

To Lenore's distress, the old lady started to cry. "Madame, what is it?"

"Willowood is where all the Lanier ladies are discarded when they give notice to quit."

"Oh, Madame Lanier." Lenore knelt by Madame Lanier's chair. "Please don't say that; I am not ready to die, and I'm going to Willowood."

"You're young, and will only be there because Alfred wants you to tend me before I stick my spoon in the wall."

Fortunately, Daisy entered and poured two glasses of the cordial. Lenore resumed her chair. "Mamère, please listen to me. We are both to be at Willowood, and, I'm sure, will deal extremely comfortably with one another, but not if you are missish all the time. Come, let us drink to our happiness and whistle the others to Jericho." She raised her glass.

"Will you let me have brandy?" asked the old lady suspiciously.

Lenore burst into laughter. "Rest easy on that head; I consider brandy, at times, very good for the blood."

Madame Lanier, pleased, drank her ratafia in one gulp. "You're full of gig, ain't you?"

"Not always, but I'm determined to try and like Willowood. Does it have a garden?"

"Pour me another," commanded the old lady. Lenore, deciding to indulge her, filled the glass half full, and watched its contents disappear immediately.

"You called me Mamère." The voice was sharp.

"It was my name for my own grandmother; please, may I call you Mamère?"

"Ninnyhammer, you already have," cackled the old lady. "Now, about Willowood. It has two gardens, kitchen and flower."

"Splendid!"

The widows Lanier chatted companionably and, when Lenore rose to leave, the old lady snapped, "Come kiss me! Eric did evince some signs of sense for once in his life, getting buckled to you. You persuade me that we'll rub along tolerably even in that desert Willowood."

After the visit, both ladies felt their future brighter.

While awaiting word from Sir Alfred on the date for travel to Willowood, Lenore experienced a nagging urge to see again the home where she and Eric had lived so lightheartedly. It was a bittersweet pilgrimage —her heart lay heavy as she slowly walked down the familiar street. Suddenly she heard her name shouted. "Mrs. Lanier, ma'am, Mrs. Lanier." A huge man ran across the road. As he drew near she recognized him.

"Abel, oh, Abel, I am glad to see you."

"And I you, ma'am. I've been here every day in hopes of catching you." The big man stepped in front of her and almost saluted.

"Oh, Abel." Lenore let the tears flow down her cheeks.

Abel grasped her elbow lightly. "Steady now, ma'am, the captain'd skin me red if he knew I made you cry."

"I cry because I'm so rejoiced to see you. When did you get back from the Penn, and what are you doing now?"

"Waiting for you, ma'am."

"Me?" Lenore asked, startled.

"If you'd be so good as to walk with me to the bench in the park there," he pointed across the cobblestones, "I'll give you the ins and outs."

"Of course, Abel." Lenore fell in step. When seated, Abel nodded toward the house. "It looks neat, but it's too quiet—no dashing in and out like the old days, when you and the captain lived there."

"Abel, is it true, you have been here each day?"

"On this very bench, ma'am, watching and hoping."

"Why? You could have gone to Sir Alfred and he—"

"Not him, ma'am, not that toplofty bell wire. No, ma'am, I felt if good could prevail, you'd come and I'd catch you."

"It did, and here I am. Do you bring news from the Penn?"

"No, ma'am, I left there quickly as I could."

"Why do you wish to see me?" Lenore was puzzled.

"Well, ma'am, I trod beside the captain since he was a young varmint—eyed him in mischief and out—and dressed him myself, for the best maneuver he ever accomplished—wedding you. Careful, ma'am," he said, seeing Lenore's eyes brim. "When he died, my life fell crosswise. Oh, I tried to report to another officer." Abel shook his head. "Not for the likes of me, not that one. At last I came to a great understanding—I was homesick. Not for England, though I love her, but for living near the captain and you. Now, I'm not so daft as to think I could have it as with the captain, but I judged that to serve you would be the next best to being with him."

"Serve me?" Lenore stammered.

"Yes, ma'am. You were a big part of the captain's life, and if I serve you, it would be beyond anything great."

Lenore stared up at the man whom she had known only as Eric's devoted batman, who had behaved with profound respect, but had never spoken more than a word or two except in delivery of his messages. His present outpouring touched her. She slowly smiled and Abel broke into an enormous grin.

"Abel, everything about you is outsize, even your heart, but I cannot let you do this—I have no money."

Abel threw back his large head and roared, "Who said anything about brass? I have all the Georges I want and more where they come from." He sobered. "Ma'am, in this whole world, nothing signifies to me but to be of service to you."

"Oh, Abel." Lenore then frowned. "But I'm leaving London to live in Willowood."

"Ach, the devil you say. Is that all the old lofty nip-squeeze came up with for you? That caps it right and tight. Now you definitely must have me, ma'am; Willowood hasn't been lived in for a devil's age."

"Oh!" cried Lenore.

"Just so, ma'am. You will require a strong man to put *that* household to rights."

"And the gardens?"

"Weeds knee-deep; I'd go bail on it."

"Oh, dear, Sir Alfred did not mention its condition; just said I should live there."

Abel sprang to his feet and let out a torrent of
Spanish words that Lenore could not understand, but
felt it far better she didn't. Finally finished, Abel
stared down into Lenore's upturned face. "Forgive me,
ma'am."

"Of course."

"Mrs. Lanier," Abel spoke in formal tones, "it
would not only give me pleasure, but I'm now convinced it my deepest duty to stand guard for my captain's widow."

"There's more, Abel. Madame Lanier is to reside
at Willowood also."

"Hoo, the old dragon?" Abel chortled loudly.

"Abel!" Lenore tried to sound severe.

"Oh, ma'am, I'm acquainted with that one. She and
I have crossed swords before—had some rare scrow
rows, we two—but I love the old harridan, with her
tongue like a fiddlestick."

"Abel, she may not want you."

"Be easy on that head, ma'am, she'll give me Turk-
ish treatment and be happy as a grig."

Lenore had doubts, but, looking up at the bib
man who grinned at her so eagerly, she said, "Abel,
you lift my spirits—I have a friend."

"You can put your blunt on it, ma'am." Abel sat
down. "Now, ma'am, we have some things to discuss.
When do you leave London?"

"I'm not certain."

"No matter, I've not unpacked since I left the Penn,
just in case you needed me quickly, so any hour will
suit. How do we go?"

"I can't say; Sir Alfred is making the arrangements."

"Where are you staying, ma'am? I'll come by each
day to discover your plays."

A wave of relief washed over Lenore for the protection of a man of strength and kindness. "Oh, Abel, I'm thankful to have you! I stay at Lady Leticia Ware's—come, walk there with me."

The huge man shortened his stride and Lenore lengthened hers—together they paced in perfect rhythm.

13

Riding through the streets on the way to pick up Madame Lanier, Lenore wondered if she would ever see London again. She sighed, then scolded herself for being missish. When the horses stopped in front of Madame Lanier's house, Lenore leaned forward to watch Abel run up the steps to the front door, which opened before he could knock. Daisy pointed to the luggage and Abel carried the bags to the carriage and stored them; finished, he went up the steps and bowed to Madame Lanier, who appeared in the doorway.

"Hello, jackawarts; see you're as handsome as ever," the old lady greeted him.

Abel's ugly face broke into a grin. "Don't try to cut a wheedle with me, madame, 'twon't serve. Take my arm." Abel crooked his elbow.

"No such thing; don't you think I can go down the stairs of my own house?" The house, she said to herself, no longer to be home.

Lenore, seeing the old lady's face crumble, called, as if impatient, "Mamère, please hurry. I'm anxious to see Willowood in daylight."

Daisy put her arm around the old lady's waist and led her down the steps. Abel, without a word, lifted the slight figure into the seat beside Lenore, who tucked a robe snugly as Daisy kissed Madame Lanier's hand and ran into the house. Before the door closed the carriage rolled on its way.

Lenore let Eric's grandmother cry herself to sleep.

Lady Leticia had provided a picnic lunch and Lenore suggested they eat in the woods by the side of the road. Nibbling on glazed ham and a slice of bread and butter, the old lady said, "Ain't smelled grass in an eon; new green in the trees—pretty. Maybe Willowood won't be so dreadful." The concession raised Lenore's spirits.

On first sight Willowood appeared buried in vines. Lenore cried out in dismay, but Abel laughed and declared himself the best pruner and trimmer in England. On entering the house, although it had been cleaned, the smell of disuse hung heavy in the shabby, elegant rooms. Abel, who had visited Willowood often, lit the fire in the morning room and hurried off to lay wood in the other fireplaces. Lenore, after seating Mamère close to the fire where she soon dozed again, went to set the old lady's bedroom in order.

After Abel had, with the aid of the coachman, put the baggage and boxes in their proper places, he urged Lenore, "Come outside, ma'am; the sun shines, and tomorrow I'll massacre the vines." Preceding her through the choked paths, he pointed out that the garden beds offered promise—a few sturdy plants bloomed, despite the tangle of neglect.

Lenore suddenly smiled. "Abel, I really can garden here."

"Ma'am." Abel sounded shocked. "A lady like yourself does not garden—you gather and arrange flowers."

"Fustian! I intend to dig, plant, weed, and grow the most beautiful blooms in the county."

Abel raised his eyebrows. "It will be some go, ma'am, with the palace nearby."

"Palace?"

"Home of the Duke of Asherwood. Didn't the captain tell you tales of his boyhood friend?"

"Yes-s-s, but he referred to him as Mills or some such name—called him a jolly lad."

"His name, ma'am, is Myles Milford William Asherwood, Duke of Asherwood; a sprightly youngster, but now entitled 'the Dour Duke;' had a misalliance —he is almost a recluse."

"What's that got to say to anything about my flower beds?"

"Ma'am, the duke's gardens are reputed among the finest in the land."

Lenore tossed her head. "I expect to enter a caveat with him there—in a small way, of course."

Abel laughed and suggested they finish the indoor tasks so he could start the outdoor work in the morning. Mamère, now awake, regaled Lenore with memories of Eric and Alfred as children. Later Abel brought cold partridges, a basket of pastries, and tea. After the repast Madame Lanier announced she would go upstairs; she rose and tottered. Lenore sprang up and cried, "Mamère, what is it?"

"Twisted my ankle at the picnic."

"Oh, dear, you can't climb the stairs. We'll fix a bed for you here."

"Fiddlesticks! Old Abel, here, can carry me up and down stairs; it'll be nice to be in a strong man's arms again."

The peccancy caused Lenore to blush and Abel to laugh. Stepping forward and picking the old lady up lightly, he leered at her. "Don't be on the catch for me, my lady, I ain't in Petticoat Lane." The remark pleased them both and mildly shocked Lenore.

The next morning Abel woke to hear Lenore stirring in the kitchen. He joined her, all apologies. "Ma'am, I overslept."

"I don't wonder at it; yesterday you moved mountains. Now don't act as if you are in for a scold. Have some tea. I've made a total of the necessary items for the larder and the garden." She handed Abel the list and pointed to the table. "There'll be eggs in a minute."

"Mrs. Lanier, you should not be cooking; 'tisn't work for a lady—"

"Abel," Lenore cut in, "true, I am a lady, but was brought up in a vicarage, where our living often ran thin. When my mother died I learned to cook and to do all the household chores, and I did them for many years. Be warned, I'll perform numerous tasks you judge a lady should not do, but you must help and not put yourself in a taking over me."

A great lady, thought Abel, but only said, "Yes, ma'am."

"Check the list to see if I've forgotten needed things," said Lenore as she busied herself at the stove. While Abel ate, she took Mamère her eggs, toast, and tea.

"Did you sleep well?" she asked the sleepy old lady.

"Not a wink," said Mamère.

"Oh dear, your ankle?"

"No, the quiet."

Lenore sighed. "How sad. . . . Well, you can stay in bed and nap all day."

"Sassbox, put the tray on the table and get me out of bed. After breakfast bring me writing materials; I intend to write my friends to tell them what they're missing, not being able to live in the country."

Uncertain as to the tenor of this remark, Lenore helped the old lady rise, then, seeing her ensconced in a large chair, explained that other duties demanded attention, but that she would see her later.

So began the settling into Willowood. Soon unpacked, Lenore turned her thoughts to the garden. Abel, true to his bragging, pruned the vines into submission, then spaded the earth and prepared the soil for planting. Lenore's flower bed stretched from the fence to the front of the stone house, which had mellowed to soft yellow. Diamond-paned windows, freed of the vines, reflected the sunshine. The vegetable bed, under Abel's care, was to be sown in the rich soil behind the house, near the succession house, with its glass panes painted white to protect seedlings. Lenore rejoiced. "I can start hundreds," she said.

Mamère brought gaiety to Willowood. She and Abel carried on an outrageous flirtation in the most lurid terms they could utter, charming themselves beyond belief.

One day, on one of his frequent visits to the village shops, Abel came home accompanied by a dark-haired, almost beautiful, woman. He announced, in response to Lenore's unspoken question, that the Spanish woman—Maria Lopez Brown, widow of a soldier—would cook for them because the señora longed to chat in her native tongue.

Surprised, Lenore studied the woman's shy face and sad eyes. "You do cook?" she asked in Spanish. The gush of response was incomprehensible to Lenore, but Abel quickly translated. "She says, yes."

Lenore, not fond of the kitchen, sighed in relief. "*Bien!*" which precipitated another deluge of words. Abel interpreted, "She says, thank you," then hurried the woman off to collect her belongings.

Later Lenore told Abel that Maria would have the room next to her own, and asked, "What of Maria's wages?" Abel replied loftily that Maria was a jewel beyond price and would accept no offered sum, and left the room.

Maria proved a joy. She sang while cooking her special brand of delectable meals, and within a few days—of her own accord—took over most of the household chores.

Lenore, feeling guilty, asked Abel about Maria's continual hunt for tasks. He explained that, being trained to hard work, she reveled in the fact that she need not fear being black and blue from beatings. Lenore gasped.

Lenore soon noticed more and more periods when Maria's singing and Abel's rolling Spanish mingled boomingly.

The gardens at Willowood flourished, and on the day Heath fell into their lives, he came as an exciting new interest. When the deep concern for his injuries abated, they all relished having the young man in the house. Mamère toddled across the hall each day to tell him tales—all discreet—of past hunting parties, wonderful horses ridden over the fields, and magnificent banquets served to people of note and beauty.

Abel tended the boy with the tenderness of a nanny. Once it was revealed that he had been on the Penn,

Heath could not get his fill of adventures Abel related. The yarns grew elaborate, with Captain Eric Lanier, the unfailing hero, superbly aided by his extraordinary batman. Heath drank in every word. Lenore finally felt compelled to warn Heath that Abel might be spinning a bit of moonglow. Heath grinned and assured her he was not a flat and knew a Banbury tale when he heard one.

Maria sang gleefully as she exercised her skill on the choice foods provided by the duke, stirred to further culinary efforts by Heath's eager appetite.

14

Seated at her desk, Lenore, recalling Heath's stay at Willowood, tried not to dwell on her own feelings, but could not push them away. Memories kept bursting like bubbles in her mind: her quaking fear for Heath; her shaking that night she had stood up to the duke; her easement when she thought of piquet to divert him; her anger at his generosity, despite its being a most timely windfall; guilt at her lack of appreciation and her surly treatment of His Grace. She felt pride in her ripping up of Doctor Sagout, and gratitude in the duke's agreement that the treatment of bleeding a patient was a barbarous custom.

Urging Heath to leave his bed had been daring, and she had trembled a little at the duke's ire, for Heath might have had a relapse. Fortunately his recovery sped rapidly and the duke had taken him home; she had not laid eyes on Heath or the duke since.

Lenore sighed and tried to snip off her thoughts, but found it impossible—she missed the duke, the man with whom she brangled, the man who let her win at piquet, the man who was kind or angry by spurts—the Dour Duke. She found herself longing to see his scowling face. With reluctance she finally admitted—green-headed as it was—that she loved His Grace.

Then why had she been so havey-cavey as to run away when he came for Heath? Maybe she should write a note and inquire as to the boy's health . . . No! that would be forward. I'm behaving like a schoolgirl—forget him!—he is a morose man, a recluse, and in all probability, I'll never encounter him again.

At that moment she heard the familiar clop of the duke's matched grays stopping at her gate. For an instant she wondered whether her imagination was playing tricks, so strong was her desire to hear just that sound. Rushing to the window, she saw the duke alight from his carriage. She ran to the mirror, arranged her hair, pinched her cheeks, smoothed her dress—thankful for its pretty fit.

When Abel announced the duke, Mrs. Eric Lanier sat straight at her desk, a pen moving busily across a sheet of stationery. When the duke entered, he saw the quarrelsome female just ending a letter.

"Come in, Duke, and sit by the fire. I will be free shortly."

Moving stiffly to the proffered chair, he watched the lady of "good sense" sign her name with a flourish, then deliberately seal an envelope and address it. He would have been puzzled had he seen the inside sheet —a scribble without meaning.

Lenore rose and so did the duke. She approached him, holding out her hand. He bowed over it.

"I trust Heath is mending nicely," said Lenore in a cool voice.

"He is better," conceded the duke.

"I'm delighted, but not struck with wonderment." Lenore sat down. Had she looked at His Grace, she would have noted him flush, irritated by her placid rightness.

"We miss Heath: he was game as a pebble while here."

The duke said nothing, just stared at the floor. Lenore tried again. "Let me send for some refreshments. Brandy or . . ."

"Nothing, thank you," muttered the duke.

Lenore gazed at the distraught man. "What is it, Your Grace? What troubles you?"

The duke raised his eyes to hers. "Have you heard the gossip, Mrs. Lanier?"

"No." Lenore shook her head.

"Then let me enlighten you about the whole of it." The duke, speaking in a low voice, told of Charles's arrival and history. Lenore uttered no word until he had finished, then she startled him by clapping her hands. "Why, Duke, how famous—a second son to love and cherish, a brother for Heath—why, sir, you are blessed!"

The duke, who had not considered Charles as other than an additional woe in his already overburdened life, grew angry. "Madam, you are tipping me a rise."

"Insulting you?" Ire flooded Lenore. "Well, that caps the globe! You are fortunate enough to have another son to carry on your name and be a comfort to you later. I congratulate you, and you claim I give offense. Sir, you have no observance of civility."

The duke, now thoroughly beside himself, rose and shouted, "Madam, I did not come to evaluate Charles's effect on my life."

"No? Then inform me quickly what you do come to talk about," Lenore demanded angrily.

"I came here to ask you to be my duchess," blurted the duke.

"What?" Lenore's reply came to her lips almost as a shout.

"I came to ask you to be my duchess," repeated the duke harshly.

"Sir, you've flown into alts!" Lenore asserted in positive tones.

The duke, having voiced the terrible question, calmed. "No, madam, I am here to request you to be my duchess, and I so do."

Lenore, quite in pieces, asked, "You want me to be your duchess?"

"Yes," said the duke succinctly. "It is exactly what I want."

"Your wife?" whispered the bemused Lenore.

The duke took a deep breath, then answered quietly, "No, madam—my duchess."

Lenore stared at the duke as the meaning of his words engulfed her—his duchess, but not his wife. She dropped her eyes, her hands clenched. She shook her head in confusion. "But if I become your duchess, we would have to marry."

"Yes, you will be the Duchess of Asherwood, so treated by everyone." The duke spoke coldly.

Everyone—except the man standing before her— the man she had missed so achingly, so longed to see.

He did not desire her as his wife, but why, then, his duchess? She frowned at the duke. "Why, Your Grace?"

The duke, having anticipated the dreaded query, responded swiftly. "It has become imperative that I open my London residence and have a duchess at the head of my household."

Lenore was stunned. She blinked. "Open your city home? You? Why, you are a recluse, almost never seen even by your own villagers."

"Yes, for some years, but now . . ." The duke paused —he felt an urge to confide in Lenore, whose upturned eyes stared so intensely, but no, he was sworn to secrecy—his plans to be withheld especially from his duchess. "Madam, a deep obligation demands a complete turnabout in my life—not only is there to be a duchess, but, when in London, the Duke and Duchess of Asherwood must blossom into the pink of the *ton*."

Totally unstrung, Lenore waved her hand airily. "Duke, you're roasting me!"

"No, madam, I am not," said the duke bitterly.

"But you don't care a fig for the *ton*."

"True, but I am going to bend my will to become the first consequence, and I shall succeed."

Lenore exclaimed wildly, "Good Lord, Duke, and you think I could be in the pink of fashion? Looby, you should go to London and marry a high-flyer."

"I have asked you to be my duchess, madam," the duke said freezingly. "Please give me your answer."

Puzzled emotions overwhelmed Lenore, but she kept her eyes lowered so the duke should not see her face. Suddenly, like a clap of thunder, she broke into laughter that soon mounted into gales, with tears rolling down her cheeks as she struggled for breath.

"Madam," said the affronted duke, "I've said nothing to make you fall into whoops."

"Oh, Duke," cried Lenore, when she could speak.
"It is hey-go-mad, if you can see. Here am I, a widow,
with not a feather to fly with, banished to live out
my days in Willowood, then out of nowhere, like a
thunderbolt, I am offered for by a duke—one of the
most renowned in England. Not as his wife, but to be
his duchess." Lenore giggled. "Just cast your mind on
what Alfred and Martha would say."

"The devil, I don't give a rush for any thoughts of
theirs or anyone's. How, madam, are you going to
resolve my offer?"

Lenore wiped her eyes and, still amused, rose and
rang for Abel. The duke, uneasy, asked, "Am I to be
sent away?"

"You should be, you know, but first—Ah, Abel,
bring some brandy, please." Then turning to the duke
she said, "I consider it only fair to warn you of the
dangers of installing me as your duchess."

The duke frowned. "I find your levity distasteful,
nor do I relish a brandy."

"But you may be most anxious for one later."

Abel's entrance stopped His Grace's possible retort.

"Thank you, Abel," said Lenore as he poured.
"That will be all."

"Now, Your Grace," Lenore said, resuming her seat,
"if I am to become the Duchess of Asherwood, go to
London—you did say enter the *ton?*"

"Yes, madam." The duke sighed and sat down.

"Then, sir, I have some requirements to be met."
She paused for a long moment; the duke waited.

"First, Mamère must join us." The duke groaned.

"She loves London—Oh come, sir, surely your home
is big enough for the wicked lady, whose joy would

pass all bounds. Next, I could not possibly do without Maria and Abel, who I expect will be publishing their banns any day."

"You voice only details, madam, though I had not anticipated Madame Lanier's presence." Noting Lenore's expression, he added hastily, "However, she will be welcome."

"Good!" Then Lenorre spoke firmly. "And this I demand: I will want to bring up Charles. Heath approaches so near my age, I could not be his mother, but Charles—"

"No! Madam, I plan to send the boy to school; it is fully settled."

Lenore spoke evenly. "You wish me to be your duchess, Your Grace?"

"Yes."

"But not your wife."

The duke drew his brows together. "Yes, madam."

"Then it follows that, as Duchess of Asherwood, I will bear no sons." The duke lowered his eyes. "Why, then, are you determined to deny my request concerning Charles?"

"The Duchess of Asherwood will have no time for—"

"Your Grace." Lenore stood and started for the door. "I bid you good morning."

The duke struggled with his wrathful urge to fling himself from the room, but his compelling necessity struck him—she had to be the duchess, for he knew no other female appropriate to the role.

"Lenore, wait!" He sprang from his chair.

His use of her name gave Lenore pause. When he stood towering over her, she turned up questioning eyes.

"If you want the boy, he will stay." The words were strangled.

Lenore, in a quiet voice, said, "Your Grace, I will never refer to this matter again, I promise." She smiled. "And if you still wish it, I gladly accept your offer."

Startled by her swift capitulation, the duke stared into her eyes and found them warm and gentle. Stepping back, he bowed. "Mrs. Lanier, you do me great honor." From his pocket he brought forth an elaborate jewel box. "Madam—Lenore—every duke in my family has presented his duchess-to-be the Asherwood pearls on their betrothal day." He handed her the velvet box.

Lenore caught her breath when she saw the pearls, lying like drops of cream tinged with pink, against the black velvet. "Oh, Myles, they are magnificent!" Then she quickly raised her eyes in fear she had uttered his given name too soon. Their glances clung for an instant, then the duke broke out, "Madam, you will forgive me if I leave; I have many duties to be attended to in the next fortnight. We will wed in the private chapel of the palace the last Friday of the month, and depart for London shortly thereafter."

"Two sennight from Friday? Sir, you cannot expect me to be ready in that short period—impossible! There is Willowood to close, preparations for the ceremony—" She shook her head. "You do not allow enough hours, and what of the banns?"

"The vicar will assist in procuring a special license. Willowood? Mr. and Mrs. Clough can see to it after you are gone. I hope you wish a small wedding with perhaps a dinner to follow."

"Yes, yes, of course, but my bridal gown, and dresses for London—"

"What is worn for our marriage ceremony does not signify. However, when in London, the Duchess of Asherwood must not only be in the pink of fashion, she must set the styles. I expect you to be the most envied lady of the *ton*—but all in due time."

"Good God!" cried Lenore, falling into a chair, for she did not crave to faint at His Grace's feet.

The duke frowned on her coldly. "I shall leave now. We will next meet in the chapel. Everyone at the palace will have instructions to aid you in your plans. Request what you wish and spare no time to lick penny thoughts." He bowed. "Good-bye, Lenore." He started toward the hall, but Lenore stopped him.

"Myles," she called softly, "I feel like a moth stirring in my cocoon, about to become a butterfly."

The duke, with no use for fanciful notions, walked out and closed the door.

Lenore burst into tears, then found herself laughing. I am a fool, she mused, and happy as a grig. He chose me to be his duchess, which means he has some regard for me. Don't be a gudgeon! It's because you are the only lady of his acquaintance. He gave me his mother's pearls! Yes, but he would so endow any female he elected to marry. He is a toplofty monster and I'm queer in the attic. Why was I such an April gowk as to agree to be his duchess when he lacks a *tendre* for me? Why didn't I behave like a diamond with an air of *à la modilité* and proclaim—"No, Your Grace, I do not intend to marry, but to wear willow for Captain Lanier the rest of my life."

Lenore's good sense bubbled up. Fustian! Eric loved me, but adored gaming; he would have had us on our knees to Alfred every month or so. She hugged herself. Hoy, the Duchess of Asherwood will not have to hang on anyone's sleeve. She frowned. But Alfred and everyone will tattle that I'm making a creampot marriage. Am I? No! I'd wed the duke and live my life as a poor crofter's wife, for he is the top of the trees and I love him! She sighed. If only he loved me. Well, he doesn't, but he favors me to the extent that he is willing to trust me to be his duchess. . . . Trusts me. Lenore snatched at the conceit. He considers me pretty well behaved enough to cut a dash with the *ton*; he has faith I can lend countenance to his household and put a needed touch on many parts of his life. Trust! And trust, Lenore Carey Lanier, is a mighty sturdy pin to hang a marriage on.

Lenore opened the jewel box and lifted out the strand of pearls and laid them across her palm.

Could he be playing me a hoax? Lenore winced. Oh, no he is not cruel. No, but—Lenore hated to admit the newborn idea—he could have had an aberration, a derangement brought on by his tragic and withdrawn life. Lenore frowned. He says he will not see me until the wedding. Is he escaping to London with the determination not to return? Oh, Lord! She picked up the pearls. Will Clough be on the doorstep in the morning to explain that His Grace is ill and . . . Torn in mind, Lenore sighed. It is possible. I must guard my tongue and not announce his proposal to a soul—not Mamère, not the vicar, not anyone. She fell into a sad trance.

A knock on the door roused her. "Come in."

"Ma'am, a boy from the palace brought this." Abel handed her a letter. She thanked him as he left, and glanced listlessly at the envelope. Going to her desk, she slit the flap and withdrew a single sheet.

Dear Mrs. Lanier,
His Grace has just informed me of his forth-

coming nuptials. Only a quinzy throat prevents me from rushing to call on the future Duchess of Asherwood, but my joy at the news is unreined.

The duke has instructed me, as his solicitor, to deposit each month, starting immediately, the sum of one hundred pounds—

Lenore stared, stupefied, at the magnanimity of the amount

—to your account.

Would you be so kind as to send me the name of your bank or, if you prefer, your solicitor.

I await with the greatest pleasure your coming to London as the duchess.

Your obedient servant,
Roger Pettibone

Lenore cried. So it is true—I am to be the Duchess of Asherwood. Myles could never deceive his solicitor! Her heart sang. Picking up Mr. Pettibone's note, she whispered, "Sir, I will provide for him a duchess of the first stare." Folding the sheet, she caught sight of Alfred's letter, cutting her allowance. Well, Alfred, your words condemned me to poverty, but now, sir, I am to be a duchess, a leader of fashion, live in London, with an allowance you and Martha would find mind-boggling. Dear Lord, what a turnabout! She laughed, then sobered. All true, but what obligation could be of such import that the Dour Duke abandons Asherwood to descend on London, bent on cutting a figure in society? And with a lost-down-the-wind widow on his arm? She shook her head. The quizzes will consider him run quite mad. Why is he so . . . ? Is it a commitment to a female . . . ? Now I run crazy; such a debt would be settled by marriage—unless he wishes to avoid a misalliance. No! It is outside his character.

Revenge? Against whom? If the gossip in the village can be believed, he has no active enemies—Lenore giggled—save old Tom Doone, who refuses to pay his rent, thereby hating both the duke and Mr. Endfield.

A favor for a friend? Lenore's eyes narrowed. Yes, he would do a favor for a friend . . . but to pay so long a price? What intimate could demand so much? The vicar? Lenore smiled. David Thomas would far prefer to save his Grace's soul than fling him to the temptations of London. Then whom? He must be a cherished friend to command—but why a duchess? I'm all around in my head in a circle that can run forever. Who? Why? Suddenly her heart sang. No matter—I am going to be the best Duchess of all Asherwood, then maybe . . . Stop! They're all romantical notions—whoosh! Looby, I've a million tasks, but first, to inform Mamère; won't she chirp merry? Abel—will he scowl and say, "Ma'am, the captain would be in dismals"; or "Ma'am, the captain . . ." What difference! Poor Eric is booked, but I'm sure he'd rather me married to the duke than dependent on Alfred's pennies all my life. Alfred! I must write him!

Rushing to her desk, she picked up her pen, but numerous sheets of crushed paper fell into the basket before, satisfied, she wrote:

Dear Alfred,
My news will be of surprise to you, and I plea your fondness for Eric, plus any small regard you have for me, will keep you silent about my disclosure. No syllable to anyone, I beg!

Today, Myles Asherwood offered for me and I accepted.

As you are now thinking, I immediately thought of your grandmother. Please rest easy on that head; she is very dear to me and I want her with us always.

Because of the forthcoming events, unless you deem other gates, Willowood will be closed, all care being taken as to its appointments.

My gratitude for past kindnesses,
Your obedient servant,
L. L.

Sealing the note, Lenore gave it to Abel to post, and went upstairs.

Mamère, seated by the window, greeted Lenore. "Come in, come in, young lady. Maria told me when I woke from my nap that you'd been closeted with the duke a long time. Don't suppose he had enough sense to make an offer for you, though he had time enough to wed and bed you."

"Mamère!" remonstrated Lenore.

"No, I don't guess he did, the cawker."

"My dear madame," Lenore said loftily, "there you're out; the duke did make an offer for me."

"Good Lord—he did? Didn't think he had the courage to offer for any female," the old lady said, sighing. "But I suppose you, with your Gothic notions, flew up in the boughs and convinced him you would wear willow forever rather than be the Duchess of Asherwood—"

"You're a trifle off the hinge, Mamère," Lenore said lightly. "I informed the duke I would be his duchess; and I've ordered Abel to bring us brandy to celebrate."

"Dear God in heaven, you do have some brains after all."

Abel knocked and entered. The old lady slapped the arm of her chair. "Don't be a slowtop, Abel, and pour me plenty. Your needle-witted mistress is going to marry the duke and I want to drink to her happiness."

Abel turned to Lenore. "Ma'am, is it true?"

His look of incredulity made her laugh. "Yes, Abel, His Grace and I will wed."

His ugly face lit up. "Oh, ma'am, this is famous news. The duke is a great gun, bang-up to the echo. All joy to you, ma'am." Then unable to contain himself, he added, "The whole village will be agog—everyone has been hoping that you and the duke would call on the vicar."

"What?" cried Lenore. "How dare they? Oh! So that's why everyone snapped their mouths like turtles when I passed by. Well! Of all the chuckle-headed rattles!"

"Oh, ma'am, the entire county will be gleeful for you and the duke."

Lenore, too angry to respond, heard a mewing sound. Turning, she asked, "Mamère, what is it?"

"You're going to leave Willowood, and I will have to stay here all alone until I stick my spoon in the wall," wailed Madame Lanier.

"Don't talk slum, Mamère, you're an impious old lady indeed, to think I would leave you alone here or anywhere—Hah! You, Abel, and Maria are coming with me—and hark this, darling worry crow—to London."

"London?!" The old lady's voice rose. "No bobbery? 'Tis true?"

Lenore nodded.

"Nuts for us!"

"Mamère!"

"Here, you flippery fellow, give me a brandy, then pour me two more—I'm going to London!"

Abel, handing her the drink, said, "Sip on it, madame, there's only half a glass left in the bottle."

"Step back, you shabster, I want to toast the best granddaughter a lady ever had, even if she is only an in-law. Here, my dearest Lenore, may you be happy as the Duchess of Asherwood and hold for a long trig." Draining her glass, she added, "Now, jackawarts, fill up another and I will sip on that!"

Abel looked at Lenore, who nodded, then asked, "Ma'am, may I tell Maria?"

"Indeed so, Abel," Lenore, concentrating on the brandy she twirled in her glass, remarked lightly. "And, Abel, if you have not done so, I suggest you offer for dear Maria right away."

"Madame!"

The two ladies had the experience of seeing the huge man turn into a fiery statue. For an instant, Lenore feared the blood might burst through his cheeks. She said soothingly, "Be easy, Abel, she'll have you; I've seen the darling glances pointed your way."

"Ma'am," said Abel in a choked voice, "I never meant to be leg-shackled."

"Exactly," said Lenore, laughing, "but think on it, and you'll realize you threw your handkerchief almost the day you brought Maria to the house."

The color drained from his face. "The captain would never approve."

"Maybe not," agreed Lenore, remembering how Eric had always wanted Abel near for his beckoning. "But now it would be a bad backcast not to wed Maria. She'll make you a splendid wife."

Madame Lanier cut in, "Don't act like a Johnny Raw, you popinjay, you and Maria have been smelling of April and May for months." She made a mock pout. "It's given me the dismals to watch, because I ain't young enough to snatch you myself. Go make the offer and don't be an anapo while doing it."

Abel looked daggers at this advice, but catching himself, said with dignity, "If you say so, my ladies, I shall do as you wish." He bowed and left the room.

"The gudgeon; he's carried a soft heart for Maria ever since she first drowned him in Spanish; just too zany to know it," the old lady cackled. "Enow for that; tell me every word Bunky said to you."

Lenore gave a polite version of the duke's offer and as an ending, she unboxed the pearls.

Mamère, her eyes dancing, exclaimed, "Humph, he did it up to the knocker this time. Why are we going to London? Thought Bunky hated the place."

"I'm in the dark, Mamère. He spoke of an obligation which demands he open his house there."

"Well, I don't give a button why, as long as it's fixed that I'm headed for London."

"You are; I couldn't go without you, darling."

"Stop talking sweet," grumbled Madame Lanier, "and give me some more."

"No, peagoose, you've had all you dare; any more and you'd be drunk as a drum."

"Nipsqueeze, I swear you're a Methodist!" grumbled the old lady, then slyly added, "I have in my mind the bedchamber I want in London."

"You've been in the house?" exclaimed Lenore. "Tell me of it this instant!"

" 'Course I have. It's big—big rooms, high ceilings—I want the bedroom overlooking the Square, where I can see something besides flowers and vegetables.

Nasty trick the Twiddlepoop played, sending me down here to see only posies and eatables I don't even like." Her voice began to falter. Lenore, seeing her nod off, sat quietly until the old lady fell asleep, then, taking the brandy decanter, left.

15

On the way back to the palace the duke was bemused to find himself not only eased of mind, but rather gratified with his visit to the lady he would wed. True, she had flown into the boughs anent Charles, but other gates she did appear a female of poise. She had grasped the tenor of his offer quickly, and had neither given way to hysterics nor cried insult. Her insistence that Madame Lanier become part of the London household rankled, but he would not have to deal with the old vixen, praise be. All in all the duke felt he had carried the disagreeable duty off to admiration.

Met by Clough, the duke gave orders that Heath and Charles be sent for, and that he and Mrs. Clough come to the library immediately.

When the Cloughs stood before him, the duke told of his forthcoming marriage, to be followed by the household's move to London. Clough broke into a wide grin and Mrs. Clough into tears.

"Good God, Mrs. Clough," cried the duke. "Don't you want to go to the city?"

Clough answered, "She weeps for pleasure, Your Grace; we have longed to go to London for many years."

"Then stop being missish, Mrs. Clough." The duke did not attach value to crying over good news.

"Oh, Your Grace." The woman swallowed her sobs. "Not just that, but your offering for the sweetest, kindest lady I ever met—Mrs. Lanier, so good to Heath, so considerate of my comfort—no words can express how glad I'll be to serve her. She'll make you a marvelous wife, sir."

The duke frowned. "That will be all, Clough. The wedding is to be the last Friday of the month. I'll instruct you shortly about the preparations."

"Yes, Your Grace, and thank you, sir. Come, you silly old woman." He put his arm around his wife's shoulder and led her from the room.

"Females!" growled the duke.

There was a rap on the door and Heath, wearing riding clothes, entered, dragging Charles behind him. "Father, Charles has had his second lesson and he already handles a horse like a whipster of promise."

The duke, moving around the desk, studied his sons. Heath appeared more in health. The miniature of himself was trying hard to hide behind his brother. Anger surged through the duke. Heath, from the time he was able to stand, even after having been given harsh scolds, had never cringed, but this child clung like a limpet to Heath, though he had had no dealings with rough snubs.

"Stop shielding the boy," growled the duke. "Hedge off—let him be on his own."

Heath, smiling down at Charles, said, "Little brother, your father will go on in a gusty way until you image he is going to draw your cork. But don't let your knees knock together for it is all flummery. Our father is as good as ever twanged—face up to him."

Startled by Heath's words, the duke felt his anger drain away. He stared first at Heath, then down on his younger son, now braced, with his legs slightly apart, his hands half coiled, as if prepared to receive any blows rained on him.

"Good God, Charles, have you never dealt with men before?"

"Only my fath—Mr. Sanford, sir."

"Were you afraid of him?" It cost the duke an effort to ask.

"Yes and no, sir."

"Your mother wrote him a caring man."

"Yes, sir." Charles hung his head.

"Well, I am your true father; when you talk to me, stand straight and meet me eye to eye."

"Yes, sir." Charles threw back his shoulders and uncurled his hands.

"That's better. Come, I have something to say to you both. Sit around the fire." The duke filled two glasses and brought them to his sons. "Watered wine for you, Charles. Don't drink until you have heard my message."

"What is it, Father?"

"This morning I made an offer for Mrs. Lanier and she received it favorably."

Both boys gazed at him, stunned—Heath from surprise, and Charles because he did not fathom the duke's meaning.

"Don't sit there with your mouths at half cock, you stupid lads—say your say."

Heath recovered and declared, "I'm bowled out—you are going to marry Mrs. Lanier?"

"Yes, sapskull, I am going to marry Mrs. Eric Lanier."

"Father!" Heath jumped up. "That is the most famous news I have ever heard in my whole life. Mrs. Lanier is incomparable, and you're the luckiest man in England, sir. Congratulations!" Heath extended his hand and the duke shook it. They turned to Charles, who stared from one to the other, bewildered. Heath laughed. "Charles, you fortunate young varmint, you are to have a new mother—a darling; you'll love her."

"A new mother?" Charles wavered uncertainly.

"Yes, and you'll meet her as soon as I can arrange it." Heath picked up his brandy and handed the wine-glass to Charles. "Arise, Charles, and drink a toast with me. Father, my deepest good wishes for your happiness." Heath drank and Charles followed suit, making a small moue at the taste of the wine.

"When do you wed, Father?"

"The last Friday of the month."

Heath laughed. "No put-offs for you, eh?"

"No," responded the duke, "but there's more."

"More? How could there be?"

"I'm moving the household to London as soon as possible after the wedding. We go when the Grosvenor Square house is pulled together."

Heath stared at the duke, then whispered, "London? We are going to London?"

The duke nodded.

Heath paused for an instant, then carefully put Charles's glass down with his own on the table, grabbed the boy, and, before the duke's astonished eyes, began to skip in circles, singing at the top of his voice, "We are going to London town, London Town,

London Town; we are going to London Town, so early in the morning."

The duke heard them out, then shouted, "Stop it, you anapos, enough! Get on your way and leave me some peace."

Heath halted, picked up Charles, and, in a breathless tone, said, "Sir, I have always thought you up to snuff, but I didn't dream you brilliant to the point that you would wed the charming Mrs. Lanier and take us to London. Maybe you're a genius, Father."

The duke was pleased. He growled, "Cut your stick!"

Over Heath's shoulder, Charles piped up, "Goodbye, sir. I am most glad to be with you, Father."

"Looby," cried Heath and whirled them both out of the room.

The duke grunted and went to the desk to read a letter from Mr. Endfield. Then he rang for Clough.

"Clough, please have Mrs. Clough prepare the west bedrooms; Mr. Endfield arrives tomorrow with a Mr. Cornby and a Mr. Foster; they will stay two days. I intend to join their party for a sojourn in London. Mr. Pettibone, if better, will leave for London also. Pack my baggage with clothes for two sennights."

"Yes, Your Grace. You will be missed."

"Ummm." The duke started to sort his other mail. Clough still waited before him.

"What is it?"

"Forgive me, Your Grace, but you have given no instructions concerning your wedding, and if you are to be in London, I wonder . . . ?"

The duke stared at his valet, then shouted, "Damme, I know nothing about things of that nature. Isn't it the custom for the bride's family to set up the trappings?"

"Yes, sir. However, in this case, may I hint that you discuss the happening with the vicar."

"Bother all females; they should be at the bottom of the sea."

"Sir," remonstrated Clough in a sad voice.

"Oh, don't let it signify. Here, I'll write a note of invitation for dinner tonight to the vicar; see that Henderson delivers it and waits to bring him back." The duke wrote hastily, dismissed Clough, then returned to his mail and did not notice that he had forgotten his pondering hour.

The vicar arrived rather breathless. "Your Grace," he said upon entering. " 'Urgent business,' your note read. Is all well?"

"No more than the regular hobble; didn't mean to alarm you. Come, sit down and have a brandy as I explain." The duke poured, handed the vicar, now seated, a glass, then sat opposite his friend. The vicar, relieved, asked, "What is it?"

The duke frowned. "Sir, you may take all the blame on your head. Today, I offered to Mrs. Lanier, and she accepted."

The vicar raised his glass high. "Heaven be praised; that is the greatest of tidings. Myles, I drink to your wisdom and years of shackled bliss."

"Thank you," said the duke in arctic tones. "Now that you have embarked me on this ocean of confusion—I lack all points about weddings, and I wed the last Friday of the month."

"Better and better." The vicar paused. "Your Grace, I—er—er—" He blushed.

"Well, out with it. What mischief now, sir?"

The vicar took a deep breath. "Myles, I've such trust in your foresight, so after our last conversation, I decided that, if you made your offer, and if the lady accepted, you would not wish to publish banns—giving the on-dits a chance to prattle—so I had drawn a special license of marriage for the Duke of Asherwood and Mrs. Eric Lanier, widow."

"The devil you say," the duke roared. "How dare you?! I should call you out!"

"It was an act of faith and hope," countered the embarrassed vicar.

"Fustian! Again, I repeat, how dare you rub bat in my affairs? Of all the notions, that caps the globe! You must be a cracked brain!"

"Maybe, Myles, maybe." The vicar shook his head.

The duke glared at his friend and suddenly said quietly, "David, you are a fly cove!"

The vicar smiled. "Duke, sometimes the Lord works in mysterious ways."

"Hoy, He has more conduct than to play such a dashed smoky trick. It's all in your dish, you sneaking screw."

The vicar grinned. "Myles, I accept all censure willingly. Let us not quarrel; you are free to wed Mrs. Lanier any day and the world will rejoice."

"Ha, to see me tenanted for life to the lady with whom I mill at the tip of a hat—a pretty piece of business!"

"Myles, if you wed in bad skin, you will grass yourself. The lady is your choice and—"

"Your choice," snapped the duke.

"Thank you." The vicar laughed.

"Damme, everyone is in high gig about my marriage except me; for me, it is Dead Sea fruit."

"Won't be, once it's brought to book," the vicar said softly.

The duke sighed. "Well, what are the duties of the ceremony?"

"Myles, why not leave the plays to Mrs. Lanier and myself?"

"Can I? Is there nought I must do?"

"You must appear, but other gates I can think of nothing."

Much relieved, the duke said, "A small affair, David. The marriage will stir enough scandal broth without our giving a raree-show."

"Have no concern, Myles. The lady, being the daughter of a vicar, is knowledgeable about the whats and wherefores—she must have noted a great variety of weddings."

"I suppose the flummery is for the females." The duke then said under his breath, "I wish I could cry off."

"Don't be a clodpole, Myles." The vicar's voice was sharp.

"I can do nothing," mourned the duke.

"Yes, you—you can give me another brandy and then dinner. Your self-pity makes me hungry."

As the duke filled the vicar's glass he said, "Devil take you, David, I would call you out if I did not have to go to London in two days."

"Good Lord, Myles, I know not one thing about either pistols or swords; you'd draw claret if I even spied the weapons. However, I will beat you to flinders at chess tonight." The vicar frowned, then asked offhandedly, "When do you return from London?"

"Don't gull me, David. I promise to be at the chapel in time for the wedding. I only go to prepare the Grosvenor Square house."

The talk turned to houses, later to books, and after dinner the duke won two hard-fought chess games from the vicar.

The two men parted on the best of terms.

16

The next morning, when his sons stepped through the doors of the breakfast room, the duke swallowed hard to keep from choking. Setting down his coffee cup, he inquired as to why they were dressed like Bond Street fripples. Heath explained that he was taking Charles to introduce him to Mrs. Lanier. The duke hoped the widow would not be blinded when she clapped eyes on such sartorial elegance.

Charles, dressed in his best shortcoat, unused to eating with the duke, kept his eyes on his plate.

Heath, feeling well-pleased by his attire of yellow pantaloons, frilled shirt, long tailcoat of blue, his belcher neckcloth tied by Clough himself, ate heartily of a breakfast of crimped cod, buttered eggs, toast, and two cups of tea.

After the meal Heath requested the tilbury be brought around, seated Charles beside him, and bowled down the drive at a spanking pace. On the road he let Charles take the reins, thus filling the boy with exalted pride. At Willowood they jumped out of the tilbury, Heath tied the horse to the post, and Charles opened the gate as they saw Lenore on her knees, weeding the flower bed. Lenore stood as the brothers opened the gate, then she curtsied. "I have never had such niff-naff gentlemen call on me in my memory. Welcome, sirs."

Heath bowed. "Mrs. Lanier, may I present my brother, Charles."

Viewing the thin boy, who so mirrored the duke, Lenore's heart jumped. "Charles, it gives me the deepest pleasure to meet you."

Charles, too shy to speak to most strangers, but overcome by the excitement of the drive, shrilled, "Brother let me take the ribbons!"

"Famous," said Lenore, beaming. "I'm sure you drove to the inch."

Becoming aware of the beautiful lady before him, Charles stepped behind Heath. Astonishingly the lady did not try to coax him forward; instead she did an extraordinary thing—she winked at Heath, saying, "If you gentlemen will follow me . . ." She turned and started on the path around the house where there stood a small building. "My succession house," announced Lenore, adding, "Please wait." She entered the glass building and almost immediately reappeared with a moving bundle of fur.

"Charles, hold out your hands, please."

Charles, rather slowly, did as he was told, and the amazing lady placed a wiggling puppy in his arms. The bundle had presence of mind to lick Charles's face forthwith, thereby sealing a perfect friendship. Charles looked up at the lady's face searchingly. She laughed. "Indeed, yes, the puppy is yours. The vicar's dog, Ginger, had nine of the darlings six weeks ago, and last night I bamboozled Mrs. Thomas into giving me this one, just for you."

Charles, hardly believing such a miracle to be his, asked, "Oh, Heath, may I keep him?"

His brother responded sternly, "Charles, don't be

an anapo. It would pass all bounds to naysay such a magnificent gift."

Such an expression of joy flooded the child's face that the other two broke into laughter. Charles then stood very straight—a difficult task with the puppy squirming—and bowed. "Mrs. Lanier, I wish to thank you. Thank you."

The unusual lady then reached into her apron pocket and brought forth a tiny collar and leash. "Here, put these around his neck and bring him into the house. You must decide on a name for him."

Charles gaped at her, then turned to Heath, who shrugged. "I cannot name him, little Brother. Let me help you with that collar."

Clasping the leash firmly, Charles put the puppy on the ground. The puppy, completely satisfied with the way life was going, jumped into Charles's arms and wiggled with glee.

Heath asked Lenore if they dare take him into the house.

"No, but in he goes anyway; come." In the morning room Lenore rang for Abel, who appeared promptly. "Abel, this is Master Charles, Master Heath's brother."

From his great height Abel smiled at Charles and said, "Master Charles, that is quite a puppy you have. What's his name?"

"It's—it's—Wiggles!" exploded Charles. "Yes—Wiggles!"

"Never has there been a dog better named, Master Charles."

"Abel," said Lenore, "please bring some cakes and cookies for my guests; I will be down shortly."

Left alone, Charles asked, "Brother, is she to be our new mother?"

"Yes," replied Heath, eyeing the boy nervously.

"Well," mused Charles aloud, "I think I'm going to like her very much—yes, very, very much. You like her, don't you?"

"I like her very much, Charles, very, very much."

"Uh-huh." Charles paused. "I never had a dog before—do you like his name?" Heath nodded. "I can hardly wait to show him to Father and Mrs. P.; won't they be excited!"

Heath had doubts. Mrs. Peablossom had often proclaimed herself pleased to work at the palace to get away from those pesky hounds at her home. The duke also had strong opinions on the subject of dogs—"Keep them in the stable where they belong; no gentleman has canines cavorting under his feet." Heath decided to discreetly escort Wiggles into the palace.

Abel entered with pastries and cakes, followed by Lenore, now clad in yellow muslin that made her eyes green as emeralds.

Heath, gazing at the smiling Lenore, could contain himself no longer; he put his arms around her waist, lifted her, and swung her around, shouting, "You're going to be my mother, you're going to be my mother!"

"Put me down, you shocking scrub oaf," cried Lenore, half horrified and half amused.

"Certainly, Mother, darling," said Heath as he set her on her feet. He then stepped back and bowed most formally. "My dearest Mrs. Lanier, I am chirping merry."

"Heath, you are about in your head. I may be a terrible mother," asserted Lenore as she straightened her dress and tucked in a wispy lock of hair.

Charles, who had watched his brother with mouth open, jumped up, ran to Lenore, and threw his arms about her waist, shouting, "I am chirping merry too. May I call you Mother?"

Lenore, smiling down on the boy's upturned face, cupped his cheek in her hand. "If you will, Charles, I too will be chirping merry."

Wiggles, craving attention, gave a sharp bark.

"Looby," cried Heath. "Take him to the garden, Charles, before he has an overset." Charles snatched the leash and hurried from the room.

Lenore sat on the couch, saying as she did so, "What a dear boy Charles is; and you, Heath, you reassure me. I confess I feared you might want to scotch the affair."

Heath sat beside her and said, "Madam peagoose, why would I?"

"Because I am a rolled-up widow, and in many ways quite beneath your father's touch."

"What flummery! Father is a duke, but he is also a dour and morose man. However, given half a chance, you'll bring him kindness, fun, and love; something even a duke cannot have just by being born a duke. Oh, Father's gotten the better part of the bargain."

Lenore, to cover her confusion at Heath's words, said, "I want to make a duchess of the first stare. I'm not certain—"

"Balderdash, you will be a gorgeous duchess; the London diamonds will turn blue."

"Oh, no, why, I don't even know how to handle a horse."

Heath gasped. "My gracious—a deplorable lack in your education, madam." He heaved a great sigh. "I fear I have only two alternatives; one to tell the vicar to forbid the banns, the other to teach you to ride myself. We start tomorrow."

"Don't be rattle-brained. I'm afraid of horses. Besides, I have no riding clothes."

"Utterly outrageous, madam. No one has ever mounted a steed without proper riding apparel, except perhaps Lady Godiva, of course." Heath nodded sagely.

"Cabbagehead!" Lenore laughed. "Be serious for a moment—do you suppose I could learn?"

"My dear Mrs. Lanier, if I cannot teach you to handle a horse, I should be given such a bear garden jaw by Henderson that I might take flight into alt."

"Methinks you're crazy already to assume I can learn."

"And the driving of a carriage, madam—tomorrow at eleven!"

"Now I know you're queer in the attic—yes—at eleven!" Lenore smiled. "And thank you. Now we must introduce Charles to Mamère."

"I'll get him." Heath left and, reentering the house, met Lenore in the hall. He held on to the protesting Charles, sullen because his beloved dog had to undergo the indignity of being tied to the gate post.

"She let him in the house before," said Charles with truth and justice on his side.

"Not this time, little Brother."

Lenore, who faced the front door, said, "Charles, Wiggles is asleep."

Somewhat pacified, Charles went with the others.

"Heath has brought Charles to see you, Mamère."

"Well, bring him in where I can inspect him." Heath took Charles and stood him before the old lady, who, when she peered, shrieked, "Good God, it's Bunky gone young! Why didn't you tell me he's the duke all over again?"

"I thought I had," murmured Lenore.

"Come closer, little Bunky, and let me see you."

Charles, given a push by Heath, stepped forward to let the frightening ancient gaze into his face. "The duke and you—two halfpennies in a purse—it's eerie." The old lady leaned back. Peeking under her eyelids at Lenore, putting her hand to her heart, she said, "Oh, my, I've such a taking, Lenore, get me some brandy."

"Hoy," said Lenore, laughing, "a small glass of ratafia will set you to rights," and hurried from the room.

"Ratafia," snorted the old lady, "you'd think I was a chit of a girl."

"Oh, no," chirped Charles. "I think you are a very old lady—aren't you?"

Mamère glared at the boy for an instant—Heath held his breath—then she cackled, "Yes, you scrub of a brat, I'm a very ancient lady, but it ain't polite of you to say so."

Charles flushed. "Oh, I am sorry, I—I—"

"Don't put yourself in a kicker, young Bunky; I know you can't fool varmints, or make them keep their tongues. Go sit down, I want to talk to your brother about London."

Charles skittered over to stand by Heath's chair.

When Lenore returned, the old lady was informing Heath about where a gentleman did or did not go in the city. After drinking her ratafia, Mamère's head began to nod and Lenore led the boy downstairs.

Wiggles's delirious welcome awaited them. After thanking Lenore, the boys drove off, Charles torn between wanting to take the reins and petting his new friend.

At the palace two carriages standing in the driveway permitted Heath to drive to the garden entrance and use the back staircase, thereby avoiding the duke. He left it to Charles to present Wiggles to Mrs. Peablossom.

At that moment the two of his guests who had arrived from London sat with the duke in the library, poring over plans for the Grosvenor Square house—Mr. Cornby, the architect; and Mr. Foster, the decorator.

Mr. Cornby's structural ideas, with a few minor details adjusted, pleased the duke. However, listening to Mr. Foster's suggestions for decorating, and inspecting the materials presented, the duke felt dissatisfied. The samples, though handsome, bothered him in some way. Suddenly Lenore's auburn hair and emerald eyes flashed into his mind; the colors before him ran to red and pink. Slightly shocked that Lenore had appeared so vividly to him, he asked Mr. Foster if he had the same materials in gold and green.

"Certainly, Your Grace," responded the decorator, digging into his bag and drawing forth two swatches the duke judged far more suitable. Shortly all plans were completed.

"A brandy, sirs, and afterward, should you care to ride, I can mount you." The two men accepted, each confessing to packing riding clothes in hope, for the duke's stable was known far and wide. Word was sent to Henderson and soon the three were galloping over the duke's acres.

The duke's table was as renowned as his stable. The men conceded the justice of its repute—soup *à la reine,* fillet of turbot with Italian sauce, dressed lobster, chicken, spinach with croutons, asparagus, Rhenish cream, baskets of pastries, and wines from the duke's cellar.

After coffee, served in the library, Mr. Cornby proposed a round of whist, a prompting he later rued, for the duke and Mr. Pettibone, his health improved and his fondness for whist unimpaired, relieved the two men from London of a goodly amount of gold.

17

The next morning Heath and Charles, by request, breakfasted with their father at an early hour. The duke had a list of do's and don'ts to be their guide in his absence. Though long, it was not oppressive.

Then a discussion arose, for Heath announced that —first, because he had been delayed by his fall, and second, because there could be no question that London was an education in itself—he would not return to Oxford for the midterm, but, his scope widened, would gladly take up his studies in the spring.

The duke accepted none of such frippery. Heath was to appear for his midterm. Heath shook his head and urged the duke to remember the sad plight of fathers who ordered reluctant sons to college, only to see them haunt the gambling halls and cockfights. The duke pointed out that such fathers were woodenheaded and, should Heath so behave, he would find himself in the Army in a wink, where he might learn to be a man—though the duke doubted it. Heath grinned, and proclaimed he would not go to Oxford at this time, but if the duke was overset, by all means—let it be a pair of colors. The duke, turning a deep shade of red, roared that he was not above letting a balky son have a cat-o'-nine-tails.

Charles, who had been silent through the altercation, screamed, "Oh, no, not a cat-o'-nine-tails," and burst into tears.

Flabbergasted, his father and brother gaped at him.

The duke, who had never used a whip on a human being, demanded, "What is it?"

Charles stood, unbuttoning his coat and almost ripping off his shirt, and cried, "Look, Father, look what happened to me." He turned his back so the duke and Heath could see the cross marks of weals that permanently scarred his flesh.

The duke went white. "Good God! Did Sanford do that? If he weren't already dead, I'd run him through myself. Your mother permitted him to beat you?"

"No, sir, he only thrashed me when she was out of the house."

"Didn't you tell her?"

"No." The boy shook his head. "Mr. Sanford warned me that if I tattled, he would beat me harder the next time."

"May he be damned in hell," shouted the duke.

"You won't, Father, will you—you won't whip Heath?" Charles pleaded breathlessly.

"Never, Son, my word on it. I was bamming him." The duke glared. "Didn't your mother see those?"

"Oh, yes, but she was told I had fallen out of a tree." Charles, now reassured, was putting on his shirt. Seeing the duke's face, he added, "She sent for the doctor, sir, and he treated me most kindly; put balm on them—and Mother cried."

The duke turned to Heath, who was sitting like a statue of gray marble. "Did you know of this?"

Heath's voice shook as he responded, "No . . . no . . . I did not. Mrs. Peablossom tends him and she has never said a word to me."

"Send for her," thundered the duke.

"No, Father, no." Charles grabbed the duke's arm. "She is so good to me, and often cries when she bathes me. She did not tell you because I begged her not to; I made her promise."

"Why? Why didn't you want her to tell, little Brother?" Heath asked in low tones.

Charles looked frightened, then whispered, "I was afraid Father would send me away."

The duke, horrified, asked, "Why, Son, did you imagine I would do such an outrage?"

"Because Mother told me that to be an Asherwood you had to be perfect—that the Asherwoods could not abide anyone who wasn't."

The duke gripped the arms of his chair until his knuckles were white. "Charles, come here." The boy moved close to the duke and waited. "Charles, you are my son. Your back does not signify. You are my son, and I will never send you away."

Charles smiled, and replied lightly, "Oh, I don't worry about it anymore. Mrs. Lanier is going to be my mother now; she loves me, and would not allow you to send me away—ever!"

The duke, whose mind had been anywhere but on the widow, gazed at Charles—struck dumb. Suddenly he became aware of a sound, a sound that could not be any other than suppressed mirth. He turned to Heath, who was struggling, but losing his battle to contain himself. The duke's dagger glance undid him completely and he fell into outright gales of laughter.

Charles, sensing the lessening tension, ran to Heath, by now doubled over, and pounded him on the back, saying, "What is it? What are you laughing at?"

The duke, feeling he had had enough of enough, stood and left the room.

After the guests had breakfasted, and preparations for the journey to London were completed, the household gathered to help the travelers arrange themselves and their luggage in the two carriages.

The duke, saying good-bye to the boys in the hall, announced coldly that Heath would be permitted to skip the midterm—the duke hoped that London might settle him—and that he would be expected to study under the tutor who was to join the household. "Besides," the duke added, "you might help Mrs. Lanier care for Charles."

Heath grinned as he shook hands. "Father, you are a genius!"

The duke's farewell to Charles differed. Putting his two hands on the child's shoulders and peering down into Charles's upturned face, he said, "I'm happy you're here, Son." Tousling the boy's hair, he strode out the front door. He did not glance back, though both boys followed him to the portico and waved good-bye until the carriages were beyond the gates.

"What is a genius?" asked Charles as the household went their various ways.

"A brainy gentlemen whom you and I can admire. Now hurry, go don your riding clothes; Mrs. Lanier expects us."

"May I bring Wiggles?"

"No, you stupid, Wiggles will have to be more grown up before he can be with horses."

"Like me?" piped Charles.

"Like you, you brat of a boy. Come on—I'll race you upstairs."

Lenore stood at the gate when the boys rode up the lane—Heath leading a third horse, a large mare known for her gentleness. Lenore stared aghast. "Glory, you don't expect me to get up on that, do you?"

"Of course, Mother," replied Charles in a superior tone. " 'Tis nothing," then, deflated, added, "but Brother will have to show you how; I've never ridden sidesaddle."

"I'll need a ladder to mount that high," vowed Lenore.

"Her name is Wisty," Charles explained. "I learned to ride on her, but now I ride Orant; he's a goer," added the boy proudly.

Assisted by Heath, Lenore was in the saddle. She wanted to put her arms around Wisty's neck to hold on, but after Heath had paced Wisty back and forth and Charles instructed Lenore in the use of the reins, she grew accustomed to the motion, then realized it was fun perching on a moving animal she could control. Finally she asked if she might ride by herself, and to her delight found Wisty always obedient.

The lesson finished, Heath assured Lenore she would be a whip in no time.

"Fustian," said Lenore, sighing, "but I crave to try. Come, we need refreshments." She led them through the gate. To Lenore's astonishment, Abel was busy in her flower garden—an unheard-of display of husbandry. "Abel, can I believe my eyes?"

"Well ma'am"—Abel rose and blushed—"I imaged this . . . er . . . weeds . . . a caterpillar . . ."

"Splendid; perhaps you might work here each day."

"No, ma'am." Abel shook his head. "I'll . . . I can't . . . not me . . . my vegetables . . . You ride . . . well, ma'am," he finally said, and fled.

When he appeared in the garden with cakes, pastries, and tea, Heath hailed him. "Abel, I'm going to make Mrs. Lanier the best horsewoman in London."

"Hoy," laughed Lenore. "A Herculean labor you've set yourself."

"He can do it." Charles nodded his head. "Look what he's done for me."

Wanting a word alone with Lenore, Heath said, "Abel, take this whipster and have him water the horses; it's warm today."

"Well," Abel said, grinning, "Master Charles, do you know about horses? Wager you can't point out a fetlock."

"Looby, that's an easy one," scoffed Charles, following in the big man's wake.

"Mother, darling," Heath said, frowning, "I have a miserable story for you. I wish it could be untold, but I must inform you."

"What is it, Heath? Something about your father?" Lenore was anxious.

"No, he left for London in fine fettle." Heath then repeated what had occurred at breakfast concerning Charles. Lenore gasped at the cruelty. "I wish I might lay a cat-o'-nine-tails on the evil man—horrible! Horrible!"

"If he were not dead, I'm sure Father would see him receive some dire punishment. I've never seen Father more infuriated."

"And you, Heath?"

"I was so overset I shook, but I decided to take another revenge. Charles will never experience another moment where he is uncertain of whether he is cherished—not while I live."

"Heath, I can understand why your father adores you."

"Oh, Mother, you come on too strong there." Heath laughed. "I've always sensed he had a fondness for me, despite his desperate struggle to conceal his weakness. You see, I'm unforgivably flawed—I resemble my mother."

Lenore's reply was unspoken, for Charles ran to them.

"I do too recognize fetlocks; Abel said I have a great grasp about horses. He gave me sugar to feed them."

"Oh, Charles." Lenore took the slightly abashed boy in her arms and hugged him. "You are knowledgeable to a trivet and will be a nonesuch when you are older."

"Thank you." Charles felt shy, and said, "Brother, I think we should go home now," then solemnly to Lenore, "You see, Wiggles needs me."

"Indeed so." Lenore rose and walked with the boys to the gate. Good-byes said, Lenore stepped into the lane to wave her soon-to-be sons out of sight. Crossing to the stone fence, she gazed over the fields. Her sons! She felt uneasy, as if she were galloping on a wild horse into the unknown; where was she going? How did she dare? It was so swift! On and on . . . She heard horses' hooves clang on the stones; they seemed to grow louder and louder as if pursuing her. Shaking herself, she turned and saw the vicar riding toward her.

"Lenore!" the vicar called. "Just the person I want to see."

He reined up, dismounted, and tied his horse to the post.

"At this moment, David, I cannot think of anyone I would rather welcome. Come in." She opened the gate.

"Not even the duke?" teased the vicar, and stared, dumbfounded, to see Lenore blush a deep red.

"He's gone to London, as you are well aware; or maybe you aren't." Lenore was flustered.

Thunder above, can it be she has a tendre for Myles? the cleric pondered as he shut the gate. Good heavens! Maybe I let her blush signify too much. The vicar tried to comfort himself, yet he sensed that he must be alert to further signs. Confused thoughts raced through his mind as he followed her.

"You just missed Charles and Heath," Lenore said as they walked. "Heath is teaching me to ride and as I have no riding clothes, this old dress had to suffice." She smoothed her faded gown.

"Riding? Excellent! Myles will be pleased." He gave Lenore a side glance. Now quite in control, she only smiled. The vicar admonished himself, for in urging Myles to offer for Lenore, he had considered only the duke's interests. He sincerely appraised her as an ideal wife for his friend; her goodness, her lightness of spirit, her acceptance of hardship, her bright mind, all had convinced him she would make an extraordinary Duchess of Asherwood.

Her assent to the duke's offer had never for a moment put into his head the possibility that it was a creampot marriage for Lenore—any sensible lady would prefer being a duchess to being a widow banished to Willowood. That she might have a depth of fondness for the duke had never crossed his mind. What a coil, thought the vicar, for he knew Myles

had no sentiment for the "brangling female" he loudly proclaimed troublesome.

Lenore broke the silence. "You concede that an
Asherwood must ride and handle the ribbons—and
what better teacher in the county than Heath?"

"None, except his father." The vicar inwardly
winced at his own shamelessness in trying to trip her.

"How is Rachel?" asked Lenore blandly.

Smiling, the vicar thought to himself, What a great
duchess, cool as rain! then responded to her question.
"My darling wife is in high spirits, prattling with
anyone and everyone about the mightily approved
forthcoming nuptials of the glorious Mrs. Lanier and
the Dour Duke, now renamed 'that fortunate man!' "

To his horror, Lenore burst into tears.

"Lenore!"

"Oh, David," Lenore sobbed, "I don't believe I can
marry him."

His fears confirmed, the vicar sat quietly and let
Lenore cry for a moment, then asked, "Is it because
you have a tendre for Myles, Lenore?"

Lenore raised her eyes to his and whispered, "Oh, do
not say that aloud, please."

"We are alone, I see no harm in it. It is not ill-
behaved to love his Grace—he is a worthy man."

"Indeed so, but he does not love me," wailed
Lenore. "He does not even want me as his wife, only
his duchess—" She stopped, aghast that she had told
what she felt she should never reveal.

You stupid fool, Myles, was the vicar's first reaction as he fought to keep his face calm and to find
the right words. He finally said, "Lenore, you're in a
devil of a fix." Lenore nodded vigorously. "Let us
think on it together."

Lenore slowly dried her eyes; she trusted her friend and awaited what he might find to say.

The Reverend David Thomas took a deep breath. "Lenore, it is I who put the notion of an offer for you into the duke's head." Lenore's eyes grew round and the vicar nodded. "He desperately needs a duchess and to me it seemed perfect that she be you. I so told Myles. As you can imagine, my suggestion was ill-received; he had made your acquaintance far too recently, and the fratches between you two were foremost in his thoughts." He laughed. "His Grace is not used to being crossed; your temerity quite upset him. However, Myles is not a nodcock, and once the seed was in place, it germinated. Though he did not like it by half, he came to see the possibilities of the proposal, even its wisdom."

"Wisdom?!" cried Lenore. "I sometimes think it foolish beyond permission. Good heavens, he could marry any lady in England."

"Perhaps," conceded the vicar, "but he could not be happy with 'any lady in England.' "

"He hates females," Lenore said bitterly.

"Yes," the vicar continued in soothing tones, "most females—with reason. Consider his past: He did not know his mother, who died shortly after his birth; he wed, at eighteen, a beauty, but—so I have been told— an empty-headed chatterer who ran off with another man, leaving him a son to bring up."

"Who he immediately abandoned to carouse about Europe," Lenore snapped.

"Quite so, where, soon titled 'the rake of Europe,' he had dealings mostly with light skirts and fancy pieces, who hardly increased his regard for the fair sex. If I were a man who wagers, I'd place a bit of brass that females were the reason he became a re-cluse."

Lenore tossed her head. "He need not have shut himself away. He could have gone to London or—anywhere."

The vicar's brows drew together. "No, he hated London for the snubs received after his elopement, and he refused to permit the *ton* another chance to give a second put-down."

"Hoy, what self deception! The *ton* would have given him royal treatment—the Duke of Asherwood, free—every daughter and mother in London to be on the catch for!"

The vicar smiled with guileless eyes. "Oh, yes, but you must concede, my dear, His Grace did not have a needle-witted lady to tell him so."

"Now you're smoking me," said Lenore, laughing.

"Yes, a little. But the duke, lacking a wise female, chose to live an almost monastic life and mourn his fate."

"Stupid!"

"Indubitably, but he convinced himself that his business affairs, books, and correspondence would suffice, and for a short time they did. What he didn't realize, as the years passed, was that he was sinking into boredom."

"Boredom!"

"Exactly. He became bored to the bone; he does not smile, and I've never heard him laugh. The villagers dubbed him the Dour Duke—a misnomer. They should have called him the Bored Duke."

"You are his friend; couldn't you have . . . ?"

The vicar shook his head. "I once adjured him to entertain guests, and experienced a hard set-down. No,

I could only discuss books and theories, and play piquet or chess with him."

"His seclusion—so unnecessary and sad," Lenore said impatiently.

"Dismal, until that glorious day Heath landed outside your gate."

"Do you call it glorious?"

He laughed. "A most fortuitous tumble; it's crossed my mind that the snake who frightened Heath's horse may have been trying to atone for his ancestor who gave so much trouble to Adam and Eve."

"Vicar!"

The cleric's eyes twinkled. "My dear Lenore, you must grant that Heath's fall, unlike Adam's, had led to the most fortunate of circumstances. Think on it—from that blessed day to this, the duke has had not a minute's ennui; he's been far too busy. Oh, I'm certain he feels put upon, even beset, but he is not bored."

Lenore sat back and stared at the vicar, who added, "Now, I grant Charles's arrival might have shaken him out of his lethargy, but even without Charles, you and Madame Lanier enlivened his life."

Lenore leaned forward. "And his obligation—do you know of that?"

The vicar shook his head. "In a way, however, I can truthfully aver I have not a thread to its nature. Just as you cognize, he must have a duchess, go to London, but why, or what is to happen, I haven't the wisp of a notion. But I am totally of the belief that whatever his undertaking, it's an honorable one, for the duke is an upright man. What signifies is that he has paid you a great compliment—he trusts you."

Lenore nodded and said, "True," then added wistfully, "but he does not love me."

The vicar studied Lenore—she is so beautiful, he mused. Suddenly he threw back his head and guffawed and clapped his hands. Lenore started.

"Lenore, I am only a poor vicar, who should never, never bet; but you are going to be very rich, and I wish my sons to go to Oxford, so I now wager their education—a large sum—that the Duke of Asherwood will fall deeply in love with the Duchess of Asherwood before the first anniversary of their marriage!" He gazed at her in gleeful challenge.

Lenore stared at him, then broke into laughter. "Hoy! Don't gull me, sir, I know all about vicars." She waved her hand airily. "Just how, hey-go-mad Vicar, would you pay such a wager if you lost?"

"Oh, unquestionably it would take me the rest of my life—but I won't lose," the vicar blithely assured her.

"Vicar, you are a good, fine, darling man, and I am cheered because you are my friend, but, dear David, you are definitely dicked in the nob."

"No, not crazy, dear lady," the vicar said, standing, "but I may be in for a trimming shortly, for Madame Lanier has been peeking at us through the curtains these last few minutes and is now giving me very distinct waves, commanding my presence."

Rising, Lenore faced the vicar, who said, in earnest tones, "You are to wed Myles, Lenore. What qualms you harbor are trivial compared to the joy you'll bring to the many who eagerly await the new duchess."

Lenore held her eyes upon the vicar and smiled so sweetly, he had the sudden desire to kiss her. Forgive me, my dearest Rachel, snapped his mind in quick remorse.

"Come, David, the longer you delay, the more time Mamère has to concoct shockers." Lenore laughed and turned to go down the path. Following her, the vicar thought, Myles, you are an unmitigated saphead!

At the foot of the stairs Lenore asked the vicar to bring Rachel for tea the next day so they could plan the arrangements for the wedding.

"With pleasure; now remember, our wager is fixed right and tight—Oxford for my sons."

"Gudgeon," said Lenore, smiling, and left him so she could gather a bouquet for Rachel. Cutting early roses, Lenore hummed as she selected blooms for her basket. Bending over to flick a worm from a leaf, she heard a carriage stop at the gate. Uncertain whether to gather some dandelions or go to the house, she saw Abel come out the door.

"Ma'am," said the scowling Abel, "the Twiddlepoop is here."

"Who?"

"Sir Alfred, the captain's brother, is in the morning room."

"Here, Abel, please give these to the vicar." Lenore handed him the basket, smoothed her dress, wondered if she should change it, shrugged, patted her hair, and hoped Alfred did not plan to ring a peal over her head.

"Good afternoon, Alfred." Lenore extended her hand to her red-faced, elegant brother-in-law, who rocked back and forth on his heels at the fireplace. Oh, dear, he intends to come the ugly, decided Lenore as she waited for him to speak.

"What is the meaning of this, Lenore?" fumed the angry man, ignoring her hand.

"Closing Willowood?" ventured Lenore. "It will certainly be—"

"To hell with Willowood; I refer to your catch of the duke."

"Oh, come now, Alfred, you know I could never do that."

"Well, you have!"

"No, no, it was he who fell tail over top into action; knocked me bandy, I assure you." Lenore wondered why Alfred always inspired her to use such low language.

"That's a loud one; Myles hasn't been hanging out for a wife since he left for Europe."

"Has he not? Well, I can hardly be privy to such knowledge, can I?" Lenore said tranquilly.

"Don't toy with me," said Alfred terribly. "How did you encounter him in the first place? He never leaves the palace."

" 'Tis easy to answer—Heath went up in a whisen-dine, landing on our doorstep. Abel carried him in, poor boy, and he had to remain on a repairing lease. The duke came each day to visit him."

"Affording you the chance to turn him up sweet," sneered the furious Alfred.

"Hardly," said Lenore, laughing. "We nearly came to cuffs every time we sighted each other."

"Then why the devil would he offer for you? Good God, you haven't a groat."

"Maybe he's well-to-pass enough not to yearn to dangle after a rich wife."

Alfred, who had found his Martha's charms considerably enhanced by her plump purse, stared at Lenore suspiciously, but no flicker of expression gave her away. He continued, "If you two brangle all the time, can't see why he—"

"Might it be," said Lenore helpfully, "he has a tendre for me?"

Alfred studied her for an instant, then said judiciously, "No, Myles loved Harriet Featherheath to flinders—made a fool of himself over her—he ain't going to let any female shumguzzle him again."

"But he does want me to be his duchess, Alfred," Lenore pointed out politely.

"Well, he has some damn reason other than your pretty face, and I'd like to know it." Alfred continued, "In fact, if you're expecting April and May, you're more hen-witted than I thought. Why are you getting buckled to him anyway?" asked the exasperated man.

Careful, Lenore said to herself, he's got you on thin ice, then she giggled. "Really, Alfred, how can you, of all people, pose such a silly question? Here am I, well up the river Tick, offered for by one of the richest dukes in England—you've windmills in your head even to ask."

"Umm, guess your motive is plain as a pikestaff, but his? Can't see why he wants to be leg-shackled to you, or any female for that matter."

"Alfred! I thought you were happy with Martha," Lenore feigned shock.

"Don't roast me, Lenore—only two causes for a man to get riveted—love or blunt. Can't see Myles wants brass—has it. Love?" he regarded Lenore closely, then shrugged.

Lenore sought another subject. "I hope you plan to see your grandmother; she will be overset—"

"Maybe later; now I want to learn about the Grosvenor Square house. Martha says there is activity there; men coming and going, drapes pulled open."

"Indeed so; after our marriage, we expect to live there."

"What?" His shout made Lenore jump.

"Yes," Lenore improvised wildly, "Myles is giving me a season in London as a wedding present."

A canny expression came over Alfred's face. "So he not only takes a bride, but goes to London. Odd, isn't it?"

"I can't see why," Lenore rushed ahead, "I love London, and Mamère is ecstatic."

"Who?"

"Mamère—my pet name for your grandmother. You know she adores the city. Heath and Charles long to see—"

"What's that got to do with anything? Myles hates London; all of you put together couldn't overweigh the scales on that score."

Lenore, disliking the direction of his talk, spoke quickly. "Alfred, I realize my letter was a shock to you and, like you, I ponder why Myles would wed and go to London. Finally I've concluded that after his many years of being a stay-at-home, he has at last grown lonely—maybe bored—and that even Asherwood is palling. When on an off chance I wistfully mentioned London, Myles leaped at the words. 'You miss the city?' he asked; I nodded, then he sparred for wind a long time in thought, then blurted, 'Why not a season there?' Simple as that, Alfred." To herself, she added, Dear Lord, forgive me for this bouncer.

"Balderdash; he doesn't need you. He could go to London, be the rake of England, and diamonds, mothers, in fact all the *ton*, would receive him with wide arms."

"Yes, but now there is Charles."

"Charles? You mentioned him before; who is he?"

Lenore, relieved, eagerly related the story of the

boy's appearance, then, drawing to the finish, said, "Charles does need a mother and, according to Myles, the child is fond of me."

Alfred, standing rock still, drew out his snuffbox. "Very pretty, Lenore, but you and I both know, keeping him at Asherwood is better for a young lad than dragging him into city life."

"Oh, Alfred, how true for most boys," Lenore raced along, "but Charles is shy and, naturally, companionship is the answer, but there are so few youngsters of his age here. When you were a child, there were Eric, Myles, the Cliveton twins, and others to play with, but now"—she shrugged—"London will be best for us all. Hoy, I've forgotten refreshments. Please do let me ring for—"

"No, thank you." He peered at the upturned face for a moment. "Lenore, you tell your Banbury tale well—you may even believe it yourself."

"I have no idea what you are trying to say." Lenore hoped she looked baffled.

Alfred gave a bark of laughter. "God knows, it will be a raree-show to see the Duke of Asherwood with his Cinderella on his arm—a creampot marriage right and tight. How London will gurgle and bubble!"

"Alfred, why are you so mean?" Lenore shot at him furiously. "Eric would rejoice for me." She watched Alfred take a pinch of snuff and draw a lace-edged handkerchief from his sleeve.

"Eric was a greenhead"—Alfred dabbed his nose—"a gamester, a care-for-nobody; stupid enough to get himself booked by a French bullet—"

"Eric was a brave soldier!" Lenore, mad as fire, cut in.

Alfred continued as if Lenore had not spoken, "—leaving me to frank his widow—"

"Which you have done so generously!" Lenore flung at him.

"—all sweet and simpering, keeping her eyes cocked to hook a duke."

Lenore flamed. "Who tended your grandmother, grew a garden to fight starvation, and quite by chance met a fine gentleman—I am honored by his offer."

"Of that I am positive."

"Fool," Lenore shouted, "you should be hurrahing —no more groats will you have to dig from your reluctant purse; no more wails from your weepy wife, begrudging Mamère and me the few pence you bestow. You should shout for joy!"

"Now, Lenore, I did not travel here to—"

"Why did you come?" Lenore demanded.

"I wanted to assure myself of your secure future."

"Hoy, what a plumper. You rocked over the rough roads to give me a thundering jaw! It turns you green that the little 'nobody' Eric married is to become a duchess."

"Oh, no," Alfred sneered, "I only wished to learn why Myles is to marry so far beneath his touch."

"Then go to Asherwood and ask him," Lenore shouted.

Alfred seemed to collapse before her eyes. Sir Alfred, visualizing the duke's anger—perhaps revenge to be wrought if he learned of the slightest questioning of his bride-to-be—cried, "Good God, no! Don't even mention my visit here, I beg you. Not a word. No! No!"

Startled at the change in him, Lenore asked, "Why on earth not? Is it unnatural for you to felicitate your sister-in-law?" Lenore's voice was chilly. "To give your blessing and discuss the details of closing Willowood?"

"Yes, yes, that's it. If he, by some misfortune, learns of my being here, I came to give you my congratulations and see to the shutting of the house." He nodded his head as if it were on a spring. "But don't you tell him."

Lenore deliberated, then said, "Alfred, you are a clutch-farthing fellow and stupid beyond permission; however, I'll do as you request and not relate our conversation to Myles—he would deplore it."

Alfred rallied. "Good, now we each carry a secret; not a syllable to anyone by either you or me."

"Will you visit Mamère now?" Lenore wished him out of sight.

"No, I must go home. Martha will wonder where I—"

"Good-bye then, Alfred. We shall not meet again until London." She did not raise or extend her hand.

Alfred gazed frantically around the room, struggling for further words, then muttered, "I do not wish you ill, Lenore, please believe me."

Lenore merely nodded and waited.

With a bow, Sir Alfred Lanier took his leave.

As the door closed, Lenore, weary to the bone, lowered her head. How could Eric have had such a brother? Eric, always pleasant, never cross, and far too generous. Alfred, pinchpenny, nasty, ready to scold, and a coward. No wonder Myles—she savored the name—Myles, Myles, Myles—and fell into a doze.

18

For the next five days pelting rain kept Lenore house-bound. She went through the closets, checking her few gowns for loose buttons or needed tucks. She was amused by the image of the Duchess of Asherwood wearing clothes so often mended.

Lenore joined Mamère for the midday meal as was her custom, and expressed her relief that at last she could tend the gardens. She did not, at first, notice the conspiratorial eye-rolling exchanged between the old lady and Maria, but finally, when Maria brought the damson pie, Lenore gave voice. "I catch out a hubble-bubble here—what tricks are you hatching?" Mamère stared at her in wide-eyed innocence, but Maria giggled.

"What is it, you two mischief-makers?"

"Gull-catcher," Mamère growled. "Maria, go bring the surprise."

"*Si, si,* madame, *muy pronto,*" said Maria, and ran from the room.

"Tell me, Mamère!" quizzed Lenore.

"Patience, puss!"

Maria returned carrying a large box, placed it on the table, lifted the lid, and drew out a cloud of palest yellow. Holding it up so Lenore could see, Maria smiled as Lenore gasped. It was a gown of gleaming—

almost white—satin, Empire in style, sheathed by cob-web-fine cream lace, the sleeves long, and at each cuff—as at the neck—were bands of tiny seed pearls.

When she could speak, Lenore whispered, "It is the most magnificent dress I have ever seen!"

"Maria made it," Mamère proclaimed.

"Oh, Maria!" Lenore, stepping close, marveled at the exquisite stitching, the cunning way the jewels were set. Maria showed the back of the lovely garment, where a panel was fashioned to fall from the neckline to the floor.

"Maria, you have toiled day and night! And I un-aware you had ever held a needle in your fingers." Lifting the panel, she gasped again when she spied the lace-covered buttons marching from neck to waist.

Driven by Lenore's obvious delight, Maria fell into a torrent of Spanish, explaining how madame had supplied the materials, long wrapped away in black paper, and how together they had created the design.

"Maria," Lenore said sternly, "please pack the dress away immediately so I can hug you." Maria did as bid. Lenore embraced her, then going to Mamère, knelt beside her and kissed the old lady's cheek, her own wet with tears.

Pleased, Mamère said gruffly, "Stop your flummery; here, use my handkerchief and dry those tears, wet goose."

Standing, Lenore made a deep curtsy. "Mamère, Maria, you have given me the finest bridal gown in England. I thank you!"

"*De nada,*" professed the beaming Maria.

"Indeed so—a mere nothing"—Lenore made an airy gesture—"for which I am deeply grateful, dear fairy godmothers."

"Fustian," sputtered Mamère. "Maria, don't stand there like a slowtop; tell your news."

"Madame!" cried Maria; dropping her eyes she blushed a dark crimson.

Mamère spoke impatiently. "That pudding-hearted Abel finally gathered up his courage to make an offer —as if you couldn't guess."

"Wonderful, dear Maria. You and I wed splendid men. Abel is the kindest of kind and lucky also—he marries a sweet, good señora!"

Maria, her eyes down, said nothing.

"Maria," Mamère spoke sharply, "stop acting like a schoolgirl; you were leg-shackled before, so you should—"

Maria interrupted with a gush of Spanish. When she finished, Mamère growled, "Well, what was said?"

Lenore patted Maria's arm. "She explained to me that she became a widow before she had been wed two hours; her husband fell, shot by a stray bullet fired by a drunken wedding guest."

Mamère paused, then tossed her head. "So she is a schoolgal after all. Abel will fix that *muy pronto* when they are buckled."

"Mamère!" cried Lenore, aghast, then turned, astonished, for Maria gave a great shout of laughter.

"*Si, si,* madame, I can hardly wait." Picking up the gown box, she flounced through the door, still laughing.

Lenore did not know what to do. "Mamère," she started to remonstrate, "do you think it—"

"Proper?" The old lady chuckled. "Course it ain't, but Maria and I understand each other, so don't behave uppish with me."

Lenore, resigned, shrugged, blew a kiss to the old lady, and left, to find Maria waiting in the hall.

"Mrs. Lanier, forgive me, I should not speak so."

Lenore smiled and patted Maria's arm.

In Spanish, Maria then asked if Abel and she could see the vicar; and did Mrs. Lanier think they could be married in the garden?

"Of course," Lenore approved. "The vicar and Mrs. Thomas come for tea this evening; I'll arrange for you to talk with him."

19

When Mrs. Eric Lanier welcomed the Reverend and Mrs. David Thomas to Willowood that evening, the consequences of the visit were to ripple like waves throughout the county.

The tea started with gracious amenities, including choice pastries. Lenore explained she would be grateful if the vicar would discuss with Abel and Maria their forthcoming nuptials. The vicar nodded, and when Maria brought more cakes, teased her about Spanish beauties stealing the hearts of Englishmen, leaving the poor English maidens to wear willow.

Maria tittered nervously, and later led the cleric to the garden, where Abel paced. The vicar promptly put both at ease, then, at their request, smoothed the way for a garden wedding.

Leaving the happy couple, the vicar sighed. If only Lenore gave the duke the darling glances Maria cast

up at Abel, and the duke's eyes could soften as did
the towering man's each time he regarded his be-
trothed. Entering the morning room, he found Lenore
and Rachel, their heads together, nodding in perfect
rhythm. "You, dear ladies, look as thick as inkle
weavers spinning a thread."

Rachel bubbled happily, "Dear David, it is so exciting; we have agreed on every detail. Do sit down;
we will tell you exactly what we intend to do."

"About what?" asked the vicar blandly.

"The wedding, of course," Rachel retorted sharply,
then added, "Widgeon!"

"So it is all brought to book," said the vicar. "Tell
me, dearest wife, are the duke and I permitted to be
there?"

"David," said Rachel primly, "if you are going to be
hey-go-mad, we will not let you hear one word."

The vicar put his hand on his chest and cried,
"Please, dearest love, do not stab me to the heart; I
beg you, pray speak."

"Oh, David," Rachel said, annoyed and pleased—
she rather enjoyed being teased by her husband—
"what will Lenore think? Well, Lenore wants me to
decorate the duke's chapel at the palace."

"Very sage, Lenore," the vicar averred solemnly.

Rachel peeked at her spouse suspiciously. "What do
you mean, David, 'very sage'?"

"Only, my delight, that you are truly experienced
in decor for weddings. There has never been, to my
knowledge, one in the county, be it home or church,
that you have not adorned the space as a bower of
beauty—surely Lenore would not dare forego the
fruits of your talent."

"No, indeed!" exclaimed Lenore. "It would be
ridiculous."

"Quite right," the vicar pronounced. "I might add that when the word 'wedding' is even whispered in the county, all flowers tremble on their stalks." His voice was grave.

"Now, David, if you are going to tattle about Mrs. Clendening's peonies, I will never speak to you again," she said, then turning to Lenore, "I assure you I did not ravish her bush. When Squire Green married Clare Adams, I took only three small peonies."

"True, my love, the lone three," said the vicar, "but I will not mention it, dear one."

"I should think not!" said Rachel.

Lenore burst into a fit of choking that required a covering of her face with a handkerchief.

Rachel, after asking if Lenore was all right—and being reassured by Lenore's vigorous nods, the handkerchief firmly in place—said, "Mr. Algernon Merse will play the organ."

The vicar, not looking at Lenore, who seemed to be struggling with her cough, bowed his assent.

Rachel continued, "I want Mrs. Turtlelock to sing, but Lenore—"

"No!" boomed the vicar, startling both ladies. "Mrs. Turtlelock is a fine, upstanding member of the parish, but, my dearest, tone-deaf. Rachel, she shall not utter a note at Lenore's wedding, for she has the voice of a peahen."

"Why, David, she sings every Sunday at all services," gasped Rachel, appalled at her husband's vehemence.

"That, my dove, is how I know she sings like a peahen."

"But if she sings like er—er—" Lenore sighed, "and she does—why do you—"

"Because she has sung, without surcease, for twenty-five years," the vicar said grimly, "and I am not brave enough to naysay her."

"David!" Rachel frowned. "I have never heard you declaim in this manner before; what has gotten into you?"

"Light of my life, I have yearned to say my say about Mrs. Turtlelock for, lo, these long years—at last I have, and I feel better for it. Lenore, may I have some more tea?"

"Indeed, yes," Lenore said, laughing. "To the vicar go the spoils."

"Lenore." The vicar scowled at her. "That is atrocious!"

"Thank you, sir." Lenore rose, curtsied, then poured the tea.

"I most sincerely hope Mrs. Turtlelock never learns what you have just said, David," said Rachel.

The vicar leaned forward and in a dire tone muttered, "If she does, love, I will know one of you two squeaked beef on me; remember that, ladies."

"David, please be more genteel," Rachel pleaded.

The vicar lifted his cup. "Come, there must be more to be said of the wedding."

Lenore said, "The chapel is so small, the service itself can be attended by only a few guests. I have no idea whom the duke will wish to invite."

"Sadly, I suspect the duke will invite no one." Seeing Lenore wince, he added cheerfully, "So you are free to ask whom you please, even Mrs. Turtlelock, if we can contrive a way to bind her mouth."

"No, I want just those of the households, and you, Rachel, and the children, of course."

"Lenore, you surprise me. Not Tom Doone?" the vicar asked, in an attempt to lift her spirits.

Shaking her head, Lenore seemed to fall into a trance.

"Well," said the practical Rachel, "and after the ceremony?"

Lenore sighed. "The duke will have to give you his plays; I have not thought on anything beyond the service."

"Why, Lenore," Rachel cried archly, "you must have pondered about some things after the wedding— all brides do that."

The vicar gazed at his wife for a long moment, then leaned over and patted her hand. "All brides are not as curious as you were, my sweet one," then, turning to Lenore, "Did not Myles request you make the arrangements? He told me he had." He did not quote the duke's words, "David, you brangle with the lady; she will mill with you until she gets every item of her list of wants."

Lenore said slowly, "Yes, but only for the ceremony."

"Oh, he couldn't have meant only that, Lenore," Rachel said unhappily. "Why, the wedding wouldn't be any fun at all."

The vicar blinked, then said loyally, "She's right, Lenore; there must be at least a dinner so Rachel will not feel deprived."

"Fine, a dinner, then," Lenore replied without interest.

"Lenore, you are far away; you must be thinking on something—what?" The vicar smiled.

"Well . . ." Lenore paused, then shook her head.

"Oh, for heaven's sake, tell us," cried Rachel. "I hate unspoken thoughts."

"Verily," said the vicar in a low voice.

"Just memories of when I was a little girl—" Lenore

stopped, then added, "It is far too long a price; I'm sure Myles would—"

"My dear Lenore," the vicar spoke earnestly. "Nothing is too expensive for Myles; he is wealthy beyond imagination, and can afford the most elaborate plan you could conceive. What happened when you were a little girl?"

"When I was eight," Lenore spoke in a low voice, "a very rich man was wed in my father's church. His gift to his bride—at her behest—was a village festival." She brightened. "Oh, the fun I had; there were games of all kinds for us children, with prizes—I won a blue hair ribbon—horses for the young men to race, favors, tables of food, and at night dancing and fireworks. It was glorious!" Lenore paused, a little frightened, for Rachel and the vicar were staring at her open-mouthed. Suddenly the vicar threw back his head and roared, "Lenore, that is the most magnificent notion ever hatched in these parts; it would throw the whole county into spasms of joy! By Jupiter, we must do it!"

"But Myles may not—"

"We'll surprise Myles," chortled the vicar.

"Shock, most likely; he'd consider me crazy as bedlam."

"Oh, but you are," the vicar assured her. "Totally and completely in alt—but how everyone will adore the hey-gone-mad duchess."

Rachel, who had been sitting perfectly still since Lenore had mentioned the festival, suddenly shouted, "Nuts to us!" then clapped her hand to her mouth. Lenore and her husband eyed her in astonishment.

In an effort to redeem herself Rachel folded her hands in her lap and said in a pious voice, "Lenore, you have proposed a splendid endeavor; I am sure the dear duke cannot help but be grateful to you. His Grace is a generous man and can't but rejoice in a duchess who thinks of others. The vicar and I shall be delighted to organize every detail, will we not, dear?"

Rachel's eyebrows rose as she saw her hearers dissolve into loud laughter in front of her eyes. "Really!" was all she could muster to express her displeasure. She decided to ignore such childish behavior and to explain her intentions.

"I have run many occasions of a similar nature. True, I have not overseen a festival, but I am sure the village will assist—the children, the men, and of course, the women."

Lenore, wiping her eyes during this declaration, went to Rachel and put her arms around her friend. "Rachel, not to let you take the reins and run would be a terrible deprivation to the world; therefore, I place the festival in your hands."

"You mean there is going to be one?" Rachel asked in an awed voice.

"Only if you promise to take full charge."

"There, David, do you hear that?" asked the exuberant lady.

The vicar suffered some qualms—that his sweet Rachel could run a vicarage, not perfectly, but comfortably; that their seven young ones were well brought up by her superb neglect; that her way with flowers was magical he could swear to—but that she could carry out the myriad details of a festival? He sighed, for he knew his services would be called upon frequently. Then he laughed to himself. She is my love, let us proceed. "Ladies, there's much to be done; we needs throw our heads together."

After an exciting discussion of the whys and wherefores, the afternoon gone, they parted with declarations that of course they were running mad, but wasn't it famous fun?

20

Henderson cursed as he drew tight rein on the horses to avoid running down the denizens of London who thronged the cobblestoned streets. "Make way, sap-skulls, make way!" he yelled at the drab crowds who turned sullen eyes to watch the elegant carriage roll by on its way to Mr. Pettibone's office, where he took leave of the party.

Impatient, the duke groaned whenever a wheel dropped into a water-filled hole. "London is the devil's town," he shouted once when the carriage tilted dangerously, throwing the three passengers into a heap.

" 'Tis the embargo, Your Grace," explained Mr. Cornby.

"Nappy's deviltry."

The rationale did not please the duke.

Turning into Grosvenor Square, the duke viewed his house and swore at its neglected exterior. "Dammit, why didn't Pettibone inform me?" An unfair question, for his solicitor had bemoaned the appearance of the house many times, only to be put off by the duke's shrug of indifference.

"Bricks and paint immediately, Cornby," ordered the duke as the three alighted from the carriage.

"The work has already begun, Your Grace—Mr. Endfield's directions—the masons are pointing up the bricks on the back outside staircase first, for they are a menace, threatening anyone who steps out into the rear garden."

"Which, I assume, is in gorgeous bloom," said His Grace sardonically.

"It's a pitiful sight, Your Grace." Mr. Cornby shook his head.

"Well, Foster, isn't the garden your affair?"

"The beds are being replanted and will be abloom shortly," Mr. Foster assured him.

"Put the monger on the railing replacement today, Cornby," barked the duke as he jiggled the wrought-iron railing of the half-moon steps fronting the house.

"Your Grace." Madcape opened the door and bowed. "It pleases us both to welcome you." He stepped back to permit his wife to curtsy.

"Mrs. Madcape, Madcape." The duke nodded. "Is the library in readiness?"

"Most certainly, Your Grace, even to the dusting of each book; the dining room and your bedchamber are prepared also."

"The other rooms?" asked His Grace.

"They await Mr. Foster." Madcape bobbed his head toward the rotund decorator, who said, "The workmen start tomorrow morning, Your Grace, if you find it convenient."

The immediate repast of Flemish soup, oysters in batter, glazed ham, mushroom fritters, ratafia biscuits, followed by celarate cream and port did much to assuage the duke's temper.

After his guests took their leave, the duke entered the library, where he had spent little time as a boy. Reacquainting himself, he sampled volumes from the shelves that lined the four walls; sat at the desk at which his father had always seemed absorbed in shuffling papers; opened one by one the now empty drawers; tried the wing chair beside the fireplace; and stared out the window that faced the side street leading to the Square.

Father did well to purchase a piece of ground bordered by a road on two sides, the duke concluded. Going to the corner, he climbed the stairs that swung around a center pole leading to his bedroom. He was very content with the living arrangement that offered him the privacy he craved.

Over the fireplace a large portrait of his mother, the former duchess, dominated the bedroom. Studying his mother's set features and overly elaborate gown, he felt a thread of annoyance at his disloyal recognition that she had neither the beauty nor the eyes of intelligence that were Lenore's.

Noting that his portmanteaus had been unpacked and his clothes put away, he hurried downstairs to read and dine, then to retire as the clock chimed nine.

The next morning, roused by the clamor of workmen's tools, His Grace woke far earlier than was his wont. He rang for Madcape who, disheveled, breathless, and cross, brought tea and toast.

"The house is bedlam, Your Grace; a man can't put his mind to his tasks—Madcape, where is this; Madcape, get that; everything slibber-slabber."

"Do the best you can," the duke said consolingly. "Are Mr. Cornby and Foster here?"

"Them two was at the door before sunup," replied the henchman. "Scared Mrs. Madcape witless with their poundings on the door."

"I'll go down; maybe—"

"No, Your Grace, it's messy; best stay out of the whole affair."

Heeding Madcape's advice, the duke ordered that his carriage be at the steps in half an hour.

Henderson, grumpy, heavy-eyed, greeted the duke sourly. "Where in the name of hell would a gentleman want to go at this hour? Sun's scarce up."

"Keep your tongue between your teeth, if you don't want it removed." The duke's tone held the old man silent. "Drive through the park."

Henderson, muttering about trumpery notions, did as bidden.

Rolling along under the trees, the duke recalled riding in the park with the beautiful Miss Featherheath when they had been so wildly in love. . . . What would have fallen out if they had stayed in London near her family?—His Grace winced—Only Mr. Featherheath could have been endured. Suddenly he called to his groom to take him to the Featherheath residence.

The duke arrived just as Harriet's father was sitting down to breakfast. Mr. Featherheath was a plump gentleman whose round face beguiled new acquaintances into a belief in his innocence in the affairs of the world. This was usually an evaluation later to be altered—sometimes at great expense—for Mr. Featherheath had an intricate intellect and a waggish heart.

His Grace, soothed by the gentleman's warm welcome, accepted his invitation to break bread with him.

"Wicks, take His Grace's driver to the kitchen and feed him," the older man bade his butler. "Now, Myles, no talk of importance while we eat; like to concentrate on my viands."

Well worth the concentration, thought the duke as he consumed buttered eggs, sirloin, hot biscuits, pastries, and coffee; then peeled an orange for the finish.

In the book room the duke recited the circumstances of Heath's accident. Mr. Featherheath clucked sympathetically. Learning of Charles's arrival, he roared his pleasure. "Your son! Instead of that demi-beau Sanford's. By the Good Lord, 'tis the greatest news! I'm not averse to telling you, Myles, I grieved over a grandson born of Hat's marriage with the left hand; now to find the boy's no Bartholomew baby—dash it, Myles, I'm happy! What's the lad like—you say he resembles you?"

"Me to the inch, sir."

"Better and better. Smart like you?" Charles's grandfather asked, "not here and therein like my Hat, is he?"

"Rest easy on that score, sir, he has your brain behind my facade."

"Perfect, eh?"

"I'd so vow."

"By God, I'm glad." Mr. Featherheath beamed. "Now, sir, what about yourself?"

The duke paused.

"Well, Myles?"

Taking a deep breath, the duke poured forth his intent to make Lenore Carey Lanier his duchess.

"By Jupiter, this is a day! Wicks! Wicks . . . oh, there you are, what hour is it?—no matter—bring the brandy . . . time to celebrate."

Mr. Featherheath raised his glass. "To the finest duke in the realm; may you hold for a long life and rejoice each year of it!"

"My gratitude, sir." His Grace lifted his glass.

"Lenore Carey, eh? Vicar's daughter, you say? Hoy, I knew her mother and father—mother beautiful beyond belief—the vicar a gentle scholar. And the widow Lanier?" he inquired, cocking his head.

"You will find her lovely," said the duke.

Missing the dryness in His Grace's tone, the old man said, "Well, Myles, my blessings; you are a fortunate man."

To forestall further discussion the duke rose, announced he must cut his stick, thanked his protesting host, promised to bring Heath and Charles to see their grandfather, and took his leave.

Henderson, in a better mood, drove slowly while the duke marked the changes wrought during his absence. Once he had the carriage wait as he entered the temporary building housing the Elgin Marbles, one of the new sights of London. On Bond Street he sauntered past the stores to observe the newest fashions, and lunched at Fenton on St. James's, a hotel whose cuisine pleased him.

The city is empty, the duke concluded late in the afternoon, and ordered Henderson to drive home. Once in the house, he told Madcape, "I can't eat here; the odors of paint and paste will make me ill—they're horrendous!"

To the duke dining out could only mean a visit to White's, the club where he had never relinquished his membership. When he stepped through the famous portals, he saw no one in the so-often-crowded hall— Damn London, doesn't anyone stay . . . ? he thought.

"Good evening, Myles."

The duke whirled around and beheld Sir Alfred Lanier. Standing beside Alfred was a gentleman elegantly dressed entirely in black satin save for a snowy white neckpiece that cradled a large jeweled pin.

His Grace bowed. "Alfred! You surprise me. In London in the off-season?"

"Oh, I'm—I'm just here on business. Martha and the children are in Bath. I've been traveling the countryside." He eyed the duke closely, then added, "And you, Myles, your presence in London at any time is enough to bowl me out. Boring, isn't it? A desert, but I by chance encountered an oasis. Myles, allow me to present the Marquis de Chondefon. Pierre, the Duke of Asherwood."

His Grace nodded coldly.

"La!" said the marquis, bowing. "*Vraiment,* I am French, an accident of birth, Your Grace—alas, one which Englishmen find abhorrent. However, such a misfortune does not prevent me from being delighted to meet you."

"Wasted, wasted, Pierre," Sir Alfred said. "The duke doesn't care a fig that you are French; he is by nature grave."

"*Bon!* Then let us invite the duke to dine with us."

"I have no desire to clunter in, Marquis," said the duke politely.

"Don't be a gudgeon, Myles," Sir Alfred drawled, "come along."

During the meal the talk was noncommittal, except when the visitor from France exclaimed over the particularly delectable English fare. Over port the marquis asked if His Grace gamed.

"Seldom—I prefer whist or piquet."

"*Mais, oui,* we must have a rubber," the French-

man said, beaming. "Alfred, a game of whist—maybe
we can find a fourth."

"Not likely," responded Alfred, casting his eyes
around the nearly vacant room. "I see only Lord
Jerald, but he fuzzes the cards and I don't play with
cheats. However, I have an engagement of import
and will leave you to piquet."

The marquis protested, but the duke said nothing.

"Myles," Sir Alfred remarked, "it comes to my
ears that there is work afoot on your London house."

"Quite so, I expect to spend the season here."

"What?" cried Sir Alfred. "So, at last you are bored
with Asherwood."

The duke frowned. "Bored? Well, I suppose you
could use the word; I never have."

Sir Alfred baited the duke. "Every eligible daughter's mother's heart will beat the faster when the news
of your arrival is announced."

"They need not," replied the duke, "I will not be in
Petticoat Lane."

"Don't tell me you intend to become the recluse of
Grosvenor Square," said Alfred.

"No!" barked the duke.

"Good, Martha will be delighted to send you cards.
Oh, by the way, have you seen my grandmother?"

"Yes, once or twice—she gave me a good scold," replied the duke. He was ready for the next question.

"And my beautiful sister-in-law?"

"Yes—Heath was tossed from his horse on their
doorstep; both ladies were gracious to him."

"Did you not find Lenore lovely?" queried the relentless man.

His Grace felt his anger rise. "Fairly, but there are
many diamonds more so in London."

"Hoy," persisted Sir Alfred. "But in Asherwood, she is an imcomparable."

"Really, Alfred." The duke's tone was icy. "You sound like the mother of an eligible daughter."

Turning red, Sir Alfred rose. "Myles, such a thought never crossed my mind—it is just usual for dukes not to marry nobodies. I bid you both good night." He bowed, whirled, and walked away.

"Methinks you drew claret, your Grace," said the marquis, laughing, as he watched Sir Alfred leave. "Or did he?" he added, as he saw the duke's scowl.

"Neither," replied the duke coldly. "Alfred and I have been at points since we were in nankeens. A game or two of piquet?"

"Splendid!"

The two men found a table in an alcove, called for cards, and silently began to play.

The duke took the first rubber with ease. "*Tiens!* My hand is out," declared the marquis.

"You have not played for a while?"

"Alas, no . . . I come from a country where gentlemen are interested only in philosophy, poetry, and music."

"Not war?"

"*Certainement,* all men are forced to be by the scourge of Europe, but, as here, gentlemen do not discuss war in their clubs but, sadly, in Germany they do not game either. Have you been there?"

"Germany? No," replied the duke.

"A dull country; I far prefer England if I cannot be in France. Have you been to my country, Duke?"

"Yes."

"Ah, *ma chère* France—so sad. I do not return until the 'scourge' is gone."

"It could be many years," exclaimed the duke.

"Perhaps," the marquis said, sighing. "So I must drift from land to land. My chateau and vineyards are preserved by my brother. I am often homesick for my France; did you not lose your heart to her charms?"

The duke spoke the truth. "I did not see them, for I was drunk during my entire sojourn."

"*Mon Dieu!*"

"Did not my May-game behavior reach your ears? It was well prattled about all over the Continent, I am told."

The marquis stared at the frowning duke—piquet forgotten—then threw back his head and laughed. "You? Are you the 'Rake of Europe'? It can't be."

The duke made no reply. The marquis gasped, saying, "Tales of your outrages at court kept France in glee for months. Champagne poured down the most delicious bodices; meringue in pretty faces; no lady's skirt safe from your uplifting fingers." The marquis, wiping his eyes, continued, "Even Josephine fled from your wandering hands. *Mon Dieu,* you could tell merry tales."

"Not so, sir!" The duke's voice froze the marquis. "I have absolutely no memory of those disgraceful solecisms—not one—I assure you."

The marquis spoke quickly. "Sir, I had no desire to offend you—my deepest apologies if I have done so."

His Grace shook his head. "No, I take no umbrage, for I have no right. My actions passed all bounds, I must suppose, but they have never been cataloged before—I am ashamed."

"Did you know that you were called by many '*La comète de rire?*' You appeared, and France was made risible, then you vanished and left a trail of sad loss."

"Good God!" The duke flushed.

"A few considered you *Le Diable* in disguise, but most loved you. Where did you disappear to, Your Grace, I make bold to ask?"

"Italy, where I became ill. Upon recovery I returned to Asherwood."

"There to be titled the 'Dour Duke,' I am informed."

"I had much to be dour about. Who fed you the scandal broth—Alfred?"

The marquis shrugged, "All London chatters; whether it was Alfred or no, I cannot say."

The men resumed their game, then the marquis, having regained his skill, they played until a late hour. Gathering the cards, the marquis paid his opponent a small amount.

The duke offered to drop the marquis off at his hotel, Clarendon's, and inquired if the marquis intended a long stay.

"No, I sail back to Germany in a day or two, but shall revisit England later."

On parting, both men expressed the hope of meeting again.

21

The next morning, when the duke came out into the sunshine, he was surprised to see the waiting Henderson ramrod straight and lips tight.

"Well, Henderson?" asked His Grace as he bent to climb into his carriage.

"Order me to Tattersall's," said the old man from the side of his mouth. "Do it loud! Say you're interested in a horse."

Bemused but having no plans of his own, the duke did as bid, saying, "Henderson, take me to Tattersall's," in a carrying tone. "There's a horse there I've heard about."

"Immediately, Your Grace."

Slightly annoyed, the duke wondered why his groom was acting so strangely.

At the horse mart Henderson spoke first as he helped the duke alight. "You do want me to go over the horse you mentioned, don't you, sir?" he said in a high voice.

"Indeed, yes." His Grace decided to humor the old man.

Once in the building, Henderson led the duke to a horse stall well away from the men inspecting Tattersall's offerings.

asked, "Myles, about your wedding—er—do you wish me to attend?"

"Good God, no!" The duke jumped up. "You stay right here in London."

"That bad, eh? Is she such an antidote?"

"Ugly? No, she is bound to put every female in London into dismals. And you, you gasseted flirt, will probably develop a tendre for her—every other male seems to. Good-bye, Pettibone." The duke walked out, leaving his solicitor open-mouthed.

22

During the remainder of his London stay, the duke swung from moments of high elation as he led the spies a maze chase—rides to no destination, or to spots totally uninteresting to his followers—to spells of gloom as he sat in his library, wondering who employed the spies and the nature of the threat they posed to his plans.

The day the duke set out for Asherwood—in his carriage, with two traveling carriages in tandem—he experienced relief in leaving the city, but his mood was dampened by dread of the morrow, his wedding day.

On the road, comfortably fed, rocked by the roll and sway of the carriage, he fell into somnolence. When he woke, heavy-eyed, he peered out the small window and recognized fields around the Village of Asherwood. He closed his eyelids again and dozed.

Startled by a shout, he looked out and saw one of the tenants on the estate waving his cap and yelling. His Grace, assuming he must be dreaming, lay back, only to hear more shouts as a group of children ran beside the wheels calling, "Your Grace, hurrah for Your Grace." Puzzled, the duke watched the boys and girls fall away from the fast-rolling vehicle. Near the village others along the road hallooed and waved; men doffed their hats and women curtsied, one or two threw kisses. Inside the green square of Asherwood, the duke gaped, for by the side of the road, Tom Doone—his disgruntled tenant, who for years had made no bones of his hatred for the duke and never saw His Grace that he did not turn his back and spit —Tom Doone, cap in hand, bent in a sweeping bow.

The duke could not believe his senses.

Farther along the way to the palace, a tilbury appeared, driven at a fast pace. The duke recognized the vicar.

Pondering the amazing behavior of his villagers, the duke came to the somber conclusion that they were mocking him. He filled with rage. On the ride up his long driveway his anger rose high, and when at last the carriage drew to a stop, he leaped out, snarled at the waiting Cloughs, strode to the vicar, and roared, "Vicar, come with me," then stormed into the palace.

Once inside the library, he whirled on his friend. "What craziness is this, Vicar?"

"Welcome home, Your Grace—I'm delighted to see you." The vicar smiled.

"Don't try to turn me up sweet; tell me what the

devil has gotten into the villagers? Every damn last one of them has flown into alt—they mock me!"

"Oh, no, Myles, you are beside the bridge; they've gone into raptures and wish to show you that you are a complete hand—a buck of the first head."

"Stop talking slum. Why are they running mad?"

"It is your wedding gift, Myles."

"My what?" shouted the duke.

"Your wedding present to your future duchess."

"Ah!" The duke threw back his head and snorted. "So she's at the bottom of this!" Scowling, he pinned the vicar with a cold eye. "Pray enlighten me. What am I bestowing on the duchess-to-be that causes all within miles to run short of sheet?"

"Not crazy, Myles—joyous!"

"No put-offs, sir, explain!"

"Your gift to your bride, Myles, is a festival for the whole village."

"Good God." The duke stepped back as if struck.

"A full-blown festival with races, games, judging, prizes, food, and in the evening, dancing and fireworks," the vicar informed the duke.

The duke stared at his grinning friend, then wheeled and poured himself a large glass of brandy, which he downed quickly. He approached the vicar. "I should draw your cork for this!"

"Glory, Myles, you cannot image it my choice—heaven forbid. I've not had a decent meal since Lenore propounded the brilliant idea."

"Damme, sir, what are you babbling about?" the duke shouted.

"A festival, Myles, a festival. Can we sit down—I am almost too tired to stand, so busy have I been."

"Install yourself, then, you pigeon." The duke

poured two brandies, giving one to the vicar. "Now tell me what flimflam Mrs. Lanier used to wheedle you into such flummery?"

Taking a goodly draft, the vicar began. "You may recall, Myles, you required Lenore to make the plans for the wedding and told me to assist her in whatever she planned?"

"Cawker that I was, yes; I remember."

"Precisely. Well, the dear lady, in discussing all with Rachel and me, wistfully recaptured a delight of her childhood—a festival for the village given by a wealthy man to his bride—her one desired present."

"What a Jack Adams!" murmured the duke.

"Maybe, but for Lenore the day is cherished as one of the most memorable of her childhood." The vicar laughed. "She won a blue hair ribbon playing a game."

"Famous." The duke's tone was arctic. "And she desires to repeat history, is that it?"

"To the trivet; the county has been in high gig ever since—the news flew like fire."

"And this absurdity is my token to the soon-to-be Duchess of Asherwood! Does she hope to win another hair ribbon?"

"Hoy!" chortled the vicar, then he sobered. "Myles, it is splendid, ingenious, and generous."

"With my blunt," said the duke darkly.

The vicar was reproachful. "Myles, no nipsqueeze, you, and you're rich as a new-shorn lamb."

"Humph, I'll be at point nonplus shortly if the future duchess has many whims of such liberality."

"Oh, she thought on that; it took some cozening to bring her to book."

"So I can blame you!"

"Yes, you can lay that on my dish. The instant she spoke of it, I sensed what has fallen out would happen—the villagers have never been so excited—man, woman, and child working for and anticipating the glorious day."

"And when might that be?" asked the duke acidly.

The vicar paled. "Tomorrow, Myles, is your wedding day."

The duke paused and said, "I'm gapped right and tight, am I not?"

The vicar took a deep breath, straightened in his chair, and, speaking with great courage to the cold, angry man across from him, said, "Happily, I think you are."

The men stared at each other in silence. Finally the duke spoke. "Tell me, what has this to do with your meals?"

The vicar gave a shout of relieved laughter. "Myles, I have made the monumental discovery that my sweet, gentle Rachel is a female of ability and power—she could run the country. She has cajoled the women, bullied the men, and run the legs off the children to ensure that every detail of the gala flows smooth as cream. Her interest in preparing food is at low ebb."

"David, 'tis understandable—power to a female is a heady thing—she has nose-led you, I can see."

The vicar grinned. "I, sir, have knocked under like a meek bit of clay."

The duke snorted. "You sound like a proper varmint, if not cow-hearted."

The vicar replied lightly, "I'm not such a flat that I do not realize when I'm under the cat's paw, but there I stand, most cheerfully, for the festival has turned the village into an Eden; everyone has something to do; everyone has much to say; everyone is too thronged to fight. It's famous fun and my Rachel bears off the palm for keeping watch and ward."

"Very tidy! But may I ask, in all this kicking up a lark, has anyone thought on the marriage ceremony itself?"

"Myles"—the vicar was contrite—"forgive me! You are to be wed in your own chapel in the morning at ten."

"Ten! Why, I'm scarce awake at that hour. It's un-heard-of, no one is wed—Ah! I see—the festival."

The vicar nodded glumly. "The rites are to be attended by only a small number. However, there will be a dinner party on the terrace at night, so your guests can enjoy the fireworks."

"Good, it pleases me that there will be some observance of civility. It crossed my mind that the lady in question might wish to have the ceremony as the opening shot of the festival. Who has been invited to the dinner—the county?"

The vicar replied with dignity, "No, Myles, only the first families—names garnered from Mr. Endfield's list—have all accepted."

"Doomed to be an insipid squeeze," the duke said, sighing. "So it begins." He paused. "Wish me well, David, for it is all bitter to me—I do not want to be wed, I do not want to reside in London, I do not want to become a Bond Street fripple, and I am forced to do it all." The duke shuddered. "It goes against my pluck."

The vicar shook his head. "Myles, you misplace your woes. You marry an incomparable, who will make London a joyous city; she'll be the darling of the *ton*, and make your household a charming one. She's a paragon, Myles; you're in luck."

"By Jupiter, I think you have a tendre for the lady," the duke exclaimed and watched his friend turn red. For a minute the vicar did not speak, then said, "She is very beautiful, a delightful female, Myles, but Rachel has my heart locked tight." The vicar rose. "I must return to the lady of my adoring or she will give me a mighty trimming for eluding my duties."

As the men shook hands the vicar spoke. "Myles, you are a top-of-the-tree Corinthian and I wish you all good in this world—and the next." He laughed, then added, "One word of caution, if I may. The lady you wed is an unaware temptress and will have many men in London dangling after her; but she is needle-witted and pretty-behaved, so you need never fear or look green at her."

The duke, astonished, would have spoken, but the vicar hurried out the door, pleased that he had given the duke reason to consider his bride-to-be in a new light.

23

Lemon sunlight filtered through gently blown curtains, waking Lenore. For an instant she lay quiet, then her eyes widened. Today I become the Duchess of Asherwood—how awesome—and how ridiculous. Trying to visualize herself in the large palace, she winced. I've never entered the vast edifice, and tonight I'm to be its mistress—what fustian! She sighed, and thought, There is much to do; I must get up. Is he awake? Is he lying in bed, wondering what a devilish crunch he is getting himself into? Is he miserable and scared as I am? Stupid! Lenore threw back the covers and swung from her bed. I'm not miserable and scared—I'm excited! She pulled the bell rope and soon Maria found her peering out the window.

"Maria, it's a glorious day."

"*Si, si,* blessing for your *nupcias,* ma'am."

"Thank you, Maria."

"Madame Lanier asks you join her for breakfast."

Entering the old lady's room, Lenore stopped short. Surrounded by carrying cases, a large open trunk next to him, Abel stood like a colossus, holding a tiny dress to his shoulders.

"Come in, come, young lady," came a voice from the window, "and close the door. Abel is helping me select my gown for today. Do you like that one—hold it up, jackawarts."

Careful to avoid Abel's eye, Lenore studied the dress and announced it would do splendidly.

"Show her the other choice—don't tear it!"

Both costumes being years behind the mode, Lenore chose the first, for it lacked the clashing scarlet and green stripes that pained the eye.

"Now get out my turban." Abel lay the striped gown over the back of a chair and drew from the trunk a turban—almost a yard across—made of purple velvet adorned with strings of pearls, feathers, and bits of tarnished silver lace. "Give it to me—it's gorgeous!" The old lady popped it on her head, thereby rendering her appearance that of a crumpled mushroom.

"Well, don't stand there like a bubblehead; it's my favorite, and many pretty words were tossed to me when I wore it. Will it do?"

"Beautifully, dear Mamère," Lenore managed to say.

"Go away, baldcock, I want to advise the bride. Sit down, child; Maria left your breakfast on the table."

Lenore sat down to eat her omelette.

"So today you become a duchess, eh?"

Lenore nodded.

"I hope you understand what being one entails, young lady."

"I haven't a thread of a notion, Mamère."

"Looby, young people are so sapskull today. There wasn't one budding lady in my day who did not comprehend what becoming a duchess meant to the pin."

"Please tell me," said Lenore placidly.

"Well, first you'll be one of the most respected ladies in the land; people will bow and scrape and—"

"Oh, dear, I don't want that."

"Humph, you'll get it no matter your preference. Then you are going to be wealthy beyond belief. Bunky has had six honeyfalls of vast proportions that I am aware of; heaven only knows what his gingerbread is—but it's sizable."

"Mamère, you frighten me."

"Don't be a peagoose, being rich is grand. Now, the real question is what kind of a duchess you are to become—a high-flyer who tries to spend all Bunky's brass on gewgaws and clothes, with a large cicisbeo at your heels?"

"Cicisbeo? Mamère! I've never sought admirers," protested Lenore.

"No, but I'll bet a monkey, you'll have to fight them

off in London. But back to the question—or, are you going to be a duchess who tends her husband, children, and household—dull and respectable?"

Lenore released her pent-up glee in laughter. "Hark! Madame Lanier, I'm going to be—me!"

"Good! Now, about the wedding—I'll give you away."

"What?"

"I lay in bed last night and it came to me like a bolt of lightning that you had no one to do the honors, so I am the one. You ain't mine to bestow exactly, but I'm the only family you have, so I intend to hand you over to Bunky."

"Mamère, I'm charmed and would choose no other, but are you certain you can go through with the commotion?"

"Farradiddle, 'course I can. If I stick my spoon in the wall afterward, I'll have done just what I had my heart set on, but I won't, missy, because I'm going to London and the devil himself can't hinder me. Now give me a kiss and go dress."

Lenore hugged the old lady. In her own room she indulged in a long hot bath. Wrapping herself in a dressing gown, she awaited Maria.

Later, Lenore, arrayed in her pale yellow wedding gown, allowed Maria to dress her hair. Maria gathered the auburn tresses into curls and pinned them on the top of Lenore's head, then let three curls fall softly down the back, and made ringlets at the side of Lenore's cheeks, finally adding a small crown of lace.

Lenore, delighted with her reflection, said, "Maria, you are a stylist of talent."

"*Gracias,*" Maria said, beaming.

Abel waited in the hall, his eyes fixed on Lenore as she came down the stairs.

"Ma'am, you are as lovely as the day you married the captain." He handed her a box. Nestled in the tissue lining was a muff of white satin covered with pale yellow roses, white daisies, and maidenhair fern.

"Oh, Abel!"

"Ma'am, if the captain could, he would wish you the best. I do so for the both of us."

Lenore let a tear roll down her cheek. "Thank you, dear friend."

"Whishee, now, ma'am." Abel whirled a handkerchief from his pocket and presented it to her. To his relief, the sound of horses' hooves announced the approach of the duke's carriage.

Henderson in full regalia sat proud. The boys alighted and hurried to the house. Maria came downstairs and announced Madame Lanier ready; Abel was to go immediately to fetch her.

Heath, greeting Lenore, swore her, on his honor, the most breathtaking lady in the world.

"I would say the universe," chirped Charles loftily.

When Mamère, in Abel's arms, appeared, there fell a silence. Her gown of plum velvet was adorned with wide gold lace at neck and sleeves. She wore her paisley shawl, and her head was topped by the turban, now awry. Her rope of gold jingled, and her numerous rings—far too large for her fingers—sparkled on clutched hands. However, it was her face that focused the stare of the gathering—a mask of flour white, a large dot of crimson on each cheek, slashed scarlet lips, and black lines painted around her eyes.

Heath gave Charles a quite unnecessary warning nudge, as the boy gaped, too awed to speak.

At Lenore's behest Heath held the door to allow Abel, carrying Mamère, to proceed to the carriage. Seated, the old lady rearranged her turban and held her head high, eyes straight and focused.

Lenore sat beside Mamère, who did not betray that she was aware of the bride's presence. Heath and Charles faced the ladies, Abel joined Henderson, and Maria waved the party off—she was to be picked up later by the vicar's wife and older children.

The drive to the chapel was almost silent, Lenore fighting her qualms of inadequacy, Madame Lanier remembering other rides and other places, Heath nervous about his responsibilities as best man, and Charles fascinated by the intricacies of Mamère's apparel.

Once Lenore sighed, and Heath, to bolster himself as well as Lenore, said, "It will all be fine, Mother, darling." The comment roused Mamère. "Most assuredly, young man—and you, varmint, take your ogles off me—I'm not a raree-show."

Charles blushed and peeked at Lenore, who smiled sweetly. He felt better, and manfully stared out the window for the rest of the journey.

When the drive was over, Heath jumped out and assisted Lenore to alight. Charles followed, then Abel lifted Madame Lanier and carried her, as ordered, into the chapel and down the aisle to the front pew.

In place, the old lady waved Abel away and studied Rachel's profusion of flowers. At the organ Mr. Algernon Merse, perceiving a guest, played softly.

The vicar entered the chancel, and upon seeing Madame Lanier, nearly dropped his prayer book. He decided to warn the duke that what appeared to be a top-heavy gnome was Mamère. He went to the amazing lady, who announced in a loud whisper, "I am to give the bride away—and don't you try to stop me."

"Never!" vowed the Reverend David Thomas, and, with a bow, hastened up the aisle to speak to Lenore, whom he spied entering the small room by the entrance. He passed Charles, who explained that Heath had told him to sit still in the second pew, to listen to the service, and to save a place for Heath after he had done his duties as best man.

The vicar greeted Heath, suggested he join his father, then smiled on the pale bride. Lenore said nothing until Heath had kissed her and left.

"Oh, David, is he in deep dismals—not Heath—the duke?"

The vicar, an honest man, gave a distressed reply. "Lenore, he is a man carved in ice."

"Oh, dear, maybe I should cry off," Lenore mourned.

"Never! To slab off now would be a shabby ploy. Myles is a slowtop, but to naysay today—oh, no." He smiled. "Besides, if you did, I could never win my wager, and my sons would be ignorant anapos."

From sheer nervousness Lenore giggled. "Oh, David, I feel such an April gowk."

"And you like an angel," said the vicar, sighing. "Ha, I hear Rachel and the children. We begin as soon as all are seated. When Mr. Merse plays the opening notes of the wedding march, you start down the aisle. May God go with you, dear Lenore." He gave her such a glance that, had Rachel seen it, she would have rapped his knuckles with her fan.

Alone, Lenore began to tremble. The strains of the march sounded, then she prayed, Help me to be a good duchess. . . . Amen." Stepping out the door, she slowly started her march to the waiting duke. He is stone! thought Lenore as she moved to take her place at his side.

The duke, arrayed in pure-white satin breeches, silk hose, a dark green watered-silk coat, his linen snowy —tied in a perfect *trône d'amour*—stood, a statue.

The vicar, watching Lenore, who seemed to float down the aisle, glanced at the rock-rigid duke, and felt an urge to plant a facer on his friend and yell, "Look at her, you fool, she loves you." Instead, he sighed and spoke the familiar words, "Dearly beloved, we are gathered together . . ." He read in a calm voice. When he asked the old question "Who giveth this woman to be married to this man?" he blinked as Madame Lanier, in a strong voice, replied, "I do, and he better be good to her!" All eyes, except Lenore's, flew to His Grace, who lifted his head a quarter of an inch.

Lenore's responses were low; the duke's clear and chiseled. When the vicar pronounced them man and wife, he added, as if it were a command, "You may kiss the bride." The duke gave the vicar a stabbing glare, then gazing over Lenore's head, put his lips to her forehead, turned, and held out his arm.

Elegantly riveted, thought the duke sourly as he moved into the aisle.

Charles had not once taken his eyes from his new mother; now, quite beside himself, before Heath could collar him, he slipped from the pew, threw his arms around Lenore's waist, and gazed up at her adoringly. The duke stopped; Lenore cupped the boy's face, leaned over, and whispered in his ear. Then kissing his cheek, she slipped the muff of flowers from her arm and gave it to Charles, then replaced her hand on the duke's newly extended arm as he led her to the portico. From the chapel Charles's voice rang out. "Maria, my mother said to give you this."

The duke dropped his arm and spoke. "Madam, you

will wish to dress for the festival; Mrs. Clough will take you to your room." He started down the curved cloister.

Lenore, keeping pace, felt touched by ire. "Thank you, I am very eager to attend the festival."

"I hope you do not attempt to win a hair ribbon; I shall be glad to furnish any you may need."

Now truly angry, Lenore flushed. "Perhaps it would be wise for you to come and see that I behave satisfactorily."

"As I can conceive of nothing that would bore me more, I shall forego the pleasure."

"And as I can think of naught that would throw a mightier damper on the whole affair for everyone than your presence, I commend you for your consideration."

Neither spoke again until they reached Mrs. Clough, who beamed on them. "Such happiness! May God bless you both."

The duke snorted, "Show the duchess to her room, please."

Lenore, her face scarlet, chin high, blindly followed Mrs. Clough into the immense hall and up the curving staircase.

Mrs. Clough wisely held her tongue. Opening the door to the bedchamber, she said quietly, "I will send Maria as soon as possible."

Though her sight was blurred by tears, Lenore realized she had entered the most magnificent bedroom she had ever beheld.

It was a corner room; its windows, draped in white satin, ran almost to the floor. Raised on a dais between two windows along the west wall stood a blue-velvet-covered bed with a canopy of carved wood that supported folds of gold brocade. Along one wall a door opened into a dressing room lined with closets and cupboards; another door led to the chamber for bathing. Between them was a long mirror. A marble fireplace, a door on each side, filled the other inner wall.

Chairs and sofas gleamed, their mahogany frames upholstered in yellow satin, shot through with garlands of bright ribbons. Glass-hung candelabras twinkled pleasingly, while vases of flowers vied with each other to please the bride.

Taken unaware by the room's charm, Lenore felt her anger ebb. She looked out on the gardens and caught her breath. Formal paths of emerald green wound through beds where blooms flourished in brilliant profusion. Lenore made a moue, recalling how she had once proudly shown the duke her garden at Willowood, and his polite praise. The duke—suddenly her anger flared anew. He is a monster; how could he be so icy? She felt the urge to scream. I am a fool to have wed him. She burst into tears, then as suddenly, with a shake, dried her eyes. Stop being missish; you knew that he despised the prospect of marrying you—or any female, she added to console herself. But he did, and now you are the Duchess of Asherwood. She moved to the mirror. Duchess, she remonstrated to her reflection, you have an obligation to be —she peered closely into the glass—yourself. Cheered, she admired her gown, then slowly struggled to undo the buttons within reach.

Maria's knock won a quick "Do come in."

When Maria came to a pause in her spate of grateful Spanish for Lenore's gift, Lenore urged her to hurry the dressing for the festival. From her few clothes brought the day before to hang, rather lost, in the large closets of the palace, Lenore had selected a pale violet muslin, a lace shawl, and a straw hat that tied under the chin with white chiffon.

A knock at the door sent Maria to admit a footman who announced that the marquis and his brother awaited downstairs. Lenore snatched her bag and gloves and ran. Charles, halfway up the stairs, took her hand, then, laughing, they marched soldier-straight down the remaining stairs, saluted Heath, who swung in step ahead of them, and ordered, "Off to the festival fray, troops."

The first sight of the festival field, dotted with stalls and tents and thronging with men, women, and children, caused Lenore to exclaim, "Glory, the whole world is here!"

"Thanks to your contrivance, Mother, darling."

"And your father's generosity," Lenore added quickly.

"Why are we sitting here?" Charles jumped from the carriage. "The fun's over there; come on."

As the three walked into the crowd Charles had an immediate and exalted experience—a group of boys about his own age gathered to hurl the most outrageous insults to and about him, thereby offering him the exquisite pleasure of coming to cuffs with a lad a bit taller than himself. They milled disgracefully over the grass, fists flying. For a time the excitement was intense, but as neither lad could cast the deciding blow, the watching boys grew bored and finally shouted, "Oh, come on, you two anapos, let's get some ices."

Charles, clothes ripped, blood on his nose, and the promise of a glorious black eye, grinned at Lenore and Heath, then, breathing hard, said, "See you later," and strutted off with his erstwhile deadly enemy, who threw his arm around Charles's shoulders as they trudged after the others.

Lenore had been restrained by Heath from interposing in the fracas. She waited until Charles was out of earshot, then exploded. "He could have been killed!"

"Never!" said Heath, laughing. "He has had a flaming victory and made a bosom bow for life."

"Horrible!" cried Lenore.

"Splendid!" retorted Heath. "Ah, there is Mrs. Thomas; let's join her." Reluctantly Lenore took his proffered arm, her eyes on Charles until he vanished in the maze of stalls.

On their approach to the booth, where Rachel held the reins of the festival in tight control, Lenore cringed slightly to see men tip their caps and women curtsy as she passed. Bow and scrape. So this is what Mamère meant. She smiled and nodded in response, thus creating a ripple of flattering comments in her wake.

Heath's face lighted up when he espied the vicar's fifteen-year-old daughter, Donna, standing shyly behind her mother. He bowed and said, "Donna, I've seen you for a long time. Shall we inspect the stalls together?" The girl, who had grown into a very pretty young lady, blushed, but stepped to his side. Turning to Lenore, Heath asked, "Will you be all right, Mother?"

"No," responded Lenore solemnly. "I expect I shall be eaten by lions and mauled by tigers." She laughed, "Go along, you two."

Rachel gave directions to a farmer who wanted to reach the pen for prize pigs, then whirled and hugged Lenore.

"Lenore, dear, what a lovely wedding!"

Lenore feigned sternness. "Rachel, you are the vicar's wife: 'tis improper to tell bouncers."

Rachel demurred, "Really, Lenore, I don't take your meaning; it was an extraordinarily beautiful affair."

"Indeed so, thanks to your flowers."

"No, no." Rachel fussed "You and the duke—"

"Peagoose, don't try to wrap it up in clean linen; why not say—Did not Mamère behave dreadfully and Charles—what a hubble-bubble." Lenore giggled.

"Lenore," chided her friend, "I'd never utter such words."

"True, but you'd think them."

"Now, Lenore." Rachel, flustered, reddened.

"To your duties, darling; here come a gaggle of females."

Both were soon surrounded by chatter, urging, then insisting the duchess and Rachel be judges of the handiwork, pickles, cakes, candies, fruits, jellies, jams, and pastries. A no would be unaccepted.

Spying Mrs. Turtlelock, Lenore said, "It requires three judges surely; Mrs. Turtlelock, will you be so good as to assist Mrs. Thomas and me in our task? I'm certain you are far more knowledgeable than I."

Overjoyed to have the new duchess select her, Mrs. Turtlelock let her resentment at not being asked to sing in the palace chapel drain from her heart.

Shepherded, the three judges moved from stall to stall and sniffed, tasted, sipped, touched, fingered, and after much nodding and pursing of lips, drew a list of the winners. They were so lavish in their praise, and complained so satisfactorily at the horrors of their dilemmas in decision, that the losers' feelings of disappointment were assuaged.

Old Mrs. Thompson, who had not even bowed to Mrs. Turtlelock in three years, applauded her high wisdom in choosing the only pickles worthy of consideration—hers.

The prizes were to be awarded later from the raised platform in front of the tea tent. The judges were invited to join the winners and losers at the elaborate tea now being readied. Lenore exclaimed herself bound to burst if another nibble passed her lips—so many delicious tidbits had she tasted—and she wished to watch the young people and later return for refreshments. Rachel and Mrs. Turtlelock borrowed Lenore's excuse, and the three walked to the area where the races were already in progress.

Lenore could not locate Charles, but finally spied a ragamuffin hobbling along in a three-legged race. Moving closer, she concluded it must indeed be her new son—grass-stained; muddy from head to toe; his black eye scarcely noticeable, so dirty his face; his clothes ripped; and apparently he had lost a shoe.

Charles had run every race, played every game, and though he never won, his enthusiasm did not sag. His cheers and screams egged his mates on to great efforts —he was among the first chosen for any team.

Noting Lenore's expression, Rachel assured her that Charles thrived, and would she please observe the vicar's third son—surely as bedraggled as Charles.

Espying the ladies, Charles limped toward them, sniffed, and grinned. "Did you see the race, Mother? We came in third, Ratsy and I." Lenore surmised Ratsy to be Charles's early combatant, for he stood nearby.

"Ratsy's my best friend, rides a horse too." Further extolling of Ratsy's charms was cut short by a distant voice. "Hey, Ratsy, Charley, you're in this one—hurry!"

"Have to go." Charles half hopped as fast as he could, then, removing the encumbering shoe, crouched to run the next event.

"Ratsy? Charley?" Lenore, bewildered, queried.

Mrs. Turtlelock laughed. "The boy is farmer Ratsmore's lad—everyone calls him 'Ratsy.' He's a good boy, the oldest of five, all girls except himself. A bit quick of fists because he doesn't want anyone to think him cossetted by so many females. His mother moans she can hardly keep him decently covered, he is so quick to wrestle, jump fences, climb trees."

"But 'Charley'! Charles is the duke's son."

Rachel laughed. "To be called Charley means that the boys in the village are willing to overlook Charles's misfortune in being a duke's son—a high tribute indeed."

"Glory, I've much to learn." Lenore shook her head.

Heath, who had been preparing his horse for the cross country, hailed her.

"Heath, have you seen Charles?" asked Lenore.

"Looks famous, doesn't he?" Heath beamed approvingly.

"How can you say so; he looks like a care for nobodies."

"Oh, no, he is just hey-go-mad to be in every stunt. A right one, that brother of mine," bragged Heath.

At the finish of Charles's race, they observed the boys forming a circle around the vicar, who had scheduled the day's program to interrupt sports with stories, giving the lads pause to catch their breath.

"Oh, do let us go," cried Rachel. "David is preparing to tell the most dreadful shockers—all about the wild west in America. He reads tales in magazines about Indians and cowboys, then makes up—Oh, they are beyond permission."

"And the boys eat them up," chimed in Mrs. Turtlelock.

"He used to tell me stories as rewards for good lessons," Heath said judicially. "I listened with never a doubt that each word was gospel—still think so, Mrs. Thomas; can there by any question?" Heath leered at the lady wickedly.

"Now, Heath, you know full well—" Rachel started, then caught Heath's eye. "Hoy, you're gulling me, jackanapes. . . ."

Laughing, they moved to see Heath swing onto his horse's back and attach himself to the group of young men jockeying for position to attain a good start for the cross country—a long and grueling test of stamina for horse and rider.

The ladies lingered for the starting gun, waved until the racers were out of sight, then drifted back to the refreshment tent to view the young and old parade the field. Many came to thank Lenore and praise Rachel for the festival.

The vicar appeared with Charles—whose clothing hung shredded here and there—in tow, and announced that the boy had won the wrestling bout, and was a young blade worthy of this honor. Charles accepted the praise, the proffered tea and ginger cake, and ate four sugar buns.

"Hey, Charley, let's go swimming," called Ratsy from the edge of the tent.

"Yes!" replied Charles. "Excuse me, Mother . . ."

Lenore grabbed his arm. "Charles, you don't know how to swim."

"Yes, I do, Mr. Sanford taught me."

Taken aback by the casual mention of Mr. Sanford, whose death by drowning Charles must have remembered, Lenore said nothing.

"Rest easy, Lenore," the vicar assured her, "I'll be with the boys and I suggest you come too—an amusing spectacle."

"But he has no swimming apparel," Lenore objected nervously.

"He can swim in his nankeens, Your Grace," decided Ratsy. "Usually we swim naked, but today it's a bit crowded."

Lenore looked a bit surprised.

"Do you think it shocking?" asked Rachel. "All the boys in the village swim unencumbered, and"—she rolled her eyes at her husband—"even the fathers when they can sneak off!"

"Why, my very dearest, *what* an innuendo!"

"Don't play the innocent with me, David Thomas, I've seen you men down their diving and running—" she stopped, bewildered, as all except Charles and Ratsy broke into laughter. Gasping, she added hastily, "From a great distance, of course," a statement that markedly increased the hearers' enjoyment.

"My heart of hearts," exclaimed the vicar appreciatively, when he could speak, "life without you would be a desert! Come on boys—last one in is a sloth's tail."

"I think you are all horrid." Rachel tossed her head.

"Oh, we are," affirmed Lenore, "totally lacking in gentility—really quite dreadful." She began to giggle.

Rachel, eyeing Lenore, gave a titter and soon the whole tent fell into an uproar again and only calmed when Mr. Endfield entered and informed Rachel it was time to award the prizes.

"Come, Lenore, Mrs. Turtlelock," Rachel urged. "Prize time—you too, Mr. Endfield. The duchess will give them out as you, sir, hand them to her."

"Must I?" Lenore hung back.

"Certainly," Rachel responded with authority, and bustled the two ladies onto the platform in front of the tea tent.

In his library, the duke sat at his desk, considering with no pleasure whatever his new state—he was married, soon to leave Asherwood to the possible return of the spies following him, who might curtail his movements in London until his obligation should be met. Gloomily he frowned at his inkwell, then gradually became aware of the sour sound of bagpipes playing a lively tune.

The festival! He turned his head and looked through the French doors bringing into view bright peaks of tents towering above the treetops; he listened to the strains of the music.

Flags on the poles of the tents made spots of flashing color, and a kite lazed against the blue of the sky.

Suddenly distant yells of encouragement reached the duke's ears. Most of the county must be there; bet even old Humfort, who never misses any function— that pop must be a starting pistol—Rachel should be pleased; she evidently has done a bang-up job and deserves the thanks. The whole estate is teeming with zaniness—the south meadow is—the south meadow . . . ? Good God, the south meadow!

The duke jumped up, threw open the French doors, leaped over the low parapet, and started for the festival. Damme, Endfield knew that meadow had a special crop for the blue bloods; why in hell would he let it be trampled flat by every boot in the countryside?

In rapid strides he covered the distance and came upon the back of the tea tent. Circling the tent, he paused. Before him on the raised platform, Lenore, Rachel, Mrs. Turtlelock, and Mr. Endfield stood facing a crowd who gazed up and were quiet as Lenore spoke. "Mrs. Eulai Thompson wins the prize for her delicious pickles." Mr. Endfield gave Lenore a blue ribbon and she, in turn, placed it in the hand of Mrs. Thompson. The crowd applauded politely.

Continuing to watch, the duke was distracted by a group of boys brawling behind him. Scruffy varmints, thought the duke, and caught his breath as one mud-filthy boy landed a square hit on the nose of his opponent, then fell on his victim to thrash furiously; finally, seated on his defeated foe's chest, the winner panted in victory.

By good fortune no flash of recognition struck either father or son.

Turning back to the roster, the duke's temper flared anew and he climbed the two steps to the platform, bent on giving Mr. Endfield what the duke felt would be a well-deserved trimming.

"Endfield!" growled the irate duke in angered tones, "explain to me what—" He got no further, for his voice was drowned by sounds—handclapping, shouts, whistles. Astonished, His Grace stared at the cheering and waving crowd below him, who, having caught his attention, increased their halloos—"The duke, the duke, hurrah for the duke"—men, women, and children were running closer, eager to catch sight of His Grace.

Dumbfounded, the duke slowly raised his hand—an

action that increased the crowd's excitement. "Speak, Duke, speak," a few called, an urging quickly taken up until it became a chant.

The duke shot a side-glance at Lenore, who clapped and nodded. Bewildered, the duke took a step forward and a thunderous silence fell.

The duke spoke. "Thank you, friends"—there was a roar of approval—"thank you, but your appreciation is misdirected. It is"—the duke swallowed—"the duchess and Mrs. Thomas who provided what I hope is a pleasurable day for you all." He turned and bowed to Rachel and Lenore.

The crowd broke into delighted yells of gratitude. Blushing, both ladies smiled and waved.

To Lenore the duke muttered, "I'm off to the palace," and fled on back the way he had come. Walking home through the woods he experienced a sensation quite puzzling to him—well-being, even a touch of warmth. The duke was strangely unversed in happiness.

After the duke's withdrawal, there lingered confusion, but Rachel clapped for silence and the award-giving resumed.

Her task completed, Lenore suggested, "Dear Rachel, if you ensure it proper, I should like to walk to where the lads are swimming—er—in nankeens."

"Stop gulling me, Lenore." Rachel slapped Lenore's hand lightly. "This way."

A throng of ladies, accompanied by one or two gentlemen who felt lucky to have been in the tea tent this day, strolled across the grass to a bend in the river where the water was alive with boys, splashing, diving, a few even swimming.

Lenore caught her breath when she spied Charles gripping a tree limb, high above the river, kicking his heels and shrieking, "Get out of my way, you ninnyhammers!" As she stared Charles let go, and holding his nose, landed in the water.

"Oh, Lord," she murmured as she waited to see if her new son would emerge. He did, and swam over, scrambling to the bank. Relieved, Lenore lowered herself on the grass to let her heart stop thumping; the others moved ahead, leaving her alone. Hearing a rustling sound, she turned her head and saw Tom Doone approaching from upriver.

"Your Grace." The raggedy man removed his grimy hat and bobbed a bow.

Lenore hesitated, then responded, "Good afternoon, Mr. Doone."

Tom Doone crouched near, thereby inundating her with strange aromas.

"Tom, Duchess, call me Tom."

"If you wish, Tom." Lenore wanted to put her handkerchief to her nose, but not to offend the old man, so refrained.

"You've probably heard, Duchess, that I don't hold with the Dour Duke." Tom glanced around for a place to spit, but thought better of it.

"Well, I—"

"No harm, Duchess, he twangs his way and I twang mine; but this day he done a good thing—took a fine bride. Only smart act he's ever done in his life."

"Why, Tom, thank you," said Lenore, touched.

"Yes, sir—the best—so I brought you a gift. 'Tain't much, but it's a beauty." So saying, he pulled from his shirt a dripping, filthy rag and put it in Lenore's lap. "Open it, Duchess, it's a humdinger."

Stunned, Lenore lifted a corner of the sopping cloth, revealing a large brook trout, gills flapping slowly.

"Ain't that a nacky? Must weigh five or six—easy, Your Grace"—Lenore jumped as the fish gave an expiring leap and slid down the front of her bodice—" 't'won't do you a bit of harm."

Lenore, gazing down at her soaked dress, fought tears.

"Well, Duchess, ain't you going to say something?"

"Ye—es, Tom." She turned to meet his eager stare. "How can I accept your—" Tom's brows drew together. "On the other hand, I can't resist." With a show of bravery, she touched the fish.

"My God, I knew you was a muffin," cried the delighted Tom. "Most females wouldn't touch the critter with a stick, but my duchess—she's no nick ninny."

Lenore, amused by being called Tom Doone's duchess, said, "I'm pleased with the present, Tom—the duke will be too."

"Ah, ma'am, you ain't to tell the duke about this!" Tom whined. Lenore realized the generous Tom had been poaching on the duke's river. All damage done, she laughed. "Tom, it's lucky for you there aren't many weddings, for you might land in jail. I won't squeal, I promise."

"You're a good 'un, Duchess. Just give it to 'Orrendous 'Enry; he'll take it to old Clough, then the duke, none the wiser, can feast hearty." The fisherman rose.

"I will, Tom, and thank you."

The old man shuffled off and Lenore stared at the bundle, picked up the dripping mess, and laid it on the grass.

At that moment the Reverend and Mrs. David Thomas and Charles reached her.

Charles, hair matted down, nankeens clinging,

shoes and shirt abandoned, glowed with excitement. "Mother, it was more great by half." He shook a few drops of water over her. "What's that?"

"It's a present from Tom Doone." Lenore glanced up at Rachel and David, who had backed away.

"Hoy," David said, "Tom's fish is as regular at weddings as Rachel's flowers, but I never dreamed he'd have the courage to give you one. Congratulations, Duchess."

"Thank you," said Lenore dryly, and stood, shaking out her dress. "Charles, you are garbed just about in mode to carry the gift to the carriage."

"Oh, that nasty old man," cried Rachel. "Imagine his smelling you up like that—he should be run out of the county."

"And lose the best poacher in England?" exclaimed the vicar, shaken. "What gets into you, light of my life?"

Lenore asked, "Can't we hide the fish and—"

"Never!" shouted the vicar, then lowering his voice to a threatening whisper, hissed, "At this very instant, two eyes pierce your every move; like an Indian, unseen, but alert. You will be stalked to the palace door. One false step, one trace of disgust, and you will be scalped!" The vicar made a frightening slice to his forehead.

"Charles," the vicar said reasonably, "run ahead of us. You, gentle wife, and I shall escort our leige lord's lady to the conveyance—at a respectful distance, of course—two paces at least."

"Is it that troublesome?" asked Lenore pitifully.

"It is, Your Grace." The vicar bowed.

Lenore turned to Rachel, whose eyes peered sadly over her carefully held handkerchief.

Lenore laughed heartily. "Well, now being quite

outside the touch of genteel society, I shall be like your Indian—unseen, but alert, as we stalk 'Orrendous 'Enry, who will never let me step foot in the duke's carriage—ever!"

"Rest easy, Lenore," said Rachel. "If Henderson is niff-naff, David will be glad to drive you to the palace, won't you, dearest?"

The vicar sighed.

Threading through the woods, the party skirted the meadow where the festivities continued.

When Henderson spied Charles, the duchess, and the Thomases, he leaped from his perch, prepared to welcome them. As they neared, he sniffed. "So the old devil got to you, eh? 'Twas a fool thing to accept it, Your Grace; guess I'll—"

"Accept it!" cried Lenore. "He tossed it in my lap before I could—"

"Like him, like him; know'd that one since he was Satan's youngest imp. Well, you just prattle a moment while I line up the seats." Muttering imprecation on Tom Doone's soul, the groom drew out a folded linen cloth, flapped it open, covering the interior surfaces. "Now, Duchess, whenever you're set to go. Charles, you ride with me, Her Grace is going to do enow damage without your adding your waftings."

Lenore rolled her eyes to the sky, waved good-bye, and holding her skirts tight to her body, climbed into the carriage.

At the palace, Lenore, her eyes searching for the lurking Tom Doone, who remained hidden, grabbed Charles's hand, flew up the stairs past the footman in the hall, who swiveled his head sharply in their wake.

"A bath, Charles, now!" She gave him a little push. Once behind her own closed door she rang for Mrs.

Clough, tore off her clothes, and threw them in a pile.

"A bath immediately, please, Mrs. Clough." Lenore tied the belt of her robe with a fierce yank.

Mrs. Clough broke into a small smile. "Old Tom, Your Grace?"

"Tossed it in my lap, Mrs. Clough."

"You were lucky; he usually throws it *at* the bride. Luke Lancey's bride broke her ankle trying not to be hit by his bigheartedness."

"A strange gesture of generosity! Do hurry, please."

Immersed in a hot bath, lavished with lavender salts, Lenore felt soothed. The festival had been famous fun, and Myles had appeared at the festivities. Lenore sang a few notes.

"Your Grace," Mrs. Clough called through the door, "you must make haste; the duke has requested you go to the library as soon as possible."

Unused to being ordered about, Lenore dressed slowly, to Mrs. Clough's fretful impatience. "Please, Duchess, the duke waits."

So he does, thought Lenore, taking extra care with her hair. This morning he was rude; this evening he issues commands. I love him, but I will not be his slave.

The duke, standing at the fireplace, for the first time that day looked directly at his bride. She is beautiful, he admitted to himself. "Come in, Lenore, would you enjoy a glass of wine?"

"No, thank you, but do have one yourself." She walked to the center of the room and peered about her. "I'm not sure I've ever seen so many books."

"The Asherwoods have always collected; whether it is a strength or a weakness, I do not speculate."

"I shall wish to read some of them." Lenore moved

to the wall beside the fireplace, book-lined from floor to ceiling, reached for a volume, opened it, and perused the lines, then flipped to the next page.

The duke frowned. "You read Latin?"

"Yes."

"And Greek, I suppose," he sneered slightly.

Lenore nodded. "Yes, my father insisted I learn the classics."

Good God, an educated female, the duke thought ruefully.

Lenore replaced the book, and turning to the duke said, "You sent for me?"

"Please sit down." The duke sipped his wine while she did as bid. "Lenore, you find your bedchamber comfortable, I trust?"

"Indeed so, very," she said, her answer made terse by uncertainty.

"Did you note the doors on either side of the fireplace?"

"Yes."

"This morning the doors were locked; tonight each is unlocked."

For an instant Lenore's heart leaped, but the chilly mien of the duke dispelled any fancies she might have held. "I can only assume they give onto your bedroom," Lenore said quietly.

"One does, the other opens to my dressing closet."

"Do not be afraid, Myles; neither shall ever be set into motion by me," Lenore affirmed coldly.

"You slip past the point, Lenore."

"That being your desire that the household be hoaxed into believing we are lovers."

"You speak frankly, madam," said the flushed duke.

"How I say it does not signify; the charade is of

import to you." She paused. "I shall play fairly. . . . Should we not be ready to welcome our guests?" Her voice did not betray her cold anger.

Baffled by her utter calm, the duke started to speak, but catching her eye, instead wheeled and led her to the drawing room. Lenore, on entering, halted, overwhelmed by the size and beauty of another great room. Gentian-blue brocade walls shimmered in the light of myriad tapers crowned by tiny sedate flames, whose reflections danced wildly in the glass prisms of the tiered chandeliers. The fireplace, hooded by a rounding stone mantel embossed with the Asherwood coat of arms, served as a frame for banked flowers—its warm-weather adornment. Chairs and sofas of light-green velvet were set along the walls, interrupted by windows draped to the floor in pale-pink satin. Huge folding screens of ebony wood, ornamented in gold, hid the doors to the terrace.

"My mother had the room done," the duke explained. "It was incomplete when she died, but my father continued the work. He never entertained here, and I have only rarely." He moved to the fireplace and indicated that Lenore stand at his left.

"An extraordinary room." Lenore gazed at the painted ceiling.

Before either could say more the first arrivals of the twenty expected guests were announced. The duke greeted each and presented to Lenore those whom she did not know. She was soon encircled by ladies and gentlemen, curious to discover the nature of the new duchess. It did not seem long before Clough oversaw the folding of the screens and announced dinner.

The party drifted out onto the terrace, where the guests found their places at the table. Lenore and the

duke were seated at either end—candelabras and
tureens of fruit and flowers prevented their seeing
each other.

Footmen served soup *à la reine*, fillets of turbot
with Italian sauce, wax baskets of prawn and crayfish,
pickled crab, rump of beef *à la Mantua* with asparagus, broiled mushrooms, spinach, and croutons.
Each course was accompanied by wines. Orange soufflé,
baskets of pastries, fruits, and nuts completed the
meal.

As course succeeded course the duke heard frequent
laughter from Lenore's end of the table, contrasting
sharply with the polite dull prattle around him.
Once a burst of mirth made the lady on his right
start.

Dinner over, Lenore led the ladies into the drawing room for coffee. The men's talk, at first torpid,
soon fell into lively chatter over the after-dinner
wines, liqueurs, and spirits—a wide choice.

Clough approached and spoke quietly to the duke,
who murmured a word to the gentlemen seated near
him, then followed his henchman into the hall.

Inside the front door stood a man wearing a long
black cap. Seeing the duke, he spoke in French.
"Your Grace, I am M. DuLac, here at the request
of your good friend. I carry a letter explaining my
strange intrusion. Will you be so good as to read its
message."

The duke accepted the extended note and opened
it.

Dear Myles,
    M. DuLac is the most accomplished couturier
in France. I send him to you so he may create for

your duchess *les robes* required for her London season.

Treat him well, my friend, he is a genius. His skill is my dowry to you and your duchess.

Folding the letter, the duke, in French, welcomed the weary traveler, bade Clough prepare the yellow bedroom immediately, then asked if M. DuLac spoke English.

"Perfectly, sir; I have endured the miserable crossings from my country to yours with regularity."

"Again, I welcome you." The duke bowed. "Though I am at sea in the realm of lady's apparel I'm sure you are an artist, but I'm puzzled as to how you can carry out your plays so far from the shops of London."

"Your Grace, I do not come empty-handed. In the traveling carriage are all the materials I require—brought from France. I need only a room, a mirror, and la, the duchess, *naturellement*." Then smiling wanly, he said, "*Alors*, I must rest—you have guests—so if you permit, I shall retire."

"As you wish, sir—Ah, Clough, is the room ready?"

"Yes, Your Grace; if the gentleman will follow me."

"Oh, Duke," the Frenchman said hurriedly, "the boxes must be unloaded immediately; there are many."

The duke spoke to his footman. "Peacemake, tend to the baggage; put it in the sewing—no, too small—the Blue Room, and have mirrors moved there before morning."

"One more moment, Your Grace, the weary French-man said, "I prefer to breakfast in my room if pos-sible, then to receive Her Grace midmorning."

"I will explain to the duchess. Good night, M. DuLac."

"Thank you, and *bon soir*, sir." He followed Clough up the stairs.

Returning to the terrace, the duke found the display of fireworks already blazing the sky. The ladies gave screams of pleasure, the gentlemen nodded approval as burst succeeded burst of color—each more brilliant than its predecessor. The final explosion of golden stars spread over the dark night and lingered pleasingly. The heavens black at last, the guests made their farewells, thanking the duchess and duke, many adding, "How happy you must be, Duke, to have such a charming bride," or similar messages. His Grace accepted the plaudits stoically.

After the final departure, he requested Lenore to come to the library. "Please sit down. Would you like refreshments?" Lenore shook her head and seated herself by the fireplace. The duke poured a brandy, then sat opposite her.

"My compliments for a delightful dinner party."

Lenore, surprised at his praise, said, "Thank you."

"A strange event took place tonight; we have received a most unusual gift. A friend in France has sent a couturier—a M. DuLac—he—"

"M. DuLac!" Lenore cried. "*The* M. DuLac? The famous M. DuLac, who robes the ladies of the French Court?"

Startled, the duke replied, "Why, I collect he must be, though I have never heard of him."

"*Bon Dieu*—you have never heard of the most renowned couturier in the world? Why, when he comes to Madame Fanchon's for a showing, the ladies of the *ton* fight for the privilege of buying just one gown." Then she asked anxiously, "He is the same M. DuLac, is he not?"

Bewildered, the duke nodded. "Yes, I am persuaded so."

"You say he is a gift?"

"He was sent to design your wardrobe for London."

"Oh, Lord." Lenore made as if to rise. "I must go to London at once and purchase every yard of material I can unearth."

"It isn't necessary; he has brought all yardage with him from France."

Lenore's eyes opened wide. "No! Oh, Myles, is it true? I think I'm dreaming. No one, no one in the world has ever had more than one, or, at the outside, two gowns designed by M. DuLac—even Josephine—and you say . . . I am dreaming." She pinched her arm.

"Lenore," said the duke coldly, "M. DuLac, I trust, is asleep upstairs, and tomorrow midmorning wishes to see you in the Blue Room."

To his intense displeasure Lenore broke into tears.

"Good God, madam, stop that."

"I can't help it, Myles, I have never had such a day in my life." She sniffed, trying to stem her sobs.

Conceding the truth of her statement, the duke said, not unkindly, "Go to bed, Lenore."

She rose dutifully, wiping her eyes. "Thank your friend in France, Myles." She hurried to the door. "It's been the most glorious day, Myles . . . good night."

The duke pondered: What kind of female have I married—demands to peruse my library one minute, the next cries with joy when a French fripple arrives to make her gowns—reads Latin and Greek, but is hey-go-mad enough to keep a dinner table in an uproar—elects to give the village a festival, but fratches at the wink of an eye—yet has the devotion of my sons and household. The duke shook his head and went to bed. His last misty thought was, as he drifted to sleep —But she does not prattle. . . .

At the vicarage the weary vicar as he removed his clericals spoke to his wife, already tucked between the sheets. "My beloved, I feel today has been historic in the annals of Asherwood, don't you?" His beloved's response was a gentle puffing snore.

24

The next morning Lenore woke amazingly rested. In anticipation of the momentous event to come, she dressed with pinpoint precision, bemoaning her out-of-mode garments, but determined to commit no sartorial solecism.

At the instant designated, Lenore, Maria by her side, knocked on the door of the Blue Room and opened it. What met her eyes caused her to stop short. The chamber burst, like the rockets of the night before, in a riot of color. Unrolled bolts of satin, silk muslin, gauze, transparent fabric, velvet, lace, gold, and silver tissue draped every chair, sofa, table, and footstool. The bed appeared as if covered by a mad quilt. Large boxes placed about the room overflowed with feathers, ribbons, trim, wax fruits, furs, and other bits, giving the appearance of sacrifices on altars of savage tribes placating strange demons.

At dead center of this tumult of color, his back toward her, crouched a man garbed from neck to ankle in purple. Lenore suppressed an urge to giggle, for M. DuLac reminded her of a giant spider in a web of hues. Suddenly the Frenchman intoned in a deep voice, "Duchess, please frame yourself by the closed door; I wish to regard you for the first time thus." Maria leaped to one side and Lenore posed herself at the doorway.

Slowly M. DuLac pivoted, fixed Lenore with a fierce gaze, raked her from head to toe, then raising his hand, described a circular motion. Dutifully Lenore revolved full about. Suddenly M. DuLac threw up his head, kissed his fingertips, and tossed the kiss into the air.

"*Magnifique!* Come!" he waved Lenore to him. "I am happy for the first moment since I embarked on the dreadful sailing and the riding of your monstrous roads." He bowed. "Your beauty, my dear Duchess, banishes the horrors."

Lenore blushed.

M. DuLac scolded, "*Tiens*, madam, there can be no mirror that does not proclaim the truth, *oui?*" He raised his finger to the ceiling. "*Mais, oui*, now you are beautiful, but enfolded in the gowns I create, you will elicit gasps of wonder!" Stepping back, he studied Lenore again, then reached forward to stare into her face, picked up a curl, and growled, "*Bon!*" Letting the tress fall, he clapped his hands. "*Alors*, we begin." Whipping out a tape measure from his pocket, he tossed it to Maria. "Take Her Grace's measurements in the order I command; there will be no reason to write them down—I memorize." Leaning against a table, he folded his arms and went into a trance.

"M. DuLac, may I express two desires?" Lenore asked meekly.

The Frenchman nodded.

"Thank you; then please will you create a riding habit first?"

"Ah! I envision one in rich bottle-green and one in sapphire-blue, trimmed in sable."

Lenore paused.

"One request, Duchess; the second?"

Lenore hesitated, then said, "Please, may my gowns be simple; I am not a female who likes fuss in my dress."

"Madam, you view life through my eyes! *Bon!* Each morning we will contrive together." The Frenchman subsided into his thrall. "The measurements to start at the neck."

The measures completed, M. DuLac bowed, asked that the household seamstress be sent for, as he must pursue his work *tout de suite*.

Maria hurried out to enlist Mrs. Peacemake's services. Lenore thanked the couturier, then sought her bed to rest, in an effort to avert a lurking ache behind her eyes. Maria, her errand finished, knocked, then opened Lenore's door. Since her mistress was asleep, she tiptoed away.

25

The days pending departure for London raced by, busy for everyone.

The duke, relieved at no sign of spies at Asherwood, consulted the vicar on the best method of concealing their messages back and forth, and both enjoyed immensely setting up a code involving horses, Henderson, Peacemake, and Rachel—her name mentioned, the true sign that all went well.

The duke paid his yearly visits to his tenants and villagers—an undertaking of some days—and listened with polite ennui to the praises heaped upon himself and, more especially, his duchess.

Lenore lamented the lack of minutes in the day. Each morning she stood patiently as M. DuLac spun his magic threads. After the midday meal, she rode or took the reins with Heath and Charles, both of whom insisted she would undoubtedly become a complete hand.

Often the three visited Mamère and heard her bitter complaints about the new maid, sent from the palace. "She's a dowd—won't give me my brandy—oh, no, not she—only ratafia and I have to fake a faint to command that."

Lenore spoke to the disapproving maid, ordering

one glass of brandy before dinner for Madame Lanier.

Lenore found she could distract the old lady by talk of the wedding of Maria and Abel.

As planned, the marriage was performed under the arbor at Willowood on a day when the air was like wine. Maria beaming, Abel ramrod straight, they paid strict attention as the vicar read the age-old service.

During the toast-giving—much to everyone's surprise—the duke came around the corner of the house.

"Father!" shrieked Charles.

As his brother ran and threw himself at the duke, Heath froze.

"Stand back, jackanapes," said the duke. Over the boy's head his eyes met his older son's. For an instant the memory of his father's rebuff—upon his return from abroad—gripped Heath; then he grinned. The duke expelled his breath, tousled Charles's hair, and stepped up to felicitate the bride and groom, then obeyed Mamère's louder order of, "Duke—come here!"

"Madame." He bent to kiss her hand. In his ear she said in a low tone, "You're a top-of-the-trees Corinthian, Bunky."

Surprised, the duke murmered, "Thank you, Mamère."

"Hoy, Mamère, eh?" chortled the old lady. "Lenore is turning you up sweet."

Angered, the duke muttered, "Hardly, madame," and walked away.

"Paperskull!" Mamère called after him.

The duke, striding to leave, stopped, accosted by the vicar.

"Myles, are you cutting your stick?"

"As fast as possible; stand off."

"Let me accompany you to your mount." The two men fell in step. "What oversets you, Myles?"

"I am weary to the bone of the praises, paeans, lauds, and 'how lucky I ams' sung of the duchess on every side."

The vicar sighed. "Why don't you try to fathom this entire agreement on her virtues?"

"Oh, I realize she is lovely—I'm not blind—she is obviously kind. Heaven knows I've been informed often enough—educated, intelligent—a paragon!"

"Could a duke require more in a duchess?"

"No—" the duke faltered, "no, I suppose not."

"Then count your blessings, Myles," exhorted the vicar.

"That one, David," the duke said coldly, "is the least comforting of all platitudes extant." So saying, he swung on his horse and rode off.

The vicar watched the duke vanish, then began to whistle. Racing back to the party, he sought Rachel—chatting with Lenore—grabbed her and kissed her heartily, then holding her in a hug, he said, over her shoulder, "My love, our sons, Samuel, William, Mark, and John—have I forgotten any?—will all be Oxford bred, trust my words." His eyes slid to Lenore.

"Flummery," said Lenore ruefully. "He did not even glance this way."

"A most encouraging manifestation," averred the vicar.

"David!" said the flustered Rachel, her cheeks burning as she disengaged herself. "We must go home at once!"

"Oh, my avid darling." The vicar leered beamingly. "Your ardent desire is my joyous command."

"David!" squeaked the outraged Rachel. "'Tis the stew for dinner; I'm afraid it will burn!"

"Alas," sighed the vicar in such a doleful tone that Lenore whipped out her handkerchief.

"Oh, dear," asked Rachel, turning to Lenore, "is your cough still troubling you?"

Lenore gave up and went into gales of laughter.

"Really, Lenore," Rachel said severely, "I don't understand you or David."

"Better so, my dearest," soothed her husband, "for I must rely on you for proper observance of civility."

"And I too, darling Rachel," Lenore proclaimed, wiping her eyes.

"Silly bleaters," said Rachel, hugging Lenore good-bye, then leaving to gather her children.

"I shall miss your lack of proper conduct, Duchess," said the vicar with a bow.

"And I yours, Vicar," laughed Lenore, giving him her hand.

26

On the afternoon before leaving for London Lenore made her adieus to Mamère, now in high spirits caused by the restoration of Maria and Abel to Willowood.

"Well, Duchess, you are to be launched into the *ton*—too bad I ain't there to guide you."

"You soon will be, my dearest."

"Humph, well, try not to grass yourself before I arrive."

"And after you come?" Lenore laughed. "Have I your permission to get into trouble?"

"Saucebox!"

"I promise to behave."

"Just be yourself, missy; you're an incomparable." A tear ran down the old lady's cheek, which she brushed aside impatiently.

Lenore hugged her and withdrew to find Maria and Abel waiting to say good-bye. Good wishes and farewells done, Lenore said, "Take our dearest dragon a brandy; she has a touch of the dismals."

That night, Rachel, the vicar, and their daughter Donna dined at the palace. Noting the underlying sadness of the affair, M. DuLac made a rare concession—he invited the ladies to see the result of his creativity. Heath teased Donna into a game of backgammon, and Charles, quite put out by his brother's attention to a silly female, retired to play with Wiggles. The duke bore the vicar off for a game of chess. The vicar, with forbearance, allowed the duke to win two of the three games.

The evening passed rapidly. Hugs, handshakes, shoulder clappings, promises to write, and an easily stolen kiss in the playroom rendered the parting sweet but sad.

The Reverend David Thomas, musing on how empty Asherwood would become on the morrow, was silent on the drive to the vicarage, thus allowing Rachel to reflect on the possibilities of converting the French touches of elegance she had seen into her own needlework, and Donna to gaze dreamily into space, afloat on the charms of the Marquis of Asher-wood.

27

The long-awaited morning dawned cold and threatened rain. When the three carriages rolled to a stop at the palace portico, Clough and Peacemake, assigned to seeing to the distribution of trunks, boxes, and carrying cases, kept footmen and maids running.

Lenore, Heath, and the duke were to ride in His Grace's carriage; Charles to go with Mr. and Mrs. Clough; the third traveling carriage to convey the luggage.

All readied, there were tears. Mrs. Peablossom threw her apron over her face and sobbed, Mrs. Peacemake cried openly, and Peacemake bit his lower lip as the travelers took their places.

A dreadful moment presented itself when Wiggles almost escaped from under Mrs. Clough's cloak. In this deceiving of His Grace, whatever guilt stirred in the upright woman's breast evaporated when she thought of Charles's dismay should the duke forbid Wiggles to go to London.

Once they were under way the trip went smoothly. A midday meal and a change of horses at a country inn broke the monotony. Near London the rain clouds disappeared, revealing a brilliant evening sky.

Had it not been the hour when residents of Grosvenor Square took their rides in the park, more curtains would have discreetly twitched. Those who did see the three carriages rumble down the side street into the Square and stop before the palatial house on the corner proclaimed it a sight most unusual; the duke in his greatcoat, leading the duchess, garbed in a long sable cape, up the marble steps; the two boys in redding coats; the country couple who promptly took charge as a swarm of footmen unloaded the luggage. The doors of the house finally closed. The carriages clattering off in tandem, lit by the sunset, held every eye.

"It was a raree-show," vowed the witnesses.

Few ladies and gentlemen did not regret their absence from Grosvenor Square that afternoon.

28

Sir Alfred Lanier considered breakfast "the most rewarding repast of the day."

Seated at the head of the long dining table, he relished his unvarying plate of eggs and sirloin, toast, pastries, and coffee. *The Morning Post Gazette*'s financial section at hand, his wife, Lady Martha, opposite, quite removed by the expanse of mahogany, his lordship was content. He nodded to the footman to refill his coffee cup, then to peel an orange—a daily procedure. He spread the newspaper and brought it close to his nearsighted eyes in anticipation of satisfactory news of his holdings. He read, nodded, and peeked over the paper periodically to see if Lady Martha's occasional clucks signaled her desire to pass on tidbits of gossip or merely to comment on the doings of society, printed in *The Gazette* she held inches from her face. Lady Martha also suffered from impaired vision and, like her husband, succumbed to vanity, the word spectacles never mentioned.

A congenial silence filled the room.

Suddenly his lordship heard an agonizing shriek; lowering his paper, he saw his wife collapse in a dead faint, her head falling backward. Jumping from his chair, he ran to her, telling the footman to fetch smelling salts from the sideboard. Chafing his wife's hands, he called, "Martha, Martha!" The footman placed the salts under her ladyship's nose, and gradually she roused, only to slap the newspaper that covered her breakfast and faint anew. Again the smelling salts were applied, and again returning to consciousness she pounded the newspaper. To his lordship's horror he thought he heard her murmur, "Whore, whore!"

Sir Alfred ordered his wife to be carried to the sofa in the morning room—her favorite resting spot. The footman lifted the lady, who wept tears down the front of his uniform. Sir Alfred picked up *The Gazette* and followed. Once in the morning room he demanded a glass of ratafia be brought, then tried to soothe his sobbing wife. All of a sudden she sat up, and jabbing her forefinger at the paper he held, cried, "Read it, read it!" Stepping to the window, Sir Alfred studied the columns until he found a heading that read, NUPTIALS OF THE DUKE OF ASHERWOOD—under-

neath, in smaller print—the announcement of the
duke's marriage to Lenore Carey Lanier, widow of
Captain Eric Lanier. Sir Alfred read the notice
through, then, feigning surprise, exclaimed, "Good
Lord—a devil of a coil!"

"How dare she?" screamed her ladyship.

"I'm fairly capped as to how they would even
meet," her husband said. "It's common gossip that
Myles never leaves the palace except on his annual
visits to the villagers and trips to London on business."

"Ha!" exploded his wife. "That wily Lenore would
find a way! I always said she was on the catch to be
elegantly riveted. Consider how she hoaxed your
brother—a mere boy—into marriage."

In view of the fact that his "mere boy" brother had
been thirty when he wed, Sir Alfred remonstrated
gently, "Now, Martha . . ."

"This time she's flung her cap over the windmill
for far bigger game—a duke no less!" Lady Martha
laughed harshly.

"Martha, you cannot—"

"No, humph, I wager she went head over teakettle
to nab him; I'm surprised he would be such a green-
top as to not catch out her bobbery."

"Martha, we do not know what occurred. Lenore
is extremely beautiful—"

This faux pas cost his lordship dearly, for his wife
snorted, then raved that it would not astound her if
his lordship himself had a tendre for the "beautiful"
Lenore, who seemed to be able to turn all men round
her thumb; but it was acceptable to herself, for no
lady would compete with a light skirt; and he need
not think it would cause her any loss of sleep, because
the Paphian had now wed the rich duke and would

never cast her favors on a mere lord. Out of breath, her ladyship sipped her ratafia, allowing Sir Alfred to say, "Martha, take a damper; I don't have a tendre for anyone but you, my dearest—mark it well!" He took her hand and kissed it. "My love, what boggles me is, what's to be done when they come to London?"

"What!" shrieked Lady Martha.

"Surely you read the duke plans to open his Grosvenor Square house for the season?" He waved the newspaper.

"I didn't read that far; give me the paper."

Sir Alfred handed her *The Gazette* and brought a candle. Lady Martha, slightly breathless, perused the entire article. Throwing the paper aside, she announced firmly, "Well, they need not think we are going to have anything to do with them—everyone knows he was the Rake of Europe, and when I finish, the *ton* will be well twigged to the duchess."

"No!" The word expelled like the slap of two pieces of wood. "No, my dear wife, you will not make mischief for either the duke or the duchess!"

Lady Martha gaped at her husband in amazement; she had never experienced him in so forceful an aspect. "What's come over you? You've always vowed you hated Myles Asherwood." Her voice shook.

"Quite so, my dear, but hear me carefully, Martha. The duke has a mortgage on my acres in Asherwood and controls companies in which I have large interests. This marriage is against my pluck as much as yours, but should the duke hear a breath of gossip you had a word in, I could be ruined. Are you listening, Martha?"

Sulkily his wife replied, "Yes." She paused. "But do I have to be civil to them? I simply will not entertain those two; you cannot ask me to."

Sir Alfred thought a minute, then said, "No, you need not receive them, but you must put watch and ward on your conversation at every turn."

"It won't be easy," said the sullen Martha, pouting. "They're bound to be the topic of the *ton*."

"Without doubt, but you are to keep your tongue still."

"Oh, Alfred, what am I to do? Everyone will quiz me about the misalliance."

"Exercise your constant charge to the children—'tell the truth'—that you are as surprised as your friends, but have no further knowledge of the affair."

"But they will demand to hear about Lenore."

This time his lordship took care in his response. "Inform them that you hardly were acquainted with the lady; that Eric whisked her to the Penn so soon after they were married, she was nearly a stranger, and since her return you have not laid eyes on her."

"And I don't want to," said Martha fiercely.

"Don't," roared his lordship, "under threat of the rack, say such a thing abroad, Martha; you must be discreet, I warn you!"

Martha was beset. "What a hobble!" she moaned.

"Granted," agreed Sir Alfred, "but now you'd better dress, for I am of the strong opinion you can expect morning callers shortly. Come, my darling, and remember, step lightly, other gates you may find us and the children punting on the Tick—the duke would not hesitate to ruin me." He helped her rise, and putting an arm around her, led her upstairs.

Sir Alfred's prediction proved sound. Shortly the morning room was crowded with ladies and gentlemen eager to discuss the latest wonder. Those not acquainted with either the duke or duchess quickly learned that the high sticklers of the *ton* did not ap-

prove the duke or creampot marriages, and leaned
toward not accepting the newly wed couple into polite
society despite the duke's high rank. These sentiments
soothed Martha's troubled heart and she confined
herself to listen more than talk. Her seeming lack of
knowledge soon sent most who had come to the supposed font of gossip concerning the duchess on their
way.

Sir Alfred did not make an appearance—not an unusual absence—but shut himself in his library, checking his account books as was his wont each morning.
A footman brought his lordship the post. Glancing
through the letters, Sir Alfred saw the Duke of Asherwood's frank, and ripped the envelope open to read
rapidly.

> Dear Lanier,
>
> This is written to inform you that your grand-
> mother is—at the request of the duchess—joining
> my household in London.
>
> As this allows you to close Willowood, I am
> sure it will win your approval.
>
> > Sincerely yours,
> > Asherwood

Sir Alfred felt relief, for evidently Lenore had not
prattled to the duke. Moreover, if they could put up
with the old vixen—fine! However, on reflection, he
realized that leaving her care to the duke would put
him under further obligation to His Grace, an onus
he did not welcome.

Pursing his lips, he took pen and wrote a note, explaining his appreciation of the duchess and duke's
kindness to his grandmother, but under no circum-
stance could he permit her to reside in the duke's

home unless the duke accept an allowance for expenses her care might incur, therefore he was sending a sum—a like total to be forwarded each quarter.

After thought, he enclosed an amount far more sizable than ever given his grandmother directly. He sighed, then ordered the missive be taken to Grosvenor Square immediately.

29

The duke, who had withheld the announcement of his marriage from *The Morning Post Gazette* until his household's arrival in London, awaited curiously the reactions that might be forthcoming.

When Sir Alfred's note was delivered, the duke, upon reading it, wagered to himself the enclosed a larger sum than Mamère had ever enjoyed. He laid the money draft aside to give the old lady when she arrived, thinking, *Let her enjoy its largess; I don't want any of Alfred's blunt.* It occurred to him to send for Lenore to read Alfred's note, but he decided he'd better not, for Lenore would be thong.

He judged correctly—Lenore was busy.

The night before, when the duke had led her through the heavy carved wood front door, she had stood stunned at the sight of the enormous hall—the wide marble staircase facing her across the parquet floor; the closed doors on her left and right, and be-

tween the doors, niches in the walls, in each a marble
statue of a man, nearly life-size, and almost nude.
Lenore was taken aback. The statues were undoubtedly fine works of art, but her upbringing in the
vicarage had not included acceptance of lifelike naked
gentlemen, no matter how masterly the artist's hand.
Embarrassed, she listened as the duke presented Mr.
and Mrs. Madcape. Not looking up, Lenore greeted
each pleasantly, then requested, "Mrs. Madcape, would
you kindly show me to my bedroom; I am weary."
To the duke she said, "If you will excuse me, I would
like dinner served in my room."

The duke bowed. "I will wish you a good night."
He spoke to the boys, who were gazing around the
hall in wide-eyed fascination. "Heath, Charles, Madcape will take you to your quarters; you will join
me for dinner."

The Madcapes proceeded up the staircase. Heath,
seeing how white Lenore's face was, took her arm as
Charles trotted beside her.

"It will be all right, Mother, darling."

"But it's so big and cold," Lenore murmured.

Charles, who had been eyeing the marble balustrade,
put out his hand and ran it along the smooth surface. "Glory, what a slide; I can hardly wait."

"Take care, Charley, you might break your silly
neck," Heath said, only half sternly, for he totally
agreed with his brother's estimate, and felt a strong
desire to have a go at it himself.

At the top of the stairs Mrs. Madcape said, "We
go to the right, Your Grace, and the young gentlemen to the left."

The boys kissed Lenore and swung in behind Madcape.

Lenore gasped as she followed Mrs. Madcape down

the hall, for again there were niches, but these differed in that they were filled with statues of females in the most outrageous lack of attire. Lenore, miserable, wanted to cry, but when Mrs. Madcape opened a door and nodded welcome, she stepped into a room that drove away her distress.

In shape the room was a replica of her bedchamber at Asherwood, yet slightly smaller and of different decor. The walls were paneled in botttle blue-green satin; the windows curtained in white cotton and draped in white velvet. The fireplace held Lenore in a thrall. Deeply recessed, framed by an unusually wide band of intricately carved marble, and topped by a mantelshelf, it cradled a briskly burning fire that threw dancing light on the flanking chairs, done in rose velvet. On the mantel a French clock ticked softly, and two Sevres vases bulged with flowers. Opposite the fireplace stood an inlaid desk and chair, behind which—to Lenore's joy—a bookcase, its lower shelves hidden by cupboard doors of gleaming white, fit flush with the wall between the windows. The bed's carved bedposts supported no canopy.

The dressing room and bathing room doors were faced with long mirrors—later Mrs. Madcape showed Lenore that when open they allowed a view from three sides, the third reflection from the mirror that hung on the wall between them.

Lenore noted that unlike her bedroom at the palace, only one door beside the fireplace opened into the duke's chamber.

Mrs. Madcape helped her disrobe, brought dinner, then took her leave. Lenore, drowsy, sat by the fire and wondered about past duchesses who had slept in the room.

The next morning Lenore dressed in an old dress,

rang for breakfast, requesting Mrs. Clough, who entered carrying the tray of tea and toast, to stay so together they could unpack.

"Your Grace, Mrs. Madcape and I plan to do so."

"My gowns, yes, but my books I wish to place myself. We will dust each, and I need you to hold the chair for the top shelves. I'm—"

"Your Grace." Mrs. Clough's tone held reproach. "You must not climb, 'tis labor for a footman." She tugged the bellpull.

Lenore sighed—being a duchess has some drawbacks—but resigned herself to directing the young Fenwick, who did as she ordered, patiently arranging and rearranging at her behest.

"Thank you, Fenwick." Lenore smiled at the serious youth, who at that instant fell in love with the new duchess.

"Come, Mrs. Clough, let's go see how the boys fare."

When Mrs. Clough knocked on Heath's door, Charles piped, "Wait a minute, just a minute." There was a scraping sound bespeaking a heavy object being moved, then the door flew open.

"Gracious," said Lenore as she stepped into the room. "What a complete romp!" The furniture had been pushed to the center of the rug; parts of a dismantled bed leaned against the wall; books, candlesticks, and clothes were scattered in odd spots.

Charles, his sleeves rolled up, black smudges on his face, grinned. Wiggles, ecstatic to receive guests, jumped on Lenore, then made a slide for the open door, but Mrs. Clough shut it quickly, nearly nipping his nose.

"What on earth?" Lenore asked.

"Bro and I had a stupendous idea last night; we

decided to make this room our study and use the other for sleeping—so we are changing things about." Charles's tone implied there could be no other logical course.

"Why didn't you ask Clough or someone to help you?" Mrs. Clough was unused to even young gentry doing manual work.

"We wanted to do it ourselves; Heath has gone for a hammer."

Eyeing the puppy, Lenore asked, "Charles, has Wiggles been out today?"

"Oh, yes, Mother, we took him around the Square this morning."

"Charles, you know I shall have to tell your father about his being here, don't you?"

"No, Mother, I must inform Father. Bro and I had a talk and are of the same mind; I'll do it at nuncheon." Charles sighed. "I do hope Father won't banish him."

"Don't upset yourself on that score; your father is a very kind man."

"But he doesn't like dogs underfoot; Mrs. Peablossom told me so."

Just then Heath arrived, and after a few words, Lenore and Mrs. Clough left, for the boys, though polite, clearly fretted to resume their tasks.

At noon the duke met Lenore and his fresh-scrubbed sons in the hall and shepherded them into the breakfast room. "Myles, what a charming room," Lenore exclaimed justly. The walls were of pale-blue silk, the fireplace was faced with Dutch tiles, and the window overlooking the back garden was draped in mellow flowered chintz. An ebony center table covered by pink linen gleamed with silver settings that circled a tureen of fruit.

A footman held Lenore's chair as the duke and the boys arranged themselves around the table. From an ebony serving table behind Lenore the footman filled bowls of Rhemish soup.

"Myles, every room I've seen here is delightful; mine is extraordinarily pleasing to me. Thank you—it is exquisite. I'm curious. Did you have the book-case added, or has it always been there?"

"It is part of the original house; the Duchesses of Asherwood enjoyed their books at hand, though I believe my grandmother used the shelves for her collection of china. And your rooms, Heath, Charles?"

Heath responded, "Famous, Father; however, we did juggle things a bit; we moved my bed into Charles's room and his desk into mine. And my room is now our study."

The duke frowned. "It's not because you are afraid to sleep alone, is it Charles?"

Charles answered quickly, "Oh, no, sir, I'm not scared; it's just that when we are doing lessons, I won't have to run back and forth to ask Bro questions. We've put our desks back to back." Having his father's attention, Charles decided to continue rather than be under stress during the entire meal. "Father, do you like dogs?" The question drew immediate attention. The duke, taken slightly aback, answered, "Yes, in their place; they are useful in hunting, but abominable in the drawing room."

"I consider that well said, Father," Charles said judiciously. "In their proper place, dogs are splendid."

The duke spoke sternly. "Charles, you are not prattling in the hope of getting a dog, are you?"

"Oh, no, no such idea entered my mind," Charles replied with the virtue of one telling the complete truth.

Lenore and Heath waited; the silence became prolonged. Charles took a gulp. "Father, the idea of getting a dog never entered my mind, because, you see, sir, I already have one." Then to stem the anticipated wrath, Charles raced on. "His name is Wiggles—he squirms all the time almost—he's famous fun, and I will keep him in my room and take him out each day, and care for him; besides, Mother gave him to me." Charles ran out of breath; the duke's glare flew to Lenore.

"Did you give Charles a dog, Lenore?" His tone was chilly.

"Yes, indeed, the vicar's Ginger had pups and I thought Charles might enjoy one."

"You've had this creature for some time, I take it, Charles; why didn't you tell me?"

"Well—er—er—well—" Charles gave Heath a pleading look.

"Father," Heath cut in, "your dislike of dogs underfoot is thoroughly understood; at Asherwood, to keep the pup out of your way was easy—not so here. It's possible you may hear him bark, though he isn't a yapper; then again you might meet him in the halls, despite our assurances he is to be confined to our rooms."

The duke scowled at his oldest son. "How did you get him to London without my seeing or hearing him?"

"Under Mrs. Clough's cape, sir," Charles cut in.

"Mrs. Clough." He paused. "It appears my whole household has conspired against me."

"It was stupid, Myles," Lenore said quickly. "We should have informed you. Had I been aware how graciously you would accept the knowledge, I would gladly have told you long ago."

The duke stared at her, then roared, "Accepted the knowledge! I have not accepted the knowledge; I've just learned of the fustian—"

"Indeed so," said Lenore placidly. "You have learned that Charles has a dog and you have accepted the knowledge. Splendid! Charles, finish your soup, please."

Trying to put his finger on the circumlocution, the duke shook his head. The rest of the meal was eaten in silence until Lenore began to peel a pear.

"Myles," she said, "I admire you for your justice and kindness; it was wrong of us to plot against you; I'm sure the boys join me in the hope never to leave you in the dark about our doings again."

"Except at Christmas time, Father," said Charles with fine logic. "You must expect us to have secrets then."

The duke, still boggled, could think of nothing to say but "Do not let—what's his name—Wiggles?—cross my path."

"Oh, no, Father," Charles vowed.

Rising, the duke announced he expected to see them all at dinner; had he seen the loving smile Lenore gave him as he passed her chair, he would have been startled.

"Charles," said Heath as they resumed their seats, "I'm afraid you and I will never marry."

Charles, who had not given the subject much thought, asked, "Why?"

"Because, little Brother, I doubt we will ever find a female as needle-witted as our mother."

"Oh," said Charles, quite neutral about the whole idea.

"Hoy," laughed Lenore. "You'll meet so many

young ladies worth your consideration that you are bound to throw your handkerchief often."

"Most problematical, madam. Come on, Charley, better take the redeemed Wiggles for a walk. Excuse us, please, Mother."

Lenore sent the boys along, then mused as she sipped her coffee. Myles is a kind man and worthy of my affection—she sighed—if he would only notice me. He scarcely glances my way, except in anger. Oh, well, I am here and can be seen; maybe some great day . . .

Mrs. Madcape entered and invited Lenore to tour the house. Lenore, trying not to look at the niches, wondered if she could ever pass through the hall without a shiver.

On sight, the morning room depressed her—with its size, its gloom. Heavy purple-maroon draperies managed to shut out most of the daylight. The sofa and chairs done in dark-brown velvet or leather stood stark and cold. The black marble fireplace yawned like a cavern. In wide, dingy gilt frames, former dukes stared down in sternness or disdain.

"Has the room always been like this?" asked Lenore. At Mrs. Madcape's nod, Lenore frowned.

"Come see the drawing room—now used as a ball-room," urged Mrs. Madcape, crossing the hall and throwing open double doors.

"Good heavens, it's monstrous." Lenore, not wishing to step into the room, craned her neck to look down its length to the distant wall.

"The shutters have not been removed, so you cannot appreciate the appointments," Mrs. Madcape explained. "There is a balcony at the farther end; let me—"

"Thank you, no, Mrs. Madcape, I'll await more

light. May I see the kitchen? It has been brought up
to date, Mrs. Clough informs me."

Pleased by the intrusion into her domain, Mrs.
Madcape showed off the two fireplaces, each with its
side compartment for baking, the new indoor pump,
and the enormous table running down the center of
the tiled floor.

Impressed, Lenore began to discuss food prepara-
tion, baking processes, even the making of jams and
jellies, causing Mrs. Madcape later to proclaim to all
the household staff that they need not try to play
tricks on the new duchess for she was knowledgeable
to a pin in the culinary arts, and other household
matters too.

30

A week of settling in had passed. At dinner one
night the duke announced that a Doctor William
Sylvester was expected on the morrow. "A man of
erudition who will tutor you, Heath and Charles," he
explained. "He is to have the chamber next to your
study."

"What stripe of man is he, Father?"

"He is a doctor of medicine and a scholar—Oxford,
Cambridge, and the University of Edinburgh; he's to
be treated as a respected member of the household."

"Have you met him, Myles?" asked Lenore.

"No, Mr. Pettibone sent me his name and references, and I searched his background."

"Does he like to ride?" Charles asked anxiously. "I do wish he rides."

"He's a nonpareil according to Pettibone," said the duke shortly.

Heath said, "Sounds a top-of-the-trees; thank you for finding him, Father. I'm behind in my studies, and must be ready for Oxford next term."

The following afternoon Doctor William Sylvester drove into the Square in a curricle with matched grays. Fenwick, who assisted the doctor to alight, was aware that here was a personage indeed—tall, extremely handsome, garbed in a greatcoat of fine cloth, a beaver hat, and possessing mint-new luggage.

On meeting the doctor the duke thought, Good God, he's far better looking than Sanford was, and twice the gentleman. He greeted the doctor coldly.

Dr. Sylvester had not only been a physician with a large practice but a teacher of note—a pleasant man who had made friends with ease. His wife, a lady of wealth and beauty, and his three children had held his devotion. He had traveled extensively—always in demand as a speaker of wit.

One night while he lectured in Bath his London home caught fire and his wife and children perished. Grief overcame him and he fell into despondence, drink seemingly his only comfort. His practice melted away and his health shattered. Mr. Pettibone, a friend of long standing, taking him into his own home, had rescued the ill man. Hours of talk, hours of attempts to divert him, had had effect; after months, the doctor had recovered not only his health but his interest in life.

When the duke charged Mr. Pettibone to find a

tutor who was also a doctor for Heath and Charles, Mr. Pettibone seized on the coincidence, related to the duke Doctor Sylvester's story, and suggested he try the man. The duke, who had lived through a similar experience, though for different reasons, offered the position immediately. The doctor, however, hung back. Finally Mr. Pettibone told his friend bluntly it was time to get out into the world, and that the duke's household offered him an opportunity he'd be a fool to reject.

Now, over brandy, the duke inquired that if called upon, would he be willing to exercise his skills as a physician. The doctor responded, "Assuredly, sir, if needed. My knowledge is at your command." The two men discussed the duties of a tutor, and the duke was pleased by the doctor's enthusiasm and by his qualifications.

At dinner, introduced to the duchess and to his prospective pupils, the doctor proved a gracious addition; he deferred to the duke, was pleasantly polite to Lenore, talked Oxford with Heath, and reassured Charles that riding was one of his favorite sports. He then won Charles completely when he averred he could never make up his mind whether he favored horses or dogs as nature's finest creatures.

During the serving of dessert the doctor asked if whist were ever the means of whiling away an evening. The duke, who had stolen looks at Lenore as she ate, felt unexplainably buoyed, for she evinced merely courteous interest in the striking doctor. He responded, "No, but do you play piquet, Doctor?"

"One of my favorite games, Your Grace."

"Then let me give you alarm; the duchess is a master player"—Lenore stared wide-eyed at the unexpected tribute—"however, my game is chess—do you play?"

"Yes—though expertly?—alas, no."

"A game then?" asked the duke, rising.

The men took their leave. After a pause, Heath invited Lenore to inspect their new study.

"On one condition," Lenore said liltingly. "A game of jackstraws."

"Whee," shouted Charles, jumping up. "Mother, you're more fun than Wiggles!"

"Looby, image that!" Lenore rose, saying, "Last one upstairs is a silly lamb's tail," and ran from the room. The brothers looked at each other, then tore after their fleeting mother.

Fenwick, nodding at his post, jumped alert at the sight of the duchess, holding her skirts and dashing up the stairs, and the two lads, taking the steps two at a time after her.

31

The next morning Doctor Sylvester announced lessons to begin as soon as he had a chance to quiz the boys—"The questioning to begin immediately after breakfast!" The doctor smiled.

"Oh, but Mamère arrives today," objected Charles.

"Not until late afternoon, silly; she did not start

from Willowood at midnight last night," Lenore admonished.

"No put-offs, Charley." Heath rose. "Come on, let's
get it through with, then if it doesn't rain, you can
show the doctor how you ride."

They were doomed to disappointment; it did rain
—torrents.

Lenore spent the morning arranging Mamère's
room, paying special attention to the alcove, with a
bay window that extended over the front steps. She
had Madcape place a chair in the correct position so
the old lady could watch the comings and goings
through three windows, one giving view up the road,
one facing down the road, and one between—a full
panorama across the Square.

The midday meal proved a lively affair with chatter
about the quiz—both boys rolled their eyes heaven-
ward in comment—then the talk turned to the awaited
Mamère and her didos. The doctor evinced marked
curiosity in such an "outrageous old tale spinner" and
declared himself half in love already, with scarce
patience to meet her. Only the duke said nothing; he
did not share the eagerness extant.

When the meal was finished, Lenore retired to her
room to sit at the window and watch for the traveling carriages. Finally, hearing the double clop of the
horses, she ran downstairs and ordered Fenwick speed
the word. To her surprise the duke came to stand beside her as she waited impatiently for the party to
disembark. It was still pelting with rain, and so
Clough and Madcape ran out with covers to protect
Madame Lanier from being drenched.

Maria entered first; Lenore hugged her as did Mrs.
Clough, who introduced her to Mrs. Madcape. Finally,
Abel, carrying Mamère and flanked by Clough and

Madcape holding a canopy overhead, ceremoniously marched into the hall.

"Put me down, baldcock, can't see around or through you."

Lenore rushed to her as Abel set Madame Lanier on her feet. "Oh, Mamère, I'm so happy to see you!" She gathered the old lady in her arms.

"Stand back, ninnyhammer, and let me take it all in," ordered the old lady, after giving Lenore a loving pinch. She scowled at the group smiling at her. "Look at you standing about like grinning apes. Here lads, come kiss me proper." The boys rushed forward, and Charles made such an extravagant bow, all laughed except the duke, who frowned at antics.

Mamère turned to him. "Well, Duke, you look resplendent." The duke, relieved she had not called him Bunky, bowed. "Welcome, madame."

"Mrs. Clough, Clough, it pleases me to greet you," she said, then spying Dr. Sylvester, who stood away from the group, added, "Jupiter, who is this gorgeous gentleman? I like men good to gaze upon—who are you, sir?"

The doctor, recognizing the old lady's stamp, slipped quickly into her game, and before anyone could speak, stepped to her. "Madame, I am the new tutor, who has just fallen under your spell—your most obedient slave —Doctor William Sylvester." He bowed very low, then lingered over kissing her hand.

Delighted, the old lady laughed. "Hoy, a toadeater!" The doctor straightened slowly and to her joy gave her an outrageous wink.

To prevent Mamère making some shocking rejoinder to the doctor's action, Lenore quickly presented the Madcapes, assuring Mamère she would find them kindness itself. Mamère nodded. "This mountain of a man next to me is Abel; he's buckled to Maria, and I cherish them both. Take and give them some refreshments; the big one is always hungry."

Sensing the old lady's desire to be alone with the duke and duchess, the doctor said, "Madame, much as it devastates me to depart your presence, these half-lings must be educated. I anticipate our next meeting eagerly. Off we go, Heath, Charles."

The others gone, Madame Lanier stared around the hall with an eagle glance. "I see it's the same old mausoleum and the same old naked men; wager the same old naked females upstairs too. Know how they got there, Bunky?" the old lady asked. The duke scowled and shook his head.

"Your great-grandmother started it. Not long after she was married, your great-grandfather took a fancy piece and the duchess was mad as fire, so she had a niche put into the wall upstairs by her husband's door; then had a statue carved and set in right where he would pass every day. Some say it resembled his ladylove, but I never believed it. Soon—so the story goes—more and more niches were built; forget how many all told."

"But, Mamère . . ." whispered the horrified Lenore as she gazed around the hall.

"You've twigged, missy; the duchess, tired of her husband's cartes blanches, began to play his game— no gentleman in sight was safe."

"You mean . . . ?" gasped Lenore.

"Yes, these were called the Duke's Retort."

"Good God!" expelled the duke in a strangled voice —his face afire.

"Oh, don't look so hipped, Bunky, that generation had claret in its veins, not all namby-pamby like today."

The duke, too overwrought to speak, turned on his heel, went into the library, and slammed the door.

Mamère laughed. "That Gothic tale gave him a toss; may do some good—he might get rid of the ugly things."

"Mamère," asked Lenore. "Is this shocking tale known in London?"

"Ain't no tale, it's the truth! Some of my bosom bows may remember—used to whisper about it behind closed doors when we were youngsters."

Fortunately, Abel appeared at that moment, for Lenore could find no words. She finally murmured, "Mamère, you had better go to your room; you must be very tired."

"Hoy, bowled you out, have I? Humph, if these walls could chatter, they'd bring color to your cheeks —had a few flirts in this house myself."

"Abel!" commanded Lenore.

"Don't you touch me, you old bull." Mamère did not wish to be banished.

"Enough, my pretty lady bird, upstairs we go." Abel picked her up and started for the stairs.

"Put me down or I'll bang your nose 'til I draw blood."

"If you do, madame, I'll not give you the brandy I asked Mrs. Madcape to bring you." Abel jostled her lightly.

"Humph, you're a rum touch rascal," muttered Mamère, and let her head fall on his shoulder. Before they reached the beckoning Mrs. Madcape, the old lady slept.

Lenore ran to the library, knocked, and without awaiting response entered and rushed to the duke.

"Myles, this is dreadful!"

"Get that old devil out of my house today, madam," roared the duke.

"Good Lord, Myles, we can't do that; if we did, she might dangle the story all over London!"

The truth of the statement only fanned the duke's anger. "She will anyway, with that split tongue of hers."

"No, Myles, I don't think she means harm; you note she did not speak in front of anyone but you and me. My worry lies in the fact that others will recall the story—that is what signifies."

The duke glared at her. "I suppose, madam, that you are going to suggest I have the statues removed?"

Lenore, who hoped so with all her heart, said, "Perhaps some museum might welcome them."

"Each neatly tagged with the Gothic tale—you run mad."

"Maybe not, Myles, if you sent them to obscure museums far from London."

"Fustian. Some old fool would toddle in, see 'em, catch the bubble, and feed the scandal broth raw meat."

"Then why not store them at Asherwood?"

"Perhaps you would like to use them as garden statuary," sneered the duke.

Lenore felt a flash of anger. "No, Your Grace, I'd prefer them smashed to chips and used on the driveway in front of the palace."

The duke looked at her in astonishment—a brilliant solution. In a more reasonable tone, he asked, "What would you put in their place?"

"Urns for flowers," replied Lenore promptly.

"I will send for Mr. Cornby at once," said the duke coldly.

"Splendid." Lenore turned to go. When she reached the door, the duke spoke. "Please, madam, keep Madame Lanier out of my sight, and more especially, my earshot."

"Gladly!" Lenore shut the door.

32

Lenore did not see the duke for two weeks.

M. Dulac arrived the next morning and, aided by Mrs. Clough and Maria, unpacked and filled the closets with gowns, coats, capes, bonnets, shawls, scarves, bags, muffs, and gloves. He then handed Lenore a handwritten list explaining what frippery served each costume.

"M. Dulac, how can I ever thank you?" Lenore asked.

"By enhancing my creations in health and happiness, Your Grace." Lenore kissed the Frenchman on both cheeks, promised she would think of him with affection, and pled he visit on his every trip. In turn, M. Dulac vowed he would at any time be ready to create a gown for her and most *certainement* whenever he crossed the miserable Channel.

M. Dulac then went to say farewell to the duke, who expressed surprise that the couturier was not to stay with them longer.

"Thank you, Your Grace, but I must execute my pledge to Madam Fanchon to create a few gowns for the *ton*: I have a suite of rooms at Fenton."

"You will be missed, sir. Express my gratitude to my friend in France, and assure him his present has charmed the duchess and that our plays go well here." He tried to offer a gift, but M. Dulac refused, saying he used his art to delight many ladies, but this commission had permitted him to please himself—"She is so beautiful."

Toadeater, thought the duke, not realizing that the Frenchman, for one of the rare times in his life, had revealed his true feelings. The two men parted amiably.

Day after day the rains neither abated nor impeded the ever-increasing flow of carriages drawing up to the duke's door. Often there were two or three in tandem awaiting Clough or Abel to bring protection against the weather, and escort the passengers into the house—but not to call on the duke and duchess.

"Madame Lanier is back!" The news had zigzagged like lightning throughout London.

Lenore, at first startled by the parade of old ladies and gentlemen who gamely climbed up and down to the second floor—each to be greeted with whoops of joy—consulted Doctor Sylvester as to the advisability of such excitement. The doctor pointed out that not only was the pleasure good for all participants, it was to be encouraged. Lenore ordered refreshments served—though no spirits stronger than ratafia—and later had tables for cards set up permanently in Mamère's room. She questioned Maria and Abel, for they, it seemed, were running constantly to see to the needs of the throng. They laughed, claiming it a pleasure to serve

Madame Lanier and her friends, so happy, brave, and quaint.

The rains unending, Lenore found herself lonely, with the duke closeted and the boys busy with their lessons. Her depression deepened on receiving a response to her letter to Lady Leticia Ware, explaining her friend to be confined to the bedroom with loss of memory, recognizing no one.

Perforce Lenore drifted to Mamère's room and discovered herself welcome and petted. The old ladies fought to have her take a hand at whist; the elderly gentlemen flirted with old-fashioned gallantry. She was caught by the charm of the out-of-mode talk, the ancient clothes. She learned that by giggling at the quarrels that sprang up among the chatterers, they soon ceased. Mamère abused her shamefully—calling her terrible names and proclaiming her a bluestocking turned Methodist—with such loving winks and singing tones that the others began to tease her in the same cherishing way. Lenore accepted their thrusts and once in a while turned saucy to the assemblage's cackling glee.

Though soothed by the flattering attention, Lenore longed to see the duke. At last a sunny day dawned, and to Lenore's relief Mrs. Clough informed her at breakfast that the duke wished to see Her Grace an hour hence. Dressing in one of her most becoming gowns, Lenore knocked and walked into the library at the appointed moment, to find the duke exactly as he had been when she had last seen him—angry.

"What is it, Myles?" Lenore asked anxiously.

"Madam." The coldness of his tone made her quake slightly. "What is this parade of relics who pass up and down my stairs all day?"

"They are friends of Mamère's, Myles."

"They are horrors, madam," shouted the duke. "Monsters! Yesterday I came down the stairs and at the bottom stood a wraith I could almost see through; suddenly the boggard bowed and said, 'Good afternoon, Bunky,' then floated up the steps."

Lenore uncoiled like a spring into laughter.

"How dare you, madam?" cried the outraged duke.

"I can't help it, Myles, the boggard you saw is the Earl of Westham, and he does look exactly like a ghost."

"Further, madam, I will not permit Madame Lanier to turn my house into a gaming hell."

"What?! Oh, Myles, you are coming on too brown. Two tables of cards where not a farthing is exchanged does not make a gaming hell."

The duke, frustrated, took another tack. "What leaves that room in the way of gossip makes me shudder to think on."

"Oh—quite beyond permission—absolutely appalling —but only concerns those who have long since stuck their spoons in the wall. These 'relics,' as you call them, are out of touch with today's *ton*."

Bemused, the duke shook his head. "I do not see the charm Madame Lanier holds for these ghouls."

" 'Tis easy; she is a sparky, lively lady who teases, bullies, and shows them kindness. In their eyes she's famous fun; they adore to be with her and each other."

"I did not come to London to amuse the almost booked," said the duke coldly.

"I wonder why you did come to London." Lenore's tone matched his.

"You are aware that I did not move my household here idly; my purpose required long and precise planning. There have been put-offs, and the climate has delayed what needs to be done. But today I sent for you to inform you that each day not inclement we will drive or ride in the park. I have ordered the carriage for this afternoon; I expect you to accompany me."

Overjoyed, Lenore exclaimed, "Myles, I've longed to drive in the park. I will be prompt." She started for the door, then hesitated. "Myles, you are a benevolent man," she added, closing the door before he could answer.

33

Lenore, breathtakingly lovely in her olive-green coat trimmed in sable, her bonnet edged by matching fur, stepped into the open carriage and felt a surge of contentment as the duke, elegant in his greatcoat and beaver hat, seated himself at her side.

Henderson set the matched bays off at a goodly clip and soon the carriage rolled into the park. The duke, silent, searched among the many vehicles for his acquaintances of the *ton*. Suddenly he lifted his hat and bowed to a couple in an approaching curricle. Lenore quickly nodded, then saw the man and woman turn their heads away.

"They did not see us," muttered the duke. A tilbury neared, again the duke raised his hat and bowed, and again the greeted pair swung their heads. Lenore felt uneasy.

"Ah, there's Wrenham, my old friend." The duke pointed to a man on horseback. "Good evening, Wrenham," called the duke, but the rider speeded up his horse, and without a glance in their direction, rode by.

Frightened, Lenore turned to the duke and watched his face drain white. She spied a barouche occupied by friends of Eric's and hers. When the carriages drew side by side, Lenore waved, called, and smiled, only to see them stare straight ahead.

"Good God, they are going to do it again," growled the duke. Leaning forward, he said, "Henderson, take us home."

"No!" cried Lenore, catching the duke's sleeve. "Drive on, Henderson," she ordered sharply. Still holding his sleeve, she said, "Myles, talk to me—talk and look at me. Do not see any vehicle or rider here; just pin your eyes on me and chatter."

"Why should I, and what about?"

"Anything, Myles. If you are engrossed in me and do not see them, there can be no chance for their turning away. Tell me about the London house, Mr. Pettibone, your childhood—anything!"

Glowering, uncertain, the duke, gazing down at her, began to mutter about his childhood. Lenore evinced enraptured interest, laughing once at nothing.

"What are you finding humorous?" asked the duke darkly.

"I'm proving the amusing time we are enjoying."

"Fustian," growled the duke, but continued the monologue.

The agonizing hour plodded on, however, before

they reached the exit gates of the park, the duke's tales caught both his and Lenore's interest and their tension eased. Entering the house at last, Lenore followed the duke into the library, where he exploded, "Those damn town tulips and their brass-faced light skirts— may they go to Jericho!"

"What's its meaning, Myles?"

"It's the nod that the *ton* is going to turn its back on me, just as it did years ago." The duke poured himself a brandy. "The Duke and Duchess of Asherwood are not to be accepted by the *ton*." The duke drank his brandy in a toss.

"Can they do that?" asked the puzzled Lenore.

"You were there this afternoon; oh, yes, they can do that," said the duke bitterly.

Lenore felt cold. "Myles, may I have a small brandy, please?" She seated herself in a corner of the couch, and taking the proffered glass, sipped slowly, staring into the fire. Suddenly, putting her glass on the table, she spoke in a firm voice. "No, they can't!"

"Don't talk slum; they can, and obviously intend to."

"No, they *can*not! Because we are going to first. Myles, please sit down and listen. The *ton* expects to give us rough snubs by turning their backs on us, but they can hardly do so back to back; it would be silly."

"Stop posing riddles!" the duke barked.

"Myles, today we did that exactly; we couldn't be set down, for we were blind, and from today on that is how we are to behave at all times. No acknowledgment of anyone alive but you and me."

"What fustian is this?"

"Every day the *ton* rides in the park; so will we—but always enthralled in ourselves—marking the existence of no one."

"Nonsense!" said the impatient duke.

"Not so," denied Lenore, then expanded her introspection: "Let us appear everywhere—the opera, the museums, the art shows, the theater, all functions where the *ton* gathers, but to us—invisible."

"And at Almack's?" challenged the duke.

"True, we cannot go there, but it does not signify. If the plan works, the *ton* will be dying to learn why we notice no one; curiosity will consume each and every bewildered one of them."

"Ridiculous; it won't fadge."

"If you say so." Lenore paused, then said coldly, "I can be packed to return to Asherwood in two days." The duke stared at her. "Have you any other notions, Myles? You told me that it is of the first importance we blossom into the pink of the *ton*; if other gates, let us sneak off to Asherwood."

The duke paced the floor. "Today I had it dashed well hurled at me and I'm blue-deviled. From some I could expect it, but Wrenham!" He banged his fist on the desk.

"Wrenham is a Bond Street dandy, not worth a farthing of your trouble, and who, do you imagine, tied his belcher? It was a sartorial malapropism."

The duke glared at her. "Do not prattle, madam, Wrenham is—er—was a close friend."

"And will be again, if you don't skulk off to Asherwood as you did before," said Lenore pleasantly.

The duke glowered. "Madam, you are coming it too strong."

Lenore rose. "Sir, I am the Duchess of Asherwood, wed to the finest gentleman in England, and I do not intend to let the high-in-the-instep, bubble-headed ninnyhammers prevent me from taking my rightful place in London." Lenore swept to the door, then turned back. "If the *ton* wishes to make war against us, I am going to follow the drum and beat them to flinders; I hope you will enlist on my side."

The duke blinked at the slammed door.

34

Each day at the duke's residence Doctor Sylvester found himself more content. His pupils, serious students, demanded close attention: Heath's methodical mind craved logical sequence and explanations in depth; Charles's lightning-quick grasp of any presentation required that the tutor be prepared to defend deductions drawn from stated facts, and lively arguments ensued.

After Lenore's expressed concern, the doctor had taken to dropping in on Madame Lanier to note any signs of change. He discovered her a keen, perceptive lady who loved to flirt and who treated him like a lover with whom she was toying; he enjoyed the role and whispered outrageous suggestions in her ear, sending her into chortles of hilarity.

The interplay of the duke and his family intrigued the doctor. He realized the boys cared deeply for their father and idolized their new stepmother, who in turn adored the duke. What puzzled him was the duke's seeming indifference to his family. That he sheltered them elegantly could never be brought to question, but he did not appear to enjoy or cherish either his sons or his wife.

On the night of the disastrous drive through the park, the doctor sensed trouble the moment dinner was served. The duke spoke not at all. Lenore responded absently to the boys' description of their visit to the Royal Exchange, a story that most times would have amused her, for the bear's antics had been droll.

When dinner was over, the duke took his leave with no suggestion of a game of chess, thus confirming the doctor's fears. Sending the boys to their lessons, the doctor said to Lenore, "Your Grace, I am at loose ravelings this evening; I could join Madame Lanier and her friends, but I fear a scandal, for I think the darling old lady wishes to display me as her latest conquest."

This contrivance made Lenore smile. "She is a gazetted flirt and would do exactly as you predict. I hope you are not bothered by her bobbery."

"Not at all; it amuses me to be cast as the object of an experienced charmer's affection. I enjoy her wiles—she is very expert."

"She's dreadful; doesn't she shock you?"

"Duchess, it may surprise you, but once or twice I have set *her* in a bustle, bringing a blush to her cheeks."

"Incredible!" said Lenore, laughing.

"Your Grace, fully warned as to your prowess, I bravely wonder if you would consider a rubber of piquet?"

Lenore frowned. "I'm not certain. Don't you wish to read in your spare hours? You are a scholar."

The doctor chuckled. "Your Grace, each night after I have had my trimming at chess, I read far into the night, often to stay ahead of the two budding scholars I teach. However, in the early evening I prefer games." Seeing Lenore's indecision, he added, "You hesitate."

"Yes," confessed Lenore. "I'm a trifle on the fidgets and I dislike the morning-room gloom."

"Let us play here then; I'm sure a table will fit by the fire."

Reluctantly, Lenore consented, rang for a footman and, the table and chairs set, cut for deal.

The doctor, not quite believing the duke's warning, and thinking merely to distract the duchess, found himself being badly beaten. "Your Grace, you are rapidly relieving me of my brass."

Lenore looked up in surprise. "Are we wagering high stakes? None were mentioned."

"Whew, what a blessing!"

When the game was finished, the doctor said, "Thank you, Duchess. I hope to serve you tie and tick someday, but doubt the possibility—you're an expert."

"Good night, Doctor," said Lenore absently. "We shall play again."

Seeing Lenore far away in her thoughts, the doctor left.

If only Myles had been my opponent, mused Lenore. At Willowood he played, but here . . . She rose, entered the hall, paused by the library door for an instant, then continued upstairs. Drifting off to sleep, she prayed her tactics in the war on the *ton* would not fail.

35

The siege began the next day. Lenore and the duke rode through the park, the duke, pale, tight-lipped, at first incapable of speech, laying the onus on Lenore. She spoke of her father and childhood in the vicarage. From time to time she had to remind the duke to look at her instead of staring straight ahead but, finally, his attention caught, he listened and later asked questions.

The magnificent carriage and matched grays, driven with elegant precision by the see-nobody Henderson, left astonishment and bemusement in its path. The *ton*—well prepared to snub the duke, pondered what words of the duchess's held the duke so engrossed, thereby depriving them of their anticipated giving of rebuffs.

The duke, not displeased at the bewildered faces he saw out of the corner of his eye, told Lenore, "Damme, I think the battle well broached."

" 'Tis only the opening shot, Myles," responded the determined Lenore.

At dinner, in a lighter mood, the duke announced, "Heath, Charles, tomorrow morning we go to call on your grandfather."

"Grandfather?" Heath queried.

Charles turned to Lenore. "I didn't know you had a father, Mother."

"Not your present mother's father," the duke spoke sharply. "Your own mother's father—Mr. Winslow Featherheath."

Charles, befuddled for an instant, then said in a small voice, "Oh."

"A fine gentleman—you remember him, Heath."

"No, Father, I'm sorry, I don't."

"Well, you'll meet him in the morning; he expects us."

"Bro, we must walk Wiggles. May we go now?" Charles asked.

"Will you please excuse us, Mother, Father?" Heath rose.

The duke nodded. After the boys had gone, the duke said, "I can't see why they cannot take interest in meeting their grandfather."

"They're frightened, Myles; old gentlemen can be awesome."

"Featherheath isn't; he was the only member in Harriet's family I could abide."

"Good! Myles, you are very wise to introduce them to him, especially Charles."

The duke stared at her but said nothing.

The next forenoon Mr. Featherheath welcomed the duke and his sons in the morning room. Refreshments having been brought, the old gentleman studied his grandsons as they drank their tea.

"Charles, come here and let me feast my eyes on you."

Charles, with some hesitation, stood before his grandfather, who said, "Humph, you have a dog and you ride."

"Yes, sir," replied Charles, perplexed as to how he knew.

"Are you a young whip?"

"No, sir, Bro is—I'm just learning—he's teaching me," Charles answered proudly.

Heath broke in, "He's going to be a nonpareil when he's older, sir."

Charles, elated by Heath's praise, flung out, "Heath is a nonpareil already—I just couldn't think of the word before—he is bang-up to the echo in everything, sir."

"Stop talking slum, little Brother," Heath said quickly.

"But he is, sir." Charles nodded vigorously to his charmed grandfather.

"Will you two stop 'sirring' me; I'm your grandfather," the old man spoke in gruff delight. "Heath, you are the spit of my daughter—don't try to answer that silly comment, but I had to say it."

"I understand, Grandfather."

"Now, I hope to cast my ogles on you two often, but today I wish to talk to your father, so would you be good enough to go to the book room? I had Wicks put out some games and periodicals—Wicks!" the old man shouted.

Wicks entered and led the boys from the room.

"Damme, Myles, they're a couple of up-to-the-knocker grandsons. I'm damn pleased! Now, pour some brandy and we'll drink to them."

The duke rose and filled the glasses. "I have brought the boys for a purpose, sir, as you can freely imagine."

"Certainly, you don't want your miniature—Charles —regarded as a result of a marriage with your left hand."

"Precise to the pin," said the duke, grateful to be spared explanations.

"Nor do I! Since the day you wrote about him, I have been proclaiming to one and all that I could scarce wait for you to arrive in London so I might view my grandsons—sons, you will note."

"Sir, I am relieved."

"You are not such a cawker as to think I want a grandson of mine ill thought of? Having lent my ear to the on-dit in this town for years, I did some spreading prattle on my own. Did more than talk though; every grandchild I have is peeled to meet his cousins. Minute I alert 'em, there'll be invitations to parties, picnics, rides in the park, and any other devilment young'uns conjure up."

"Just the thing, sir." The duke spoke warmly.

"Least I can do. My daughter, Hat, was a fool." The old man sighed. "And I guess she paid for it; however, neither you nor Charles is going to, if I can contrive other gates. Fill up our glasses and tell me how old Madame Lanier is; had an eye for her once myself; almost landed in the soup."

"Why not come and see her; all London does," said the duke ruefully.

"Do they? Humph, in that case, I may toddle over myself one day. She was full of gig as a young gel and—"

"Still true—do come—any time," he said, then to his own surprise the duke added, "I wish you to meet the duchess."

"Hear all over town she's a beauty. Do the grandsons like her?"

"They love her."

"Famous! Boys need a good mother. You happy with her?"

The duke paused, for he had never given a thought as to whether he was happy being married to Lenore.

Mr. Featherheath laughed. "Think on it, Duke," then shouted, "Wicks!"

36

Each day that the weather allowed, the duke and Lenore executed their strategy of battle. The lovely duchess, seated beside the perfectly appointed duke, appeared in the park—eyes only for each other—and disappeared again, leaving those eager to snub dashed. On-dit first bubbled, then boiled.

The opening of the opera signaled officially the beginning of the London season. No member of the *ton* dared miss it, save for dire reasons. Ladies, dazzlingly bejeweled, fluttered down the aisles, escorted by their gentlemen, attired in cutaway tails and silk or satin coats, the neckcloths tied in a variety of styles, their hair done in the latest mode—a fashion set by Beau Brummel himself. Once seated, all ladies' eyes flew upward, as did the gentlemen's—quizzing glasses raised—to the duke's box, so many years empty. The box lay dark. Triumphant nods throughout the house proclaimed that the Duke and Duchess of Asherwood would not venture to appear.

When the curtain for the first interval descended and the light brightened, a rustle of gasps ran over

the house. The duchess, in pure-white satin, adorned
by the Asherwood emeralds—the necklace of deep green
twinkled, stirred gently by Lenore's breathing—her
red-brown hair nesting an emerald of size, surrounded
by diamonds, sat resting her arms on the railing of
the box, her entire attention given to the duke, who
leaned forward in his chair to enlighten her—as to
what?

The gentlemen, moving from box to box to greet
friends, tried to catch a glimpse of anyone who might
enter the duke's box, but no one did.

Lenore lifted her opera glass and swept the house,
then commented to the duke, who raised his glass to
linger row by row, then box by box. A lively dialogue
ensued and many wondered—What are they saying?

When the curtain lowered for the second interval,
every head swung as one to the duke's box, making
Lenore want to laugh so much that she hid her face
with her program and whispered to the duke, " 'I'm
dying, Egypt, dying'; pray say something so I may
laugh."

The duke said, "Don't be a flosstop," which sent
her into peals of laughter. "Stop it!" ordered the duke,
a command that heightened her amusement.

When the final curtain fell—the duke's box was
empty.

During the ride home Lenore giggled. "The wid-
geons, staring as if we were in a circus ring."

"Did you enjoy the opera?" the duke asked.

"Oh, Myles, glorious! The color, the costumes, the
lights, and who cannot love Mozart—Figaro, Figaro,"
she chanted. "I do hope we will go again."

"We have to," the duke said glumly.

"Don't you like opera, Myles?"

"No."

"Then why go?"

"One must be seen at the opera."

"Fiddle! Next time I will take the boys; Doctor Sylvester can squire me and you can stay home."

"Madam," the duke flared. "You are not to be seen with Doctor Sylvester except in my presence—ever!"

Charmed this time by the duke's temper, Lenore said, "As you wish, Myles."

During the rest of the ride home neither spoke.

On entering the hall, Lenore handed her cape to Maria, who was waiting, then followed the duke into the library.

"I want to replace the emeralds." She unfastened the clasp and undid the pin in her hair. "Thank you for allowing me to wear them; they are magnificent."

"The duchess has always worn the Asherwood emeralds to the opening night of the opera." He poured a brandy.

"Then I am doubly grateful. Good night, Myles."

Fenwick, at his post, was startled to see the duchess dance around the hall, humming to herself. Spying him, she circled and said to him, "Fenwick, did you know that only *the* Duchesses of Asherwood can wear the emeralds to the opening night at the opera?" And before he could respond, she danced to the stairs and ran up them lightly.

37

Mr. Oliver Cordyne, artisan, art dealer, and patron of aspiring artists, in pleased astonishment congratulated himself on his daring venture. For his annual showing of paintings by unrecognized artists he had rented a large circular room, domed by glass, so paned as to shed almost perfect light on the landscapes, still lifes, portraits, watercolors, miniatures, and sketches displayed. Never had his invitations—even for shows by noted artists—drawn so many members of the *ton*, who before him drifted in a slow counterclockwise circle around the room, greeting friends, giving cursory glances at the paintings, one or two pausing to purchase. He noted a strange air of expectancy among his guests: darting eyes, shakes of heads, shrugs. Suddenly a ripple of words ran like a stream around the crowd—"They're here," "Here they come." The circle, as if by command, stopped its rotation and the *ton* swung to stare fixedly at the wall of art.

Puzzled, Mr. Cordyne looked to the entrance and saw the elegant Duke and Duchess of Asherwood framed in the doorway; he rushed to greet the distinguished pair.

Lenore, eyeing the solid ring of backs, whispered to the duke, "Glory, what devout connoisseurs!" and laughed.

"Welcome to the Cordyne Gallery, Your Grace. I am Mr. Oliver Cordyne."

"Mr. Cordyne," said the duke with a slight bow, "would you be so kind as to set up an easel right here so we may consider one by one the paintings I have listed." The duke extended a sheet of paper. Mr. Cordyne paled—he had never had such a request— but took the sheet. A quick glance told him that the duke had selected the seven finest canvases in the collection—two Constables, a Valley, a Cox watercolor, two Cotman etchings, and a Martin landscape. In the deadly silence Mr. Cordyne looked at the expectant duke, the smiling duchess, then clapped his hands. Three assistants sprang to his side—orders whispered, the men dashed off in various directions.

"May we bring you chairs?" asked the dealer.

"No, thank you," said the duke, lifting his head from a confidence he had been murmuring into Lenore's ear.

The members of the *ton* held their breath as the assistants parted them, removed the requested paintings from the walls, and returned to Mr. Cordyne, who balanced the Cox watercolor carefully on the easel. He started to speak, but the duke cut in. "It's unnecessary, sir, for you to enlarge; please, if you have no further use for it, may I have the list."

Lenore and the duke studied the watercolor, consulted inaudibly, then the duke waved his hand for it to be replaced.

Slowly members of the *ton* began to turn from the wall; by the duke's fourth hand wave, the entire circle faced the duke and duchess in utter stillness.

Suddenly, Lord Wrenham, who had been watching the proceedings from across the room, could withstand it no longer.

"Good afternoon, Duke." His words rang like snapped icy branches in a deep forest.

The duke swept the crowd, then spying Wrenham, said, "Good afternoon, Wrenham," in a cold voice, and swung back to the easel. Lenore pulled his sleeve and whispered. The duke immediately stepped toward the middle of the room and called, "Wrenham, how are you?" Surprised, Wrenham pushed through the others and approached the duke, who put both hands on Wrenham's shoulders. "Old friend, I'm delighted to see you. You appear in top health. Come, you have not met the duchess." He led the lord to Lenore.

"Lenore, may I present my old friend Lord Wrenham."

"I'm happy to meet you, my lord; Myles has spoken of you often."

Wrenham blushed and kissed Lenore's hand.

The *ton*, agog, gasped at this chink in their ranks.

Lenore indicated the easel and asked, "Is not young Constable a pleasing artist?"

Wrenham, conscious of the dagger stares shot his way, merely nodded.

"Lenore," said the duke, "we are in luck; Wrenham is home to a peg anent art; always dashing in and out of galleries as I remember—let him advise you."

"Indeed so," said Lenore. As the remaining pictures were shown she conferred with His Lordship to confirm her own likes or dislikes.

The paintings viewed, Lenore and the duke checked their choices, then handed the list to Wrenham, who gave a word or two of approval.

Mr. Cordyne again received the paper and was overwhelmed to find five of the seven paintings marked for delivery. Profuse with his thanks, he moved to escort his new departing patrons. Wrenham paused for an instant, then hurriedly left with the duke and duchess.

"May we drive you anywhere?" asked Lenore with a smile.

Wrenham bowed. "Thank you, Your Grace, but I go to my club just around the corner. To the duke he said, "Myles, you are a most fortunate man," then walked rapidly away.

"Lord Wrenham is a man of courage," remarked Lenore on the way home.

Reentering the gallery, Mr. Cordyne found it in an uproar. His assistants rushed to him, their hands full of orders.

Mr. Constable, who had hovered near his land-scapes in hope of selling one or two, was astounded to find every one marked "sold" in a matter of minutes. The artists fortunate to have been favored by the duke and Wrenham were soon swamped by buyers, some of whom took pictures off the wall to hunt down Mr. Cordyne or an assistant who could accept their money.

Within the hour the gallery was empty of people, and the walls almost bare of paintings.

Mr. Cordyne, elatedly busy, did not until late at night wonder how the duke had compiled his catalogue of the most select works of art, for there had been no preview. He puzzled for days, but never connected the visit of the solicitor representing the owner of the building, who had walked around the gallery to discuss possible damage to the walls, where the paintings hung—a Mr. Pettibone.

38

Lady Sally Jersey made her first appearance of the season at the opening gala at Almack's. She had returned to her London home only late the night before from a long trip abroad. She had nearly foregone the occasion, but finding her household in order by dinner time, changed her mind.

On entering Almack's, a rush of friends escorted her to her customary place; she had a pleasant word for each who came to welcome her. When the small crowd finally dispersed, she languidly surveyed the brilliantly lighted room and noted with some surprise that many stood in clusters, talking despite the lively dance music being played.

"Why are there so few dancers, Bella?" she asked her close friend seated next to her.

"Haven't you heard?" Lady Bella sounded taken aback. Lady Jersey shook her head. Lady Bella Dickam clasped her hands to her bosom, entranced. It was a rare ear that had not already been filled to brimming over with the tale of the Duke and Duchess of Asherwood. Taking a deep breath, she launched into the lively on-dit.

Lady Jersey listened, asked the proper questions, smiled or frowned at the appropriate places, giving

Lady Bella enormous satisfaction. At last, out of
truth, and gossip, Lady Bella inquired of her friend
"What do you think of it, Sally?"

Lady Jersey drew her ostrich fan idly through her
fingers. "The duchess must be fascinating."

Lady Bella, slightly dashed, for she longed to hear
the judgments of the astute Lady Jersey, pouted. "Is
that all you have to say?"

Lady Jersey smiled. "Has Wrenham left town?"

"Why, yes, he left the morning after the art show
to go to his hunt box in Melton county."

"Wrenham's a wise man." Lady Jersey fell silent.

Her friend, feeling rebuffed in some way, asked
"Don't you consider the duke and duchess out of
civility?"

"I've not had time to think on it, my dearest Bella."
Lady Jersey patted Bella's hand. "But thank you for
enlightening me; I would far prefer to hear your version than any other."

Lady Bella, soothed by the compliment, promised
to report further developments.

Pleading fatigue, Lady Jersey left shortly.

Later, Lady Jersey, tucked in her bed by her abigail,
examined the extraordinary tale she had heard. She
trusted Bella to have told the truth of what she knew.
Bella, not the brightest of ladies, however, was not
one to embellish. The tale propounded questions:
Why had Myles—Lady Jersey had known the duke
since boyhood—after years as a recluse, unseen, unheard—suddenly acquired a wife, moved to London,
and attempted to take his place in the *ton?* Why had
Lenore—Lady Jersey remembered the beautiful bride
of Captain Lanier—wed the duke? Lady Jersey dismissed the creampot marriage gossip as nonsense. The
ton's conspiracy to reject the duke announced itself

as pure malice. True, Myles had made a stupid but natural boy's mistake, eloping with the empty-headed Harriet; true, he had been titled "the Rake of Europe"—not that a single member of society was able to make explicit or describe his wicked excesses.

Lady Jersey was bemused by Bella's account of the duke and duchess's ride in the park and her almost breathless recitation of their odd behavior since that day. "They do not see us!" Bella had exclaimed. "We could be murals—they go everywhere, except to parties, to which they are not invited." On mentioning Cordyne's Gallery, Bella had lowered her voice. "Wrenham spoke to him—I could almost say shouted—I tell you, Sally, it was dramatic—'Good afternoon, Duke,' just as clear as a trumpet. And the duke greeted Wrenham with warmth, then introduced him to the duchess, consulted him on pictures, treated him as if nothing had ever been amiss in the whole *ton*. It rocked us all, I assure you."

Lady Jersey lay back on her pillow and laughed—the sly turntablers—snubbed the snubbers—famous! What a caper! Was it Myles or Lenore who instigated the luscious swing-around? Concocting plans of her own, Lady Jersey drifted into sleep.

39

The next morning Lenore sat with Mamère, who resentfully suffered a slight indisposition from the damp weather. Abel knocked, entered, and solemnly announced that Lady Jersey awaited Her Grace in the morning room. Lenore, startled, requested Abel to repeat the name, then, elated, threw a kiss to Mamère, ran to her room, pinned a corsage of violets on her bodice, peeked in the mirror and, reassured, flew downstairs.

The morning room seemed less forbidding with the lovely Lady Jersey seated by the fire, extending her ungloved hand.

"Ah, Lenore, how pleasant to rewelcome you to London; you have been in other climes since last we met." Lady Jersey's voice was half amused, half kind.

"Lady Jersey"—Lenore spoke with gravity—"seeing you again gives me cause for great rejoicing."

A simple truth, thought Lady Jersey as she drew Lenore to sit next to her on the sofa. "Come, tell me of your adventures since Captain Lanier's dashing bride left London for the Penn—to return as the Duchess of Asherwood."

Lenore caught her breath; to confide in the gracious lady tempted her, but by doing so she might betray Myles. "It charms me to be requested to talk about myself to a sympathetic listener, but first let me offer you refreshment."

A sparring for wind, concluded Lady Jersey. Very wise. "Some ratafia and cakes would be welcome."

Lenore rang, gave instructions to Abel, then seated herself in a chair opposite her guest. "I'm sorry Myles is away this morning, and the boys out riding—they will be disappointed to miss you."

Ha, she does not wish to confide. "It's you I came to see, Lenore. As I recall, the last time we met was at poor dear Leticia's, just before you sailed."

Lenore nodded. "I remember. Well, the trip was difficult, and the Penn not a comfortable place for wives, but Eric and I were as happy as could be under the conditions." She dropped her eyes.

A bouncer, assessed Lady Jersey—I must watch the little duchess—her face reveals more than her tongue.

"Eric's death was saddening—to recite the ensuing troubles that beset me before sailing to England would be painful to us both."

"Of course, my dear, please do not," drawled Lady Jersey.

Abel entered and served the wine and cakes.

"And here?" Lady Jersey resumed.

"Here, two extreme pieces of good fortune befell me—Eric's batman of years, Abel—the man you just saw—sought me out and offered to serve me. The other —Eric's brother, Alfred, asked me to tend his wonderful grandmother, Madame Lanier."

"Then buried you both in Wilowood," Lady Jersey said ruefully, "where you were expected to *wear* willow forever." She laughed. "What a comeuppance for the clutch-farthing Alfred when you rose like a phoenix."

Lenore blushed. "Oh, quite by chance, Lady Jersey.

Mamère—that is my name for Madame Lanier—and I were content at Willowood—"

"Madame Lanier content? Tell me, in the country, into whose ears did she pour forth her scandalous stories—yours?"

"Oh, no, I'm far too schoolgirlish." Lenore giggled. "She told them to the vicar."

"The vicar?" Lady Jersey gasped.

"Indeed so, the Reverend David Thomas, who has an understanding heart and who listened with patience. He did Mamère worlds of good."

"Lenore, you are coming it too brown," said Lady Jersey, laughing.

" 'Tis true; of course, he didn't listen, but feigned his shock and horror expertly."

"Very proper. Now tell me how you encountered Myles."

"Heath was thrown from his horse near the gate of Willowood and Abel carried him into the house. While Heath mended, the duke came to visit him—"

"And thereby developed a tendre for Eric's lovely widow—how romantic!"

Lenore felt the color rise to her face. "He kindly asked me to be his duchess."

Lady Jersey noted the blush, but also that Lenore did not drop her eyes. "A splendid twist of events. What made Myles decide to come to London? His devotion to Asherwood is ingrained."

"Please have more ratafia." Lenore rose and poured the wine. Careful, she warned herself, but said, "Myles learned I love London," she said, smiling, "almost as much as Mamère does. Heath too wanted to visit the city, and Charles demands to go where Heath goes. You could call it a present to us all."

Bravo, well said, thought Lady Jersey; she's in the

tradition of Asherwood Duchesses—needle-witted and in this case, loyal. Aloud she said, "Tell me about Charles."

Relieved, Lenore described the boy, his amazing resemblance to the duke, and the story of his introduction into the household.

Lady Jersey watched Lenore through hooded eyes. So the little duchess is deeply in love with the Dour Duke. Does he love her? Probably not—what a hobble!

When Lenore finished, Lady Jersey said, "Myles is a most fortunate man; I will tell him when I see him. Please do not blush again, you make me feel old—haven't blushed in years." She laughed. "Let me explain the reason for my visit. I came to invite you to my Birthday Ball." She reached into her bag and drew forth a large cream-white envelope and laid it on the table. "It is sometimes an insipid squeeze, but at my friends' insistence, I give it each year. The invitations were posted during my absence and I did not hear until last night that you and Myles had moved to London. I came today to be made sure that you will attend."

Lenore felt tears spring to her eyes. Lady Jersey's ball, given at the first of the season, ranked as the most important party of the year; to be omitted from her invitation list spelt doom to any member of the *ton*. Her eyes bright Lenore smiled at the most understanding of ladies. "Thank you, Lady Jersey."

Lady Jersey rose and put on her gloves, saying, "You will come?" Lenore nodded. Lady Jersey looked around the room and said briskly, "Order Myles to redo this room—it's a Gothic horror."

Lenore went to the elegant Lady Jersey and kissed her cheek. "Dear friend, I have no words."

Lady Jersey smiled. "Inform Madame Lanier I'll visit her soon; today I cannot be plied with brandy and wicked tales. Good-bye, little Duchess."

When Lady Jersey had gone, Lenore burst into tears.

When the duke returned, Fenwick, who had observed Lenore crying, told the duke that the duchess was in the morning room. The unusual announcement, coming from his footman, drove the duke to seek Lenore. Finding her in tears, the duke said, "What is it? What has happened?"

"Oh, Myles." Lenore waved the open invitation. "Lady Jersey called this morning to invite us to her Birthday Ball." She dried her eyes.

"Sally Jersey?"

"Yes. She was so kindly; she called me 'little Duchess.'"

"Good God!"

"She is the dearest lady in the world, and wants you to redo this room."

"What?"

"She says it's a 'Gothic horror.'"

"How dare she call my morning room a horror!"

"Because it is, Myles."

The duke stared around the gloomy room. "It's been like this since my great-grandfather's day."

Lenore was silent.

"And she says I should redecorate?"

"Yes, but I'm certain she'll forgive you if you do not wish to change it," Lenore spoke hastily.

"Wish to?" The duke glared at the portrait of his great-grandfather. "I hate this room and have ever since I was a boy; those faces scowl down at me and make me feel small every time I'm here."

"Then remove them," suggested Lenore practically.

The duke turned on her. "They are my ancestors, madam!" he shouted.

Lenore stood up. "Myles, to live with portraits that haunt you is outside of enough—indeed absurd," she said as she left.

Walking around the room, the duke studied each dreary painting, then, gazing up at his great-grandfather, muttered, "By God, sir, you may have met your match."

40

Mr. Winslow Featherheath, true to his word, alerted his family. An invitation for the celebration of George C. Featherheath's seventeenth birthday was posted to Heath and Charles Asherwood. Neither boy wanted to accept, but a word from their father settled the matter.

Old Mr. Featherheath, hugging a secret that tickled him, insisted that every last one of his grandchildren attend the party at the Brooks Featherheath home.

When Heath, uneasy, and Charles, cross, entered their uncle's hall, their cousin, George C. Featherheath, was coming from upstairs.

"Glory," squealed Charles. "Bro—look!"

Heath, giving his coat to the footman, turned and

gasped, for the figure coming down the stairs was himself. Charles watched, wide-eyed, as the two frowning
cousins approached each other.

"Damme, you're me," said Heath's reflection.

"Like a mirror," agreed Heath.

"I'm George Featherheath."

"I'm Heath Asherwood."

They stared at each other, awed; suddenly George
gave a shout of laughter. "What a shock—you me, me
you! Come, Coz, let's bowl over the family." He put
his arm around Heath's shoulder and headed for the
drawing room doors.

"Wait, wait," screamed Charles, "I'm Cousin
Charles; let me go first so I can see the fun."

"Right you are, little Coz." George clapped Charles
on his head. "Lead on, MacDuff." The footman threw
open the doors and Charles strutted through, followed by Heath and George. Those near the door
goggled—two Georges?—impossible! Neither cousin
said a word and walked forward slowly.

"Good God!" shouted George's father when he saw
his son in duplicate. "He must be Asherwood!" "Is,"
said old Mr. Featherheath, chortling at the effect of
his surprise—which he had nurtured since first seeing
Heath.

"Father," said George grandly, "meet *me*."

His father studied Heath, then laughed. "Young
man, this is an amazing pleasure, but whether I can
put up with double Georges is problematical."

Heath bowed. "Sir, now that I am recovered from
shock, I count this an auspicious day; may I present
my brother, Charles."

Looking down at Charles, Mr. Brooks Featherheath groaned. "Am I to be startled yet again?—I am—
you, Charles, are the duke whittled down."

"Thank you, sir," said Charles solemnly. "You could not pleasure me more; my father is a top-of-the-trees." The pronouncement brought amused grins.

"Introduce your cousins to your mother, George, she is on the sofa over there." Mr. Brooks Featherheath indicated the way and followed to watch his wife's reactions.

Her son caught her attention. "Mother, I want you to meet my cousin Heath." George stepped aside to let her see his copy.

"Good Lord!" said the astonished lady. "George, you come right here and stand by me so that I may know my own child."

"Mother, I am I." George bowed, adding, "This is Heath's brother, Charles."

Mrs. Featherheath smiled at Charles, who bowed, then turned her eyes up to Heath again. "I will never be able to tell you two boys apart—never—you're two pebbles in a pouch. Let's see, Heath, do you have a mole on your—"

"Mother!" George cut in, aghast.

The lady looked bewildered amid the titters of amusement. George grabbed Heath and rapidly retreated to another part of the large room. Heath laughed. "I don't have a mole on me, Coz; please reassure your mother that she can easily distinguish you from me."

George shook his head. "Females!" Heath could not comprehend whether George referred to his mother, or the group of pretty girls staring at them with open mouths.

Charles, who had followed his host and brother, slowed, considering the girls a gaggle of silly bleaters, and seeing a boy his own age eyeing him, he swerved. "Are you a cousin?"

"No, I'm the Earl of Laudersdown," replied the boy timidly.

"I'm Charles Asherwood, and I hope you have another name, 'cause I can't call you Earl of Lau—whatever you said—all day."

The young earl, the only child of a widowed mother, petted beyond belief, shy, stared with hungry eyes at what might be a miraculous onset.

"I'd like to be called Nick," he said tentatively.

"Nick it is then; you can call me Charley. Do you ride?"

"Yes."

"Well, then, let's go riding some day; my brother takes me every good day—would take you too if I asked him."

The young Earl of Laudersdown could scarcely credit his ears. He did ride—between his tutor and his groom—but never had he dreamed of riding with anyone his age.

"Come on, Nick, let's find something to eat." Charles stepped out toward the end of the room and a table laden with food that had caught his eye. In a trance, the young earl started to follow the only boy who had ever asked him to do anything.

"Clarence, where are you going, dear?" sang out an overly sweet voice. In agony—had his new friend heard?—the earl turned and said, "Just to get some food."

"All right, dear, but eat carefully; you know what too many sweets do to you, Clarence."

"Yes, Mother." The earl spun quickly, fearing his new-found friend might have flown in disgust, but Charley stood staunch.

"She called you Clarence; guess you like Nick better," said Charles.

"Uh-huh. When Father died, my mother insisted on calling me that—Father called me Clar."

"Well, you're Nick to me; come on—let's eat."

The boys stuffed themselves happily, agreeing on many things—chestnuts better than grays—females horrendous—boxing probably the best sport—the earl confessing he did not know how, but receiving assurance Charley would teach him—the cakes were fine—and they would have more. Other lads joined them and soon seven or eight boys chatted, bragged, pushed, poked, and ate; mindful, however, of parental presence.

So Heath and Charles were introduced to the sons and daughters of the *ton*.

That night the Earl of Laudersdown, mildest of boys, gentle in obedience, threw himself to the floor and howled in his first temper tantrum, by which he elicited a promise from his agitated mother that he would be allowed to ride, see, and be with the Asherwood scions whenever he wished.

41

On the night of the ball, the great bronze statues that flanked Lady Jersey's massive doorway, their arms aloft, held bowls of fire that cast flickering light on London's new-fallen snow. The doors open, light fell on the red carpet that ran down the steps to the curb. Footmen lined the carpet, ready to assist guests from the conveyances to the entrance hall.

At the insistence of Lady Jersey, the duke's carriage was the first to arrive. Entering the large foyer, Lenore and His Grace were greeted by their hostess, who led the way up the marble stairs to the landing by the ballroom. The Lady took her place, and, motioning, announced, "You are to receive with me, dear Asherwoods—do not naysay me, Myles; I will not accept a no."

The duke said sharply, "Madam, do you wish to make us a raree-show?"

"Yes, I think I do," replied his hostess genially.

"Then let me tell you, we will—"

"Be delighted," cut in Lenore. "Where shall we stand?"

"Right next to me, Lenore, and, Myles, you stand next to Lenore."

Lenore stepped forward, but the duke stood still.

"Oh, Myles," said Lady Jersey, "don't be high in the instep—it's my birthday."

Lenore watched the duke and her eyes widened; he seemed to melt. His rigid body relaxed, his chin lowered, and he bowed. "Dear Lady Jersey—Sally—forgive me—the honor stuns me; I also suffer stage fright."

"Fudge! Hurry, people are arriving." The duke moved to Lenore's side. Sir William and Lady Bella Dickam were climbing the stairs. Lady Jersey welcomed the couple. "William, Bella, so glad you're here; you know my good friends—Myles and Lenore."

In the hollow instant that ensued was born the first of the struggles that were to threaten Lenore all evening—her urge to laugh. Sir William and Lady Bella stood, unable to move, each with eyes staring, chin dropped.

The silence lengthening, Lenore spoke. "It is pleasant to see you both." Lady Bella snapped her lips, bowed her head slightly, and glided into the ballroom; Sir William would have trod in her footsteps had not the duke said, "Bill, do you still race? I'd like to match my chestnuts against yours someday."

Sir William blinked and said sourly, "I don't race anymore, sir," and hastened to join his wife.

To each newcomer Lady Jersey repeated the words, "You remember my friends Myles and Lenore," or, if uncertain, "I desire you to meet my friends the Duke and Duchess of Asherwood."

With suppressed amusement Lenore noted the reactions of the members of the *ton* as they were confronted by the de trop, now comfortably under the sanction of the magnificent Lady Jersey. First the startled unbelief, succeeded by a spectrum of responses —a stiff bow, a muttered word, a relieved smile, a gush of released words, even a hug from one or two old friends.

The staircase became crowded, the ladies garbed and bejeweled in the pink of fashion; however, each quickly became aware she held not a candle to Lady Jersey and her favored guest.

Lady Jersey's ample figure was cleverly draped in green chiffon, lightened by the sparkle of diamonds. Lenore was in an Empire gown of scarlet silken velvet, the bodice cut low and filled with tiers of gossamer lace, the skirt flowing from the waist, the hem ringed in sable in a simple design of exquisite harmony. Many a lady sighed—snagged by the hook of feeling overdressed.

Lenore listened, astonished, as the duke, usually so taciturn, spoke pleasantly to those who came his way, often referring to past events involving the greeter and himself. Lenore was pleased. He is being cordial, she thought. Hoo, if only he would smile.

The duke wondered if he might not lose his mind as he wrestled to remember names and the past. Noting the ease of manner Lenore displayed he felt bitter —she is enjoying herself; this is the life she likes—God, that I were back in Asherwood—"Good evening, Lady Vaga." He stared into the pinched face of the nastiest old lady in London.

"Humph," growled Lady Vaga. "See you've got yourself another pretty one. Think you can hold on to this one?"

The duke said nothing.

When Lord Alfred Lanier and Lady Martha entered the great door of Lady Jersey's home, Lady Martha felt blue-deviled. The day before, her husband had brought home an unexpected guest, and had insisted she write a note to Lady Jersey requesting they might bring the gentleman to the ball.

"It is beyond permission to make such a request," Lady Martha had protested.

"Write the note, Martha," had been her husband's reply.

"But he is French!" cried her distracted ladyship.

"He is the Marquis de Chondefon, and concerning his country his sympathies are correct," said Sir Alfred coldly.

"What is your acquaintance, Alfred?"

"The marquis and I have corresponded over the years—now write, Martha." It was a command.

Later in the day the Lanier coachman returned with a note saying Lord Lanier's guest would be welcome at the ball. Martha's mind was relieved, but her unease did not lessen.

Dressing for the ball, she had given her abigail fits.

Donning a new gown fashioned by Madame Fanchon Martha studied her reflection and wanted to cry—the gown bespoke expense, but screamed dowdiness—too many ribbons, too much lace—grotesque. Furious, she forced her frightened maid to do her hair over three times before the poor girl received a "humph" of faint approval.

Being late, Lady Martha hurried down the stairs, pausing as she saw their guest. The marquis was clad in black satin from chest to heel. His white linen, cradling an enormous brooch of rubies, sapphires, and diamonds, dazzled her. That the marquis was slim, tall, and handsome with gleaming black hair, and of pronounced elegance, did not please Lady Martha— beside him her husband, as he presented the marquis, looked plump and frumpy in his white breeches and three-year-old yellow coat, and with his quizzing glass and heavy gold watch fob.

Bowing over her hand, the marquis said, "Lord Alfred, your lady will make many eyes turn this evening." Martha pondered his words during the drive to Lady Jersey's.

In the large entrance hall, awaiting her husband and the marquis, Lady Martha had a sense of dread, though she smiled and nodded to those near her. At last the marquis and Alfred stepped to her side, and the three began to make their way slowly up the stairs. Suddenly Lady Martha clutched her husband's arm. "I may faint," she hissed. "Look!" Alfred followed her nod and blinked, but before he could speak, Lady Jersey was extending her hand.

"Lord Alfred, Lady Martha, how nice of you to come."

His lordship recovered enough to kiss Lady Jersey's hand and to ask if he might present the Marquis de

Chondefon. Lady Jersey gave the Frenchman a long glance, then extended her fingertips to the man in black, who slowly kissed them, and said, "A lady as beautiful as she is gracious; thank you for allowing me to be in your presence on this occasion. Whatever your years, you belie them."

"You spin a fine phrase, sir." Lady Jersey laughed. "I want you to meet the Duke and Duchess of Asherwood."

Lenore, who had been watching the shaken Laniers, turned to the marquis, who gave a nod, then spoke to the duke. "Your Grace, by Jupiter, my luck holds; I had not expected to encounter you so soon upon my return"—the two men shook hands—"nor to have the added pleasure of meeting your duchess." His eyes blazed into Lenore's for an instant. "Myles, you are indeed a fortunate man."

"So Germany palled, Pierre?" said the duke.

"Rapidly! Duke, we must chat later. Now I retard the receiving line." He bowed and entered the ballroom.

Lenore started to ask the duke about the marquis, but heard her hostess say, "No need to introduce you, for you're long acquainted with my dear Lenore."

Sir Alfred found his voice. "Good evening, Lenore."

"Alfred, Martha." Lenore smiled. "I'm pleased to see you; I'd hoped to welcome you sooner at Grosvenor Square, but realize you are taken up with many duties. Myles, here are Martha and Alfred."

The duke frowned. "Good evening, Martha; good evening, Lanier; thanks for the blunt."

The expressed gratitude electrified his lordship into hurrying his wife into the ballroom.

"What blunt, Alfred?" asked Lady Martha as she was pushed.

"Never mind, I'll explain later."

Martha stopped as if she had encountered a wall—she had had more than enough—the marquis, the duke and duchess, and now this. "No, you will tell me now."

Versed in his Martha's moods, Alfred pled, "It's nothing, Martha," then sensing rejection, added, "I send a pittance each quarter to the duke to tend my grandmother's wants."

"A pittance? How much?" his lady demanded.

"Martha, we are at a ball, let us not discuss money."

"What amount, Alfred?" Her voice was low and strong.

Alfred sighed and named the correct sum—for Martha would unendingly seek the truth.

"What!" Lady Martha hissed, then a slow glittering smile lit her face. "I'm delighted to learn you can be so generous, Alfred; yes, I shall recall it in the future." With that, her ladyship whirled and approached the marquis. "Ah, dear Marquis, do allow me to present you to some of the lovely ladies here tonight; you will surely wish to dance when the music begins."

"Yes, but first I dance with you, Lady Martha, the other diamonds must wait."

Sir Hubert Wrenham, among the last to climb the stairs, caused Lady Jersey to clap her hands. "Now the dancing can begin; Wrenham always has my first dance pledged. Come, Lenore, Myles, join us for the set." Taking Wrenham's hand, she led the way to the center of the floor and signaled the musicians to play the opening bars.

Each step correct, each change executed perfectly, Lady Jersey's set drew admiring glances.

"Myles," said Lenore, "you dance as if born to it."

The duke made no response.

When the music ceased, Lady Jersey smiled. "Wrenham is a splendid partner, but, Myles, you've not forgotten your dancing skill—a charming set. Oh, dear, I must mingle—do enjoy yourselves."

"Wrenham, is there a card room?" asked the duke. "I could sustain a brandy and a rubber of whist."

"Later, Myles," Wrenham answered absently. "Sally prefers we dance awhile—ah, Miss Codswell is free—excuse me."

"Don't you like to dance?" asked Lenore.

"No," said the duke.

"Sad. Come, we must converse with Martha and Alfred."

"Good Lord, why?"

"Because Mamère wishes to see Alfred and frets because he has not come near since her return—oh, I know she calls him the Twiddlepoop, but he is her grandson." As she spoke Lenore walked across the room and the duke followed.

Lady Martha, her spirits lifted—the marquis had not only danced with elegance, but had given her compliments on her grace and lightness—commented, "Alfred, all men should learn to dance as does the marquis."

"If all men were as idle as the marquis, they too could dance like fripples."

"Good heavens, it's them." Martha held up her fan to cover her comment.

"Keep your tongue gentle, Martha," admonished Alfred as he rose to offer Lenore his chair.

"Martha, Alfred"—Lenore ignored the chair—"I'm aware you have obligations and invitations, but Mamère, your grandmother, misses you; I hope you will soon visit her."

"How is she?" asked Alfred.

"Other than aches caused by the wretched weather, she is well."

"Snappish as ever, I presume," commented Lady Martha.

Lenore laughed. "Indeed so, but adored. She draws like a magnet—legions of friends march to see her."

"House is like a club," muttered the duke.

"Really," said Alfred. "If she's a burden—"

"Didn't say that!" the duke retorted.

"No, but if she—"

"Livens up the place," the duke announced. "Never know whom I'll meet; one old boggard almost called me out the other day when I tried to give him an assist up the stairs."

"Truly, Duke," Lady Martha expounded, "I'm surprised at your patience. I, myself, can't abide a person who is almost booked." The lady shuddered.

"Then it is to be hoped that you acquire age slowly," said the duke, walking away.

"Alfred, what did he mean?" whined Lady Martha.

Lenore said hastily, "Alfred, come and see your grandmother; it would please her. Bring the children, Martha. Good night." Lenore left Alfred to deal with his wife.

Lady Jersey moved from group to group, exchanging a word or two with each guest. She was listening to Lady Vaga scolding her for her misguided friendship with the duke and his latest when a voice whispered into her ear, "Dear lady, let us waltz."

Startled, she swung and recognized the marquis, his glance full of mischief.

"It is an unseemly dance," she muttered under Lady Vaga's carrying tone.

"Lady Jersey," said the marquis in a voice loud enough to cause the chatter around them to cease, "you have a guest in dire need of your attention; may I escort you to where you are so wanted?" The marquis presented his arm.

"Excuse me, Lady Vaga." Lady Jersey allowed the Frenchman to lead her to a quiet corner.

"Who needs me?" inquired Lady Jersey.

"I do," replied the marquis.

"You are in perfect health as far as my eyes tell me; what afflicts you?" The lady, glad to be free of Lady Vaga, was amused.

"Dear lady, I yearn to waltz!"

"Sir," Lady Jersey said haughtily, "you are bold; I do not indulge in such a low dance."

"Fustian, sweetest Lady, do not gull me, nor proclaim that in your travels you did not waltz—my ears would disbelieve you."

Lady Jersey, who had not only learned to waltz, but loved the lilt of the music, studied the marquis, who smiled with quirked eyebrow.

"Sir, your audacity tempts me." She looked around the room at her guests. It will throw them into spasms, she concluded, but what better time than tonight. To the marquis she said, "The musicians may not know the music."

"Madam, you cannot conceive I would ask this delicious favor if I had not, with foresight, laid my plays. When I raise my forefinger, there will be angelic music enough for even you—come!"

"You are outrageous, sir," vowed her ladyship, but placed her hand on his sleeve and moved with him to the center of the floor.

On the opening chords of the strange rhythm, guests paused to see what their hostess planned—what they saw made them gasp.

In the center of the room, facing Lady Jersey, the

marquis bowed, placed one arm around his hostess's waist, raised high his opened hand, into which Lady Jersey tucked her own, and rested her free hand on his shoulder. To the music, the couple began to glide— there was a stunned silence—Lady Jersey was waltzing!

"The waltz!"—"She's waltzing!" hissed throughout the room as the pair revolved gracefully, quickening their steps as the beat grew faster.

"Beautiful, beautiful," murmured the marquis.

"Shocking, shocking," replied his partner, who followed his intricate whirls with pleasure.

The chatter, at first subdued, rose as the onlookers found voice: "Deplorable . . . delicious . . . charming . . . never would I . . . I wish I . . ."

"Shameless! A dance for Haymarket wares," Lady Vaga proclaimed shrilly, adding, "No genteel young lady should be permitted to see such devil's doings," a remark that caused two mothers to drag protesting daughters from the room.

The duke, noting quizzing glasses raised and heads shaking, whispered to Lenore, "Do you, among your other accomplishments, waltz?"

"Yes, indeed!" replied Lenore brightly.

"Wrenham," ordered the duke in a preemptory tone, "find yourself a partner," then slipped his arm around Lenore's waist and glided onto the floor.

Wrenham, with a grin, encircled the young lady standing next to him and waltzed away so quickly she had no time to demur. He was in luck, for Miss Welton had been—in secret—learning the forbidden dance from her brother, Captain Welton, and made no misstep in Wrenham's clasp.

"Captain Welton," cried a young lady in a pained voice, "your sister is waltzing!"

"Jupiter, so she is!" he said, and immediately sought his fiancée to march her onto the floor.

Suddenly a few parents were given an unexpected comeuppance as they saw their sons and daughters entwine members of the opposite sex and whirl to the lively music, seemingly as if they had waltzed from the time they were in leading strings.

Lady Welton had the presence of mind to faint.

When the music stopped, Lady Jersey was surrounded by young people who thanked her for breaking the taboo against the dance they had practiced in hiding for months. Lady Jersey laughed and went to face those not so kindly disposed.

"Myles," said Lenore, fanning herself, "you waltz like a dancing master."

"Madam, where did you acquire the steps so perfectly?"

"On the Penn. There's Lily Chiswick—let's go chat with her."

"You may; I'm going to play whist." The duke escorted Lenore, bowed to Lady Lily, and after seeing the ladies seated, moved to the card room.

"Oh, Lenore, what an elegant gentleman your duke is," Lady Lily said, sighing. "It must be heaven to be a duchess."

"Now, Lily, you've loved Tommy Chiswick since you both were in bibs."

"I suppose so, but he cannot waltz, and vows he will not learn." Lady Lily pouted.

"He will." Lenore laughed, then said, "How are your children—there are five now . . . ?"

"Six." Then Lady Lily embarked on the history of each, ranging from the youngest to the eldest. Lenore listened, but during the description of a bout of measles, she became aware that the Marquis de Chondefon, no matter where he moved to chat with others, had eyes only for her. He did not dance, but moving from group to group, edged nearer. Agitated, Lenore spied Lord Wrenham. Jumping up, she said, "Lily, I'm promised for this dance," and rushed away, leaving Lady Lily openmouthed in the middle of a fascinating account of her Tommy's broken leg.

Wrenham, pinned by Lady Greenshot and her homely daughter, was flustered at his deliverance.

"Lord Wrenham, have you forgotten you asked me for this dance?" Lenore laid her hand on his arm.

"Er—what?—oh, yes, certainly, certainly, Your Grace—stupid thing for me to do—our dance, of course." He bowed to his captors, and escorted Lenore to their place in a set. At his first opportunity he inquired, "Did I ask you to dance, Duchess?"

"Of course not, silly, I just wanted to get away from"—Lenore caught herself—"a bore." To herself she said, Forgive me, Lily. . . .

Lord Wrenham's brow cleared. "Oh, good, for a minute I feared I was aging—bad memory—senile—that sort of thing. And I thank you; Lady Greenshot teetered on the edge of pushing that gel of hers into my arms. It caps the globe the way mothers are always trying to make me dance with their plainer daughters. Why is it, do you suppose?"

"Because you're so kind—you do as bid."

"Flummery." Wrenham stepped back for a bow.

The dance over, Lenore returned to Lady Lily and apologized for the interruption, which proved not to be one; Lady Lily took up her tale exactly where she had left off, telling the penitent Lenore the full details of Tommy's broken ankle.

There were other cuts into the monologue; guests

joined the ladies to say a few words; some, who had been most haughty in the receiving line, had decided that the duchess might be worth at least a probe of her civility.

"Time for supper." The duke and Tommy Chiswick stepped before their ladies.

"Tommy, you've lost a goodly sum at whist; I can tell—your eyes squint!"

"A fairish amount, my love, but not to be worried about; would have lost more if the duke hadn't been my partner for the last rubber. Myles, you are beyond anything great at whist."

On that note the party went down the stairs for supper. As the gentlemen sought plates of lobster and garnishments, Lenore gazed around the supper room, then relaxed—the marquis, his back to her, was seated opposite Lady Jersey.

Her relief was short-lived; when the parties entered the ballroom, Lady Jersey brought the marquis to Lenore and the duke.

"Myles," Lady Jersey announced, "we are to have another waltz—this one I wish you to dance with me. Lenore cannot mind, for I have brought her the finest waltzer present—outside yourself, of course—as her partner, if she so chooses." Lady Jersey took the duke's arm and signaled the musicians to play, then faced the duke, who waltzed her away.

Lenore did not glance at the marquis, who teased, "Oh, to think that I must acknowledge the presence of a man in black who stares me out of countenance . . . why does he do so?" The words so paralleled her thoughts that Lenore winced inwardly.

"You are mistaken, sir, I—"

"Careful, Your Grace, you do not want to tell a bouncer."

"I think we should dance," said Lenore firmly.

"And leave the question to burn in your mind all night—unfair—let us sit and chat." He led her to a sofa. "I stare at you, Your Grace, because your beauty entraps my eyes."

"Fustian, this room is full of diamonds."

"Whose eyes are as empty as the stones, whereas yours are full of warmth and intelligence."

"I will not listen to you!" Lenore whispered.

"Why not? Ladies like to be told they're beautiful. *Mais, oui,* you fear I may have a tendre for you and you do not wish to be disloyal to your splendid duke."

"Sir, I must leave you." Lenore started to rise.

"I have no tendre for you, Your Grace; please sit down."

"You confuse me," admitted Lenore. "Why have you made me uncomfortable all evening?"

"*Mon Dieu,* I had no such desire; I admire loveliness." He shrugged. "I presume it's because I'm French."

"Are you aware that my husband was killed at the Penn?" Lenore asked tartly.

"Eric? Yes, and I lament it bitterly—Eric and I were close friends at one time."

"How can that be?" asked Lenore. "He never spoke of you."

"He called me Pierre."

"Pierre? Not Pierre, *le parfait?*" Lenore stared at the marquis.

"*Oui,* he used the name sometimes."

"Why, Eric often said to me, 'If Pierre were here, he could do—this or that'; or, 'What would Pierre *le parfait* do now?'" Indeed so, Marquis; in a way I know you well."

"*Bon,* so now we can be friends." The marquis smiled.

"Yes, but you must not stare at me."

"My dear Duchess, I'm not sure I can submit to such a cruel deprivation, but"—the marquis sighed— "I will try."

"Silly." Lenore laughed and rose. "Let us finish the waltz; I confess my envy of Lady Jersey when you danced together."

The duke, at first annoyed by being the cynosure of Lady Jersey's guests' attention, experienced a sting of abandonment when Lenore and the marquis captured the heed of the assemblage.

"Your little duchess glows, Myles . . . don't scowl at me—you will have to live with the fact that Lenore lights up any room she enters." Lady Jersey smiled up at the duke, his face so near to her own.

"I shall count it one of my blessings," said the duke dryly, and swung his partner into a spin as the music played its final flourish.

When the music stilled, the marquis held Lenore for an instant. "Friends?" Lenore nodded and stepped away. The marquis extended his arm. "*Tiens,* please then call me Pierre." He escorted her to Lady Jersey and the duke.

"Lenore, Marquis." Lady Jersey smiled. "Myles and I turned quite green when you joined the dancing. Ah, Wrenham, you appear on time for the last set. Come, Lenore, Myles, we'll make the set; Marquis, find yourself a diamond."

"I already have done so, but she deserts me for— for—" The marquis eyed Wrenham sternly as he sought words, then he shrugged, saying, "Later, charming lady," and moved away.

Lenore offered her thanks and good-nights to Lady

Jersey, who whispered in her ear, "Lenore, you are turning the duke up sweet, bless you!"

During the drive home Lenore, lulled by the motion of the carriage, let her head fall back. She dozed.

The duke, reviewing the night's events, took satisfaction in the invitation proffered by Chiswick to meet at Brooks the next evening.

At the turn of a corner, Lenore's head rolled gently, coming to rest on the duke's shoulder. His first impulse was to wake his duchess, but looking down into her face, pale and quiet, he paused. She must be weary; God knows I am. He continued his musing on Lady Jersey's remark. "The little duchess is in the Asherwood tradition, Myles; intellect above all."

Her words alleviated some of the pain he had felt for years concerning his marriage to the rattlebox Harriet. However, remembering his response to the lady's comment, he frowned. "Thank you, Sally, and she is beautiful too." What madness made him utter those words? He bent to look at the sleeping Lenore and sighed; it could not be denied, his duchess was lovely.

The wheel of the carriage rolled over a stone and Lenore woke. Startled, she peered up at the duke. For an instant she gazed into his eyes, then she jerked her head and sat up straight. Feeling a blush rush to her face, she said, "Myles, I fell asleep. I'm sorry."

For no reason he could explain, the duke was angered. "It is all right," he said icily and did not speak again.

When the footman handed Lenore down at the door, she gave a smothered good night, running up the stairs to her room before the duke entered the house.

"Females," muttered the duke, in dudgeon, as Clough helped him to retire.

42

For Lenore the next day passed in a bustle. Rising later than usual, she had dutifully gone to Mamère's room to describe the ball. After a few sentences, she was interrupted by the sound of a heavy crash outside the door. Rushing to the hall, she found the workmen had accidentally dropped a statue taken from its niche—it lay in pieces.

She ran back to Mamère. "Good Lord, the men have dropped and broken a statue."

"Splendid!" commented Mamère.

"But they are works of art."

Mamère laid her claim as a critic. "Ugly as sin, by third-rate sculptors—rubbishy—good riddance."

"Oh dear, Myles—"

"Wouldn't have been done if he hadn't ordered it, and don't you go cluntering in with any missish sentiment."

Further discussion was stemmed by the appearance of Abel, who announced, "The Twiddlepoop is downstairs."

"Abel!" remonstrated Lenore. "That is no way to speak of Sir Alfred."

"How did you know his name, ma'am?" asked Abel.

The expression on Lenore's face sent Mamère into chortles. "Abel, I'll see him presently; Lenore, get me up and give me my oldest robe and shawl; don't want the nip farthing to think I'm cosseted or he'll cut my jointure."

"Nonsense—he'll think the duke's hard-fisted and dibs you of your blunt."

"Oh—my best outfit then. Did you or Bunky build a fire under him last night?" asked Mamère as she leaned on Lenore's arm and walked to her favorite chair.

"I explained I hoped he, Martha, and the children would call."

"Wagfeather, you know I don't want to see the fubsy-faced Martha or her brats, though I may when the young ones are older. Do you always have to wrap everything in clean linen?"

"Mamère, I'm sure their feelings about visits and yours are two halfpennies in a purse."

"Pert, ain't you, Duchess?" snapped Madame Lanier.

Lenore whirled, and picking up a shawl from the closet shelf, placed it around the old lady's shoulders. Mamère caught Lenore's hand. "Forgive me, child, for I love you more than tongue can tell."

Lenore kissed Mamère's cheek and said, "Then, you wicked old lady, be nice to the Twiddlepoop," and took her leave.

43

The duke, startled from sleep by a heavy crash, rang for Clough.

"What was that noise—it woke me."

"I'm sorry, Your Grace, one of the statues fell as the men were removing them."

"Flippery fellows—tell them to have a care. I'd like my breakfast."

"Immediately, Your Grace." Clough lit the fire as he spoke. "Shall I send Fenwick to help you dress?"

"I'll dress later." The duke lay back, watching the glowing flames, his thoughts on Lady Jersey's ball. Was it a success or failure? Certainly most were friendly—Wrenham, Chiswick, the men in the card room. Every time I spied Lenore when she was not dancing, she was amidst a crowd of ladies. The duke frowned. What devilish impulse made me waltz—I behaved like a Bond Street dandy. The duke threw off the bedclothes, donned his dressing robe of red velvet, and flung himself into a chair beside the fire.

Clough returned with the breakfast tray. "Your Grace, here are some notes brought by coachmen; the post has not come." He laid a pile of various-size envelopes on the tray.

"Slit them open for me, Clough; I'll read them after

I eat." Clough did as bidden, then stood behind the duke's chair.

Eyeing the stack as he drank his coffee, the duke lifted the top note, perused its contents, then hastily read the others. When he had finished, he sighed.

"Good news, Your Grace?"

"Very, Clough." The duke rose. "First my bath—I'll wear my blue superfine today."

Dressed, the duke told Clough to request the duchess to come to the library. Leaving his room by the main hall, he watched the workmen for a few minutes, then started downstairs to be met by an onrush of boys racing up the steps.

"Good morning, Duke"—"Hello, Your Grace." The boys slowed slightly to make passage for him, then sped up the remaining stairs. Good God, what is this? The duke looked up to see the boys enter his sons' study. Continuing, he passed the morning room door and heard his name called; peering into the dark room, he saw Sir Alfred.

"Good morning, Alfred; have you come to see your grandmother?"

"Yes, but I'm glad to see you, Myles. Last night there was no time to congratulate you on your marriage to Lenore."

"Thank you." The duke nodded.

"I do confess, however, I was bowled out when Lenore's note reached me, and Martha was even more surprised when she read your announcement in *The Gazette*."

"I'm sure you were."

"Not, of course, as to why Lenore wished to wed you—plain as a pikestaff—but why you, Myles, would get tenanted for life to Eric's widow"—Sir Alfred shrugged—"leave Asherwood, set up this household—all an astonishment."

The duke's eyes glittered. "Could it be conceived that I had a tendre for Lenore?"

"Oh, Myles, come now! I've known you since we were in shortcoats. I watched you head over tail for Harriet Featherheath, then later, after her didos, flee from England, and later still, burnt in the socket, pop into a clam shell and snap it shut. Don't try to cozen me that you cast your ogles on Lenore and—bang—burst like a skyrocket over London for love. Do you take me for a Johnny Raw?"

"Alfred, the history of Asherwood has been plain—when a duke meets an incomparable, he weds her if he can."

"Oh, I've heard the Gothic tales, but Lenore is far beneath your touch."

"Eric did not think her beneath his," said the duke mildly.

"Eric was a dashed fool. Martha and I tried to cozen him against getting buckled to a country miss without a feather—"

"To fly with," the duke cut in, "poor—the besetting sin for you and Martha; but for me a trifle of no account."

Sir Alfred shrugged. "Well, her beauty may have caught you, just as it did Eric, but to come to London—why? You have always hated—"

"Alfred." The duke pinned him with his eyes. "When your sons, and all the distaff members of one's household, yearn for a season in London, a wise head capitulates."

"Now you're talking about my grandmother."

"Her boredom at Willowood lent a note to the orchestration."

"You're a bigger fool than I'd have wagered if you let her allow to weigh in the pleadings."

"Pleadings?" the duke growled. "She never mentioned coming to London, or her unhappiness at Willowood; I gleaned it during our talks."

"Talks? Don't tell me you can converse with her; all I get is put-downs and rough snubs; it's why I visit rarely."

"Really." The duke studied Sir Alfred. "Perhaps you don't have the secret of chatter with ancients."

"What's that?"

The duke took a deep breath. "You ask the aged about the past."

"Hoo, I'm not interested in the doings of long ago."

"No, but the old are. Ask your grandmother about the bygone days; you may find the past—er—enlightening."

"Hm-m, maybe I will try a question or two; might stop her ringing peels over my head."

"More than likely." The duke rose. "You will excuse me, I've business I must tend." He bowed and left the room.

Alfred thought over his conversation with the duke —Maybe Myles was right—ask about the dim, dark days, listen carefully—maybe Grandmother wouldn't find me such a dull fellow after all.

Lenore interrupted his musings. "Good morning, Alfred, Mamère will see you now. I'm sorry you had to wait so long, but she wanted to appear her best for you. Abel will show you the way."

"Thank you, Lenore—er—Martha sent her good wishes and hopes she will see you soon."

What a bouncer, Lenore thought as she led Alfred to the hall where Abel waited. Proceeding to the library, she was surprised by the duke's greeting. Holding envelopes spread like cards he said, "In front of you, Lenore, behold seven invitations from members of the pink of the *ton*."

He has forgotten his attitude of the night before, Lenore concluded, and said coldly, "I'm sure they are gratifying to you."

"These were delivered by hand; I'm of the belief the post will bring more."

"I sincerely hope so." Lenore's voice drew the duke's attention.

"Aren't you pleased? You should be, it was your ingenious plays that brought the *ton* around."

"I'm glad if you are set up."

"It means we can entertain," the duke expounded. "We can start with a rout, then perhaps a Venetian breakfast."

"I don't see how; the holidays are nearly upon us and the morning room is not yet begun."

The duke glowered. "You don't let Lady Jersey's prattle signify, do you?"

"Of course, hers is an excellent suggestion—the room is depressing beyond belief. You yourself said you hated—"

"I said I disliked the portraits, but they can be removed and the new paintings hung—Why are you shaking your head?"

"Because the portraits have been there for heaven knows how long; the walls must be badly marked."

"Then we will entertain and leave all as is." The duke dismissed the whole redoing with a wave of his hand.

"We cannot invite guests until the room is lightened."

"Madam," roared the duke, "Madame Lanier can turn my house into a gaming hell; Heath and Charles can inundate us with young varmints; but *I* cannot have my friends unless I spend a fortune to redecorate half my house?"

Lenore spoke quietly. "To ignore Lady Jersey's wish would be uncivil—she has been a dear friend."

The duke glared at the duchess.

Lenore nodded. "Send for Mr. Foster today; make your plans, and begin work as soon as possible; then after the holidays we can entertain every day if you wish."

"I'll be bound if I'll send for Foster. Damme, I've no time for such nonsense; I'm busy for the next sennight."

Lenore waited.

"What a coil; females bullocking a man to go against his pluck. Well, I wash my hands of it—you deal with Foster!"

He was surprised to see his duchess's face light up. "Oh, Myles, could I? I never have, you know—and to think you would trust me to redo—"

"Lenore, you pass all bounds; you come in here sunk in dismals, and now—"

"Myles, all my life I've wanted to beautify—I can visualize exactly—"

"Best listen to Foster, he's—"

"Oh, I will." Lenore rose. "I'm going to study the room. Will you send for Mr. Foster, please?" She started for the door. "I've only a moment or two; I have to go shopping."

"What about the invitations?" The duke picked them up.

"Accept those you wish, Myles," Lenore replied lightly.

Throwing open the doors of the morning room, Lenore frowned at its darkness. It must be a light room—it must be. Standing below the paintings, Lenore cocked her head—you, gentlemen, will be banished, your stags, horses and dogs with you. She touched one of the almost-black velvet draperies. How long have you hung guard at the windows? You deserve a rest. Glancing at the tall clock in the corner, Lenore spoke aloud, "You, clock, have the only touch of welcome here; you may remain—Oh, glory, are you telling the correct time? I must fly. Maria and Henderson will freeze."

Running upstairs to her room, Lenore gathered her bonnet, cape, and reticule, and started down the steps, stopping on seeing Alfred clinging to the broad railing as if he feared falling.

"Alfred! Are you ill? You look as if you have seen a ghost."

"I have just seen Grandmother," Sir Alfred said in a hoarse whisper.

"Is she ill?" Lenore felt alarm.

"Oh, no, not she—I. Has she ever"—he fumbled for a word—"reminisced with you?"

Lenore laughed. "She's been recounting her wicked stories."

Sir Alfred shuddered. "She used words I did not know the meaning of—then explained them."

Noting his ashen face, Lenore touched his hand. "Alfred, you're shaking; come to the morning room, there is a fire." Seeing Charles come out of the study, she called, "Charles, bring me the coverlet that's on the chair in my room, please." She took Sir Alfred's arm. "Come."

"I must leave." Sir Alfred took a tentative step.

"Not until you have a warming drink—"

"God, no, Grandmother plied me with brandy—I'm quite bosky."

"Then do come and rest." Lenore urged him slowly down the stairs. She saw the footman enter the hall. "Fenwick, tell Henderson I'm delayed."

"No! Fenwick, just help me to my carriage." Sir Alfred, now at the foot of the stairs, stood erect and walked stiff-legged to the door.

Fenwick and Lenore saw Sir Alfred safe in his carriage. Forgetting Charles, Lenore entered her own waiting carriage and ordered Henderson to take her to the Pantheon Bazaar.

Charles, impatient to return to the study, hurried into Lenore's room, snatched the fringed coverlet from the back of the chair, and swung to leave. The shawl resisted, and turning back to find the trouble, Charles froze. Before him the wall beside the fireplace was moving, making an ever-widening gap. Terrified, Charles dropped the shawl, screamed, and tried to run, but his feet tangled in the coverlet and he fell forward.

Heart pounding, eyes shut tight, he lay awaiting his fate—a boggard—no, Bro says there are no ghosts— a man with a knife!—Why is he so quiet? I'm going to have to look—there'll be a skeleton, I know it; Father is a duke. Lifting an eyelid and twisting his head, Charles saw a stair tread. Getting to his knees, he viewed a second step. Untangling the shawl, he stood, then peered into the opening. Jackawarts, it's only an old flight of stairs going to the ceiling. Picking up the hanging end of the shawl, he found that the fringe had caught on a node of the carving that decorated the fireplace. Disengaging the fringe, he pushed the node—the stem of a bunch of marble grapes—and the door slid closed.

Whee—a secret staircase! He pulled the stem and again the wall slid aside. Where does it go? I'll bet there's a room up there full of jewels and gold hidden by a pirate, I'll bet! Tempted to venture through the wall, Charles put his foot on the lower step, then quickly withdrew it. What if the wall closed? I could holler and scream and no one would hear me. Imagining himself in the dark, his heart raced. I'd rot away and no one would ever find me, even Mother—Oh, the shawl! He pushed the node in place, snatched up the cause of his discovery, and ran from the room.

But the duchess had gone. Charles returned to replace the shawl. He tested the wall, then ran to the study to tell Heath of his discovery, but the room crowded with boys made him decide to wait until he had Heath alone.

At the Bazaar Lenore and Maria left Henderson and entered a shop. Lenore's Christmas list ran no great length; it was the duke's custom to distribute largess to his household, so she felt no need other than to select the presents she wished to give, bought by monies from her own tiny income.

A Jobba shawl for Mamère, a frilled shirt for Heath, two games—speculation and a new jackstraws—for Charles were soon purchased, as well as one gift the duke had requested she select—a bracelet for Lady Jersey.

In the jewelry shop Lenore lingered over a tray of gold bracelets, eager to find one that she thought would please Lady Jersey. One by one she held the delicate chains aloft, finally choosing two she felt worthy. She slipped one on her wrist.

"Precisely, Your Grace—perfect." The marquis stood at her elbow, smiling down on her.

"Hoy, sir, how can you know? Good morning."

"Any lady of taste would adore the trinket." The

marquis picked up her hand and studied the linked chain.

"I also like it, and succumb to your judgment," said Lenore, smiling.

"Your wrist will enhance it, dear Duchess."

"Oh, the bracelet is not for me," Lenore said hastily, slipping the chain from her arm.

"Alas, its charms are dimmed already."

"It's for Lady Jersey." Lenore nodded to the clerk.

"Ah, the dear lady will welcome such a gift."

Lenore rose and arranged the purchase, then turning to the marquis, resplendent in his deep-blue greatcoat, said, "Now, may I assist you in selecting—"

"My dear Duchess, I plan no shopping. A moment ago as I passed, I saw the fairest lady of them all in a dilemma—gallantry bade me enter." The marquis bowed.

"Fustian," said Lenore, laughing, as she accepted her package from the clerk.

"Duchess, complete boredom drove me into the cold; to encounter you is exquisite deliverance. May I join you on your rounds so my life will be sweet again—can I be of service to you?"

"Not unless you can suggest a pleasing gift for the duke."

"Your Grace, a Herculean labor you set me."

"Indeed so—it has plagued me for weeks."

The marquis waved his hand. "A jeweled fob for his waistcoat."

Lenore chuckled. "He would ask me if I thought him a London nob."

"Ah, jewels and quizzing glasses wiped out in a swoop. A cane, perchance?"

"You think me dwindling into the grave, madam?"
Lenore imitated the duke's growl.

"*Mais, oui;* then, of course, you must buy him a
charging steed."

Lenore laughed. "He would then be certain that I
had flown into alt. No, it must be of a simple nature."

"Difficult . . . difficult . . ." The marquis put his
finger to his lips in thought. "Ah, a book—the duke
does read?" Seeing Lenore frown, he said quickly,
"No, no, no, I mean—His Grace enjoys books, journals, periodicals?"

"Yes, he spends hours over them." Lenore smiled
again.

"Then a book is to be considered seriously. Fortune
rains upon us; there is a shop around the corner
—Tollands, small but select; we can walk."

Leaving the jewelry shop, Lenore dismissed Maria
with instructions that she and Henderson follow. The
marquis offered Lenore his arm and she, fearing the
strong wind that threatened to blow her away, took
it.

Tollands, small, dark, crowded with tables, each
covered with the widest choice of reading materials,
delighted Lenore. The marquis led her first to the
tiny fireplace.

"Because the selection of a book for the duke is of
high import, dear Duchess, allow me to ask a few
questions."

"No romances; novels are eliminated immediately."

"Do you not approve of them?"

"Oh, yes, I rather enjoy them—but the duke . . ."
Lenore shook her head.

"Quite so." The marquis became serious. "Does
he like opera. Or opera singers?"

"Heavens, no; he goes, but most reluctantly."

"Art?"

"Ye-es," replied Lenore, "but he prefers to perceive rather than read."

"Understandable. Does he read French books?"

"He reads French; why do you ask?"

"There are many books on the revolution; one might interest him."

"I doubt it; he evinces little interest in politics."

The marquis stared at her. "You surprise me; having lived in France, I'd think him piqued by her woes."

"He is far more concerned with the troubles of England—so harsh, since the embargo."

"Ah, the dreadful presumer—emperor of France indeed"—the marquis's voice dropped to a whisper— "the duke must despise him."

"I have no idea; we do not speak of affairs abroad." Lenore moved to the tables.

"I am an imbecile! You wish to find a book and I speak of the unspeakable. Pardon! Allow me to go to Mr. Tolland and elicit his aid in our pursuit." The marquis left.

Lenore began reading titles—either of no appeal or already on the duke's shelves.

He buys so many, thought Lenore as she moved from display to display: Byron, Shelley . . . he has the poets . . . Shakespeare? An entire shelf, she knew, was devoted to his works. Passing a table of second-hand books, she glanced at a book, then paused— Newton's *Principia*—ah, science. She picked up the worn copy and opened its cover. Casually she read the handwritten inscription, then stared at the cramped script—it can't be! She moved to the dingy window and reread the faded writing:

To my dear friend Edmund Halley
With deep gratitude and affection,
               Isaac Newton

Lenore stood stunned. Could it be that the shop-keeper did not realize what a rarity he had? It's priceless! She noted the modest sum penciled in the corner. Incredible!—I must inform Mr. Tolland. She went to the back of the shop, where in a glassed cage, the marquis conversed with another man, elderly and bent. Lenore knocked on the small glass window; they did not seem to hear. She rapped harder and finally the old man, whom she presumed to be Mr. Tolland, scowled at her through thick spectacles. "Open the window, please," said Lenore.

"Madam, don't you see that I am engaged with this gentleman?"

"I'm sorry, but I have found a book of great worth and think you should be told." She tried to hand the book through the opening only to have it pushed back to her.

"But, Mr. Tolland, it is a signed copy of Newton's *Principia!*"

"Ha, science, dry as dust—even signed it's worthless. Now please leave the gentleman and myself to our—"

"Mr. Tolland, I wish to purchase this book, but think it is—" Lenore pleaded.

"Then find my lazy helper and pay him; if you plan to fret, pay him an extra pound—Cliffy!" the old man shouted and slammed the window.

Baffled, Lenore looked at the marquis, who had watched the exchange with amusement. Seeing him nod, she turned to face the scrubby boy who seemed to spring from nowhere.

Lenore paid him, adding the extra pound. She felt a surge of happiness. What good luck, finding such an unusual gift—Myles will be surprised. Tucking the package in her reticule, she wished the marquis would hurry; she wanted to go home to study the treasure. When the marquis appeared, she exclaimed, "Marquis, I'm overcome with gratitude for your bringing me here. Did you ever hear of such a felicity? I wonder if Mr. Tolland is queer in the attic—selling this wonder so cheaply?"

"Dear Duchess, I am overjoyed for you."

Lenore started for the door. "I must leave." She stopped. "Marquis, you did not have anything to do with—no, you couldn't have—forgive me."

"No, Your Grace, I had nothing to do with your transaction, but you were not alone in receiving the smiles of the gods. Stacked in Tolland's office are some new books not as yet to be sold. One title intrigued me, for it bespeaks your character." The marquis drew from his coat a book and handed it to Lenore.

"*Sense and Sensibility,*" Lenore read aloud and laughed. "Sir, you flatter me. Hmm, written by Jane Austen—I've never heard of her."

"A new author, the old man told me; in fact the book is not supposed to go on display at this time; I had a hard time wheedling him."

Lenore held out her hand. "Sir, I am doubly in your debt. Thank you for the book—*Sense and Sensibility,* an intriguing title. Can I drive you anywhere?" They went into the cold.

"No, dear Duchess, I must return to Sir Alfred's. Tonight I'll have the pleasure of seeing the duke at Brooks's. Do not be fearful; I will keep your literary secret."

"Silly, you wouldn't play me such a bobbery as to tattle."

"No, but there is one condition, Your Grace."

"Sir, you threaten me?" Lenore laughed.

"Exactly. I shall expose your trickery unless you call me Pierre."

"A shocking toll, sir; thank you and good-bye, Pierre." Lenore let the marquis hand her into the carriage.

Excited by her purchase, Lenore gave no further thought to the marquis. At last in her room, almost frightened that the inscription might have disappeared, she opened the *Principia* and leafed through the pages, then, reassured, hid the book under her jewel box.

Entering the dining room for dinner, she was surprised to find not only the boys and Doctor Sylvester but the duke awaiting her. When the footman had finished placing the bowls of Flemish soup around the table, she said, "Myles, I thought you were going to Brooks's tonight."

"I am, later; how did you know?"

"Why, I—er—I ran into the marquis while I shopped, and he told me he expected to see you there tonight." Lenore felt color creep into her face.

"So you are already developing a cicisbeo." The duke was unaware that for the first time he was teasing his duchess.

"Not fair, Myles." Lenore sensed she was developing a true blush. "The marquis, by chance, saw me in the jewelry shop and came in."

"And did he, by chance, of course, buy Your Grace a pretty bauble?" The duke was annoyed at her discomfort.

"Myles, that is an outrageous question." Lenore's

anger added color to her blush. "I was selecting a bracelet for Lady Jersey and he merely helped me in my choice."

In mounting anger the duke said, "The marquis is either a gentleman or a nipfarthing; few who dangle after a duchess would not insist on an ever-so-tiny token in appreciation of her beauty—an amazing lack of civility."

Lenore bit her lip. She did not dare reveal that the marquis had given her a book—so innocent when she had accepted it, and now proclaimed the play of an accomplished flirt. *If I tell him, he will demand to know what I was doing in Tollands.*

What is she hiding from me? wondered the duke. *Why is she in fidgets? Good God, is she—always the properly behaved, the open of countenance—changing?*

The duke, forgetting his grandmother, reminded himself that the Duchesses of Asherwood do not indulge in cartes blanches; it is beneath them. "What is it, Charles?" His voice was harsh.

"Father," Charles asked for the third time, "does this house have a secret room?"

For an instant the duke did not absorb Charles's meaning, but finally said, "Certainly not. What put that loose-screw notion into your head?"

Charles had prepared for the question. "I read a tale the other day about an old house and wondered—"

"Doctor Sylvester," the duke interrupted, "with a large library at your disposal, is there nothing better for my son to read?"

Taken aback, the doctor exclaimed, "Your Grace—"

Charles jumped in. "I saw the story in *The Morning Post Gazette,* Father; it was about a house in Ireland."

"Ireland and England are two different places, Charles," the duke said stiffly. "I know of no secret rooms here or in Asherwood."

"Thank you, Father." Charles returned to his dinner.

Heath regarded his brother and thought, You've been subdued all day, little Brother; we will have a chat tonight.

Glancing at the duchess, who had paled, the duke saw she ate almost nothing and decided he would make a point of seeing the marquis at Brooks's.

Lenore, hearing little of what Charles and the others had said, wondered why she had permitted the duke's words to put her in such a taking. She had done nothing amiss, her only crime deceiving Myles about the book, but only in the attempt to prevent his learning of her gift. I'm pudding-hearted for nothing. The marquis has no tendre for me and I love only Myles. She glanced at the duke and caught him frowning at her. My, he is in hips about Pierre—maybe it is a good omen! Cheered, she ate a large piece of damson pie and determined to start reading the novel *Sense and Sensibility* before the day was done.

After the duke rose and bowed, saying, "Good night, all," the others soon dispersed.

As was their custom, the boys studied the prepared papers for the next day's lessons. Heath finished first; rising from his desk, he asked, "The usual, Charles?"

"I suppose so."

Heath pulled the bell cord and the footman, by prearrangement, appeared with the nightly tray of biscuits and milk. Seated by the fire, Heath scrutinized his brother. "All right, Charley, out with it—have you found a secret room?"

"Oh, Bro, how did you guess?"

"Your questions at dinner were odd."

"Well, I haven't—not a room—not exactly—but I found a staircase that may lead to one."

"Looby, how did you do that?"

Charles, pent to the bursting point, poured forth the story, from Lenore's request for her shawl to his folding and replacing the shawl. He omitted his fear of boggards, evil men, and skeletons.

"Whew! You must have been scared!"

"Only a little at the first," Charles conceded.

"You're a cool fish, Charles . . . it's true, isn't it? You're not making a Gothic out of whole cloth?"

" 'Course I'm not," Charles bristled. "I don't tell shockers, anyway, not long ones like this."

"I believe you, little Brother," Heath soothed. "By Jupiter, a secret staircase—never heard of one—just in books. What are we going to do?"

"Well, I hoped you and I could—er—explore a bit."

"You mean go up the stairs to see what's there?"

"Uh-huh. You go up and I'll watch—so you won't get closed in."

Heath stared at his bland-faced brother. "You delegate me to find the hidden room?"

Charles nodded. "Think of it, Bro, there may be great treasure—and you'd be the first to discover it."

"Hoy, most likely mice, cobwebs—even a rat or two."

"But it's worth a peek," Charles pointed out.

Heath grinned. "Yes, Sir Francis, I suppose it is."

"Sir Francis, who's he?"

"Anapo, you've just been studying about Sir Francis Drake."

Charles did not deign to make response to such a pedant, but asked, "When can we go?"

Heath bit into a biscuit, sipped his milk, then said,

"Everyone will have to be either out of the house or too thong to bother with us. Can't have even George or Nicky with us."

"We'll send them home if the others are out of the way."

"We'll have to tell Father, you realize."

"Certainly, Bro, but not until we can maybe lay treasure at his feet—think on that!"

"Don't hoax yourself, you scrubby schoolboy."

The boys speculated on what they might find until Doctor Sylvester came and reminded them it was well past bedtime.

44

At Brooks's the duke handed his greatcoat to the porter, who gave him a note full of apologies from Chiswick—his wife had suddenly taken ill—nothing serious, but he was not free for the evening. Disappointed, the duke decided to see if any other friend was in the Club.

There was an intake of breath when the gamesters saw the duke, framed in the doorway of the brilliantly lighted gaming room, elegant in his white satin breeches, his superfine coat of brown, and his belcher, tied to strike envy in the heart of every would-be dandy present. Sweeping the room to note those at the table, the duke saw the marquis detach himself from a group and walk toward him. The marquis bowed. "Your Grace, this is a pleasure." The marquis could not go unnoticed in his garb of black satin, contrasting with the stylish arrangement of his pure-white linen, the folds of which held a pin of rubies and diamonds.

The most distinguished figures to be seen in the Club moved away from the entrance.

"I had the great good fortune to encounter the duchess this afternoon, Duke."

"So she told me."

"Undecided between two bracelets for Lady Jersey, she graciously permitted me to resolve the matter. Have you seen the bauble?"

"No, not yet."

"A charming trifle, though either bracelet would have pleased Lady Jersey, for the duchess has ex-quisite taste." The marquis spoke lightly.

"I presume I should thank you on behalf of the duchess, and I do."

"Not at all, Duke, you are to be complimented for taste and wisdom in your choice of a duchess. I dis-covered today she is a lady of sense and sensibility." His glance slid to the duke's face.

"Yes." For some reason the marquis's comment irked.

She didn't tell him, concluded the marquis, then said, "*Assez!* Englishmen find praise for their wives embarrassing; my apologies, sir." The marquis smiled.

"Oh, no; however I am puzzled how you could learn so much about the lady in so brief a meeting."

"Ah, Your Grace." The marquis laughed. "Your duchess is of open countenance; one can read her face like a—er—book."

"I find her a Greek text," muttered the duke.

"The fate of husbands whose wives are active in the attic."

The duke stared at the marquis. "Good God, I've been told that she is beautiful, kind, good, charming, educated, but clever—I have not heard that."

The marquis laughed. "Englishmen—obtuse."

Disconcerted, the duke changed the subject. "Do you game tonight?"

"*Oui*, I feel lucky and optimistic—and you, Duke?"

The duke hesitated.

"Myles, Marquis, here—this table," Wrenham called, waving. "I've ordered drinks."

With an exchange of nods of agreement, the two men joined Wrenham.

Whatever luck the marquis depended upon soon deserted him, but his optimism never fagged. Each loss seemed to inspire him to a deeper urge to wager. Once, after he had lost an amount large even for Brooks's, Wrenham urged caution, but the marquis laughed. "Order another round of drinks, sir, then watch me recoup."

The duke, whose every wager brought him gold, finally announced he'd play no longer.

"Ah, Duke, *mon ami*, I'll walk you to your carriage—but I shall return," the marquis quickly assured the men around the table.

In the hall, the marquis slumped against the wall.

"You're drunk," observed the duke mildly.

"As a wheelbarrow," confirmed the marquis.

"And short of flimsies," surmised the duke.

"Quite out of town," muttered the marquis.

"Here." The duke held out his bag of winnings.

"No!" The marquis glared. "No gift—I will give you a note."

"Don't be a fool—take it."

The marquis straightened. "You, sir, may be the Duke of Asherwood, but I am the Marquis de Chondefon and I accept no alms. A note, Duke—do you understand me, sir?"

"Perfectly. If you insist—a note." The duke asked the porter for writing materials and said, "What is the sum in the bag?"

The marquis poured the gold on a nearby table and the duke counted an amount sufficient to cover the marquis's losses and permit him further play.

"Good God," exclaimed the duke. "My luck was in tonight." He did not add that he had mingled his winnings with his own gold in the velvet bag.

The marquis snatched the pen and scrawled his name on the note. "Your Grace, I thank you." He swung on his heel and staggered to the doorway of the gaming room; there he paused, threw back his head, and strolled into the brightly lit room.

The duke shrugged and tore up the note, tossing the pieces into the street as he entered his carriage.

45

Heath and Charles did not have to wait many days before they could investigate the secret door. One afternoon the house was empty except for Mamère, who was napping, and the household was busy preparing for the holidays. The boys, armed with can-

dles, entered Lenore's room and Charles showed Heath
how the node worked. After studying the opening,
Heath took a candle, placed his foot on the first
step, paused, then climbed to the fourth step, where
he had to stop, for his head brushed the ceiling. Holding the candle aloft, he turned to inspect the back
wall. To brace himself he placed his free hand on the
top step, curling his thumb under the edge. What
happened next so startled him that he backed down.
The wall at the head of the stairs slid open and a
rush of musky air blew out his candle.

"What did you do? What did you do?" squealed
Charles.

"I'm not sure," said Heath, holding a handkerchief
over his nose.

"You must have done something—it opened."

"Let me see, I went up as far as I could and then
leaned—that's it—I put my thumb under the stair
tread and my weight must have caused the—whatever
it is—to work. Here—relight my candle—I'm going up
again."

"Are you going into the secret room?"

"Not yet; not until I find how the zany wall works."
Heath climbed and placed his thumb as before, then
pressed, and the wall closed. "That's it!" Heath
announced.

"Well, open it and go see what's up there." Charles
danced with impatience.

Heath opened the wall. "Whew! It smells terrible."

"Never mind. Look in and tell me what you see."

Holding high his relighted candle, Heath peered
into the aperture. "Good Lord, the room's enormous!"
Heath waited until his eyes adjusted to the dim
light. "It covers the whole house."

"Is there any jewelery or gold?" Charles queried.

"Can't see anything much—some bundles in the corner."

"I'm coming up," Charles proclaimed.

"Not on your life, Charles." Heath came down to face the boy. "There's just a big empty room up there, and you aren't going up until I find a way to open that door from the inside."

Charles gaped at his brother. "You mean you are going into that room and closing the wall?"

"No, you're going to close the wall and I'm going to discover how it works."

"You're diked in the nob; I'm not letting you go into that smelly place and then shut the wall on you— what if I couldn't open it and you were stuck there?"

"Don't be a Johnny Raw; if I don't find the trick of it, you can raise an alarm."

"Oh, Bro, I'm scared."

"Well, I'm not—here we go."

Charles, feeling shaky, followed Heath up the stairs. Heath stepped into the room, turned, and grinned down at the boy. "Ready? All right, push the bar."

Charles reluctantly did as bid, then hit the closed wall with his fist. "Can you hear me, Bro?" There was no answer. Charles sat down on a step and placed his hand on the bar. Find it fast, Bro, hurry. After what seemed a dreadful wait, the wall slid open.

"I'm coming up." Charles rose.

"Not yet. Go down and put a chair in to block the lower door; I'm not certain it can be opened from this side."

Charles raced down the stairs, grabbed a small chair, and tilted it so the wall could not slide closed. Then crawling over the barricade, he ran up the steps to stand beside Heath.

The room before them was so large that the boys

could barely discern the opposite wall. The disagreeable mustiness, the floor thick with dust, the round windows laced with cobwebs, bespoke years of disuse. In one corner stood trunks, and a cloth covered a rectangular shape.

Heath said, "Here, I'll show you how the wall slides." He pushed the node on the molding by the opening—the wall closed. "I found it fairly quickly because it's about the same height on this false column as the one by the fireplace."

"Let's get some air." Both boys tried, but the porthole windows would not budge. Moving to the opposite end of the vast room, they stared for an instant at two closed doors facing them on the back wall.

Charles went to the one on the right and tugged it ajar; a brick wall blocked the outlet. "Bro, I'll wager, beyond this there is a hall to the stairs that run up outside the back of the house."

"Won't take your wager—I'd lose. What's behind the other door?"

Heath opened the left-hand door to see a blank wall filling the space. Suddenly the wall slowly toppled away from them. Charles grabbed Heath as the wall fell part way and then with a thud, came to rest. For an instant the boys did nothing, then Heath said, "It's false, and only propped." Both rushed to peek around the edge of the doorframe.

"It's a hall; the panel fell against a banister. Come on." Charles scrambled through the narrow opening. Heath followed, and once in the small area, the boys lifted the false panel and leaned it upright, out of their way.

Suddenly both boys froze—they heard Abel's voice calling, "Maria," followed by a spate of Spanish.

"We're over the servants' quarters," whispered

Heath. "These stairs go down there. Listen . . ." There was the sound of a door closing below and, on a bare floor, footsteps that faded as they listened.

"Come on." Heath moved to the staircase and tiptoed down the flight, Charles at his heels. At the bottom, a door faced them. Heath turned the handle slowly, shoved the door open, and pushed a curtain aside. There was a long corridor leading to the kitchen staircase.

"What shall we do?" asked Charles.

"Go back the way we came."

"Are we to put the panel back?" Charles asked as they went up the steps. Heath shook his head. Once again in the large room, Charles wanted to examine the trunks, but Heath, crossing the room, said, "They can wait. You go downstairs; I'll close the door up here."

Charles clambered down the steep steps, picked up the blocking chair, and almost ran into Lenore, just entering the bedroom. Lenore and Charles stared at each other, then Charles, dropping the chair, swung around in an effort to climb out of sight, thereby running into Heath as he stepped into the room.

"Charles, Heath, what in the world? Look at you—you're filthy! Good Lord—the wall!"

"Mother, I can explain," Heath said breathlessly. "We've done no harm; it's a wall that slides open."

"*What?*"

"Look, I'll show you." Charles pressed the node and the wall closed.

"Glory; what's behind it—stairs? Where do they go?"

"To a secret room that runs the length of the house."

"Secret room—how can that be?"

Heath said, "Not secret, but it has been sealed off

and there are two doors at the farther end. One is bricked up, the other leads to a staircase to the servants' hall."

"Well, you two have been busy this afternoon." Lenore removed her bonnet and coat. "How did you discover—"

"Your shawl, Mother. Remember when you asked me to get it? Well, the fringe caught on the molding and triggered the sliding wall. Gave me a start."

"Indeed so. Is there anything up there?"

"Only some old trunks and a picture or frame covered by hollands," Heath responded.

"Are there any—er—mice or rats?"

"Oh, no, Mother," Charles assured her.

"My shawl, imagine. . . . And now?"

"We haven't had time to think about it; we'll have to tell Father, of course," Heath said.

Lenore smiled. "First both of you go and bathe, you chimney sweeps! And keep your tongue between your teeth—no word to anyone—we'll talk later."

After the boys left, Lenore tried the node and peered up the stairwell, then closed the wall and rang for Maria.

Later the duke impatiently watched Lenore, gowned in pale yellow, descend the hall stairs. "We'll be late! Lady Vaga considers promptness a virtue; she expects—"

"To have her every whim obeyed." Lenore buttoned her gloves and allowed Maria to drape a velvet cape across her shoulders as Clough assisted the duke into his greatcoat. In the carriage the duke said, "I find you strange, madam; Lady Vaga's invitation—"

"Is her recognition that we are now declared to be of the pink of the *ton*."

"Exactly—not to be seen at Lady Vaga's *Evening with Euterpe* is an exclusion to be feared."

"Indeed so; once Eric and I were commanded by Alfred to accept her invitation to the *Evening with Euterpe*—silly name—and were seated in rows like children in a schoolroom, then tortured by the caterwauling of a female crow and the scratchings of mishandled violins. I wanted to scream that night, and tonight I may."

"Madam, the Duchess of Asherwood does not scream."

Lenore laughed. "Then never let me encounter a mouse. Forgive me, Myles, I'm a trifle on the fidgets and Lady Vaga scares me."

Waiting in line to greet the formidable Lady Vaga, Lenore and the duke chatted with those around them. Finally the duke bowed and kissed their hostess's hand. The lady boomed, "Well, Duke, I can see you and your duchess are determined to make the rest of us look like mushrooms and dowds. Wouldn't have invited you, except I wanted to see if you were too high in the instep to give an appearance."

"You are too kind," the furious duke murmured.

Lady Vaga's glance swiftly swept Lenore from head to toe, then met Lenore's eyes in a piercing stare.

Lenore was startled for a moment, then thought, She's like Mamère—frightened and lonely. On impulse, Lenore gathered Lady Vaga in her arms and whispered in her ear, "Hold your fire, you wicked old lady, 'cause like it or not, I'm going to be your friend."

Astounded, Lady Vaga gave Lenore a fierce glare, then said, "Maybe the duke ain't the fool I thought him."

"Then you'll have nuncheon with Madame Lanier and me tomorrow," Lenore announced.

"No!" Lady Vaga barked. "Haven't spoken to that wet goose in forty years and—"

"Famous, you'll have much to say to each other; we'll expect you at one sharp." Lenore started to walk away.

"Don't count on it," Lady Vaga called after her.

"What did you say to her?" queried the duke.

"I called her a wicked old lady and ordered her to come for nuncheon tomorrow."

"Good God, she'll chew you into small pieces."

"No, she'll come and, with Mamère, rip the *ton* of the past forty years into ribbons and become Mamère's bosom bow. There are the Chiswicks; I want to speak to Lily."

Chairs and people impeded their progress. A voice behind Lenore said, "I know a secret room, Duke." Lenore started and turned to see the marquis standing behind the duke.

"Ah, good evening, Duchess," he then whispered, leaning between them. "Behind yon center pillar there's a narrow door giving onto an oasis where refreshments and cards await."

The duke spoke. "A noble thought, sir, but I cannot abandon the duchess in this swirling squeeze."

"*Mon Dieu,* you don't imagine I would cut up so extremely stiff as to desert the duchess—if you are alert, you may see Lady Jersey gliding even now into the very portal; soon she will vanish—a rubber of whist for four."

"Lenore does not play whist," the duke proclaimed.

"Myles, you forget the Penn. Pierre, we will be happy to be rescued." She did not see the duke's frown.

The marquis beamed. "Move softly then, for to be observed would invite interruption—you first, dear lady."

Lenore made her way, pausing to express pleasure at Lily Chiswick's improved health.

Edging nearer to escape, the duke watched the marquis disappear through the wall. Just beyond the pillar Sir Alfred Lanier stepped in His Grace's path. "Myles, good evening. Have you seen the marquis?"

"Saw him a minute ago, but don't see him now."

"Martha sent me to find him; she wants him to sit with us. Well, I'd best continue the search." Sir Alfred moved on.

"Welcome, Myles. The cards are all dealt; you're to play with me," Lady Jersey said as the duke slid into the room.

The game began. Later a large score mounted under Lenore's name.

"Good Lord, Myles, you should send your little duchess to Brooks's; she'd sweep the field," Lady Jersey exclaimed.

"*Tiens!* The duke's been harboring a whist wizard under his roof and he didn't even know she played—I'll never understand Englishmen."

"Cease!" Lenore waved her hand. "I've been lucky."

"And skilled, little Duchess, and now I have the ill fortune to be the marquis's partner."

Later, the cards dealt, the marquis said, "Lady Jersey, if you succeed with the play of this hand, I'll take you to dinner before the opera next week."

"Thank you, no; I'm not overly fond of opera, even when well sung, and there hasn't been a singer worth listening to since Grassini returned to France."

"Ah, Grassini! *Quelle voix!*" The marquis kissed his fingertips and tossed it into the air. "Don't you agree, Duke?"

"I haven't heard her sing."

"Never to have heard or seen *la magnifique* Grassini

—*tragique!* She's worshiped in France—even the emperor is at her feet."

"Allow me to play the hand, gentlemen," Lady Jersey commanded. She played and won.

"Well done!" The marquis clapped his hands. "Grassini's absence from London is my loss."

"Hoy, deal the cards, Myles, it's late," said Lady Jersey.

The duke said, "If you enjoy opera, Marquis, join us in our box next week."

"I accept, sir."

At the end of the next round the score permitted Lenore to jingle a handful of gold coins into her reticule.

The marquis said, "I have a favor to ask of you, Duke; tomorrow I go to Tattersall's to select some horses. You are a nonpareil, and your advice would be greatly valued. Could you meet me there?"

The duke nodded. "Tattersall's is a place I enjoy—shall we say, eleven o'clock?"

"Perfect! Now, dear Lady Jersey, though you have broken my heart"—the marquis kissed her hand—"I will persist; some night, when you are starving, will you accept my offer to dine?"

"When I am starving?" Lady Jersey laughed and smoothed the side of her gown. "I cannot wait that length of time—I am free tomorrow evening."

"*Je suis heureux!*"

Lady Jersey kissed Lenore. "Good night, little Duchess, Myles, Frenchman; thank you for an unexpectedly charming evening." She slipped out the door.

"Do you wish supper?" the duke asked Lenore.

"No, I want to go home."

In the carriage Lenore said, "I heard Grassini once; she is very beautiful and sings like an angel."

"If she returns to London, I will hear her," replied the duke. "Right now I am far more curious to see what horses the marquis intends to purchase."

"It must mean that he plans to be in London some period of time."

"A prospect you contemplate, I'm sure, with the greatest pleasure," the duke said acidly.

"Indeed so; Lady Jersey will be so delighted."

Both fell silent.

Lenore read late into the night.

46

The next morning Lenore arrived for breakfast to find the boys and the doctor finishing their tea. "Disgraceful, I overslept." Noting that the boys were preparing to rise, she continued, "Have you told Doctor Sylvester of your discovery of the secret room?"

"Oh, no, Mother, not a word." Charles shook his head.

"Then do so as I feast on oranges. You first, Charles; start with my sending you for the shawl."

"Well, Mother sent me to get her . . ." Charles flew into the story. Doctor Sylvester listened with mounting excitement to the tale of finding the secret staircase.

"How absolutely extraordinary!" he exclaimed when Charles finished. "Do you think the duke is unaware of the sliding walls, Your Grace?"

"I'm not certain, but I would wager yes. Today I want you and the boys to explore the room with me."

"Famous!" cried Charles.

"Great!" Heath beamed.

"I am curious; now, however, I must see Mamère. Meanwhile you two change to suitable old clothes; I suggest you do the same, Doctor. If you had spied your cobwebby pupils yesterday, the need would be obvious."

Later, entering Madame Lanier's room, Lenore kissed the old lady's cheek. "Good morning, Mamère, you look splendid."

"You don't in that raggedy old dress; you're not in ashes anymore, Cinderella."

"Today I have some work that may soil my gown, so—But I have something to tell you—you and I are having a guest for nuncheon."

"I certainly hope you plan to change your gown, Duchess."

"Lady Vaga—"

"If I had worn such a tatter—*What?*"

"Lady Vaga is coming for nuncheon."

"Absolutely not!" Mamère's voice shrilled.

"Yes, I have invited her, and she is coming."

"Lewd Lucy?"

"What?"

"Lewd Lucy, that's what we used to call her."

"Mamère!" Lenore cried, "Lady Vaga is one of the highest sticklers of the *ton*."

"Well, she was anything but until she got leg-shackled to old vacant Vaga; on-dit claimed her one of those statues you broke up; ain't sure it wasn't the one outside my door."

"Oh, you can't mean that!"

" 'Course I can; everyone knew she flung her cap over the windmill in every direction. Getting dressed for balls, she used to have her gowns soaked in water so they'd cling to her fine figure—and I have to admit she had one—seen her myself in this very house, in that ballroom." The old lady pointed to the ceiling.

Lenore gaped. "Mamère, the ballroom is downstairs."

" 'Tis now; Bunky's father did that. 'Twas upstairs, but one night the Earl of Slater was so foxed, he slipped on a brick of the outside steps and broke his head. Cocked up his toes right then and there. Caused an awful palaver, so the old duke sealed up the room and built the new ballroom. Didn't Bunky tell you?"

"No."

"Well, if those walls"—she again pointed to the ceiling—"could talk, they could play ducks and drakes with those who behave so uppish these days—like Lewd Lucy."

"Oh, please don't call her that," said Lenore. "You know she is one of the first leaders of fashion."

"Well, she was wild to a fault until she married Vaga . . . brass-faced enough to have a big wedding too, then she settled down—had a quiver full of brats. When old vacant stuck his spoon in the wall, he left her so full of juice that people forgot about her hey-go-mad days—except me—I remember precisely to the pin."

"Oh, Mamère, you won't say anything to her, will you?"

"Don't worry on that score, 'cause I ain't going to talk at all; I don't speak to Lady Vaga."

"All right." Lenore rose. "Now, may I borrow Abel for the morning?"

"I don't own him," snapped the old lady.

"For which, I am sure, he is thankful. I'll see you at nuncheon, and you are to be good."

"Can't be other gates, 'cause I ain't going to open my mouth," muttered Mamère as Lenore left.

Lenore found the boys and the doctor seated on the hall steps. "Charles, get Abel and tell him to bring candles; we'll not go until you are with us."

When they returned, Abel asked, "What is this, ma'am—the young one is babbling about a secret room."

"Abel, we intend to surprise you. Now, if you will all follow me . . ." She led the way to her bedroom, then nodded for Charles to open the wall. Abel was duly astonished. He swore a few Spanish words, but at Lenore's behest, dealt out and lighted the candles. Heath led the party up the stairs and stood aside.

"See, Mother, I told you it was big."

"You hit the needle, Charles."

Doctor Sylvester went to a window. "Your Grace, when these are cleaned, they must give fine light."

"Ma'am, forgive me, but my fingers itch to open the trunks," Abel called.

"Look out, Charles," Lenore cried as the boy ran and slid on the dust floor. "Doctor, let's see the contents of the trunks."

One by one Abel lifted the creaky lids, but the trunks were empty. "Maybe one of them has a false bottom," Charles suggested.

"Shall we remove this holland?" said Dr. Sylvester.

"Nothing there but an old picture; I lifted a corner," Charles said gloomily.

"We might as well look while we're here," Lenore said. "You'll have to bring it near the light."

The large oil in its gold frame appeared dim and faded until the men set it by the window, then Lenore caught her breath. "Asherwood, seen through whirls of mist—beautiful—the colors glow even through the grime. Heath, who is the artist—Doctor, what do you think?"

"Your Grace, I'm overwhelmed; it's like no landscape I've ever beheld. Can you make out the signature, Heath?"

Heath, who had been wiping the corner where faint letters appeared, placed his candle close and read slowly, "J. M. Turner."

"Turner? It can't be—he doesn't paint in that style," Lenore exclaimed.

Heath leaned close to the markings. "Those are the letters, Mother."

"It's Asherwood, no one could mistake it. Abel, come here—what do you think?" Lenore asked.

"Lord, ma'am, it's enough to knock the wind out of a man."

"Heath?"

"Mother, I'm homesick."

"It's haunting," said the doctor. "Makes me long to visit Asherwood."

"Not me," said Charles. "I like London."

Lenore studied the painting for a minute. "Please, will you bring it to my room." She surveyed the dusty walls and added, "There's nothing more of interest here; let's go downstairs."

Charles demurred, wanting to stay in the ballroom, but was reminded of a bath and lessons.

"All I do is bathe and have lessons."

"Perhaps, little Brother, if you were here alone, the mice might venture to make their appearance," Heath said, grinning.

"Ugh!" Charles ran ahead.

When the painting was propped by the fireplace, Lenore asked the others to give her time to ponder before divulging the find to anyone. Once alone, she gazed at the canvas for a long time. Finally, going to her desk, she penned a note, rang for the footman, and gave orders for the note to be delivered to Mr. Oliver Cordyne at his gallery—a reply to be awaited.

47

At one o'clock Lenore greeted Lady Vaga as she entered the front door. Fenwick took her wraps, and she peered around the hall.

"Huh, I see you've new decorations in the niches—good thing."

"Yes." Lenore watched her guest closely. "I didn't like the statues, although one or two upstairs were of great beauty."

Lady Vaga pinned sharp eyes on Lenore, who smiled blandly.

"Shall we go to Mamère's room?"

"Mamère? Is that what you call her?"

"It's my pet name for her."

"I called her Floss, when I was speaking to her."

Entering Mamère's room, Lenore gasped. Madame Lanier was seated in the small alcove with a tray on a stand before her; a table set for two stood at the other end of the room. Lenore moved quickly and picked up the tray. "Mamère, you are getting old; you have forgotten your friend Lady Vaga is having nuncheon with us."

"Never forgot a thing in my life."

Lenore took the tray to the table and set the third place, then pulled the bell rope and returned to Mamère. "Lady Vaga came out in the cold to see us; we'll have a brandy before nuncheon. Please, Lady Vaga, sit here, where you can see Mamère."

Mamère swung her head away violently and stared out the window.

"I'll leave, Duchess," Lady Vaga growled.

Lenore stared from one to the other, then stamped her foot. "You make me cross as crabs, both of you. Grew up together, were close for years, and I'll wager came to points over something neither can remember." She paused. "Can you? Well? A thousand shared memories you could discuss forever—No, Abel, I thought I'd ask for brandy, but I guess there isn't to be need of it."

Abel closed the door.

"Just a minute, Lenore," cried Mamère.

"A hundred hours of happy prattle between you, and you are like lumps—too starchy to say hello to each other."

Lenore took a deep breath. "Well, it's no bread and butter of mine—good afternoon." She started for the door.

"Duchess!" roared Lady Vaga.

Lenore hesitated.

"I'd talk to Floss; I came here, didn't I?"

Lenore turned to Mamère.

"Lucy shouldn't have done it," Mamère said crossly.

"Done what, Floss? Not accepted the duchess's invitation to nuncheon?"

"No—stolen Lord Gregory from under my nose, right upstairs in the ballroom."

Lenore stared at the pouty old lady and began to titter. "Good Lord, Mamère, that was over forty years ago."

"Besides," cried Lady Vaga, "the duchess stole him away from me within twenty minutes—he just vanished. Didn't you know, Floss?"

"No, I didn't." Mamère tossed her head.

"And you two ninnyhammers haven't spoken to each other for all these years? God give me strength." Lenore threw up her hands.

Mamère angled her head so she could see Lady Vaga. "Lucy, did the duchess actually steal him?"

"Just like that! I was talking to him and the duchess came up, took his arm, and said, 'I want to show you something.' They walked off and I never saw either of them again the whole night."

Lenore stared at Lady Vaga in a trance.

"Well, I ain't surprised," rejoined Mamère, "she was a gazetted flirt all right; I remember the night she . . ."

Abel entered with the brandy.

"Oh, Lenore, you didn't mean it; you were shamming." Mamère beamed. "Have a brandy, Lucy, you used to like it."

"Still do, Floss; this reminds me of the day . . ."

Lenore let the reminiscences of the two ancients flow around her.

After the meal, when there was a pause in the

stories, Lenore asked to be excused. The two old
ladies hesitated long enough to say their thank-yous
and good-byes; closing the door, Lenore heard Lady
Vaga say, "This duke's duchess is a right one."

In the hall Abel handed Lenore a note announcing
that Mr. Cordyne would arrive within the hour, prepared to restore the painting. Lenore went to the
study, now crowded with boys who hung on every
syllable of Doctor Sylvester's description of American
Indian scalpings, knives, and gore. Lenore waited
until the doctor looked up. "Your Grace?"

"May I speak to you, Doctor?"

"Be right back, boys." The doctor, stepping over
Wiggles, followed Lenore into the hall.

"Doctor, Mr. Cordyne is coming to clean the painting and needs a place to work. I cannot allow him in
the morning room—the duke might wander in—so
could you clear the study, take the boys out, or—"

"Your Grace," the doctor cut in, "it would give me
great pleasure if he used my room, then the boys
won't—"

"How generous, sir; then, with your permission,
Abel and Fenwick will bring the picture immediately."

"Duchess," the doctor said, smiling, "would you do
me the honor of being my guest when Mr. Cordyne
arrives? I'm sure you wish to hear his first comments
on the painting."

Lenore nodded. "Thank you."

Laden with an easel and odd-size boxes, Mr. Cordyne
banged on the outside door, then asked Fenwick for
the duchess, and ordered the footman to show him
where to go. Fenwick sent a maid for Lenore, who
beckoned from the head of the stairs. "Welcome, Mr.
Cordyne."

"Good afternoon, Duchess. Pray tell me—is the painting truly by Mr. Turner?"

"It is so signed," Lenore replied as she led him to the doctor's room, where Mr. Cordyne set up the easel and Abel lifted the painting in place.

"Humm," Mr. Cordyne commented, then gave a long and close scrutiny. Finally he took out a glass, bent down, stepped away, closed the glass, and turned to Lenore.

"It is his signature, Your Grace; however, the vaporous color, the vague outline of the house"—he shook his head—"it's not Mr. Turner's work."

Lenore, disappointed, asked, "Whoever the artist, do you not think it beautiful?"

Mr. Cordyne frowned. "No, it meets no standard of the Royal Academy and would be rejected on sight."

"Farradiddle! Would you hang it in your gallery?"

"I cannot respond, Duchess, until I've finished my work; fortunately only cleaning is required—the picture is undamaged."

"Good; then you must proceed. May we watch, or—"

"No, I need assistance in removing the frame, then I demand to be alone."

"Help him, Abel; I shall be in my room if you need me." Lenore felt annoyance. The painting is a rare and lovely piece of art—I don't give a fig what the Gothics at the Royal Academy think. Mr. Cordyne is a snob! She had almost reached her room when Fenwick came up the stairs and said, "Your Grace, the duke wishes to see you." She ran down the stairs.

Entering the library, she exclaimed, "Myles, I'm so glad to—" The expression on his face froze her. "What is it?"

"Madam, it has come to my attention that you and

Mr. Foster almost came to cuffs yesterday." The duke's tone was heavy.

"Fustian, we did have a good brangle, but cuffs? Ridiculous!"

"Did you enter a caveat to his every suggestion concerning the morning room?"

"I did; they were out of bounds—silly!"

"Mr. Foster is the finest decorator in London, madam."

Lenore shrugged. "I did not like his schemes, Myles."

"He did your bedroom; you say it is charming."

"Oh, come, Myles, he didn't do my room, you did; he merely followed your instructions. But every request of mine he dismissed with a wave of his hand."

"Even so, did you have to quarrel with him?"

"Yes; he insisted that the walls stay dark and urged ugly materials."

The duke rose. "Lenore, I'm not certain you know your place in my household."

"I am your duchess."

"Yes, but that does not give you leave to ride ramshackle over—"

Lenore sprang to her feet. "Your Grace"—Lenore's voice was icy—"I do not know why you made me your duchess; however, whatever your reasons, I *am* the Duchess of Asherwood, and no fat fripple is going to tell me how to redo anything." Her eyes flashed. "What a rum touch for him to tattle to you."

"He didn't."

"No? What jack-pudding did, then?"

"The marquis."

"What?!"

"At Tattersall's today Pierre mentioned that Mr. Foster was quite overset—ill in fact."

"How could he learn that?"

"Mr. Foster is redecorating the marquis's new house and was unable to meet with him today."

"Why would he do that?"

"Not meet with the marquis? Because you threw him into dismals."

"No, no. I mean why would the marquis tell you?"

"Just in passing, he casually expressed the hope that you were not in a worry today; I asked him why you should be, and he replied, 'No reason really, only Mr. Foster was blue-deviled,' and he hoped you were not."

"How considerate of the marquis. Perhaps Mr. Foster is ill and I am not because I did not eat three servings of buttered lobster, mushroom fritters, oysters in batter, two orange soufflés, and near a basket of pastries for nuncheon yesterday."

"Good God!"

"Indeed so—why do you think he is fat as a faun?"

"Nevertheless, I do not want you pulling caps with Mr. Foster or any man in my employ," the duke said coldly.

"Then instruct Mr. Foster not to treat me as if I had just left the schoolroom."

"Just don't come to points with him, Lenore."

Lenore drew a deep breath. "Either he will redo the morning room his way or my way. Decide which, Your Grace, and so inform me." She walked out of the room.

"Oh, Lord; females!" The duke paced the floor for a while, then went to the morning room, and closing the doors behind him, stood for a long time.

Lenore, in a fury, only nodded when Fenwick told her Mr. Cordyne had left and would return in the morning.

Dressing for the evening rout, Lenore wondered about the marquis. I thought him a friend—she shrugged—maybe it was a simple comment that Myles blew out of proportion.

Going downstairs to join the duke, she noticed the morning room doors wide open.

The duke stepped to the doorway. "Lenore, you are correct. The room is too dark; I've written a note to Mr. Foster telling him to follow your instructions as if they were mine."

"Myles, that was a handsome thing to do—thank you." Lenore beamed up at him.

She is beautiful, he thought. "Shall we go?" Impulsively he extended his arm and felt his duchess's hand rest lightly as they walked to the carriage; the duke experienced a sense of well-being.

The duke found the rout boring. To Lenore's joy he resorted to talking exclusively with her—about the boys, Asherwood, his youth. He asked her questions about her girlhood. Lenore was tempted to confide to him the adventure of the new-found ballroom, but refrained, content just to listen to his voice.

At home, as they said good night, Lenore told the duke he had turned a deadly flat rout into a famous evening.

The duke nodded.

48

The next morning the duke announced that because he wished to take the boys out for the morning, the doctor was free for the day. Lenore and the doctor exchanged a quick glance, which the duke caught, feeling a flash of annoyance as he did so.

"Father, I'd like to see the fisticuffs. Can we go to Jackson's?" Charles asked eagerly.

"No," growled the duke, "I have other plans," then, "Doctor, I have changed my mind—you will accompany us today."

"Father, that's not fair," Heath said. "Doctor Sylvester has had hardly a moment to himself since he arrived. He must have many—"

"What are your thoughts on the matter, Lenore?" the duke asked.

Lenore, surprised, replied, "I haven't any, Myles."

"And you, Doctor, what are your wishes?"

"Whatever way you close with the offer will be acceptable, Your Grace."

Placated by the unruffled responses, the duke said, "Heath is right—take the day, sir."

Heath rose. "Come, Charley, we must not delay."

"Yes sir." Charles jumped to his feet and followed Heath out the door.

"Myles, are your plans for the boys secret?"

"They are," the duke replied succinctly.

Standing, the doctor said, "Thank you for the time, Duke. My list is short, but Christmas is near and the shops will be crowded. Good morning."

After the doctor left, the duke frowned. "And do you, Lenore, intend to visit the shops also?"

"Heavens, no, my gifts are fixed right and tight. Besides, it's too cold to venture out."

Relieved, the duke said genially, "I plan to take the boys to Fenton's for nuncheon."

"What a treat for them." When Lenore walked with the duke to the hall, Fenwick gave her an almost imperceptible nod, which the duke, distracted by the boys running downstairs, did not see.

"We're ready, Father." Charles went to Lenore. "Mother, are you sad because you are not coming with us?"

"Heavens, no, what would one lone female do amid such a rum-gumption trio of males? Go along and have fun."

When the door was closed, Lenore asked Fenwick, "Mr. Cordyne is here?"

"Yes, Your Grace; he ordered that he not be disturbed, but that he would send word when he is finished."

"Splendid! I'll be with Madame Lanier."

Doctor Sylvester, bundled in greatcoat and scarf, and holding a beaver hat, left Mamère's room as Lenore came down the upper hall.

"Mr. Cordyne," the doctor said, grinning, "ousted me the minute I entered my room; scarce let me retrieve my outside garments. So I visit the shops early—Mr. Cordyne is a tyrant!"

"Is Mamère all right, Doctor?"

"She's extraordinarily well, considering the amount of brandy she consumed yesterday."

"Oh, I'm a fool—I forgot to remove the bottle."

"Its content was conducive to sleep, Your Grace; today only a dull ache in the head is her proud complaint?"

"Proud?"

"Certainly; she crows over her powers to drink me under the table. It bothers her that I eschew spirits; she doesn't know my history—just thinks me a dull dog. Oh, don't be distressed, Duchess. When she berates me, I reveal further shockers about my other vices, which keeps her in a hubble."

"Doctor!" Lenore laughed. "Wicked! Both of you!"

"Rest easy, Your Grace; the old lady is well—as well as she is wicked. I must go or I may melt at your feet—this coat—good-bye."

When Lenore stepped into the bedroom, all shades were drawn and Mamère lay abed.

"Good morning, Mamère."

"Forego to come near me; I suffer dreadfully." Mamère's voice was muffled. "Don't endanger yourself."

"Fiddle, you don't want my nose to tell me you had too much of the grape yesterday."

"No such thing, I'm very ill."

"I understand; however, sleep and time will pluck you up. I'll leave and let nature heal—next time curb the lavish pourings."

"You're a wench without heart, Duchess."

"Also empty-headed, leaving temptation within your reach."

The old lady giggled.

"How about Lady Vaga, is she—" Lenore started.

"Slept on this bed like a baby for two hours, then

Abel helped her to her carriage. No spine, that one."

"Oh, Mamère!" Lenore shook her head and left.

In her room Lenore wrote a long-overdue letter to Rachel and the vicar—a confused ramble destined to puzzle her friends. She had just sealed the envelope when Fenwick announced that Mr. Cordyne awaited her.

When Mr. Cordyne threw back the covering from the painting, Lenore gasped; Asherwood, the grime removed, floated, bathed in gentle, glowing colors, whirling and subtly brilliant. Lenore could not drag her eyes away. "It will never pall, forever fascinating."

"I hope you find my work adequate, Your Grace. The frame had need of repairs that I made last night."

"Sir, you have brought to life a lovely treasure—I'm in your debt."

Mr. Cordyne bowed. "Your Grace, despite the painting's unusual style, I'm now convinced the work is that of Mr. Turner, and I would deem it a privilege to hang the painting in my gallery."

As he spoke an idea came to Lenore that sent her mind racing.

"Mr. Cordyne, you are a man of perception, but now I must leave; I have much to do. Thank you for your excellent work—good-bye." She was gone.

Flighty females, thought the artist, then brightened as he realized he now had the pleasure of figuring the goodly sum he could charge His Grace.

Lenore gave Clough orders, then impatiently waited until her frequent glances out the window were rewarded by the sight of Henderson opening the curricle door for Mr. Foster. "Clough, have Abel help you bring the painting to the morning room immediately," Lenore called as she ran downstairs.

Mr. Foster, suffering an indisposition caused by what he considered the treatment at Lenore's hand—he never blamed food for any of his woes—felt put upon by the duchess's command of his prompt presence. Entering the house, he determined to deal with any call on his talents with suitable loftiness.

"Your Grace wishes to see me?" He calculated his tone one of chill.

Lenore, too excited to note his arrogance, urged him on. "Come, you're going to see the solution to our differences." She moved to the morning room—he had no choice but to follow. "Please sit there, sir."

Mr. Foster hesitated for an instant but lowered himself into the chair. From the couch Lenore watched Clough and Abel enter the room and give the scene its proper drama—Clough entered first and stood the easel with precision in front of the fireplace; Abel then balanced the covered canvas, taking care to tilt it to the inch. The task complete, both men bowed in unison and left the room.

Lenore rose and removed the cover.

Mr. Foster, eyes fastened on the painting, felt his anger drain from him. He knew he was gazing on the masterly use of both color and form. For a long time only the tick of the clock punctuated the silence; then Mr. Foster spoke. "Your Grace, the painting must be the heart of this room."

"Mr. Foster, those were the very words I desired to hear."

They looked at each other and smiled.

"Whose artistry, Duchess?"

"Mr. J. M. Turner's, sir."

"No!—can it be? I have never—"

"It is so signed."

"But it's not his style." Mr. Foster frowned, bewildered.

"No, but Mr. Cordyne is certain," Lenore answered.

Mr. Foster went to the easel and raised his quizzing glass. "If it's Mr. Turner's work or another's does not signify; we will redo the room as a setting for this jewel."

"Mr. Foster, you are knowledgeable to a pin; let inspiration flow and I cannot but be pleased."

The decorator found the redoing of this gloomy room an invigorating challenge. "Duchess, this may surprise you—I desire to start my plans this minute, here and now; paper and pen are all I require."

"Yours, sir, on the desk. I'll leave you; if you wish anything, ring for Fenwick."

Shortly Mr. Foster sent for the duchess. He had done a task that pleased him greatly.

Mr. Foster bowed. "Duchess, my plays are ready. Please sit there." He moved to the painting and with the feather of his pen lightly touched the surface. "Your Grace, consider doing the walls in this pale yellow." Color by color he wove a scheme for the draperies, the sofa, the chairs, and occasional pieces.

Lenore listened, sometimes nodding. When he had finished, she said, "Mr. Foster, your reputation as London's finest decorator is deserved—you have just shown me the reason for this."

His round face beamed. "High praise, Duchess. Now, for materials—I have listed those that might be used." He handed her his notations; harmony between them was suddenly strained—he had dictated heavy materials. Lenore dissented.

"Sir, I desire the room, like the painting, to float," she cried at one point.

"This is a formal room, Duchess."

"Precisely why no one is ever comfortable here."

Mr. Foster sighed. "If you insist, Your Grace, although I doubt the duke will approve. I'll bring samples of—"

"Let me go to the shops with you; often the perfect bolt is tucked away in a corner, unseen."

Mr. Foster's shocked tones told his dismay. "Certainly not; that would be most irregular, Your Grace. A lady doesn't—"

"Fustain; if ladies shop for cloth for gowns, why not for the far more important materials that they'll have to look upon for years? Please, let me come."

"My dear Duchess, I go to warehouses that are often unclean and sometimes full of rough men."

"I shall dress accordingly, and you can protect me." The vision of the roly-poly man in front of her, standing with fists up, made her want to laugh.

Meeting the eyes of the tiny lady, Mr. Foster decided there was no gainsaying her. "Very well, Your Grace, though I cannot approve."

"Fiddle! Can we go tomorrow? And how soon can your men begin the work?"

"You are precipitous; the duke must see the plans."

"Good Lord, no! It is all to be a surprise; you must never mention one word to him."

Mr. Foster's eyebrows shot up. "I've never heard of a husband—"

"You see, sir, he trusts me." Lenore smiled. Mr. Foster said to himself, "And me."

Lenore rose. "Tomorrow morning, then; with Christmas only a sennight away we must make haste."

"Your Grace," the man said, boggled, "you don't expect the work to be finished by—"

"Of course! It's my gift—"

"Impossible! Absolutely impossible!" The decorator shook his head vigorously.

"Mr. Foster." Lenore laid a hand on his arm. "You are a man of talent and resource. That you could not succeed in any undertaking I reject as a shabby thought—other decorators, yes, but not you."

Mr. Foster blinked and sighed. "I cannot promise—"

"Of course you can't, you can only try," Lenore agreed sweetly.

"My men will have to be here extraordinarily early tomorrow—"

Lenore smiled. "They'll be welcome. Later in the morning you and I can visit the shops. Mr. Foster, your artistry is only matched by your kindness."

On those words they parted.

That night, on the way to Lady Grafton's dance, Lenore told the duke of her cordial relations with Mr. Foster, and that the redoing would begin in the dawn of the next day—to be observed throughout by no one but herself.

49

The confusion of the week before Christmas set the duke's household in a bustle.

True to his word Mr. Foster sent a crew of men. They carried the heavy pieces of furniture to the waiting lorry, and swore heartily at the two boys who, racing into the house, dodged around them. Redford Chiswick paused to listen and was rewarded with a magnificent low epithet that he happily filed for future use against his tutor.

Later the crew were bedeviled by the fragile old ladies and gentlemen who, plodding their way up-stairs, ran the gamut of workmen trying to maneuver the large ancestral paintings to the storeroom on the second floor.

"One damn nick of them toddlers would send 'em tumbling down them damn stairs in a heap," said one workman. Abel and Clough guided and soothed the men as best they could.

After two days of being refused entry to their favor-ite gathering spot, great excitement prevailed among the young and old.

"Heath, old horse, how are you?" Lenore heard George Featherheath, Jr., yell as he passed her on her way downstairs to meet Mr. Foster.

The selection of bolts of materials of various colors, patterns, and weights was slow and tedious labor, punctuated by mild quarrels when Lenore and the decorator differed. After visiting two shops and a long session in a warehouse, Lenore declared she could go no farther until she had eaten.

Mr. Foster was dismayed. "There are no proper eating places within miles, Your Grace."

"Then an improper place, provided it's clean," teased Lenore.

"Duchess!"

"Mr. Forray," Lenore swung to the owner of the warehouse, who jumped and began rubbing his hands again, "can you tell us where we can get nuncheon? I'm faint with hunger."

Mr. Forray pursed his lips. "Your Grace, there is

no place of elegance in this neighborhood, however there's a small tea room where the soup is—Sandy"— he spoke to the boy who was rolling bolts—"run and inform Mlle. Arnot that two very important friends of mine are going to need a table and must have one now. It is beneath your touch, Duchess, but the food is very good."

Mr. Foster was soon seated opposite Lenore at a tiny table, steaming bowls of soup *à la reine* and a basket of hard rolls smothered in butter between them.

For such patrons Mlle. Arnot made the salad with her own hands. When she placed her masterpiece before Lenore, the duchess exclaimed, "It is a garden, Mlle. Arnot, and only demands your own dressing," whereupon the Frenchwoman shouted for oil and vinegar—"not the house vinegar, you *imbécile,* my own bottle"—and made a mixture that pleased even Mr. Foster's discerning palate.

The rest of the afternoon passed quickly and in harmony. In the carriage on the way home Lenore said, "We've done it, Mr. Foster; I'm pleased—and you, sir?"

"Your Grace, if you were not a duchess, I would hope to take you into my employ—your taste is flawless."

They beamed at each other.

When Lenore entered the house, a troop of boys was taking leave. They all bowed formally to Lenore except for the Earl of Laudersdown, Nicky, who came to her grinning like a cat. "I gave Charley a thump today—drew his claret." Seeing Lenore's frown he added happily, "Oh, don't worry, he's still my best friend," and ran out the door.

Lenore hurried upstairs to the study, where Heath and the doctor were putting things to rights.

"Charles—where is he? Is he badly hurt?"

"He's fine, Mother—Charley, come here," Heath called.

Charles emerged from the bedroom. "What is it, Mother?"

"Nicky said he thumped you today, leaving you bleeding."

"Oh, that." All three males began to laugh.

"What happened?" snapped Lenore.

"Your Grace, Nicky accidentally hit Charles with his elbow, unfortunately on the nose. It bled a few drops—nothing serious, I assure you."

"How could he do that?" Lenore felt annoyance.

Doctor Sylvester answered, "The room was crowded, and boys move fast. I'm always glad that no bones are broken."

"Must the room be so crowded, so many here?"

"Mother!" Charles disclaimed loudly, "of course! They're Heath's and my friends; it has to be."

"It's really Father's fault; he brought us Doctor Sylvester, who tells such famous stories and knows so many games, that the boys like to come."

"Now, Heath," the doctor remonstrated.

"It's true, Doctor."

Lenore looked around the room, then said, "Doctor, come with me, please; I wish to speak to you alone." She turned and the doctor followed her into the hall.

The doctor spoke first. "Your Grace, I believe we share an idea."

"You do?" Lenore said. "The ballroom?"

"Yes, the ballroom. After some work it would be ideal for the boys and their friends; I've given the idea much consideration. I already planned to see the duke as soon as you gave permission to reveal its discovery."

"Let's go see him now," Lenore said. "We'll explain what we propose should be done and learn his reaction." Lenore paused. "But I don't want the duke to know about the secret door and stairs from my room." She shook her head. "I realize my whim is odd, but will you kindly respect it?"

"Of course, Duchess, but if there were a fire—" the doctor frowned.

"Naturally it should be used; Heath can show you how the doors open. Also, you are to be present every time the room is occupied; the boys are never to be alone there at any time."

"You relieve my mind, Duchess."

"Then let's see the duke."

The duke, surprised to see Lenore and the doctor enter the library together, had a twinge of worry when Lenore said, "Myles, the doctor and I have something to discuss with you."

"Yes?" the duke's voice was cold.

"Myles, you have complained to me about the—I think you said—varmint that runs up and down the stairs all day."

Puzzled, the duke said, "Yes, pesky, noisy varmint."

"Well, Myles, please listen carefully. By chance Charles discovered the ballroom upstairs."

"The devil he did—how?" shouted the duke.

Lenore swallowed. "The panel in front of the door was loose and toppled onto the banister."

She does not tell bouncers well, thought the doctor.

"What banister? What are you talking about?" the duke demanded.

"The one on the top floor over the servants' quarters."

"What was the imp of Satan doing up there?"

"Your Grace"—the doctor wished to give Lenore time to recover—"you remember—boys explore."

"Explore, yes; but to pull away a panel—"

"Oh, he didn't do that; it just fell, and naturally he looked in."

The duke's tone became icy. "My father had that room sealed, and I never violated his order; however, my son is not so respectful."

"I don't know why it should be respected; it only has some empty trunks and—" Lenore stopped.

"You've seen it?" The duke glared.

"Ye-es—the doctor, the boys, and Abel and I ventured into its gloom together. It's a handsome room."

"My father commanded no one enter again, madam."

"Why on earth?"

"The Earl of Slater died because of that room."

"Not so Myles. The old duke was foxed and slipped on the outside staircase, breaking his head. Mamère told me all about it."

"Be that as it may, no one was to—"

"Why? It isn't haunted." Lenore shrugged.

"It was my father's wish!" said the duke.

"Your father has been booked for years and now your sons have need of the room."

"What?"

"Heath and Charles have so many friends—scions of the *ton* pack the study every chance they are given."

"I am aware, madam, that the house is like a school in full session."

"True, that is why—"

"Good God! Is it your idea that I throw open the ballroom for their use?"

"An excellent suggestion, Your Grace," the doctor said calmly.

"You think so?" The duke's glare swung to the doctor.

"Yes, Duke, I do."

"Why?!"

"For the benefit of your sons, Your Grace."

"Humgrudgeon! They are spoiled enough now."

"No!" Lenore's voice rang clear. "They are wonderful boys and in danger—"

"Danger?"

"Just today Charles's nose bled, hit by an elbow, because the study was so crowded."

"I should shut the house to all visitors," the duke proclaimed.

"That would be the most zany act of your life," said Lenore.

"And you, madam, propose I should—"

"Take a damper and listen to Doctor Sylvester. He's given thought on it."

"Well, Doctor?"

"Your Grace, the room is large and would serve truly well as a play space. The outside stairs would empty your hall of its clamor and the stairway to the kitchen quarters could be used if a fire broke out. Once cleaned, it would be a boys' paradise."

"Those outside stairs have not been trod in years and the doorway is bricked up," the duke argued.

"A mason could solve those problems in a flash, Myles," Lenore pointed out.

"The place must be buried in dirt."

"Amazingly not bad, Your Grace." The doctor smiled. "The lads could clean it in short order."

"What?!" the duke roared. "Do you expect the boys

—you're in queer stirrups to imagine the sons of the *ton* would do scrub work!"

The doctor laughed. "Duke, the sons of the *ton* are boys, and boys given such a room for their own use would enjoy cleaning it up."

"Never!" bellowed the duke.

"Provide buckets, brushes, cloths, and soap, Your Grace, and see what happens."

"You sound very sure, sir."

"Enough to put blunt on it, Your Grace."

"It will never come about." The duke shook his head.

"Try it, Myles." Lenore laughed. "I want to put a groat or two on it myself."

"You run mad, both of you; the masons are getting enough of my money not to waste more on your idiotic notions." He paused. "However—" Before he could continue Lenore jumped up and threw her arms around his neck. "Oh, Myles!"

Startled, the duke drew away. Lenore snatched her arms down. "Oh, I'm sorry; I was so happy—you are such a good father!" Turning fiery red, she dropped her head and whispered, "Please forgive me."

The doctor, astounded by Lenore's distress, waited an instant for the duke's any word, but the pause grew long. "Your Grace, yours is a most generous act; Heath and Charles will honor you for it."

Never taking his eyes off Lenore, the duke said, "Very well, Doctor, we will make plans later. Please leave now and take the duchess with you."

Lenore raised her head. "Thank you, Myles, for everything." The color had drained from her face, leaving her marble white.

In the hall Lenore burst into tears and allowed the doctor to lead her to her room.

"Some laudanum, Your Grace—I speak as a medical man—then rest. I will send Maria to you."

The duke was furious that Lenore had taken his involuntary withdrawal—caused by surprise—as a rebuff. He had meant no rejection of her. Dammit, why had she misread him so? Did she not realize he would not ever humiliate her? Her bowed head, scarlet countenance, her face, raised to speak, paling—all an insult to him. Why? I've shown her every courtesy, gallantry, even the indulgence due the Duchess of Asherwood. Why would she so put me down in front of the doctor?

The duke poured himself a brandy. I wish David here; I'd tell him what a shambles she has brought on my head—"She will make you a splendid duchess, Myles"—Ha! The cool clear voice of the vicar sounded. "Well, hasn't she, old friend?" The duke closed his eyes. She has—my sons adore her—the household runs smoothly—the *ton* delights in her—it's only I she rubs caveat with. The vicar's voice rang out. "Myles, perhaps you should . . ."

A knock interrupted his thought; Clough entered. "The post, Your Grace."

Accepting the pile of letters, the duke ran hastily through them; amid the many obvious invitations lay a letter from the vicar.

"Thank you, Clough, that will be all."

When Clough closed the door, the duke ripped open his friend's note.

Dear Myles,
     My French window opened a few minutes ago, letting in heavy gusts. For some reason they made me think of you. Why? Perhaps the snow, for I understand that one must be very wary of slipping

in London. Ah well, we will all welcome the thaw that must take place in the first week of February.

Rachel reads me the duchess's letters; they are full of your goings and comings—quite confusing to us. Cozen Lenore well, Myles, for she is—Rachel says—a rare and precious female.

Yuletide blessings to you all from Rachel and all the Thomases—a goodly number—and our deepest gratitude for your magnificent generosity.

Your friend and obedient servant,
David

The duke read the note twice more, then tossed it into the fire—David, I miss you. He went to the desk and consulted a calendar, then marked a date in February. So the time is set. But first Christmas . . . the boys . . . Lenore. The duke pulled the bell rope.

"Clough, have Mr. Cornby meet with me tomorrow after nuncheon—send Henderson to inform him."

Easier of mind, the duke turned his thoughts to David's "wary of slipping" warning, but of what or whom he did not know. The spies had not reappeared, and except for the *ton*'s rejection, which Lenore had overcome, there had been no hint of trouble. To what is David alerting me—no untoward event—no sign—the only Frenchman the marquis. The marquis—Pierre? A toadeater, a dandy, but dangerous? Absurd! The duke frowned. True, he hates the "scourge of Europe," but many Frenchmen do; true, he talks much about the opera; true, he dangles slightly after Lenore, but he flirts with all ladies. A popinjay! Good God, what a coil! Christmas upon us and I'm bedeviled; he pulled the bell rope savagely.

"Clough, I go to White's tonight; send Henderson here as soon as possible upon his return."

Lenore slept late, then, unhappy, she lived and relived the duke's withdrawal, and did not leave her room until the afternoon was well gone—her presence needed in the morning room. Mr. Foster, shocked by her wan and listless manner, was tempted to inquire as to her well-being, but decided it would be gauche. "I have been with the duke and Mr. Cornby, Your Grace. He took us to see the ballroom and urges that the mason remove the bricks in the doorway in all haste, for you have your heart set on it."

"Yes."

"Duchess, I disturbed you for I wish you to see the one panel that is finished to be sure the color pleases you."

Lenore stared around the walls, but ignored the panel. This room is as stark and empty as my life, she mused.

"Your Grace, please look at the panel." Mr. Foster was uneasy.

Lenore moved so she could view the soft, warm yellow. "It's like sunshine, Mr. Foster."

"Then I can have the men continue?"

"Please do." Lenore smiled at the two men gazing at her, totally unaware that they would have painted the world for her. "Thank you, Mr. Foster." She turned to go.

Mr. Foster stopped her by his gentle tone. "Your Grace, you are in the dismals and it sinks my spirits; could we have a brangle over something to pluck you up?"

Lenore looked at the moon-faced, absurd little man, whose face twisted into a concerned twinkle. She laughed. "Do you find me cheery when we quarrel?"

"It does put a sparkle in your eyes, Your Grace."

"And, to my lackluster eyes, preferable."

"Yes, Duchess," responded the decorator simply.

"Sir, you have put me in better gig already—thank you." She extended her hand and left.

Lenore made her way to Mamère's door, knocked, and walked in.

Mamère and the duke sat at the fireplace, each with a glass in hand. Lenore started to back out.

"Come in, come in," Mamère ordered. "Don't stand there like a loose screw. Bunky comes to see me when there ain't anyone around. He's been telling me the plays for the ballroom; too bad those fancy walls are silent—such tales they could tell—one night the old duchess danced there bare as a grape."

"Not in front of Lenore, madame," the duke ordered.

"Farradiddle, why must I always hold my tongue when Lenore is here—she's had two husbands."

"It isn't that I have had two husbands, Mamère, it's that I've had no lovers."

"What a pious one you are; after I was married only three months, Mr. Mitword came—oh, all right, Bunky; I can see the mere whiff of Lenore taking a lover turns you green—no gumption, this generation."

Lenore said, "Mamère, you have all the gumption

needed in this household. Myles," she added mischievously, "there is the opera tonight; if you do not care to go, I'm sure the marquis will escort me."

The old lady chuckled. "I wager he would—the most beautiful duchess in London. Well, Bunky?"

Wishing he could smother all females, the duke said, "To keep the forked tongues from wagging all over town, it behooves me to be in the box, *n'est ce pas*, madame?"

"*Mais, oui*, Bunky."

"I must leave." Lenore kissed Mamère and nodded to the duke, who held the door for her.

The duke, reseated, heard the old lady's voice. "Bunky, Lenore is a darling."

"Madame Lanier, I came today to talk about other plays altogether. I want you to invite your friends who have no family ties for Christmas dinner—Lady Vaga, the earl—any that would be alone."

The old lady stared at him. "Myles, you are the top of the trees! There's pen and paper on my desk. I'll tell you my list if you'll be so kind as to write the names." She called the names swiftly. When the duke kissed her extended hand, she whispered, "Bunky, if you'll let me, I want to kiss your cheek—There! I'm a happy old lady."

That night Lenore came downstairs and was informed that the duke would be a minute late. She smoothed her dress of pale lavender satin, cut in Empire style, and touched her hair, drawn in a Psyche knot.

The duke emerged from the library and handed Lenore a box. Opening it, Lenore caught her breath. A bunch of violets were nestled within, and a diamond cluster lay beside the blooms to serve as the pin.

"Violets in December—unheard of, Myles, and the

pin is exquisite—thank you." She put the box on the table.

"Aren't you going to wear them?" the duke asked anxiously. Lenore raised her eyes and studied his face.

"Yes, Myles, I plan to put them on in the carriage."

He sighed, and she knew he wanted to be forgiven for his snub of yesterday.

When they entered the opera box, the violets were at her waist, setting off her gown to perfection. As he placed her chair Lenore was stunned to hear her husband say, "You look very lovely tonight, Lenore." He wishes to be friends, she thought, and smiled up at him. The marquis's arrival brought an end to the comfortable silence the duke and duchess were enjoying.

On Christmas Eve, in accordance with long custom, the duke gave an evening party of dancing, singing, and refreshments for his household. As usual he forbade one morsel of the repast to be prepared in the house. While his own staff labored on the dinner for Christmas Day, outsiders cooked the hams, fowls, seperts of mutton, boiled tongues with turnips, and all the accompaniments. Desserts and pastries were placed in the kitchen, ready for the table, while hired servers lined up, waiting to perform their duties.

This Christmas party differed greatly from those at Asherwood—with the presence of a new duchess, a new son, and the duke himself, who in the past had delegated the duties of host to the Cloughs.

The huge drawing room was brilliant with blazing candles. Three musicians were ensconced on the balcony.

Promptly at the moment assigned, the duke threw open the doors and welcomed each member of his household. Lenore, at his side, admired the way of master and servants.

"Clough, old and valued friend." The duke shook hands and placed his other hand on his henchman's shoulder. "Merry Christmas!"

Lenore did not observe the duke's further greetings, for Clough was bowing before her. "Your Grace, you have lighted our lives—our Christmas is brighter; may you have a happy one."

"Why, Clough," Lenore said in delight, "you dear man, thank you! Merry Christmas!"

Mrs. Clough said softly, "Your Grace, may I confess I was a foolish old woman who turned blue when you first came, but now my heart would cringe if you were not here." Tears sprang to Lenore's eyes as she hugged the sweet-faced woman. "My darling Mrs. Clough, you are so good, and I love you."

The Madcapes expressed their joy that the duke and duchess were there.

"Thank you; you help make our stay a pleasant one."

Abel—Maria a step behind him—stood peering down at Lenore sternly. "Ma'am, the captain would wish you his happiness this night and say he is glad you are cared for by so fine a gentleman as His Grace."

"Thank you, Abel, and he would rejoice that his grandmother is so happy in your gentle hands—and a handful she is." Lenore laughed.

"She's a tartar right and tight. Maria, speak to the duchess."

Maria, who reeled volumes to Lenore each day, stood tongue-tied.

Lenore, in Spanish, said, "Maria, almost the best thing ever to happen was the day Abel brought you to me. I will never want to be without you, so please

be brave and enjoy this festive night." She kissed
Maria's cheek, saying, "Merry Christmas!" and was
glad to see the Spanish beauty melt into a shy smile.

Fenwick, staring stiffly over her head, in a choked
voice wished her the best of the season.

"Fenwick, look at me; I can't extend holiday greetings to a statue." The footman lowered his eyes, full
of love and devotion. Lenore could say nothing for an
instant as his face flooded into a dull brick-red. Then,
in a low voice, "Fenwick, it will be our secret—yours
and mine. Merry Christmas!"

Hearing her soothing words, Fenwick relaxed—She
knows and she understands—it's all I wanted. He
smiled. "A very Merry Christmas, Your Grace!"

Slightly dazed, Lenore spoke to the other maids
and footmen, who curtsied and bowed to her. Henderson brought her alert.

"Duchess, greatest day in Asherwood ever when Master Heath went up in the whisendine in front of your
house; told the duke the first day he said he was getting riveted to ye, 'Duke, you've had a rush of brains
to the head' and I was right on the needle."

"Henderson, you make this Christmas chirping
merry for me; now run and hook a pretty girl—the
dancing is about to begin."

The doctor, who had had dinner with Mr. Pettibone, arrived just as the music started. "Duchess, if
you save a set for me, it is going to be my best Christmas in a long time."

"Of course I will, Doctor. I have the greatest idea—
watch!" She signaled the musicians to stop playing,
then tugged on the duke's arm. "Myles, it's time to
dance." She gave the musicians a wave and they struck
up a lively waltz.

"Good God, not—" The duke frowned.

"Indeed so; come on." She took his hand and tugged him to the center of the floor. The duke, with a quick glance at the expectant faces of the onlookers, growled, "Females!" but placed his hand on Lenore's waist and—to his household's delight—waltzed. Cheers and squeals went up as their duke and duchess circled the dance space.

When the music drew to its close, the applause lingered until the duke clapped his hands for silence.

"You have watched the duchess and me; now we will watch you. Take your places everyone—the set is about to start."

Thus began a lively evening. The duke danced with Mrs. Clough, Mrs. Madcape, and tried to dance with Maria, but she hid her face on Abel's shoulder. Lenore had a dance with the doctor, Clough, Mr. Madcape, then Abel requested she call for a waltz and amazed everyone by showing himself as accomplished as the duke in whirling the duchess in time to the music.

Heath endeared himself by either dancing or talking with every female in the room. Charles darted amid the dancers, serving refreshments. He tried one set with Lenore but, getting hopelessly tangled, called for his father to replace him.

Just before midnight Abel and Maria slipped away and returned, Abel carrying Madame Lanier, who had been sleeping. Putting a glass of brandy in her hand, he said, "Now, my old dragon, wet your whistle and join in the caroling."

"Bring me two more, and I'll sing like a nightingale!"

"Hoy, you'd cackle like a crow."

He did not hear her reply, for the opening strains of "It Came Upon the Midnight Clear" filled the room.

When the carols had been sung, the duke opened a large basket and handed out bags—later to serve as reticules—each containing gold coins destined to brighten the receiver's eyes.

When all the gifts had been distributed, Henderson—definitely on the go, as Fenwick noted—shouted, "If there's a finer gentleman in all England than our duke, let anyone in this room step forward; I'll mill him down, so I will. I'll draw his claret, so I will." He put up his fists and reeled around, facing every direction.

"We know he's the best, old man; come along, I'll tuck you to bed." Fenwick collared the coachman, who sparred the air as he was led from the room, leaving laughter in his wake.

Mamère sleepily allowed Abel to lift her, then leaned her head on his shoulder and whispered words into his ear that later made him shout with laughter when he repeated them to the doctor.

The doctor shook his head. "I think she'd execute every outrage she suggested, given the chance."

"By Jupiter, even I'm too old for what she chatters about," Abel said, chuckling.

Within the hour the house fell quiet.

51

On Christmas morning the household came alive before dawn. Maids and footmen inspired deeply, enjoying the whiffs of delicious smells that came from
the kitchens as they hurriedly ate breakfast.

The family rose later, but in time to be ready for
Henderson to drive them to early service. The sun
dispelled the haze and the snow lay in patches as the
carriage took its place in line at St. Paul's.

Awed by the size of the cathedral and the solemnity
of the music and words, Charles was quiet; however,
on the drive to Grosvenor Square, he squirmed in anticipation of release from his Christmas secrets.

Heath, with his own secrets, tried in vain to catch
his father's eye in a meaningful exchange. The duke,
nodding to passing friends, mused on the change of
circumstances since the previous Christmas, spent in
isolation at Asherwood. Lenore, lifting her hand in a
wave now and then, wondered if the proud man seated
beside her would ever smile on her.

Doctor Sylvester peered from Madame Lanier's window. He had looked in on Mamère earlier in the day,
had found her feverish, and sent word he could not attend early service. He saw the carriage swing into the
Square. "Madame, you and I are blessed to be in this
house."

"Don't be a toadeater," snapped the old lady, "and if you don't let me attend Christmas dinner, you will be on the street by nightfall. Don't stand there lollygagging, come quack me."

Relieved by her return of temper, the doctor checked her and concluded nothing more than rest was now required, so told her farewell and that he was going to breakfast.

Mamère, giving him a leer, said, "I wish I were younger; no morsel of food would tempt you from this room."

"Indeed not, it scarcely does now." He sighed. "But I relinquish you to my arch rival—Morpheus"—he blew her a kiss—"my fickle jade."

The family was assembled when the doctor entered the breakfast room.

"How is Mamère?" Lenore asked.

"She's a trifle overcome by excitement, but can certainly join her guests for dinner."

"Oh, that's good news. Come, Doctor, before your eggs grow cold."

"Oh, please hurry, Doctor," Charles urged, "I don't see how I can abide waiting much longer. What do we do first, Father?"

"Your mother has made the plays and appears as jumpy as you are"—Lenore had spilt some coffee—"so we will put her in command and follow her instructions to the letter. Your orders, Duchess?"

Lenore, dabbing her gown with a napkin, gazed at the sober faces, then hoping to sound military, said in deep tones, "Troops will form four abreast outside the morning room—the doctor, Charles, the duke, and Heath. I will scout ahead. When you arrive at the ramparts, knock three times."

She rose and saluted. Charles giggled as she marched out of the room.

"Troops," said Heath knowingly, "it would be wise to like what we see."

"Son," said the duke, "you're growing up."

Lined in formation as commanded, the duke stood at attention, and the others straightened in rigid pose. The duke then knocked three times slowly. The doors were flung open and Lenore stood to one side. The four males relaxed and gasped—it was as if they looked into the sun itself.

The yellow walls; the white draperies; the soft tawny and rose Aubusson rug; the mint-green chairs; the golden desk, inlaid with mother-of-pearl; the tall clock—all light, all cheer.

"The ramparts have fallen. Do come in, sirs." Lenore curtsied.

Tentatively the duke moved to view the fireplace, the others still as his eyes lighted on the painting.

"Asherwood," he whispered, "Asherwood." He stepped closer. "How magnificent!" Whirling on Lenore, he asked, "Where did you get it?"

"You like it, Myles?"

"What a question! Where did you get it?"

"We found it in the ballroom."

"I really found it," Charles said.

"It is the work of Mr. James Turner, Myles."

"Turner?" the duke studied the signature. "Turner doesn't paint in this manner."

"So all agree, Myles, but Mr. Cordyne, who cleaned it, and Mr. Foster both vow it is Mr. Turner's technique."

The duke gazed at the canvas as the others roamed around admiring the room. Charles posted himself by

the Christmas presents and hoped the largest package
in the pile was for him.

"Good God!" ejaculated the duke suddenly.

"What, Myles?" All turned toward him.

The duke replied slowly, "When I was a small tot,
a scrubby boy came to our door—I remember, because so few came unexpected—and asked my mother
if he might paint Asherwood. She told him he might,
provided he show her the painting at teatime. At first
he demurred, then agreed. I dimly recall following
him, but soon lost interest, for all he did was take
paints from a messy box, and then my nurse came
and took me away. The boy might have been the
young Turner." The duke frowned in puzzlement.

"May I open this present? It has my name on it,"
Charles cut in, then gazed from face to face so eagerly
that the others took their places—the duke seating himself so he could study the painting.

Charles ripped open the large gift—it had turned
out to be for him. He shrieked with joy at the saddle
of tooled leather with brass trim.

Charles dragged forth the object of his happiness.
"Nicky will turn blue." He heaved a sigh. "Now, Bro,
your turn." He handed Heath a large flat box—the
next biggest.

"I see we sport our own Saint Nick," said the doctor to Lenore and the duke as Heath drew from the
box a superfine dress jacket with large brass buttons.

"Whee!" exclaimed Heath. "Will George's eyes bug
when he sees this." He removed his jacket and tried
on the new one. "A perfect fit, Father; how did you
know my—"

"A father too can have Christmas secrets, Son," the
duke retorted.

Charles, while Heath folded the jacket, ran from

the tree to give each a gift. Gradually the stack diminished—there were no disappointments. At one point Lenore said, "Charles, give your father that package—no, the next one—I can't stand it one more minute."

The duke slowly untied the ribbon, tore off the paper, then gazed in mild surprise at the worn book in his hand. "*Principia* by Newton," he read in an inquiring tone.

"Lift the cover," cried Lenore.

The duke did her bidding, perused the faded writing, then rose and went to the window to reread the inscription.

"Lenore!"

"Yes, yes, isn't it exciting?"

"What, Father. May I see it?" Heath leaned over his father's shoulder and read the words aloud.

"Why, it's, why—Mother, how did you find it?"

"Yes, Lenore, it's a true rarity. How . . . ?"

"I went to Tollands, and there it lay, tossed carelessly on a secondhand book table. I tried to explain to Mr. Tolland its value, but he was most lofty, saying, if I must, pay the boy an extra pound. And, Myles, that is what I did the day I met the marquis, and if I'd told you, you would have wanted to know why I was there, so I didn't." Lenore said it all in one breath.

Charles chimed in, "Oh, I can see that—lies are white at Christmas, Father."

The duke peered closely at the book, saying, "Lenore, this is an addition of worth to my library—I thank you." He bowed. "Doctor, take a look at this."

Shortly the presents were unwrapped. Lenore, arranging ribbons and tags, realized that among her gifts there was none from the duke. Don't be a mawkish fool—he's let you redo this room and have the ballroom done—most generous—and I'm a selfish fuss-budget. "I must go to Mamère," she announced.

"Let us all go," remarked the duke. The offer surprised Lenore.

"Must I, Father?" Charles asked. "I'd like"—he caught the duke's glance—"Oh, yes, Mamère should have Christmas too."

Lenore, carrying her presents, went into the hall, smiled at Fenwick, and started up the stairs.

"A moment, Lenore; hand Fenwick your presents—I want to show you something."

Fenwick jumped and relieved Lenore of her gifts and ribbons and the boys flanked the front doors as the duke held out his arm. Puzzled, Lenore rested her hand and let the duke lead her to the doors, which Heath and Charles threw open. Then she gasped—drawn up to the curb stood an elegant curricle and two matched grays—Henderson sat tall in the driver's seat.

"Merry Christmas, Lenore!" said the duke.

"Oh, Myles," cried Lenore, and burst into tears. The duke handed her his handkerchief.

Fenwick brought a cape and placed it on her shoulders. When she had dried her tears, the duke put on his greatcoat. Heath and Charles stepped back and bowed. Henderson jumped down and held the grays as the duke and Lenore ran down the steps.

"Oh, Myles, the grays are—I can't find words."

"The finest in England, Your Grace," Henderson supplied as she patted the noses of the proud creatures.

"Shall we take a drive?" asked the duke.

"Oh, yes—but Mamère?" She looked at the old lady's window to see Mamère, the doctor, and the boys waving and grinning. She laughed and threw kisses to her audience.

Lenore let the duke hand her in and when he was seated beside her, fought her desire to throw herself into his arms. Instead she smoothed the swabs. "Myles, my gratitude has no bounds."

The duke, with a slight movement of the hands, set the bays clopping in rhythm.

"What perfect movers; do you think I can ever learn to handle the reins?" Lenore asked.

"Of course. Heath will teach you."

"Oh, I hoped *you* might."

"No, I expect to be far too busy."

They rode along in silence, Lenore admiring his driving skill, of which the duke seemed unconscious.

Lenore broke the silence. "Myles, as a little girl I daydreamed of growing up and being a princess, a great actress, a famous opera singer—though why a singer I'll never understand—my voice is scarcely better than Mrs. Turtlelock's—but to the young any dream is possible. I mention this because in every role I cast myself, I rode in my own curricle pulled by matched grays, seated beside a handsome gentleman to whom I had, with condescension, entrusted the reins." She giggled. "Though I must confess the gentleman had a strong resemblance to Johnny Snow, my father's acolyte. Today is far finer than any dream because you are handsomer than Johnny Snow."

"Thank you, madam." The duke's tone was dry.

"So you can see, your gift, like the festival, enchants me. Thank you, Myles."

"Lenore, did you ever dream of a masquerade?"

"Heavens, no; I never even heard of one as a child —why?"

"I intend to give one."

"Why, Myles, what fun!"

The duke pulled to the side of the road and

stopped. "It is to be the biggest ever given, the cream of the *ton* to be invited, and—"

"Where is it to be held?" Lenore was more than ready to discuss the affair.

"At the house, of course."

"You can't get the cream of the *ton* into the house, Myles."

"We'll open the lower floor right through, including the library and breakfast room; in that way we can accommodate a large number of guests. Lenore, the ball is important; I want no expense spared—two orchestras, all the extra servants needed, flowers in profusion, and anything else you deem necessary. I will draw up the list of those to be invited and see to the printing and posting—other tasks to be yours. I'm aware I ask a lot, but—"

"Myles, I will undertake the planning gladly." Lenore paused. "I do wish Rachel were here; she's so knowledgeable about such things. But now we must go home and celebrate Mamère's Christmas."

Entering Mamère's room, they found the doctor and the boys playing jackstraws. After questions about the curricle and horses, Heath remarked that not only would he teach Lenore the fine points of driving but would demand payment—the privilege of borrowing the carriage on occasion.

"To sport a figure for some silly bleater, you can be sure," said Charles.

Heath grabbed the boy and they scuffled for a minute, then Mamère intervened. "Enow, you anapos, it's my Christmas time."

As she opened her presents Mamère told a story of how one Christmas her grandfather rode a horse into their great hall and distributed the gifts by tossing them to each child. "He had a large bag full." She sighed. "That was a long time ago. . . . Thank you for your gifts, and now go—I must rest or my doctor won't permit me my dinner."

As the festivities were over until dinner time, Lenore went to her room and packed away her gifts, singing as she thought of her curricle and grays. Myles is truly kind—a masquerade. He grows genial!

The Christmas dinner served in the drawing room was punctuated with clucks and smacks of relish as the servings appeared, each more delicious than the last. Mamère, attired in purple and wearing her turban, presided, at Lenore's insistence, at one end of the long table, and the duke at the other. By the table card of each old lady and gentleman were ivory fans for the ladies and watch fobs for the gentlemen. After dozens of reminiscences, some amusing, some tiresome, the ancients, as they left, assured Lenore and the duke that it was a most wonderful Christmas. They kissed Lenore and the bolder ladies hugged the duke. Heath and Charles stoically allowed themselves to be petted and patted. Mamère, waving good-bye until the last guest drove from the house, turned to the duke and said, "Duke, you're a darling, and I love you," then fell into Abel's arms, asleep before he reached the stairs.

"She's right, you know," said Lenore, laughing. "You are truly a great gun, Myles."

"Stop pouring the butter boat over me. Christmas is for the old and the young, and I'm neither. Good night." His Grace was certain that he had had enough of Christmas.

"Mother, I'll play jackstraws with you."

Lenore, staring at the closed library door, did not hear his offer.

"Come on, Charley, Mother is tired."

"What?" asked the dazed Lenore.

"Charles would like to play jackstraws with you, Duchess." The doctor smiled.

Lenore looked on the trio, who waited patiently, then said, "I would too—last one upstairs is a slow monkey!" She whirled and ran lightly up the stairs.

52

"Oh, Alfred, must I?" Lady Martha Lanier touched her lips with the quill of her pen.

"Yes!" Sir Alfred slapped the desk. "To eschew the Duke and Duchess of Asherwood would be an error beyond bounds."

"I don't see why; I dislike her and I judge you are not overfond of the duke, so—"

"Our feelings do not signify; to exclude the Asherwoods, who cozen my grandmother, from any party we give would rock the *ton,* and I do not choose to do so."

"Oh, I wish Eric hadn't gotten himself blown to bits on the Penn, then she wouldn't be so lofty and the most talked-about female in London. Have you seen her new curricle?"

"No, but Pierre described it to me."

"Ha, that's another thing; Pierre and the duke are as thick as thieves—gaming, riding, pleasuring together everywhere—why, when Pierre hangs on your sleeve, does he not include you in their—"

"Most simple, my dear, I don't wish to go under a cloud gaming, I have the worst seat in all London, and conversing with them gives me the fidgets."

"I thought you liked Pierre."

"I do; every night upon his return, over a brandy he regales me with the evening's sport and what was said —he is amusing. Now please get on with your list, Martha."

Exasperated, she began to write—"The Duke and"— then paused. "Alfred, did you see your heir yesterday?"

"Leon? No, should I have?"

"If you had, sir, you would pause to invite—"

"What has Leon to do with inviting . . . ?"

"Leon is your son."

"No question; resembles me to a pin."

"Well, Leon came home yesterday looking like a dipped cat."

Sir Alfred stared at her.

"Close your mouth, Alfred. Leon's clothes were stained, damp, and his fingers wrinkled."

"Martha, do try to make some sense."

"Do you know what he'd been doing? Washing the duke's windows!" she exclaimed in triumph.

"Martha, you've lost your buttons."

"Not so; like every boy in London, Leon insists on visiting the duke's at every opportunity—yesterday the duke made him scrub windows."

"Hubble-bubble! Myles wouldn't—"

"Ask Leon!"

"I will—where is he?"

"In his room; I told him to stay there until I gave him permission to leave."

Sir Alfred rang for the footman and instructed him to send his son to the library. "Martha, you stay here and finish the invitations."

Leon entered the library and faced his father across his desk. The boy's sullen expression bespoke his dejection.

"Leon," Sir Alfred asked sternly, "what does your mother tell me?"

"I don't know, sir." The factual statement stirred Sir Alfred's ire.

"Don't talk pert. Did you or did you not wash the Duke of Asherwood's windows yesterday?"

Leon gazed at his father in frustrated amazement.

"Is that what she told you?"

"Yes, and I want an explanation."

"Yes, I washed the duke's windows, though I never thought of it on that head."

"How did you think on it?"

Leon paused.

"Speak up, Leon," Sir Alfred urged not unkindly.

"Father, the most famous thing—the duke's given us a club room all our own."

"Start from the beginning, Son."

"Well, yesterday when we gathered in Heath's and Charles's study, Doctor Sylvester announced he had something to show us."

"Us?"

"Oh, our crowd—all the chaps—about eighteen of us. Well, the doctor led us down through the kitchen, then up two flights of stairs, and there was this huge room. The doctor called it the old ballroom—glory, it's big. The doctor said the duke would let us have it as a clubroom if we wanted it—"

"Traipsing through the kitchen every day?"

"No! There's an outside staircase, just not repaired yet. Father, you should see the room—"

"But the doctor said you must clean the room first?"

" 'Course not! You see, we decided that Heath and

George should be the club's leaders—they are bang-up-to-the-nines chaps, both of them. Then we discussed where we could get tables and chairs—Hacky said his father has—"

"Hacky? Do you mean the Earl of Hackingham's boy?"

"That's who; he says his mother has a slew of old chairs in the attic—do we, Father?"

"I don't know; finish your story."

"Well, Nicky said he might be able to get a table, and Willie thought his—"

"Never mind that; what about the windows?"

"While we were ganging around, making our plans, old Bed wandered off to inspect some things in a corner. He found a broom and began to sweep. Hacky saw him and asked what he was doing. Old Bed asked him if he was blind—he was sweeping—couldn't Hack see the place needed it? The rest of us drifted over, then Hacky picked up another broom. Nicky said to Charley, 'Hey, there's some rags, let's you and me dust'; I saw the windows were dirty so I asked Heath where I could get some water, and he said 'You're too small to lug water; I'll get it,' and he did, and I washed windows. It was famous fun; they're round, you know, and open, so we could do both sides."

"We?" asked his bemused father.

"Uh, huh, Chizzy, Devons, Glou, and me—those chaps couldn't stand it when they saw the fun I was having."

Sir Alfred blinked—the scions of two dukes, an earl, and a lord washing windows!

"You ought to see it, Father—'course you can't, 'cause the only grown-up allowed is Doctor Sylvester. It's almost spotless now, as far as we could reach, but Heath said he believes his father will see to the cleaning above our heads. After we mend the tables and chairs, we're going to try to get mats and bookcases; we may even set up a ring—Doctor Sylvester knows fisticuffs." His face fell. "And Mother won't even let me out of my room—I'm missing all the fun."

Sir Alfred stared at his eldest, who had always been the most languid of his children, passive, and—yes—bored. "All right, you may go to Heath's. I'll speak to your mother. Wear your oldest clothes."

"Hurrah! I'm going to ask the footman if there isn't some old thing I can take from the attic. Thanks, Father, you're bang-up to the nines too!" Leon called back as he ran out the door.

For a moment Sir Alfred savored the first words of praise he had ever elicited from his son, then returned to the morning room.

"Well, Alfred, did you find out?" Lady Martha asked.

"Yes; Myles let the boys have the old ballroom on the third floor for a clubroom, and on their own the boys are cleaning it."

"That's outrageous! I don't think my son should be washing windows, after all, he is . . . your son and will be Sir Leon Lanier one day."

Foregoing a reminder to his wife of the conditions under which his son would be Sir Leon, Sir Alfred said, "My dear, if Heath, Charley, Nicky, Hacky, Bed, Chizzy, Devon, and Glou can sweep, scrub, and wash windows, I guess my son and heir may."

"What?" shrieked his wife. "Do you tell me . . . Did those . . . ?"

"Yes."

"I never in my born days heard of such a thing—why, they are the cream of—"

"Precisely! Is the invitation list complete?"

Lady Martha rose. "Finished, and this very minute I'm going to call on Lily Chiswick; I'm sure she will feel as I do, especially about her Redford doing scrub work—he's sickly, and washing windows could easily give him influenza."

"Fiddle-faddle; Redford's strong as a horse."

"Good-bye, Alfred; I must go to poor Lily right away."

"Guard your tongue, Martha!" He winced as the door slammed.

Lady Martha's anticipation proved correct; Lady Lily was most outraged, and her morning room was abuzz with affronted mothers. Their repugnance at having their firstborns demeaned by low labor was an indulgence they all enjoyed!

Some mothers had been fortunate enough to meet their sons returning from the servile toils, thus having the authentic say-so in the discussion. Others gleaned their information from tattling tutors and butlers, and were forced to give way to their more knowledgeable sister in indignation.

Torn nankeens, filthy shirts, ripped stockings, broken fingernails, scratched faces, and cobwebby hair were enjoined to catch the attention for the speaker. Wounds were enumerated, ruined garb listed—gradually the twice-told tales spun to an end and the prattle swung on the duke, the perpetrator of the indignities.

Although she dared not contribute, the talk soothed Lady Martha—once she asked shyly if any of the ladies had seen dear Lenore's new curricle—a perfectly harmless question, she decided. The response was most gratifying; the ladies gave "dear Lenore" a proper ripping. Too beautiful not to be a flirt, far too overdressed, a new gown for every occasion—does anyone know where she purchases them?—a careless stepmother or she would not have permitted the duke . . .

Lily Chiswick confessed she had known Lenore when she was Eric's wife—as sweet a girl as you could know, but now . . . ?

Seldom silent for long, Mrs. Osterhouse, a widow of great wealth, firm convictions, and a heavy voice, proclaimed, "It was wrong of us to accept Sally Jersey's dictum to acknowledge the duke and duchess. In my opinion they are de trop completely and I for one do not intend to have anything further to do with them. You may do as you wish, but my position is clear—neither my son nor I will speak to the Asherwoods again."

There was a short pause, then a burst of uncertain murmurs broke out: "I'm not sure . . ."—"My William may not . . ."—"What will Lady Jersey think if . . ."—"I've invited them to . . ." Finally Lady Martha spoke aloud. "Mrs. Osterhouse, Helen, you can realize that however much I may approve of your suggestion, I am unable to engender your course. My husband's grandmother, Madame Lanier, is a—I won't say guest—a member of the duke's household, therefore I am obliged to . . ." She shrugged.

Mrs. Osterhouse smiled. "We understand and sympathize with your position, dear Martha, but for the rest . . ." She swept the circle with a stern eye.

"My son is my heart," averred Lady Hackingham—an avowal that drew stares, for it was well known that she viewed her children as rarely as possible—"and belittling him to the function of the most menial of servants I will not tolerate. I align myself with you, dear Mrs. Osterhouse." She rose and sat by her new ally, whom she despised.

Others nodded in agreement, giving bobs of forgiveness in Lady Martha's direction.

Sipping tea and glowing with righteousness in their display of immaculate motherhood, the ladies chatted —all innocent of their instigation of battles royal in the bosoms of their families.

53

That very night Mrs. Osterhouse chose to inform her son at dinner of her forbidding his going to the duke's home ever again; she sat astounded as she saw her son rise, throw down his napkin, and stalk out of the room, banging the door with vim.

Lady Lily, resting on her chaise longue, sent for her Redford and gently explained to the dear boy that because of his frailty, she dare not expose him to further dangers so rife at the duke's house. She nearly fainted when he uttered a completely unacceptable word and rushed from the room. Most certainly she would have fainted had she beheld her frail Redford, in frustrated rage, challenge his tutor to a mill and proceed to knock the poor man senseless.

Nicky, the Earl of Laudersdown, went into a tantrum and sent his mother into hysterics.

One lively lad of eight, when forbidden to go to Charles's home ever again, told his mother not to be a fool in a tone so reminiscent of his father's that she slapped the boy, who walked to the door, turned, and made an elaborate bow, saying, "My dear Amy, you are a fool!"—every inch his father.

Sons noted for their amiable natures became snarling rebels before their mothers' eyes. Certain ladies found their sons' low vocabularies to be far more extensive than they had thought.

Tears flowed uselessly; signs of vapors were scorned; threats to report behavior to fathers—often the ultimate weapon—were shrugged off. Finally sons were banished as mothers awaited reenforcements—fathers.

Only one lad escaped the rigors of the afternoon, for he, as he entered his home fresh from his labors, had the extreme good fortune to run into his father, who with exceeding good sense seized his bedraggled son, rushed him up the stairs, and restored him to respectability.

Mothers, exhausted, tearful, and angry, awaited eagerly their husbands' presence. The gentlemen had been away from home the night before attending a banquet in honor of Lord Codwather's thirty-fifth birthday—a dazzling affair, unattended by ladies—for the Lord was an envied bachelor as well as a party giver of renown. Wines and spirits had been abundant, and as the gentlemen had not seen fit to follow in Sir Alfred's footsteps—abstemious participation and early leave-taking—most were unavailable until evening for their family duties.

Wives who had ruled the nursery and uninterruptedly controlled the growing years of their offspring, were totally unprepared for their spouses' reactions. With varying degrees of veracity the ladies painted the picture—the duke's crimes against the young, the strictures any good mother would impose, the deplorable behavior of heirs, the obvious requirements of the parental hand, and the readoption of censure of the duke and duchess.

The fathers laughed!

"Duke got the little cawker to dirty his hands—best thing that ever happened to the halfling"—"He was tongue valiant to you, eh"—"So the apron strings ain't as tight as I feared"—"Damn good go—make a man of him"—"Ha, the wagfeathers have their knives sharpened again"—"Don't be a fool, Amy."

Abashed, the ladies railed and wailed, but to no benefit.

Lord Chiswick, the mildest man in London, said, "Lily, you've mollycoddled Redford long enough. Old Myles has proved to me there's at least some hope for our overgrown brat in nankeens. Knocked old Willow Willie senseless? Good! Now Red can go to school like any boy his age should."

"Red? Chizzy, don't you realize Redford is—"

"Red is a strapping lad, cosseted and petted to his and my distraction."

"Don't call him Red!" Horrified at the vision of her son as anything but fragile, and furthermore, his being sent away, Redford's mother wept.

"Dry out your ogles, Lily; they won't bring me around your thumb."

The Lady tossed her head. "Well, you can do all those cruel things to me, but you can't make me speak to Lenore or Myles ever again."

"Don't care a groat if you don't—your loss, not mine."

"You mean you will, even though I won't?"

"Certainly—Myles is one of my oldest friends, best whist player I know and a great gun; I'm beginning to wonder, after what you tell me, if he isn't a genius."

"Genius? Why he's so high in the instep that—look how he dresses Lenore!"

His Lordship snorted, "So that's it; you frippery females turn green when you see Lenore—"

"No!—not true, but you must concede she—"

"Is the most elegantly turned out lady in London—no question."

"Oh, go away!" Lady Lily was utterly exasperated by the failure of her perfectly logical appeal to Redford's father.

She did not suffer alone; many wives went to bed that night convinced they were married to insensitive, callous brutes.

54

On the day of her party, the first of the new year, Lady Martha Lanier woke early. She enumerated the details and arrangements. Was there enough or too much for the supper—Alfred waxed obnoxious about leftover food. Would the soprano, Madame Futon, hired at great expense, appear? Lady Martha sighed; she had wanted to employ musicians so her guests could dance, but, no—Alfred was truly stiff-necked about waltzing and nowadays everyone waltzed. She felt uneasy about those she had invited—the duke and duchess, merely by their presence, might be disruptive.

During breakfast she instructed Alfred on his duties

as host and listed the many tasks of the day ahead. Sir Alfred did not listen; he was scanning the mail.

"Good Lord, look at this." He tossed a heavy cream linen card to her. Embossed in gold was the formal invitation to Lord and Lady Lanier to attend a masquerade at the home of the Duke and Duchess of Asherwood.

"Well!" proclaimed Lady Martha, "it's about time; they have appeared everywhere and have never—"

"I wonder what it means?" asked her husband.

"It's perfectly clear; at long last they are to pay off their indebtedness."

"But a masquerade?" Sir Alfred frowned.

"Why did the invitation have to come today?" Lady Martha fretted. "It's all everyone will chatter about tonight. What showoffs! A masquerade—la! Well, I've not time to think on it today." She rose. "Alfred, don't forget to check that the champagne is properly chilled." She left Sir Alfred deep in thought.

The first snowflakes sent Lady Martha running to the window to view the sky and confirm her fears. The storm, begun in a leisurely fashion, bode ill for the evening. By nightfall the continuing swirling flakes had laid a five-inch cover on London and a chill on Lady Martha's heart. Only the brave would leave home on this night; the notes of regret, brought by bundled coachmen, were unnecessary politenesses— Lady Martha knew neither she nor any of her household would have ventured forth in the storm.

At tea Sir Alfred and the marquis tried to console the tearful lady by their assurances of attendance.

"I, for one, intend to be fully attired and ready," announced the marquis.

"I too," Sir Alfred echoed.

Lady Martha dressed slowly, spending time trying

to repair the ravage her tears had made. When she joined her husband in the hall, the footman was opening the doors to permit Mrs. Osterhouse to enter.

"Oh, Helen, I'm so glad to see you." Lady Martha hugged the enormous lady. "To come out this dreadful night?"

"Never let a few flakes deter me," Mrs. Osterhouse boomed. "Plenty of robes and a stout carriage take me anywhere. How are you, Alfred? Ah, and here's the Frenchman; good evening, Marquis." She held out her hand and gave him a glance he could only conclude was meant to be roguish.

"Madam." The marquis tested his belief by giving her hand an extra squeeze and had his own painfully pinched in return.

To have a flirt with the huge Mrs. Osterhouse lay beyond his wildest imagining. He was relieved when the doors opened and the Chiswicks stepped in from the swirl outside. Bowing to Lady Lily, he clapped his friend on the shoulder. "Chizzy, just the man I need to see," he said as he led the amiable gentleman into a corner.

"Chizzy, by all that's holy, keep me out of the clutches of that elephant," the marquis pled.

"Who? Helen Osterhouse?" Chizzy asked, puzzled.

"The very one; she is a balloon!"

"Mighty plump in the purse, Pierre."

"*Mon Dieu!* She's on the toddle this way."

"Chizzy," roared the lady, "I hear you're going to send dear Redford to school. Marquis, can you picture tearing a son from his mother's heart to send him out into—"

The marquis, who could not, nor wished to, cut in, "Excuse me, Mrs. Osterhouse, I see the Asherwoods have brought Lady Jersey." He then abandoned his friend to the dressing down given by the large lady—doubly irked by the marquis's withdrawal and Lord Chiswick's frozen indifference to her wise words.

Lady Martha's spirits had lifted slightly at the arrival of her first guests, but sank when she saw the resplendent duke and Lenore, a dream in her simple lime-velvet gown, and Lady Jersey, garbed in blue chiffon covered with silver lace.

"Lady Jersey, it is good of you to venture—"

"Fustian, I love a storm; I'm tempted to take Pierre sledding tomorrow." She laughed up at the Frenchman, who had taken his place beside her.

"For you, dear lady, I would risk my life, but spend ten minutes in the cold? No!" He beamed and led her to the drawing room.

"Lenore, Myles," Lady Martha greeted, "I hardly expected to see you this night," her voice as cold as the storm outside.

"Lady Martha," said the duke, "one can hardly resist the Lanier hospitality, no matter the weather."

Lenore, shaken by his tone, cried hurriedly, "Martha, your gown becomes you, and your hair—lovely."

"Thank you; it's flattering to have the approval of one whose own fashions are the talk of London."

Lenore blinked. She knew Martha disliked her, but the venomous tone of Martha's words hurt. She despises me. Lenore turned to Alfred, wondering if he had heard his wife's remark; if he had, his face was bland as he asked after his grandmother.

"Mamère is well," replied Lenore, "and was delighted to see you on Christmas day."

Lady Martha, though welcoming Amy Lovill, stiffened and Lenore realized she should not have mentioned Alfred's visit. Glancing at her host in fleeting apology, she encountered a flinty stare, and fled into the drawing room.

Seeing the duke and Chizzy standing by Lily's chair, she seated herself beside her friend. "Lily, darling, how are you and your dear children?" She put her hand on Lily's arm. "I hear Redford is going away to school."

"Yes, he is." Lady Lily threw off Lenore's hand and stood. "And it is all your fault. You will excuse me." Lily did not see the astonishment on Lenore's face as she watched Lily's retreating back.

"Chizzy." Lenore pulled on his sleeve. "What on earth is Lily talking about—my being responsible for Redford's going off to school?"

"Oh, just female fustian." He smiled at Lenore. "It does not signify."

"That's not true; Lily is angry and I want you to tell me why."

"Later, Lenore." Grabbing the duke's arm, he hustled him away as Mrs. Osterhouse lowered her bulk into the chair next to Lenore's.

"Duchess," the lady trumpeted, "I wish to inform you—I will not be at your masquerade, nor do I judge many will."

"Please let me ask you why, Mrs. Osterhouse." Lenore felt her head begin to ache.

"Having observed you and the duke since the time of Sally Jersey's ball, when, it can be said, she thrust you upon us, we of the *haut ton* have found you do not conduct yourselves in the gentility we deem acceptable."

Lenore gazed at the tiny eyes full of malice, buried like raisins in a vast pudding, and said, "Then it is understandable you will never wish to enter our home.

Good night, Mrs. Osterhouse." Lenore rose and walked across the floor to where Lady Vaga sat.

"Lenore, my little one, you're as white as the snow blanketing us—what is it, child?"

Lenore laughed weakly. "I'm pale at the idea you're daring such a night."

"Poof! A few sparkles never hurt anyone, although I do see Martha's party is thin; missish generation this. How is Floss, though why I ask is beyond me; she was stout as a pikestaff this afternoon—What is the matter with you, Duchess?"

"My head throbs a bit, that's all." Lenore tried to smile, but Lady Vaga saw tears well up in Lenore's eyes.

"Don't try to gull me, little lady, what troubles you?"

"Mrs. Osterhouse just gave me a fearful set-down and says no one is coming to our masquerade."

"Hoy, that one! She's as puffy as a pig, and every ounce as mean."

"She says the duke and I are not genteel enough for the *ton*."

"Devil take her—he will eventually, mark my words —genteel enough—damned nonsense. Humph, she's turned green because you are so fondly liked."

"I'm all about in my head—Martha hates me—Lily is furious with me—Mrs. Osterhouse—Oh, I wish I had not come tonight." Lenore sighed and dabbed her eyes.

"Stop those tears, young lady; here comes that fool Amy Lovill." Lady Vaga had also seen other eyes turned their way.

"Lady Vaga," Amy Lovill drawled, "because of the storm, Martha has decided to serve supper immediately; would you like me to save you a place at our table?"

"Thank you, Amy, but the duke and duchess have paid me the honor of letting me sit with them."

"Oh, yes, the duchess," Amy said in bored tones. "By the way, Lenore, your invitation arrived this afternoon. Unfortunately Cedric and I expect to be out of London that week, so of course we cannot come."

"What a silly you are, Amy; it will be the most brilliant ball of the season," Lady Vaga commented. "Lenore has just been describing some of the plans, and only the stupid will not attend."

"Then I suspect the duchess will find there are a lot of stupid people in London this season." The lady strolled off.

Lenore, held spellbound by Lady Vaga's bouncers and crushed by Amy's remarks, said nothing.

Lady Vaga, who had not taken Lenore's laments too seriously, suddenly deduced that maybe there was some mischief afoot. "Come with me; I want to see Sally Jersey—she's talking to the marquis."

Reluctantly Lenore walked beside the old lady, who proclaimed loudly enough to be heard widely, "Too bad Martha didn't get her soprano; might have cut the rattle-prattle hereabouts." Reaching Lady Jersey, she continued, "Sally, stop rolling your ogles at the marquis; I want a word with you."

Lady Jersey put her hand to her heart. "Oh, thank heaven—for a moment I thought you planned to work your wiles on Pierre—a rivalry I couldn't win."

"Keep your tongue between your teeth, saucebox," said Lady Vaga, grinning, giving the marquis a brush with her eyes. "Though I admit, thirty years ago I'd have had a shot at it."

The marquis laughed. "Why let a few years bother you, Lady Vaga? I will call on you in the morning."

"Cawker," said the pleased old lady, "I never get up before noon."

"All the better," decided the marquis with a leer.

"Now stop that flippery talk. Never entertained a gentleman in my bedroom in my life." She noted that Lenore half smiled.

"Madame, what a shocker!" The marquis shook his head. "Any gentleman lucky enough to be in your bedroom was thoroughly entertained; wouldn't you bet a monkey on it, Sally?"

"Remind me to tell you, Pierre, what fascinating tales I've heard of the trail of broken hearts strewn by Lady Vaga."

"Not one word, Sally Jersey," the old lady roared. "Don't you dare open your mouth." Her ferocity made even Lenore laugh.

Lady Jersey put her finger to her lips, then taking Lady Vaga's arm, started to withdraw. Lenore took alarm. "Lady Vaga, do not talk about me, please."

"You flatter yourself, young lady; I've more important matters to rattle about," she said, and immediately poured all of Lenore's experiences into Lady Jersey's ear, begging her to discover what these nasty females were up to. Lady Jersey, indignant, promised every aid, then said, "Lenore looks sad—we must cheer her; come on."

As the ladies whispered the marquis said to Lenore, "My dear Duchess, you are quiet tonight."

"Who would be so bold as to join in your shocking dialogue; you're as bad as Lady Vaga, and she as wicked as Mamère." Lenore sighed.

"What ails you, Lenore? You look ill."

"I do have a headache," confessed Lenore.

"Well, let's gather in the ladies and the duke and go to supper—it should help." He tucked her arm in his and awaited Lady Vaga and Lady Jersey.

Lady Jersey said, "Lady Vaga, you and I are quite in the suds; Pierre has eyes only for the gorgeous Lenore."

"Who has eyes only for His Grace, alas," said the marquis, who had noted Lenore watching the duke across the room. "To supper, ladies."

The duke, spying the party, fell in step. "Lenore, you look weary to the bone."

Giving him a wan smile, she admitted to throbbing temples.

"I advise supper, Duke; will you please give Lenore your arm, so I may escort these two ladies milling over me—such a delicious position for any gentleman."

At supper the badinage continued, but Lenore ate almost nothing and the duke, as they finished the orange soufflé, suggested that he and Lenore leave, and assured Lady Jersey he would send his carriage back for her. The marquis vowed to see her home safely.

On the way home Lenore, sobbing and almost incoherent, tried to relate to the duke what had taken place. Arriving home, the duke sent for Mrs. Clough and woke the doctor, who, after examining Lenore, announced that she had influenza and must be tended all night.

On the morning after the Alfred Laniers' party, the sun shone, but gloom as heavy as the night's storm descended on the Grosvenor Square house. During the night Lenore had become delirious and the doctor had not left her room; Mrs. Clough and Maria carried out his many orders.

Early in the morning Heath and Charles were dispatched to the George Featherheath's. The duke paced the floor and listened to Mrs. Clough's reports, given hourly. Mamère was left to the ministrations of the Madcapes, who were forbidden to go near the sick-room.

Mamère, frightened, did something she had not done in years—she prayed. Late in the morning Lady Vaga and Lady Jersey were admitted by Fenwick, whose solemn mien bespoke immediately the gravity of Lenore's illness.

"We'll see Madame Lanier, Fenwick," Lady Vaga declared, and before Fenwick could catch his breath, they moved up the stairs.

Mamère burst into wild sobs at the sight of her friends, who soothed her as best they could. Finally Lady Vaga said, "Floss, stop fountaining; it helps the little duchess not one whit." She pulled the bell rope and ordered Mrs. Madcape to bring some ratafia. Curiosity about the events at her grandson's party finally reduced Mamère's wails to heavy sighs. Lady Jersey's languid tones were punctuated by Lady Vaga's shrill denunciations as they recited the snobs that had befallen Lenore. Mamère's wrath soared.

"Helen Osterhouse! Why, her grandmother was Jilly Griftight's abigail, who seduced Jilly's brother."

"What?!"

"Certainly; she was Jilly's abigail, got in the family way, went to old Griftight, who made his son marry her."

Lady Vaga choked on her ratafia. "I never heard that."

"Oh, it was hushed up mighty quickly. Jilly was forced to claim the girl a visiting schoolchum, and as soon as her brother and the jade were married, they were whisked out of London up north, somewhere in

York. They had a son, who, when he grew up, wed a squire's daughter—methodists—they never left York." Helen was their daughter—Helen Griftight."

"How did Helen meet, let alone marry, Mr. Osterhouse?"

"Osterhouse?" Mamère laughed for the first time that day. "Paul Osterhouse was an out-and-out rake—a terror—got into trouble, fudged on a duel—hid out in York, where he met Helen—she wasn't a tub of lard then—so to save his skin and acquire some respectability, he wed her, brought her to London, and promptly drank himself to death. She's tried to get leg-shackled again ever since."

"I must be sure and ask Helen after her grandmother someday," mused Lady Jersey. "Well, enough scandal broth—what are we going to do about the masquerade? Helen Osterhouse has just enough toad-eaters to make trouble."

They paused, and Mamère began to weep quietly.

"What now, Floss?" growled Lady Vaga.

"If no one comes to the masquerade, the duke will close this house and I'll have to go back to Willo-wood."

"Good Lord!"

"I don't want to do that; I'm having fun here. And if anything should happen to Lenore . . ."

Lady Jersey, with her usual good sense, rang for Mrs. Madcape, who assured the ladies she knew just what to do for madame, and ushered them out of the room. Fenwick was told Madame Lanier would receive no further visitors that day.

In the afternoon the news from the sickroom lightened; the duchess did not seem quite so fevered.

By midevening Mrs. Clough suggested the doctor

go to the duke; she'd have his tray served there and she would sit with the duchess.

When the doctor entered the library, the duke turned ashen. "Doctor?!"

"She's slightly better, Your Grace."

"Thank God! Here, let me give you some brandy." He poured and handed the doctor a stiff portion. Abel brought a covered tray and placed it before the doctor, then said, "Is Her Grace—" He choked.

"Better, Abel, definite improvement. Thank you for dinner."

The duke never took his eyes off the doctor while he downed his drink and ate wolfishly. Finished, he shook his head and frowned at the duke.

"All right, Doctor, tell me what's on your mind."

"She frets, Duke. She doesn't make sense, mutters, 'What if . . .' then moans, 'Why would they?' then she thrashes. What causes her misery, do you know?"

"No, I don't; last night she tried to acquaint me of some happenings, but I couldn't pin her meaning down."

"We must reassure her; she's worried beyond bounds —you can conceive of no—"

"No, Doctor, I cannot."

"Well, I must go to her; I want to give her some medicine that will let her sleep."

"You need rest, Doctor; have you made provisions—"

"Yes, Maria has slept this afternoon and will attend Her Grace tonight; I'll steal a few hours."

That night Lenore, feverish and restless, had a dream—she saw the duke open the door from his dressing room, come to her side, and taking her hand, hold it for a long time. Dreaming, she heard him say,

"It's all right, Lenore, everything is going to be all right; just rest." Clinging to his hand, she fell into a deep sleep.

The next morning she dimly recognized those who tended her.

55

A few days after the Lanier party, Lord Cedric Lovill, reading in his book room, was dumbfounded when the maid announced a visitor—his father. He had not seen the old gentleman in two years, subsequent to a quarrel over money—the father had banished his son from sight. Although both lived in London, each took pains to avoid the other.

"Father! I'm delighted to see you," he said, shocked at the change in the thin figure before him.

"Cedric." The old man extended his hand. "You look stout."

"I am, Father. Do sit down; can I send for refreshments?"

"No, thank you."

There was a pause, then Cedric said, "I hope you are well, sir."

"Middling. Amy and the children?"

"All fine, thank you."

There was another pause. Then the wispy man said, "Heard you're thinking of traveling."

Cedric frowned. "Oh—no great trip; Amy wants to go to Scotland to see her sister."

"Dates all fixed?"

"Yes, we go approximately the first week in February."

"Humph, about the time of the Asherwood masquerade, ain't it?"

"Why, yes, I believe it is." Cedric was puzzled.

"Think you and Amy would hate to miss the affair."

"In a way, but Amy has her heart set on the first week in February."

"Then unset it!" snarled the old man.

"What?"

"First masquerade I've been to in years, and I want you and Amy there."

"Now, Father," Cedric said patiently, "I am sorry, but I can't disappoint Amy."

"I believe you can."

"But, sir, you're being unreasonable."

"Perhaps, but I'm bound to be more unreasonable; if you and Amy don't attend—"

"I don't understand, sir; why should you give a fig?"

"Son, you ain't got to understand, you just have to manifest yourselves. The fig I give is that your allowance will be slashed in half if I don't cast my ogles on you that night."

"Good God, Father, we'd starve!"

"For that, I don't care a fig." The old man struggled to his feet.

"But, Father—"

"Suggest you wear rags and tatters, and Amy would be just right in a dunce's cap. Good day to you, son."

"I'll walk you to the door, sir." Cedric stood up.

"Don't bother. You go see Amy."

That same evening Lady Celeste Hackingham was instructing her maid as to the arrangement of hair ornaments when two short knocks announced Lady Wilna, Celeste's mother.

"Come in, Mother." Celeste watched in the mirror as her meek, gentle mother slipped into the room.

When Lady Wilna's husband died, Lady Celeste tucked her mother in the Hackingham house as far away from her own life as possible. A tiny living room with a bed alcove had been readied. About the only times Lady Wilna saw her daughter were the permitted periodic visits as Lady Celeste dressed. The uncomplaining Lady Wilna had spent most of her days in her room until Madame Lanier's return to London; then, with the contrivance of her maid, she had been frequently absent from her small apartment.

"Mother," greeted Lady Celeste perfunctorily.

The old lady sat down as the final touches of Lady Celeste's toilet were being applied. "You are very lovely tonight, Daughter."

"Thank you, Mother; I agree, this gown becomes me—that will be all Josey—is there something you want, Mother?—I'm rather in a hurry."

"I worried about you the other night in the storm—was Lady Martha's party worth the risk?"

"Yes, as a matter of fact it was."

"Who was there? Or did the snow—"

"Oh, the usual; not as many as Martha had invited, but a fair number."

"Were the Asherwoods there?"

Lady Celeste gave her mother a quick glance, but because the quiet lady always asked for the duke and duchess, she merely replied, "Of course—they're at most parties—why do you ask?"

"I love to hear about the duchess's gowns."

"Well, the other night she looked a fright; she was far too pale for her green velvet."

"Green velvet? Light or dark?"

"Really, Mother, I don't remember."

"I wonder about her costume for the masquerade." Lady Wilna sighed.

"Something gaudy, no doubt."

"Have you selected what you're going to wear, my darling?"

"Nothing—I'm not going."

The old lady gasped. "Not going! Whatever for?"

"I choose not to."

"But Hackingham's one of the duke's best friends."

Lady Celeste tossed her head. "Oh, he may go, but I'm not."

The old lady sounded incredulous. "But, Celeste, everyone in London will be there. Are you planning to stay home alone?"

"If I must." Lady Celeste began to draw on her gloves.

"Or will Sir Winclef keep you company?"

Lady Celeste's head jerked. "What are you prattling about?"

"Dear Celeste, you forget my room is just down the hall."

Her daughter turned white. "Mother," she whispered.

"My lovely girl, your pose as the perfect wife and mother has pulled the wool over most eyes—fortunately even Hackingham's—but my eyes have been open a long time."

"Mother, what are you going to do?" Lady Celeste's voice quivered.

"Nothing, sweet girl, provided you attend the masquerade."

"And if I don't?" Lady Celeste struggled to be defiant.

"Hackingham, though well-natured, is a very proud man, Celeste."

"Mother, you wouldn't!"

Lady Wilna's wisp of a smile caused Lady Celeste to jump to her feet. "Well, I guess Mrs. Osterhouse was stupid about the whole affair." She took a breath. "Have you any ideas for my costume, Mother?"

"Heavens, no, my dearest; you know far better than I what you should represent."

Lady Celeste winced, then turned on her heel. "Good night, Mother."

"Good night, my darling."

The next day, Mrs. Osterhouse, famed for her weekly teas, sat amid her coterie. The illusion that her intelligence and charm filled her drawing room with the many who made it a ritual never to miss one of Helen's teas warmed her heart. In weighty tones she poured wisdom and on-dit on those who sat in the circle before her. The appraisal that fear of her tongue ringed the circle would have been rejected forthwith. However, to be a guest facing the hostess did give protection from having a dagger sunk into one's absent back.

Today Mrs. Osterhouse glowed with content; the room was crowded, the pastries delicious, and she had much to say.

"Of course, it is sad the duchess is so ill; one can only assume her low décolleté exposed her to the rigors of the storm the night of Martha's dance. Dear Martha was quite appalled at the depth of Lenore's neckline, were you not, Martha?" She did not wait for a response. "Naturally, in the precise sense, we cannot

lame the duchess; the knowledge about where to
lace one's neckline is a matter of breeding."

There was a rustle around the circle as remembered
owns floated to mind.

Smiling with secret understanding, Mrs. Osterhouse
poke on. "You will recall the distress of Alfred and
ear Martha when Eric wed the little waif from the
icarage?" She glanced expectantly at her guests, who
odded, even those who had never heard of Eric
anier. "Alas, poor Eric perished in loyalty to his
ountry; Alfred and Martha showed all kindness to
is widow—a home and a proper companion, Madame
anier, supplied by their generosity. You and I would
eem ourselves blessed, and wear the willow gladly,
ut not the widow Lenore; she laid herself out to
ook the duke. That accomplished, she aimed higher—
o take London by storm."

Amy Lovill, bored, intoned, "Hasn't she done just
hat?"

"It would appear so, but we sticklers of the *haut
on* are resolute; we are not falling under her—"

From the arched doorway, a footman announced in
stentorian voice, "Lady Jersey."

Every lady turned toward the doorway, thus miss-
ng the sight of their open-mouthed hostess—"giving
er the appearance of a beached whale"—accorded
ady Jersey later.

"Helen," Lady Jersey trilled, as she slowly crossed
he room, "I was on my way home from an exhaust-
ng meeting of the Board of Almack's, and yearned
or a cup of tea. I recalled your renowned hospitality."

Lady Jersey, elegant in fawn velvet, her bonnet
rimmed with an ostrich feather that curled mag-
ificently under her chin, riveted every eye.

"Delighted to see you, Sally," said Helen Osterhouse, who wasn't. "Do you desire lemon or sugar?"

"Pray, no sugar, I'm already much too ample." In view of the fact that compared to her hostess she stood a shadow, the arrow went home. "Just a touch of lemon, Helen, please." Searching the circle, Lady Jersey moved to a couch where Martha Lanier hastily made space for her; the footman followed with a tray of tea.

"I bring glad tidings!" Lady Jersey announced at large. "The little duchess mends. I have not seen her, for visitors are still forbidden, but the duke assures me she will be able to welcome us to the masquerade." Lady Jersey sipped her tea. "Helen, this is delicious; I am weary—the Board meeting at Almack's was unusually debilitating this month—it concerned the membership review." She nibbled a bite of Savoy cake. "The Board felt the rooms, this past season, were far too crowded. Therefore certain present members, unfortunately, will have to be excluded next season. May I have some more tea, Helen? It is so reviving."

An eerie silence muffled the room as each waited to hear the next syllable of the low musical voice. A fresh cup in place, Lady Jersey resumed. "As you can well imagine, the dilemma of whose names to drop was maddening. Back and forth the discussion raged until Princess Esterhazy drew up a brilliant solution."

There was a rapid intake of breath; one or two ladies so forgot themselves as to ask, "What did the Princess—"

Lady Jersey shrugged. "Her suggestion proved quite simple—let the Duke of Asherwood's masquerade serve as the measure; those in attendance will be assured vouchers for Almack's next year—a perfect criterion for of course only the crème de la crème will be present."

The pronouncement, airily given, had a devastating effect.

Ghostly pale, Mrs. Osterhouse said in hollow tones, "You refer to the duke's guest list, naturally."

"Oh, no, Helen, we'd never be so bold as to attempt to obtain the duke's invitation list—no, we plan to compile our own tally the night of the masquerade. It will serve, because any who, unless burnt in the socket, are so gauche as not to be present, would exhibit such a lack of gentility, they obviously couldn't come to scratch at Almack's." Lady Jersey rose. "Thank you for the tea, Helen, it's quite restored me. Good afternoon, Helen, ladies." Lady Jersey trailed through the archway.

A number of ladies stood as if shot and left without bidding their hostess farewell—a discourtesy quite unnoted, for their hostess had fainted.

56

Lenore's recovery was slow; she was weak and easily upset. She sought courage to relate to the duke why the post brought the many regrets, politely couched in formal terms, in response to the invitations to the masquerade. He had not mentioned the subject to her, but noting his sternness, she worried. That he might be concerned about her health did not cross her mind.

The first time she was permitted downstairs, after a quarrel with the doctor, who only gave in because she became overly excited arguing, she was astonished to find the morning room a bower of flowers.

"Ma'am," explained Abel, who at the doctor's insistence carried her and placed her in a comfortable chair by the fireplace, "they came while you lay ill. The doctor would not allow them in the bedroom."

"Glory, I should think not; I would have been positive I'd stuck my spoon in the wall."

Abel, who had not smiled for days, grinned. "You're your old self, ma'am. I'm—" He shook his head.

"Hoy, Abel, takes more than a bug or two to—Myles!" Her face lit up as the duke entered. "Abel, please bring us a cup of tea and a large—mark, I say—a large plate of pastries; I'm hungry all the time. Myles, did you ever see such a profusion of flowers? I hope the cards were kept; I must thank everyone."

"All saved, Lenore." The duke sat opposite her. "But do not bother yourself writing; you need rest."

Lenore peered at him from under her lashes. "Goodness, I'm tired of playing the invalid. I had almost a mill with Doctor Sylvester to even put my foot to the floor. He'd have cozened me until I was too weak to move."

"He told me," said the duke. "I'll never be certain your 'quick out of bed' is a prosperous theory."

"Well, here I am, hoping soon to stuff myself, whereas the doctor would condemn me to lying in bed —Ah, Abel, oooh, give me that one, please, it's the biggest." She broke a large piece of cake and munched happily. The duke studied her pinched face.

"Myles, I know I'm thin, but I'm stout—soon I'll take up the labors for the masquerade."

The duke scowled. "You can rest easy on that head—the plans and preparations are complete."

"Oh." Lenore gave a moue of disappointment. "I anticipated—who tended them?"

"I had some lively advice from Lady Jersey and Lady Vaga, and Madame Lanier dipped her oar in once or twice."

Lenore gave a low chuckle. "Quite a bevy of strong-minded females; you must be bruised."

"Although Lady Vaga and Mamère neared coming to cuffs, Lady Jersey acted the referee, and all—Come in."

Fenwick entered and brought Lenore two notes on a tray. She gave him a smile of thanks, which caused him to burst out with, "Oh, Your Grace, I'm that glad to see you fit again. While you was ill the whole house lay in dismals." He gave Lenore such a loving beam that the duke said sharply, "That will be all, Fenwick," then, after the door closed, "Good God, he has a tendre for you."

"Yes, he does," replied Lenore placidly.

"I'll get rid of him now!" The duke stood.

"No!" cried Lenore. "Sit down, Myles. He is respectful, proper to a fault, and kind beyond all bounds to me."

"How dare he even look at you? No footman should—"

"Don't be an addleplot. Fenwick serves us both equally, works long and hard. What he feels only enhances his willingness to do so—he's the perfect footman, and someday we should make him a butler."

The duke fell quiet and Lenore opened an envelope.

"Goodness, this is odd—read it." She handed the note to the duke.

My dear Duchess,

We thought other obligations stood in the way of attending your masquerade, however, by the greatest good fortune, all obstacles have cleared away.

Please now let us withdraw our regrets; we are so delighted to find we can come.

With sincere good wishes for your returning health.

The note was signed Sir William and Lady Wise.

"Hoo, read this one, Myles!"

Dear Lenore,

Like a silly, I twisted my dates and was sad we could not come, but after I got my head around, found, to my joy, we can be at your masquerade.

So you will surely recognize us; I'll be a shepherdess and Clifford will be a rabbit!

           With fondness,

The signature, "Nellie," was scrawled.

"Did Nellie refuse? I thought she was—" Lenore sighed. "Myles, you've had quite a few turndowns, haven't you? It's all my fault; let me explain about Martha's party. I tried to on the way home that night, but I guess I was too ill." She told of the snubs at Lady Martha's and Sir Alfred's party. The duke's face grew grim.

"What two-faced Januses—and some were brass-faced enough to send flowers."

"Myles, I am so sorry it happened."

"Can't see you had a thing to do with it," the duke

growled. "My error entirely for assuming their brats could get grubby without the sky falling."

"What? What are you prattling about?"

The duke explained the scrubbing of the ballroom.

"So that's why Lily and the others were in such a hubble-bubble." Lenore laughed. "And I thought I'd made some grievous mistake; I've puzzled for days as to my sins. What a relief!" Picking up her fourth pastry, Lenore grinned. "I'm going to be as fat as Mr. Foster if I'm not more prudent, but this one is to celebrate."

"Lenore, what do you think about these notes?" he tossed them on the table.

She cocked her head and spoke slowly. "Myles, I'm of the mind they are the first of a series. Hmm, watch the post—there's a change of wind." She sniffed, then burst into tears.

"Good God, Lenore, what in the—"

"Sitting in this room, chatting with you, free of fears, and these lovely pastries have choked me with happiness."

"Females!" rasped the duke in a tone so pleasing to Lenore she cried harder. The duke rang for Abel, who gently lifted the overtired duchess and carried her to her room, but not before she had given the duke such a dazzlingly tearful smile that he shook his head in bewilderment.

For the first time since the night of the Lanier party the duke left his residence.

Mr. Pettibone was surprised when his most distinguished client entered the inner office. "Your Grace." The men shook hands. "The duchess is better!"

"Yes." The duke seated himself and accepted a

brandy. "I've come to see if our plays ride smooth."

"All in readiness, Duke."

"No spies, no untoward events?"

"Not unless you begrudge your solicitor gaining fame as a bit of a right cool fish on the docks."

"Deuce take you, how?"

"One or two sailors tipped me a rise and I played ducks and drakes with their noses—broke one."

"Good Lord, you're not one for fisticuffs."

"No, not partial to them, but if the need arises . . ." Pettibone shrugged. "Did cut a wheedle with the sons of the sea that despite my niff-naff appearance, I'm no rum touch. Of course the mills took place when I first visited the waterfront—now I'm as unseen as a barnacle."

"Good! Now, about the schools; have you—"

"Prepared either way, Your Grace. I aver your only worry now is the duchess and the masquerade"—the solicitor chuckled—"where you won't recognize me— wager a groat."

"Corkbrain," said the duke. But he was reassured, and took his leave.

On order, Henderson drove the duke to Brooks Featherheath's home, where he was received by Mrs. Featherheath. After asking of the duchess's health, she explained that her husband had been gulled into taking the boys to Jackson's Boxing Saloon.

"Truly outrageous, Myles; Brooks can sometimes be restrained from being wound around George's thumb, but add Charles's eagerness and Heath's smile, and my Brooks is sunk."

"I apologize! If the boys are a burden to—"

"Burden? Nonsense, they're a joy. A mite disrespectful when I call Heath George or George Heath —throws them into whoops. Really, Myles, there's not a scrap of difference in their appearance, and both resemble Harriet, so Brooks tells me."

Harriet! Hat! Good God! The duke realized he hadn't thought of the former duchess in months, even when Heath—"Lydia, will you forgive me if I take my leave?" He rose. "I'm—I'm—"

"Of course, Myles," Lydia assured the duke. Like many ladies of kindly stupidity, Lydia Featherheath had flashes of intuitive insight. As the duke kissed her hand she whispered, "Dear Myles, I rejoice that at long last Harriet is exorcised."

Stunned by her words, the duke left quickly and directed Henderson to Grosvenor Square, growled at Fenwick that he was to be undisturbed, and rushed to his library, determined to ponder as of old. Seated by the fire, brandy in hand, he commanded his reminiscences—his meeting Hat at Almack's, her beauty, their life at Asherwood, but it would not serve. Almack's brought to mind that he and Lenore had received cards just yesterday; trying to visualize the young Harriet, she appeared with red hair and green eyes; reviewing their life at Asherwood, he slipped into musing about the vicar, the wedding, the festival, and then London. Distraught, he rang for Clough, who entered carrying the mail.

"Your Grace, these arrived a few minutes ago."

Snatching a pile of notes from the tray, the duke glanced through the franks, and judged them probable acceptances to the masquerade. Tossing them aside, he asked, "Is the duchess—"

"Sleeping, Your Grace; the doctor forbids waking her."

As Clough waited the duke thought for a moment, then asked, "Who sits with the duchess?"

"Maria, sir." Again Clough waited.

"All right, send for Mrs. Clough, Abel, and Fenwick; I require their presence—yours also, of course."

"Immediately, sir."

The duke reviewed his forthcoming directions to the members of his staff, who gathered quickly. Seated at his desk, he spoke sternly to the four standing respectfully before him.

"The orders I now give are of the weightiest importance, but even of more gravity is the necessity for secrecy—no word to the others in the house, except, Mrs. Clough, you will instruct Mrs. Madcape and Maria. Moreover, I stress, not even a faint hint is to reach the duchess."

There were nods, then "ahs" and "ohs" as the duke propounded their added duties on the night of the masquerade. When the duke had finished, each pledged aid and silence concerning the serious matter.

"Your Grace," proclaimed Abel, "if you had joined the colors, you would be a general." The others murmured agreement to Abel's high praise. The duke thanked his trusted servants and sent them back to their posts.

Meanwhile, Lenore, carried easily by Abel to her bed, had fallen into a light sleep, and after an hour wakened refreshed. Musing about the masquerade, she rang for Maria and requested she unpack the costume M. DuLac had made for the occasion. As Maria drew forth garment after garment from two large boxes, Lenore felt dismay. The bodice of the gown was so tapered from neck to waist that a lacing chemise was required; the skirt approached four feet across, its sides to be held extended by pads worn on the hips. Every inch of the heavy maroon velvet was hung with ropes of jewels, silver lace, and braid. Maria could hardly lift the extending pads and the boned lacing chemise—an instrument of torture.

"Heavens, Maria, if you could get me into the dress, I'd not be able to move."

"*Si,* Your Grace, I feared—"

"Oh, that stupid M. DuLac! What am I to do?" Lenore began to cry. At that moment Mrs. Clough knocked, entered, and understood the disaster at a glance.

"Now, Your Grace—"

"What? You can see I have no costume, and there isn't a dressmaker in London who hasn't her needle flying this minute." Lenore sobbed.

"Your Grace, do you forget that Maria is an artful seamstress and Mrs. Madcape also sews an exquisite seam?"

"Yes, but we have no material, no time, and as for ideas—it's hopeless."

"Your Grace, please hear me out. Once, before I married Mr. Clough, I served Lady Welwith, who was in the pink of fashion and attended many balls. For one masquerade she ordered a costume of great beauty, and I helped fashion it. I have not forgotten how it was made. If you wish—"

"Could you?" Lenore asked doubtfully.

"Most certainly. If I may order the carriage, I'll go to a shop where I know the finest materials are available. Maria, help me pack away these monstrosities, and then send word to Henderson."

"How can I thank you, Mrs. Clough?"

"By taking your rest, Your Grace," urged Mrs. Clough as she hung the velvet gown in the closet.

"That's all I do," said Lenore, pouting. "May I not read?"

"Of course." Mrs. Clough smiled. "Climb in bed and I'll light the candles."

Lenore snatched up *La Belle Assemblée* and settled herself in bed. After Mrs. Clough and Maria left, Lenore, reading of the latest fashions, soon nodded over the pages and slept—just as Mrs. Clough had planned. A maid sent by Mrs. Madcape tiptoed in and blew out the candles.

On waking, Lenore scarcely believed she had slept almost two hours; feeling famished, she rang for tea. Mrs. Madcape brought the tray, and Lenore eyed the pastries eagerly.

"Your Grace, Mrs. Clough asked she be informed the minute you roused; she has—"

"Oh, yes, please light more candles and send for her."

Mrs. Clough and Maria entered, followed by a maid carrying two boxes which she placed on a chair, curtsying as she left. Maria opened one box which cradled a cloud of soft green material.

"Oh, let me see." Excited, Lenore lifted the chiffon and rubbed her cheek. "Beautiful! Oh, look." She touched the length of gold tissue that hung over Maria's arm.

"What am I to be, Mrs. Clough? I can't wait another minute."

"A lady of the eleven hundreds, Your Grace."

"The eleven hundreds?" Lenore frowned. "Oh, yes—like Maid Marian?"

"Yes, though I would never have—"

"What is that?" Lenore asked of Mrs. Clough, who had lifted from one of the boxes a tall cone of stiff material.

"It's the base of the hennin, Your Grace."

"Hennin?"

"Yes, the ladies of that age wore them on their heads, with a bow of tissue tied at the peak and the ends streaming out behind them."

"Good heavens!"

"If you will sit before the mirror, Your Grace, Maria and I can pin it in place."

At Mrs. Clough's direction Maria's fingers flew; Lenore watched, fascinated. "Mrs. Clough, it hides my hair completely."

"Do you wish to display a curl or two?"

"Oh, no, I'm delighted." An elusive idea entered Lenore's mind as she studied the hennin.

"Are you weary, Your Grace; if not, we could drape the gown—"

"Mrs. Clough, you must bring to a stop this treating me as if I am dwindling into the grave—I can scarce wait to be draped." Lenore laughed, and jumped up to stand before the long mirror.

As Maria and Mrs. Madcape worked Lenore again let her thoughts play with the notion born as she viewed the hennin.

Before the pinning was completed a maid knocked and announced the doctor wished to see the duke and Her Grace in the library when she was free.

Lenore sent word she would be just a few minutes. Apprehensive, she went down the stairs. The duke greeted her quietly and led her to a chair. The doctor's expression was somber.

"What's fallen out? Tell me right now!" Lenore glanced from one man to the other.

"Your Grace," the doctor began, "please do not be distraught—it's not that serious."

"What's not?" shrilled Lenore.

"This afternoon at Jackson's Boxing Saloon, Charles tripped over a rope and broke his leg."

"Oh, the poor boy." Tears filled her eyes. "How is he—is it dire? Tell me, Doctor."

"He was lucky—a clean snap of the bone—easily set."

"What happened? Word for word."

"As I say, Charles tripped and fell; Mr. Featherheath and Heath held the leg straight as they drove him home."

"Lenore," the duke cut in, "the most fortunate turn; the doctor happened to be there waiting to see the boys; and was therefore able to set the leg immediately."

"Why didn't they bring Charles here?" demanded Lenore.

"Mr. Featherheath explained that this house is in a bustle enough right now; and they are glad to have Charles."

Lenore rose. "I must go to him."

"My dear Lenore," the duke said in a calm voice, "you could do the boy no good, and might harm yourself beyond repair. The doctor and I will see to his comfort, and Heath vows he won't leave his brother's side."

The doctor essayed to lend further weight. "The boys sent a message to you, Your Grace. Charles—I must say he had pluck to the backbone while I set his leg—said I must convince you that if his silly leg overset you, he'd run away to sea. His word 'convince' was uttered in emphatic tones." The doctor smiled. "A further threat, Your Grace; Heath proclaimed that you enjoy the masquerade or neither he nor Charles would ever play jackstraws with you again."

Lenore could not help herself—she laughed. Turning to the duke, she said, "Myles, promise you'll drive

e to see the boys the minute this dreadful weather
ases."

"Lenore, the masquerade is two days ahead; my
ead and heart are wrapped in the events of that
ight. Until it is past, I can neither see the boys my-
lf nor take you, even should the weather become
uly."

"So!" Lenore flared. "The masquerade holds your
iterest more than your sons!"

"Yes," said the duke in sharp retort.

Lenore stood. "Thank you, Doctor. I'm certain I can
ntrust Charles's care to you; therefore I shall not
et. Good evening." Head high, she left the room.

"Dammit, Your Grace, I wish you could enlighten
er."

"Well, I can't! Good night, Doctor." The duke's
oice was icy.

Most cross, Lenore went to her room and wrote,
he hoped, an entertaining letter to the boys—her as-
onishment that they would quaintly conceive that a
ere leg snap—she cried as she penned—could overset
er, and that, furthermore, she intended to beat them
o flinders when next they played jackstraws—let them
orry about that!

Giving the letter to Maria, who brought her din-
er, Lenore, as she ate, mused about the masquerade—
o important to Myles's head and heart! The wisp of
er idea of the afternoon grew and pleased her—she'd
o it! Growing drowsy, she allowed herself the wildest
reams of how the duke would, at the masquerade,
ll at her feet, proclaim his mad ardor as he saw her
weep down the stairs. Don't be a niddlecock, she told
erself, he wouldn't even know it was you—and went
ght on with her fantasies. Once she was in bed, they
ere even more bold.

57

On the day of the masquerade the freezing cold, chased by sunlight, abated to a tangy chill. Early in the morning drays drew into Grosvenor Square to deliver boxes, trays of food, flowers, tables, and chairs. Every door on the lower floor was open to permit the passage of footmen, maids, workmen, and their helpers, under the direction of Clough. Mrs. Madcape ruled the kitchen, sorting heaps of foodstuffs, checking mixtures, tasting, smelling, wielding a large salt cellar in one hand, a pepper shaker in the other. Mr. Madcape oversaw the baking and watched the two ovens with a ferocious eye. The pantry gleamed with silver buffed to diamond gloss, awaiting Mrs. Clough's choice of distribution.

Lenore, wakened by the activity, sipped her breakfast tea and gave herself a scold for being such a schoolgirl ninny the night before—he'll not notice me tonight was her melancholy conclusion. Mrs. Clough and Maria brought an end to her gloom.

"Do you wish to try on your costume at this time, Your Grace?" asked Mrs. Clough, almost buried in green chiffon. Maria held the hennin as a jewel.

"Oh, yes." Lenore jumped from her bed and ran to the dressing room. She donned proper undergarments and stood as the circle of material slipped over her head. Maria, with deft fingers, buttoned the many loops that ran down the back of the gown. Lenore then seated herself so her hair could be drawn into a top-knot and the hennin worked over it, coming to rest on Lenore's forehead. Maria wanted to place the mask, but Lenore pushed it away. "Let me see the costume first." Stepping to the long mirror, she peered at her reflection. "Oh, Mrs. Clough, Maria, how lovely!"

A rich dark-green velvet band circled her neck; from the band yards of light-green chiffon flowed to the sleeves, the cuffs of which fell to the floor. The bodice fit tightly and the belt of bejeweled velvet hugged her hips. The skirt, straight in front, flared full in the back, creating a short train.

The hennin, its pleated chiffon band snug to her head, its cone of velvet rising to a peak blunted by a bow with ends of gold tissue floating freely to her waist, delighted Lenore.

After turning, walking, and holding her arms high to show off the enormous sleeves, Lenore hugged Mrs. Clough and Maria.

"The mask, Your Grace, please try the mask." Maria was eager.

The mask of green velvet was set into the band of the hennin in a cunning way, its half-moon fitting tightly over Lenore's brows and ending at the tip of her nose. The two openings allowed Lenore to see, but concealed her eyes; tiered chiffon edging the velvet completed the disguise.

"I'm totally not me," said Lenore, laughing, "and as I suspected, you are needle geniuses."

Mrs. Clough, after checking each seam, said, "May I be excused, Your Grace?"

"What a care-for-nobody I am," said Lenore rue-fully. "Please forgive me." Mrs. Clough smiled and left. "Maria, be so good as to unbutton me—heavens, there must be a thousand loops."

Restored to her normal dress, Lenore visited Madame Lanier, pausing as she passed through the hall to listen to the shouts and banging that rose from below.

"Mamère, you've never heard such a rattle that is going on downstairs."

"Humph. And I suppose, Duchess, you've arrived to inform me that I can't go to the masquerade," snapped the old lady testily.

"Hoy, you are sour this morning. Why would you suppose—"

"I've been watching the bustle—everything the most expensive—only the pink of the *ton* expected—Bunky won't want this ugly old boggard at the feast."

"You do have the dismals, don't you? Now, if you will stop this namby-pamby pity, I'll tell you why I came to see such a dab of a creature as yourself. To-night Abel will place a large chair, like a throne, by the drawing room entry; there, I hope, you will consent to receive our guests."

"You mean play hostess?"

"Exactly; unless, of course, you feel too feeble," said Lenore impishly.

"Feeble? You run mad." She paused and eyed Lenore suspiciously, "Why ain't you—where are you going to be?"

"I'm to be a guest, dear Mamère."

"Not receive? You can't do that!"

"Indeed I can—I have a new costume and—"

"Bunky will fly up into the boughs—mad as fire!"

"Let him." Lenore waved airily.

"Lenore, you should not—no, it's—oh, well—come, my darling, what are you to wear?"

"Oh, you're a downy one; if I tell, you'll tattle to Myles."

"I will not." Mamère's indignation amused Lenore. "You're insulting me." She waited expectantly. "You mean you aren't going to tell me?"

"Precisely, my nosy one."

"Well," the old lady flounced, "then you needn't think I'm going to be your greeter, 'cause I refuse."

"As you wish, dear Mamère," Lenore conceded sweetly. "Now I must leave you; I'll send Maria to help you dress at the proper time tonight—that is, if you have a change of heart."

"Never, do you hear me? Never!" called the old lady as Lenore closed the door.

In the hall Doctor Sylvester waylaid Lenore. "Your Grace, let me look at you—my, you are better."

"I feel fine, Doctor, but what of Charles?"

"Rest easy on that head, Your Grace; I saw him yesterday afternoon and he's quite plucked up; eats hugely and is cross as sticks—a very robust sign."

"Oh, good." Lenore exulted. "Doctor, do enjoy the masquerade."

The doctor frowned.

"What is it, Doctor?"

He paused, then said, "Nothing, Your Grace, except I have the unpleasant duty of ordering you to take a long sleep this afternoon; I don't want a collapsing duchess on my conscience tonight."

"Nonsense, I'm—"

"Your Grace, please," the doctor pled.

"All right, Doctor Tyrant, but I doubt my eyes will close."

"Risk it, Duchess."

Lenore slept all afternoon.

58

"Good God, I look like a French fripple," growle
the duke as he stood before his long glass. "M. DuLa
must be queer in the stirrups to send me this rig."

Clough spoke with feeling. "Louis the Fourteent
would have been overjoyed to see you at Versailles.

"In keeping with the rest of the fools he had a
court, eh?"

Clough was stern. "Your Grace, His Majesty's cou
was peopled by the most elegant gentlemen of fashio
known to history."

"With curls to their waist?" sneered the duke. "Po
injays!" He pulled off the wig and hurled it at h
henchman. "Be damned if I'll wear curls! Give m
the hat."

"Your Grace," cried the distressed Clough, "yo
must wear the wig; the hat won't—"

"Clough!"

"Yes, Your Grace." He handed the duke the ha
"But it—"

The large felt hat with its huge plume, when th
duke clapped it on his head, sank to rest on his nos

"I won't wear a hat," shouted the duke, snatchin
the offender from his head.

Clough's fine-hewn sense of sartorial correctness r

belled. "Your Grace, gentlemen wore their hats indoors on most occasions. Without the curls and the hat, your costume will appear with a misplaced head."

Glaring at the glass, the duke had to accept the truth. The dark-blue-velvet, waist-nipped coat with the neck bow and lace, and with wide gold-embroidered edges; the white knickerbockers caught at the knee by ribbons; and the white silk stockings and buckled shoes; all topped by a head the hair of which was dressed in the latest fashionable Brutus style lent a ludicrous incongruity to his appearance. Throwing himself on a stool, the duke muttered, "Put on the curls."

With a sigh of relief Clough replaced the wig, arranged the hat to a perfect tilt, and stepped back. Seeing himself, the duke conceded the improvement.

"Now the sword, Your Grace," said Clough, in what he hoped was a coaxing voice.

"Sword? What sword?"

"You are supposed to wear a sword swung from the belt across the back, Your Grace."

"Where?" roared the duke.

"At the back, sir, almost to the knees."

"You've windmills in your head." The duke peered over his shoulder. "No man would, if he had a brain in his attic, put his sword where he neither could sit down nor even reach it if threatened—couldn't anyway with all this lace dangling over him." The duke shook his hand covered by gold lace.

"But they did, sir."

"I called them fools, didn't I?"

"You did, Your Grace," admitted Clough.

"Put that thing out of my sight—a man could stab himself to death."

Clough laid the sword aside. "There is one more—"

"What now? Is it a muff or a chemise to put over all?"

"A cane, sir." Clough lifted a long cane tied with a large scarlet bow near the top.

"What am I? A shepherdess?"

"No, but at court gentlemen did carry them, Your Grace."

"Let me have the cane," the duke roared. "It may come in use to beat you, you nodcock."

"Please, Your Grace," Clough pled, only faintly alarmed.

Turning to the long glass, the duke held the cane by its top so it ran to the floor at a ridiculous angle.

"No, Your Grace; if I may say so, it is held upright and your hand clasps below the bow—that's right, sir, away from the body—very good, Your Grace."

Posing and swearing not too quietly, the duke suddenly shouted, "This house is freezing—why?"

"Well—well—"

"Yes, you bubblehead, why? Tell me!"

"Er—er—"

"Clough!!"

"The duchess, Your Grace, ordered every window opened on the lower floor for twenty minutes during the hour before the guests are expected." The duke gazed at Clough, who hurried on. "She said she's been nearly overcome by the heat and aroma in most houses in London, and she does not wish such disagreeableness in this house."

"Well, close them," snapped the duke.

"Most will be shut by now; the time of your guests' arrival is here. May I leave now? The duke nodded, and Clough hurried from the room.

The duke, though proud, was not vain; when he

peered again at the long mirror, it was to enjoin himself to have courage—this evening is the most important in your life, sir; although you look the fool, don't be one—his final admonition before he went downstairs.

Expecting to see Lenore, he was disconcerted when he beheld Madame Lanier, resplendent in purple, painted of face, bewigged in bright red, seated in a large chair on the spot where the duchess should be standing.

Before he could speak the old lady cried, "Now, don't give me a rake-down, Bunky; Lenore asked me to hostess with you; she wants to play the game of guest—says she'll gull both of us, although she won't me."

"Damme, madame, I am not bent to games tonight—Fenwick!"

Fenwick, either by chance or choice, did not hear, as with fine aplomb he opened the doors to let in a shepherdess and an Egyptian queen, plus two court jesters, who hailed the duke by throwing themselves at his feet and shaking their bells merrily. Before the duke could rid himself of the antics, a Spanish dancer, snapping castanets, and Robin Hood entered. Then followed a continuous flow of clowns, emperors, empresses, chimney sweeps, monks, slave girls, devils, hoydens, knights—the duke lost count—one maiden in green gave him a half-curtsy, then turning her back, flicked a veil of gold tissue across his face before making a deep curtsy to Madame Lanier.

Where is the duchess? wondered the duke as he shook hands with Falstaff, then Richelieu, whom he recognized as the marquis. Cinderella and a prince were succeeded by a Dutch boy and girl and more shepherdesses and Robin Hoods. A Snow Queen of

lush proportions, all white satin and ermine trim,
whispered to him, "Where is the little duchess?" The
duke shrugged and waved his hands helplessly. "Here
somewhere, Sally; she took the notion to be a guest."

Lady Jersey's laugh rang out. "Famous, a guest at
her own party. Mamère, have you spied out the elusive
duchess?"

"Certainly," the old lady answered crisply.

"Ooh, don't tell bouncers, darling!" The Snow
Queen swept through the door. Eyeing the drawing
room, she was pleased with Lady Vaga's and her work
—to her left at the front of the room bloomed a
garden of trees, shrubs, plants, and flowers; at the
opposite end, a long table covered by linen overlaid
with lace held a great epergne overflowing with fruits
and flanked by candelabras; glasses, silver, and china
lent sparkle and color. The balcony hanging above
the table was filled by musicians; a tall candlestick
gave light to each musician's desk. Gilt chairs with red
velvet seats lined the long walls; tall vases filled with
flowers and trailing vines stood guard at the room's
four corners. Wall sconces with flickering candles
and two enormous chandeliers, dancing with diamond
brilliance, made swirls of light throughout the room.

"My most divine Queen of Snows, shall we waltz?"
Cardinal Richelieu bowed.

"Hoy, Your Eminence, you dance in skirts?"

"With you, dearest of queens, I could waltz shackled
knee and ankle."

"Farradiddle." Placing her hand on his shoulder
she asked, "Have you recognized the duchess?"

"No," replied Richelieu, "I see no one but you,"
and whirled her away.

The duke, at last relieved of his duties as host,
stood watching the dancers wheel to the music. The

maiden in green—Maid Marian, he surmised—approached him, stumbled, and reached for his support; he put out his hand and she caught it.

"I'm sorry," murmured a voice so low he barely heard the words.

"Are you steady now?" he asked.

She nodded, but did not withdraw her hand until he became aware of its warmth and smoothness; then, lingeringly, she slipped its softness from his grasp.

"Yes, thank you, dear Duke." Letting her fingers trail down his arm in a caress, she moved past him into the hall. He gazed after her as she crossed to the morning room; no female had given him so open an invitation in a long time. For an instant he felt tempted to follow, but she did not look back so he relinquished his desire. For a flickering moment he wondered if Maid Marian might be Lenore—but no— Lenore is shorter and not so slender.

A chord, strummed loudly on a small harp, caught the duke's attention.

"I twang for a word with you, Your Grace," said the strolling minstrel standing near.

"Pettibone!" gasped the duke as he recognized the man who was usually the essence of dignity and almost funereal in garb—now in a short red tunic, his long slim legs hosed in one green stocking and one red stocking. "Come." He drew his solicitor to a corner.

"I predicted"—the minstrel drew his fingers over the strings—"you would not twig to me."

"Who could?" asked the duke, "in that rig!"

"Forsooth, sir." He extended one leg and pointed his toe. "The precise reason for the costume is to display to the ladies my handsome limbs."

"Pettibone"—the duke sounded stern—"it comes as

news to me that you throw your handkerchief to females."

"And with some success for a dried-up prune at law."

"Good God, you're foxed!" exclaimed the duke.

"A bit bosky, sir, for I celebrate; preparations finished, your ship is in—you need do no more than wait."

"Thank God! And the passenger?"

"Awaiting the unloading of the luggage, about to disembark, escorted by my trusted henchmen."

"Why aren't you there?" growled the duke.

"And have my absence noted here? 'Twould be folly—No! No, my onus lifted, I go court the fair damsels and hope to find one in distress; I will flash her an exquisite leg and she will be mine." He kicked back a heel and wavered away.

The duke spoke to Fenwick, then returned to the ballroom.

The bright morning room rang with laughter, chatter, and squeals as the flirting grew bold. Maid Marian watched the forming and dissolving of groups with amusement. A chimney sweep begged her to dance, but she shook her head, her attention caught by a hooded monk seated alone in a corner, never taking his gaze from the painting of Asherwood. Her curiosity piqued, Lenore moved around the wall and sat down beside the monk.

"Magnificent, is it not, Friar?"

"Go away!" barked a low voice.

"The work of a genius," whispered Lenore.

"I mark a thousand flaws."

"Of course you do, Mr. Turner."

"Madam, how dare you?"

"Praise your picture? Admit your knowledge? Recognize you? Which, sir?"

"All, madam, are presumptuous."

"Oh, come. I praise, for those fortunate enough to see the painting can do no other; I recognized you because of my fond hope that you would come to our home this night."

"You're the Duchess of Asherwood?" The monk turned to her.

"Yes, but please do not give me away—no one but you—" She put her forefinger to her lips.

"Humph, tell me how the canvas came to light; I had forgotten it."

"The duke's sons discovered it in the ballroom on the third floor—a room a long time in disuse. I sorrow to relate the painting had been neglected, and darkened by grime. No one believed it your work until Mr. Cordyne removed the grime, and when the duke saw it, he remembered your tea with his mother."

"Hmmm—the sweet lady who stuffed me full of cakes, and gave me a gold piece for the scribble."

"Mr. Turner, I do not hang scribbles in the place of honor on these walls."

"So you like my youthful scrawl, eh? Why?"

"For the color and air that mingle to make Asherwood float."

"The Academy would laugh at you."

"I don't care a button." Lenore tossed her head.

The monk turned back and studied the painting. "Cordyne told me the duke had it—that's why I came tonight." He paused, then added, "I like the mood myself—challenging style—may go back to it someday." Forgetting Lenore, he concentrated on his own thoughts.

Finally Lenore said softly, "Please come any time to see *Asherwood*, Mr. Turner. Good night."

"Has anyone seen the duchess?" Lenore overheard as she entered the library.

"My dear, haven't you heard? The duchess has retired to the country." Spying the shepherdess who spoke with such authority, Lenore edged closer.

"Whatever for?" asked the first speaker—a doll with a large red dot on each cheek.

"Well-known—the duke is tired of her; her illness gave him the perfect excuse."

"Fustian; he is devoted to her, scarcely leaves her side."

The shepherdess leaned toward the doll; Lenore pretended interest in the whist game being played at a table beside her.

"That is because he is afraid of what she will say."

"Nonsense, she never utters a syllable she shouldn't."

"He stands next to her to guard her tongue."

"Fudge, the duchess is charming."

"Maybe, but the on-dit is that the duke suffers boredom or else brangles with her at all times."

"I don't believe such bouncers."

"Well—she's not here; Madame Lanier received us."

"Maybe she's still out of civils."

"Ill? No! Helen says—" The shepherdess put her head close to the doll's ear and whispered.

"Oh, no! Really, Celeste, you are coming on too strong; I don't want to hear anymore." The doll moved away. "I'm going for some refreshments."

For a moment Lenore, washed by waves of rage and misery, clung to the back of a chair, fighting tears. Was it true? How dare—what had that awful

Celeste confided—retired to the country—obviously absent from the masquerade. I'll tear off my mask—no, everyone would think me mad. O Lord—a new thought struck her—when we unmask, Myles will remember how I boldly clung to his arm—a ninny, I am a ninny! Suddenly she spun and made her way to the hall; a slave girl and a clown, slightly teetery from drink, were weaving up the stairs. Lenore climbed a step behind them and feigned interest in their chatter. She told the maid outside Heath's study, now a retiring room for the ladies, to send Maria to her and went to her own room.

Going to the closet, Lenore dragged out M. DuLac's gown and flung it on the bed. Struggling to unloop the buttons of her costume, she welcomed Maria.

"Hurry, Maria, I must change. Please finish the buttons, then unpack the rest of M. DuLac's costume."

"But, Your Grace—you cannot wear it."

"I have to. No put-off—just do as I say, please."

As Maria worked, she asked, "Why must you take a new costume?"

"No questions, Maria, just hurry." Maria adjusted the lacing garment.

"Lace tight," Lenore commanded, taking a deep breath.

Her waist, normally small, squeezed by the lacings, grew tiny. The pads, balanced on her hips, did not seem as heavy as she had supposed. The dress, once on, surprised her by its lightness. M. DuLac's cunning, she concluded.

"My hair, Maria, what about—"

"There is a wig, Your Grace."

"Oh—get it please."

Lenore gasped when she saw the powdered wig,

taller than the hennin and interwoven with flowers and jewels. She sat gingerly on a stool as Maria set the wig; it fit perfectly.

"I'll have to balance as I walk," said Lenore. To her surprise she found she did not, and was anxious to return to the ball at once.

Dismissing Maria, she applied a touch of rouge to hide the signs of her illness. She posed for an instant to study her reflection, amazed to find she could almost circle her waist with her hands. Lifting herself tall, she said, "Let it be known the Duchess of Asherwood *is* in residence."

In the hall there was no sound save the distant clatter in the drawing room, where tables were being set up for supper. Good, thought Lenore, I can make my entrance into the morning room—the vision of astonished faces as she appeared in the doorway made her smile. At the head of the stairs she paused, placed her hands, she hoped gracefully, on the extended sides of the skirt, preparing to take a step.

Her heart stopped!

Framed by the open front doors below stood the duke, his arms locked around the waist of a lady whose upturned lips were pressed against his, her arms circling his neck and curls.

Lenore swayed, then covered her mouth to prevent the scream rising in her throat from escaping. Marble-cold, she watched until, the kiss done, the hooded head of the lady fell to the duke's shoulder and the duke, tucking the hood to conceal her face, gently began to lead her to the staircase. Horrified, Lenore searched the hall—one glance sufficed to tell her that she alone had witnessed the tender embrace; then she fled to her room. She was shaking; nevertheless she peered through a crack in her door and saw the duke

uide his clinging love to the guest room—so long
losed and locked, but now opening to his touch.
ovingly he urged his lady in and closed the door
n them both.

"I'm going to faint—" Lenore staggered to fall
cross the bed. She would never know how long she
ay as if dead. A loud knocking roused her; aching
nd weary, her wig on the floor, she dragged herself
pright, and holding on to bed and chairs, went to
he door.

"Who is it?" she whispered.

"Fenwick, Your Grace; please may I come in?"

She turned the handle, but did not speak; her
hroat seemed closed.

"Your Grace!" Fenwick caught the tottering duch-
ss.

"Close the door—please close the door," she rasped.

Fenwick reached back with his foot and pushed
he door shut.

"Oh, Fenwick." Lenore's head fell on his chest.

The young footman held her for an instant, then
uided her to a chair and knelt beside her. "What is
, my dearest Duchess?"

Neither noticed his solecism.

Lenore just leaned her head wearily back on the
hair.

"Shall I get the doctor?"

"Oh, no." Lenore opened her eyes. "I am not ill."
he gazed at his concerned face. "Why did you come,
enwick?"

The moment of intimacy over, Fenwick rose. "The
uke sent me to find you and ask you to join him so
he supper may begin."

Had he slapped her the effect could not have been
nore jolting.

"What?" screamed Lenore, straightening in the chair. "What did you say?"

"The duke wishes you with him to escort the guests to supper," Fenwick iterated in bewildered tones.

"Good God!" Her eyes narrowed. "When did he tell you?"

"Just now, Your Grace."

"You mean this very minute?" Her voice was a hiss.

"Well, perhaps two minutes by now probably." Fenwick was flustered. "He told me to find you and I decided to try here first."

"Why?"

Fenwick, quite at sea, shrugged. "I don't know; I thought you might be here."

Lenore stared at him for an instant, then went into a frenzy of activity. "Get my wig—it's by the bed." She flew to her dressing table and applied more red to her cheeks; snatching the wig, she set it on her head; shaking her skirt, she turned and asked fiercely, "How is my appearance, Fenwick?"

"Beautiful, Your Grace." He wondered how the forlorn lady of such a short time ago could now tower so tall.

"Do I look strong?"

"Very," Fenwick conceded in hasty truth.

"Good; now let us go."

Preceding the duchess downstairs, at her command Fenwick threw open the doors to the morning room and heard the guests go quiet at the sight of the Duchess of Asherwood framed by the doorway.

Lenore's eyes sought the duke, whom she spied talking amiably with Lady Jersey—dear God, have I gone mad? Did I imagine—no!—I saw—but now he—she became conscious of the curious glances in her direction. Stretching out her hands, she walked to the duke. "I won, Myles, did I not?" Forcing a laugh, she told the silent assemblage, "I made a wager with the duke that he would never recognize me tonight, and you didn't, Myles, did you?"

"No!" The word was an icicle. "But you have kept our friends waiting long past the time for supper—shall we now go in?" He held out his arm.

Scanning his frozen visage, Lenore controlled an impulse to strike him; instead she laid an ice-cold hand on his arm.

By now all masks were off. The guests fell in behind the duke and duchess and exclaimed at the brilliance and beauty of the drawing room. Round tables were covered and skirted to the floor in red linen, crowned by silver bowls of varied fruits; each was set for six, and beside each setting was a gift—ivory fans for the ladies and jade fobs for the gentlemen.

Lenore, seated between the duke and the marquis, let the chatter flow around her. The duke, teased by the marquis for his failure to catch out his own duchess, pleaded bafflement at the variety of costumes.

"You were invisible, little Duchess, for I did not see—how could I miss that monstrosity on your head?" drawled the Snow Queen.

"Easily, Your Majesty." Lenore again forced a laugh. "You were surrounded by Robin Hoods, minstrels, jesters, clowns—even a cardinal. I'm always surprised, Lady Jersey, you aren't crushed by your admirers."

"Farradiddle; Pierre, you are the tallest—did you not spy out our Velasquez lady?"

"Hoy," Lenore cut in, "are you not aware Cardinal Richelieu gazes only on the queen?"

"I saw the duchess," announced Lady Vaga.

Lenore held her breath.

"Lenore paled at the sight of my masterful handling of a whist hand." Lady Vaga nodded to Lenore.

She knows, but has no intention of giving me away. Lenore gave the old lady a smile. "Thank you, Lady Vaga—it was masterly, but then you always play your hands with finesse." Lenore lifted her glass to the old lady.

"Well," bragged Lady Vaga, "I won a George or two from an Indian rajah; struck him cross as sticks—the greenhead. He assumed that old ladies are ripe for short shifts at the whist table—ha!"

The talk turned to gaming, allowing Lenore to wonder about the duke—He sits beside me, eating, drinking, attentive to his guests—content—Oh, Lord, he is content!—His love is here and he is . . . Taking a sip of wine, she spoke under the conversation, "Myles, other than my bobbery, has the masquerade pleased you?"

Giving her a quizzical stare, the duke replied, "Tonight has seen the culmination of my plots, my plans, my every effort"—he paused—"yes, I am well satisfied. Shortly I hope to be free."

He turned away to greet a clown who had clapped his shoulder.

Dear God, don't let me faint, prayed Lenore, and heard a voice say airily, "Myles hopes to be free from what, Duchess?"

. . . Me, but don't say it . . . She shrugged. "Free of his obligations to the *ton*—Myles longs to travel."

"Does he?" asked the marquis, surprised. "Has he plays to that end? Where does he go?"

Keeping her voice light, Lenore answered, "Oh,

eland, Scotland." She tittered. "After listening to octor Sylvester's tales, even America."

"Strange—Alfred vows Myles to be tied to Asher-ood tight and tick."

"He was until he married me—all this you see is s wedding present to me—a season in London."

"I would judge he had other obligations besides u and the *ton* in London."

"He does, of course—properties, business interests . he spends hours with Mr. Pettibone."

Lenore could have blessed Lady Vaga for distract-g the whole table by saying in a loud, thick voice,)uchess, thish is the besh masquerade I've the privi— e privi"—her voice swooped downward—"honor to tend." With those words, her huge turban nodded ntly forward and came to rest on the table.

Disturbed, Lenore started to rise.

"No, Lenore," Lady Jersey said, "let her sleep—a p will do her a kindness."

To Lenore the remainder of the night became a ur; she stood beside the duke, bade the farewells, cepted the praises and gratitude, permitted her hand be kissed, exchanged hugs, but saw no one save dy Vaga, who surprised everyone by waking and aking her adieus with aplomb.

When Fenwick closed the doors on the last depart-g guest, Lenore did not move. The duke stepped in)nt of her, and seeing her glazed eyes, said quietly, .enore, it is over."

She focused on him with a stricken look. "Oh, yles."

The duke caught her as she fainted.

Doctor Sylvester, his foot on the stairs, strode to the ke. "Put her on the couch in the morning room;

Fenwick, get my case." Hastily he undid the tigh
dress and loosened the lacings; then he held a burn
feather under her nose and chafed her hands.

Finally she moaned and opened her eyes. Lookin
around, she sighed and her head fell back on the couc
armrest.

"Good God," cried the duke, "is she—"

"She's asleep now," said the doctor. "Fenwick, ge
Maria; we must get her out of this ridiculous gown."
He lifted the exhausted Lenore and carried her up
stairs. At her bedroom door he said to the duke, "Sh
will be all right, Your Grace—she just needs sleep."

The duke went to the library and poured himsel
a long brandy. Musing before the fire, he half doze
Rousing, he concluded he'd best see to the well-bein
of his visitor. When he knocked on the guest-roor
door, it was quickly opened by Mrs. Clough.

"Thank God you're here; madame's time has come
I can't leave her and we need the doctor now."

"My God, I thought—"

"What do French quacks know," scorned Mr
Clough sharply. "Get Doctor Sylvester immediately.

The duke, though unused to commands, did as bi
finding the doctor about to retire.

"I need you, Doctor."

"Lenore?" In his agitation the doctor forgot hir
self.

"The expected patient has arrived and—"

"Oh, Lord, so soon?"

When they entered the guest room, Doctor Sylvest
rushed to the bed; the occupant pushed him awa
"I don't want you, I want Myles," moaned the beau
ful lady, now in pain. At a nod from the doctor t
duke stepped to the bedside.

"It hurts, Myles," said the plaintive voice as the duke took her hand.

In a tone no one had ever heard before, the duke said, "I'm sad, little songbird, but you will be brave and let the doctor help you."

"I don't want a doctor, I want him; if only he were here, he would know what to do."

"My dearest," said the duke soothingly, "he is indeed a great and powerful man, but he could not help you at this time. Only a doctor can assist you, and Doctor Sylvester has high skill in these matters."

Seized by a pain, the patient clutched the duke's hand so tightly he nearly cried out.

"If madam will allow me, I can make her easier," said the doctor quietly.

When his hand was released from pressure, the duke said firmly, "My dear little nightingale, please listen. You have been put under my protection by the great one and he wants the best for you; he depends on me to provide for your care, and I have called on a doctor in whom I have unquestioned trust. So you must do as the great one desires; be as brave as he would wish you to be and you will have his fine baby." The duke winced as his hand was again caught in the vise of her pain.

The doctor, who had been studying his patient closely, said, "Madam appears very healthy and should indeed have a fine baby."

"Oh," screamed the mother-to-be, "the baby—who cares about the baby—all I want is to be well so I can sing again."

After a shocked pause, the duke spoke. "You will be, little lark, but you do realize"—he stopped as she was seized with another pain—"you must know that the great one is interested in the baby; he has instructed me minutely as to its care. Come—let the doctor assist you and soon you'll be able to thrill your audiences once more."

"You promise, Myles? You swear?"

"Yes, I promise—I swear." Gently withdrawing his hand, the duke nodded to the doctor to proceed, and left the room.

So as Lenore slept, and the duke anxiously waited by the library fire, a daughter was born to Europe's most famous opera singer and the Emperor of France.

59

The next morning the house on Grosvenor Square that had blazed with light the night before stood quiet.

The mother and the new daughter slept, watched over by Mrs. Madcape, who had relieved the weary Mrs. Clough early in the morning.

Lenore lay dozing in her bed after a night of dreamless sleep.

The duke had waited the night to learn of the child's safe arrival, then had written two letters. He now reposed deep in his first untroubled sleep in months.

Doctor Sylvester slept, after thanking his Maker for what had proved an easy birth.

Mamère slept like the new baby.

The baby, the first to wake, proclaimed loudly that newborn girls are hungry, thus rousing her mother. Mrs. Madcape, an experienced mother of five, gently laid the baby in her mother's arms and softly whispered to the mother. And so peace was restored.

During the day Lenore drifted in and out of sleep. Semidreams of dismal nature caused her to frown in her sleep. "It is all over" rang like a cruel cymbal in her mind—It is all over—shortly I'll be dismissed. He will send for me, maybe tonight, and in his coldest voice say, "Lenore, you have served my plots and plans, but now the lady I love is here." Lenore, as she became more awake, had a stirring of indignation. How dare he bring his love to this house—no matter how empty our marriage—and cover his deception by a masquerade? Why did he marry me, when he planned so soon to install his mistress . . . ? Of course, the boys . . . I provided the face of respectability, and it's now established; he can introduce his love—a distant relative—brought as a companion for his sickly wife. Dear God, he already has a doctor in the household. Oh, I'll be the duchess, indeed so, but to the world a missish and out-of-civils lady—"Poor Myles—isn't he fortunate to have two such devoted people to care for his ill duchess." Wait! If I am to be sickly, why did he give me the curricle and matched grays? Oh, yes, of course—the doctor will order me to ride each day, accompanied by Maria, thus ridding the house of my presence.

The thought brought Lenore fully awake. Well, His Grace need not put himself to the trouble—I'll go away—I will leave and go . . . ! Where? Lenore sank back on the pillows . . . Lady Jersey's? She twisted in bed. "Little Duchess, I love you, but cannot have you

tempting my admirers in my own home." Lady
Vaga's . . . ? "Lord, Lenore, you're not going to let a
fancy piece spoil your being the Duchess of Asherwood? Hah! Vacant Vaga had cyprians all over the
place, but I was always Lady Vaga—take a lover and
stop being a peagoose." Rachel and David's . . . ? "My
dear Lenore, our deepest regrets that our son will
not go to Oxford, but you did take marriage vows
committing you, no matter the pain."

Nevertheless, I will go from this house, Lenore determined, and fell into sleep. Late in the afternoon
she woke and arrived at one clear decision—she would
visit Rachel and David, leaving the next day. Feeling better, she rang for Maria and asked for tea and
pastries.

"*Sí*, Your Grace—are you rested?"

"Indeed so. Has the duke—"

"His Grace has gone out to dinner."

"What?"

"So His Grace informed Abel"—Lenore smiled bitterly. He cannot face me—"and left orders that you
were to sleep as long as possible."

Stung by anger and dreading her own thoughts,
Lenore proclaimed she would dine with Madame
Lanier.

"Are you sure, Your Grace? Madame has been as
cross as a wasp today. Scolded me, ordered Abel out
and away, a pet at the doctor, and is still *al contrario,*"
Maria warned.

"Good; I would enjoy a brangle. You tell her I'm
coming and then run."

"Well, Duchess," snapped the old lady on Lenore's
entrance, "you made a raree-show of yourself last
night."

"No, darling; I didn't make any show as far as you observed; you never cast your ogles on me."

"You weren't there!"

"I was there, and made you a splendid curtsy."

"Humph, that's a bouncer—I'd know you anywhere."

"Except last night."

"Stop the put-offs—who were you?"

"Do you remember a maiden in green chiffon, wearing a hennin?"

"Good Lord—was it you running your hands all over Bunky?"

"Looby, did you see that?"

"Brass-faced you were; threw Bunky into a hubble-bubble—thought for a moment he intended to chase you into the morning room. Don't recall your curtsy, though."

"Sad—I toiled so hard to achieve it."

"Peahen!"

"Did you enjoy the party, Mamère?"

"So-so—I'm old and can't dance or flirt—hold your reins—did you say green chiffon?" Lenore nodded. "Then why was that screw-loose doctor prattling about a velvet gown you laced yourself into so snug, you fainted?"

"Mamère, an advantage in giving a ball in your own home—you can change costumes."

"Scared the duke would catch you out in the green, eh?"

"Well . . ."

"Humbug—why didn't you show me the change of costume?"

"Impossible; by the time I donned it, you were well tucked in bed—drunk as a drum, I might add."

"Eek, how dare you talk to me in that pert fashion?"

" 'Cause I love you and the truth is—"

"Nonsense—a brandy or two to sustain me in my hostess duties, for which you have not thanked me."

"Thank you; and one or two to uphold you while watching the dancing, then—"

"Enough, saucebox, I observed every civility."

"True; your sideward slump in your chair, almost landing you on the floor, can in no way be considered uncivil, except by the highest sticklers, of course."

"Stop bamming me, Duchess; if you're trying to turn me up sweet, I ain't cozened—go away!"

"But, darling, I'd hoped to dine with you—"

"No, I'm displeased with you—just leave!"

"Immediately, my dearest vixen. Good night—I hope tomorrow you will not hold everyone in bad loaf as you have today."

The old lady turned her back to Lenore.

Meeting Maria, who had the dinner tray, Lenore said she would eat in her own room. During the evening she made plans and wept.

60

The following day Lenore spent the morning shopping, and bought her ticket on the post for the trip to Asherwood. She considered visiting Charles and

Heath, but forewent the uncertain pleasure because she feared they might read her sadness and break her determination.

The duke did not appear for the midday meal and she did not inquire as to his whereabouts. In the afternoon she asked Abel to bring her baggage, swearing him to secrecy, explaining she desired a change of air. After dinner she wrote a note to the duke, placed it on her dresser, and went to bed early.

"Your Grace, Your Grace." Maria shook her. "Wake, please—the *nena*, the baby—he wants to take the baby—he has *la pistola*—the duke—"

Lenore threw back the covers. "What about the duke? Maria, slowly, tell me from the beginning! *Despacio!*"

"*Si, si*, Abel heard the man demand the duke get the baby. His Grace claimed the man mad—the man drew *la pistola*—a pistol . . . Abel came to me . . . I come to you."

"What baby?"

Maria pointed toward the guest room. "The new baby—madame's baby."

"Who is madame?"

"Madame Grassini—she gave birth to her *nena*."

"Grassini—the opera singer?"

"*Yo no sé*—the duke calls her 'little songbird.'"

"Good God! A baby!"

"*Si, si*, born in the early hours of yesterday."

Bewildered, Lenore stood sorting her thoughts.

"The man downstairs says he will announce to the whole world that His Grace is a French agent unless—"

A French agent—the duke? "Wait, Maria, let me think." French agent—Myles's obligation—dear God.

. . . "Maria, get my clothes—hurry." Lenore, her mind racing, dressed swiftly and ran with Maria down the hall and into the guest room to the bedside of the sleeping mother.

"Madame, Madame Grassini, wake up." Lenore shook the blanket-buried figure.

"What is it? Who are you?" The opera singer peered sleepily at Lenore.

"I'm the duchess; now listen carefully—there's a man downstairs holding the duke at pistol point, demanding your baby."

"Mon Dieu! Quel malheur!" the lady shrieked.

"Yes, and you and I must stop him. Get out of bed!"

"Qué?"

"Get up!"

"Are you demented? I can't put my foot to the floor."

"You must." Lenore threw back the covers and swung Madame Grassini's legs so they hung over the side of the bed.

"But I've just had my baby," wailed the new mother. "I will die!"

"Nonsense; I've seen mothers in Spain rise after the birth of a child, wash the baby, then the bed linen. Maria, help me get madame on her feet . . . Good, now take a step or two . . . See! Her clothes, Maria."

"She has none but the gown she wore here," Maria explained.

Lenore paused. "Maria, go to my room and bring the lacings of the costume and my blue muslin."

"What are you going to do to me?" cried the singer, now fully awake.

"First dress you, then we will go downstairs, and you

re to do exactly as I direct. Here, let me assist you
with your dressing."

When Maria returned, she and Lenore dressed the
confused and whimpering patient; Maria combed
madame's hair while Lenore went to the head of the
stairs and called to Abel, beckoning him to come up.
Returning to the guest room, she said, "Madame, if
you value your baby's life, you will follow my every
lead in that which I intend to do. Remember, my
name is Lenore. Ah, Abel—come in. Madame, Abel
will carry you downstairs, then we enter the library.
I will talk, but you respond to what I say as in a
play. Can you do that?"

Madame Grassini drew herself up. "It should not
be difficult, Duchess. You forget I am a leading lady in
the opera."

"Bravo! Now, Maria, take the baby to my room
and do not leave until I return, but before you do
so, dismantle the baby's bed, remove all signs of the
baby, and make madame's bed also."

Lenore, wondering what on earth she would say to
the duke and marquis, led the way.

In the library the duke was speaking to the rigid
man facing him. "I repeat to you that Madame
Grassini is a guest in my house, but when you mention a child, I'm at a loss."

"Myles, don't weary me; I have it on the highest
authority that Grassini left the opera company in
Paris because she was obviously with child."

"Your informants are codheads!"

"Stop sparring; I don't intend—"

The door to the library opened. "Myles, darling. . . ." Lenore and Madame Grassini entered arm
in arm. "Josephina and I have been at points—Oh!"
For an instant Madame Grassini had to steady Lenore

who, after a quick intake of breath, continued, "Good evening, Alfred; I was unaware you were here, or we would not have burst in—forgive me."

Both men stared in amazement. Sir Alfred dropped his hand behind his back. The duke staggered a step and braced himself at the mantel. Neither man spoke. Lenore hurried on. "Josephina and I have argued over a wager. Myles, did we or did we not see Wellesley ride by on horseback when we drove in the park today? Back and forth we've brangled—yes—no—finally we decided you should settle the fratch. Hoy, I'm being uncivil; Alfred, you, of course, are acquainted with our guest, if not in person, by fame—Madame Grassini. Josephina, this is Sir Alfred—Eric's brother." Seeing Alfred recovering his poise, Lenore paused.

"The world knows its most famous opera singer." Sir Alfred bowed, never taking his eyes off the lady.

"You are most kind." Grassini sounded bored.

"I'm sure the duke and duchess are honored to have such a visitor; I didn't realize you knew Madame Grassini, Duke."

"Oh, he didn't; Josephina is a friend of mine," Lenore cut in.

"But the marquis told me—"

"Hoy, that paperskull." Lenore laughed. "Myles, do you remember the night at Lady Vaga's? The marquis first asked if you knew Josephina, then queried Lady Jersey, but—I thought I'd fall into giggles—did not question me. The lofty coxcomb assumed me of not enough consequence to have met one of the world's most famed artistes. Alfred, I've known Josephina for years; she used to visit dear Leticia Ware's home where we met often. We've become quite bosom bows." Lenore smiled at the singer, who said, "Many the cup of tea the duchess and I drank together; I was ac

quainted with Eric also, Sir Alfred; he used to come
backstage to see me—that is before he met his 'Luscious
Lenore' as he called her; then he had eyes for no one
but my dear friend."

Lenore squeezed Josephina's arm in high approval.

"How interesting that you were a favorite of Eric's,"
Sir Alfred said sourly. "How long is your stay to be?
Lady Martha, my wife, and I would like to entertain
you."

"A day, a sennight, a month—*je ne sais pas.*" The
lady shrugged. "*Alors,* Duke, please settle our little
wager."

"Yes, Myles, did or did we not see Wellesley today?"

"No, not so, he is out of the country." The duke's
voice sounded strangled.

"Oh, Duke, you have cost me an Indian shawl," said
Grassini peevishly.

"My regrets, madame."

"Have no regrets, Myles," Lenore said lightly, "tonight's made me most happy. Good night, Alfred; we
will not interfere in your chat any longer."

"Sir Alfred," Madame Grassini chimed in, "if time
permits, I will certainly hope to receive an invitation
from you and your wife. Good night, gentlemen; come,
Lenore, I guess I'll have to give you the shawl, but I
still think . . ." The ladies were gone, leaving stunned
silence behind them.

"Well, Alfred?" the duke said finally.

"A raree-show, I admit, but that is its full content."

"Good God, man, does Grassini look big with
child?"

"No, pleasantly slender for an opera singer, but it
does not signify—she has already had the baby."

In the hall Lenore kissed Madame Grassini, who slumped into Abel's arms. "Dear Josephina, you were magnificent! Abel, have Mrs. Clough put madame to bed while you get the doctor to attend her. I'm going to the morning room and will join you later."

In the library the duke was saying, "Fustian, Alfred, must I repeat and repeat—if she had a baby"—the duke saw the door to the morning room behind Alfred's back open a crack—"the child would be here, or Josephina would be with it somewhere else."

"Exactly! Don't gammon me, Myles." Alfred drew forth his pistol, hidden while the ladies were present. "I believe the baby is in this house, and I intend to search from attic to cellar."

"By God, Alfred, you have always been a baldcock." The duke slapped the mantel. "But this is damned out of bounds!"

Alfred gave the duke a long stare. "Myles, ever since we were in nankeens I've hated you—you were a duke —rich—you married beautiful ladies—you saw the world—you had sons; now I have the chance to do all those things."

The duke saw the morning room door close.

"I had not heard that you were receiving a dukedom, or leaving Martha." The duke sounded stupefied with boredom.

"Damn you, you know I can never be a duke, but after tonight I'll be able to mount a mistress, and will have the gratitude of all Europe."

"For what will Europe owe its thanks?"

"You don't believe me; well, just listen. The new French Empress expects a child within months."

"Does she?" The duke sounded surprised. "Bonaparte must be in transports."

"He is—an heir at last, to hand his empire to," sneered Sir Alfred.

"A honeyfall, indeed," commented the duke.

"But it isn't going to happen; a more worthy claimant is to take the stage—the bastard that is here now—in this house." Alfred spoke as if he threw a dare to the duke to contradict him.

The duke broke into a low growl. "You've windmills in your head—"

"Oh, no! Proclaimed to France as Napoleon's first-born, this child will inherit the empire."

"Rubbish! By-blows do not receive a whit of consideration for succession; France would shrug or laugh —probably both."

"Not as Josephine's child."

The duke gaped. "Good God, you have gone bedlam mad; there isn't a Frenchman living that doesn't know Josephine is barren as a barrel."

"So believed until now, but the lady has been in retirement these last nine months and the on-dit runs like a river proclaiming her delicate condition."

"Whispered by the royalists and their kin, I assume."

"Already the news brings great joy; at last the beloved Josephine lies in wait; prayers rise and candles burn throughout the land."

"Bonaparte will make short shrift of these tidings." The duke waved dismissal.

"Not so; Boney adores two things—power and Josephine. France despises the Austrian Empress and loves Josephine—her child would bring rejoicing, especially as he grows to look more like his father each day. Bonaparte will have to acknowledge and favor Josephine's child, or, who knows—another revolution."

"Fixed right and tight, eh!" The duke shook h head. "Provided, of course, the by-blow was a bo and he grows to look like his father; and that Austri will allow the switch—a veritable sieve. Did the ma quis hatch this goose egg?"

"That flippery flirt? Don't be a numbskull; he's a unknowing as the baby you house, but has serve valiantly as ears and eyes—prattling to me each nigh your every move."

"Far more useful, I presume, than the spies yo hired."

"Infinitely."

"I can't see why—neither Pierre nor the spies coul learn what is naught."

Alfred put the gun in his pocket, opened his snuf box, and took a pinch. "Myles, you and others hav considered me a—I think the word is twiddlepoop— never did you evaluate me knowledgeable, but yo have misread me. Pierre and I corresponded for years it was he who recently told me about your years a the Rake of Europe, your disgraceful behavior, and your rescue by Bonaparte. Pierre landed in Englan a few months ago, full of French scandal broth Among the tidbits, he mentioned that Madam Grassini was—er—causing gossip by her affair wit Boney; and I—I mind you—put the pieces together The emperor dare not have the baby born in France or any country in the empire. Then there were possibl scenes by Grassini—perhaps more dangerous—whis pered words to the new empress—no, he would wan Grassini out of sight, but where? England, of course where his good friend could be trusted—you!"

"A brilliant Banbury tale, Alfred, but continue." The duke sat down.

"The witless marquis, though he hates Bonaparte, is devoted to Josephine. He speaks of her to me over and over. When he told of Madame Grassini being *enceinte*, he laughed and asked if I didn't think it would be great sport to confront the scourge of Europe with his Bartholomew baby. The idea struck a spark and gradually the plan fell into place—Grassini's baby —Josephine's child. The rest is easy; through channels —do not ask me—Josephine was persuaded to go into retirement—she waits impatiently to play her part in the plot that tonight I put into execution."

The duke shook his head wearily. "Alfred, whereby do you benefit?"

"Josephine restored and grateful—France happy— and best of all, you disgraced here in England."

The duke rose. "What a coil your jealousy has led you into. Enough—shall it be the basement or the ballroom first—perhaps the servants' quarters."

"All later; first I want to go to Madame Grassini's bedroom—and no tricks, Myles—a bullet through you would not fret me." He pulled his pistol from his pocket.

The duke paled, but proceeded into the hall. "May I send Fenwick to alert the lady—"

"And warn her? No! Order your servants to stand apart."

"Fenwick, Abel, go into the drawing room and do nothing until I call for you." The duke's lips were tight. "I mean it!" Then turning to Sir Alfred, he asked, "Are you sure, Alfred?"

"No put-offs," snarled Sir Alfred. "You go first. I'm behind you; my pistol is cocked."

When the two men neared the top of the stairs, they halted, stopped by a piercing scream, shrill to the ear.

"Good God," cried the duke as he and Alfred rushed up and threw open the guest room door. The scene before them paralyzed both men.

Doctor Sylvester, his neckpiece and coat awry, gripped the footboard of the bed. Madame Grassini, her gown ripped from her shoulder, cringed against her pillow.

"Doctor!" roared the duke.

"Go away," growled the doctor, leaning over the foot of the bed.

The duke grabbed him by the collar and dragged him upright. "What is the meaning of this outrage?"

The doctor sagged and leered at the duke, his words slurring. "Now, Your Grace, if you bring luscious morsels to the table, you know a starving man bites."

"You're drunk!"

The doctor rocked on his heels. "A bit bosky, perhaps, Duke, but well able to please this gorgeous creature." He turned to Madame Grassini, who shrank back.

"Get that vile man out of my room!"

The doctor giggled. "She doesn't mean it, Duke, she's—she's—" He reeled toward the bed.

"Get out!" screamed the lady.

"Doctor!" The duke spun the doctor around. "Go to your room and pack; you leave this house at once."

"Ah, Your Grace, you don't mean that; where can I go?" The doctor weaved toward the duke, who whirled and went to the door and shouted, "Fenwick!" The doctor started for the bed—Grassini screamed— though in a lower key—Alfred grabbed the doctor's arm and the doctor leaned on him. Fenwick appeared and the doctor welcomed him. "Fenwick, my old

riend, you won't let them put me out to freeze this
night, will you?"

"Come along, Doctor." Fenwick took the arms of
the man who was trying to hug him, turned him
around, and announced, "I'll take care of him, Your
Grace."

"Are you all right, madame?" asked the duke.

"No, I am miserable." She began to sob.

"Madame," assured the distraught Sir Albert, "everything is all right now—you are safe."

"Go away, both of you, and send me Mrs. Clough
or someone—Oh, why didn't I bring my own maid?"
She peered at the men. "Go! Go!" She flung her hand
as if to brush them out of the room.

The men looked at each other and stepped into the
hall in time to see Fenwick close the doctor's door.

"What of the doctor?" asked the duke.

"Dropped on the bed like a felled tree, Your Grace,
sound asleep."

"Send Mrs. Clough to Madame Grassini—immediately and then return to the drawing room."

"Shall we continue?" Alfred asked coldly.

"Haven't you seen enough? I could do with a
brandy."

"Your room, I believe," said Alfred, opening the
door and peering around the candle-lit bedroom. "I
would be indeed surprised to find a baby here, Myles,"
Alfred said, but he moved to the closet, opened the
door, and closed it with a slam. "A baby would
smother in all that finery." He walked to the other
door.

"Alfred!—that door leads to the duchess's room!"

"Then you open it," growled Sir Alfred, stepping
to the side.

"Alfred, must you? Lenore has been ill—Oh, don't look so eager, you'll find nothing."

The duke knocked and was startled when Lenore, attired in the sheerest of pink chiffon nightgowns, flung open the door and threw her arms around his neck.

"Oh, my love, did you at long last rid yourself of that dead bore? I thought you would never—Good God, what are you doing here, Alfred?" Lenore jumped away from the duke and spun to pick up a robe.

The duke, too stunned to talk, wondered if he was losing his mind.

Alfred was dazed. Eyeing the room wildly, then seeing the desk, he said lamely, "Your desk, the duke was speaking of it; Martha and I have one like it. Ours has a secret drawer; the duke and I had a bet that yours does also—we put some blunt on it."

One glance at the duke's face told Lenore the truth. She said, "You're foxed or queer in the attic or both—but come in and settle the matter."

The men entered. Alfred fumbled at the desk, making sure to eye the entire room and dressing room; nothing was out of place, and no baby.

"Finished?" Lenore demanded. "Then good night, Alfred." She opened the hall door, saying, "Good night, Myles," and smiled at the duke as he followed Alfred from the room.

After Lenore's door slammed, the duke said in bored tones, "Alfred, having made a ninny of yourself, must you continue? Mamère is asleep and the boys are away—should you not give over?"

The baffled and angry Alfred glared at the duke, who shrugged. "Well, your grandmother's room next."

"No, no, not her room!" Alfred shuddered. "The doctor's room."

The duke, suddenly confident, said, "If you wish," and led the way.

The room was dark; the doctor, lying across the bed, snored in loud rhythm. Alfred swiftly opened closets and pulled out some deep chiffonier drawers—nothing.

Returning to the hall, the duke queried, "Now the ballroom?"

Alfred as he faced the duke suddenly sensed himself beaten—he would find no baby. Distraught, uncertain, he scowled at the duke, who, recognizing the man's indecision, said, "Alfred, you've behaved like an anapo; put the gun away and come have a drink." He started for the stairs.

Reluctantly Sir Alfred followed His Grace down to the library, where the duke poured stiff brandies, handing one to Sir Alfred, who, unconvinced and defiant, drank silently and finally said, "Dammit, Myles, there is a baby, but you've concealed it well."

"I've hidden no baby, Alfred; you're free to continue the search."

"No-o." Sir Alfred drooped slightly, then rallied, "Myles, do you swear as a gentleman there is no baby secreted in this house?"

"I swear, if there is, its whereabouts is unknown to me!" The duke moved to his chair by the fireplace. "Come sit down, Alfred; had you half a brain, you'd realize that even had you found a child, the plot would fail—Bonaparte would grass you."

"To hell with Bonaparte—my plan is flawless—his son and Josephine's"—Sir Alfred lifted his glass in a toast—"Emperor of France!—and you ruined!"

"But there is no son," the duke said quietly.

"No visible son—no!—you have won thus far—but tonight does not end my search."

The duke sprang up. "Alfred, go home! You and I have had more than enough for this evening! I will wait on you in the morning at eleven."

The duke's stone-cold eyes shook Sir Alfred. "I see no purpose—"

"You will!" the duke growled. "Good night!"

For an instant a tremor of fear touched Sir Alfred, then he shrugged. "Good night, Myles," and gave a half bow to the duke, who was picking up his brandy from the table. Sir Alfred, his hand on the doorknob, turned in fury. "Asherwood, I curse the day you developed a tendre for Eric's widow!" The door slammed.

The duke dropped his glass.

Without knocking Abel and Fenwick rushed into the room. "Are you all right, Your Grace?"

"Perfectly," the duke replied. "Fenwick, clean up this glass; Abel . . ." he paused. ". . . if the duchess is awake, ask her to come here."

"We saw the carriage leave and—" Abel began.

"Just do as I request, Abel." The duke poured another brandy.

The glass cleared away, the duke stood at the mantel, impatient to see Lenore.

Lenore entered and rushed to him. "Myles—Abel says you are all right, but—"

The duke gazed down on Lenore, her beauty marred by her anxious frown. "Have no worry on that score; do you wish a brandy?"

"Heavens, no! What possessed Alfred—he runs mad."

"Please sit down, Lenore." He waited until she

hrew herself in a chair. "Tonight has been an unusual vening—I've been intimidated, shocked, bamboozled, nd insulted. Please, in the name of heaven, tell me vhat happened upstairs."

"It was a hobble, I assure you. It started when Maria woke me and said you were being threatened by man who planned to expose you as a French agent r some such thing; I assumed him, of course, to be he marquis. I nearly dropped when I saw Alfred." Noting the duke's frown, she hurried on. "Maria ex-lained about the baby and the marquis, as I sur-ised, wanting to steal her. I got up immediately to ress, and decided that if the marquis could see Madame Grassini tightly gowned and slim, he might o away. So as quickly as we could Maria and I laced p Josephina and robed her, and Abel carried her ownstairs—Josephina was understandably reluctant—"

"The story, Lenore!"

"I wish you could have seen your face when Jo-ephina and I walked in, arm in arm. I feared you ight swoon, as I nearly did when I saw Alfred. You nd Alfred stood so stricken I had to keep prattling— idn't my tongue go like a fiddlestick—and wasn't osephina marvelous—you'll scarce credit it, but she id know Eric."

"Lenore," the duke spoke sharply, "what took lace after you left the library?"

"Abel carried Josephina upstairs, and I listened at ie morning room door—did you see me?"

"I did, then . . . ?"

"Well, our ruse had failed, so, hearing Alfred still emanding to search the house, I flew upstairs. The octor was tending Josephina and—"

"Tending?" shouted the duke. "He was ape drunk!"

"Myles!" Lenore burst out, "you weren't gulled by that bobbery, were you?"

"Bobbery?"

"He hadn't even smelled a drop!"

"Don't sham it, Lenore, I saw him drunk as a wheel barrow!"

"Fiddle, he was sober—he was *acting*—I suggested he do it. To me it was apparent that if Alfred found Doctor Sylvester caring for Josephina as her doctor, he certainly would be suspicious, but if he appeared the boys' tutor trying to seduce Josephina, it would be at least credible. No one would have believed a doctor behaving so in celebration of having delivered a child!"

The duke shook his head to clear it. "But Alfred and I saw him later, sprawled on his own bed—dead drunk!"

Lenore grinned. "He *is* an actor!"

"Continue!" barked the duke.

"I heard Alfred in your bedroom and felt certain he would come to mine. I simply had to take the most drastic means to turn him about." She faltered, "I—I—" As a deep red crept into her face she said primly, "I just decided that regardless of anything, he most certainly would realize that you would never make love in the presence of a baby!"

For an instant there was silence, then a strangled noise caused Lenore to look at the duke in alarm—first a rumble, a heave, then the Dour Duke threw back his head in a shout of laughter, sounding like a long-quiescent volcano breaking forth: he rocked tears ran down his cheeks, and turning to lean on the mantel, he buried his head in his folded arms, his back shaking as he gave spurts of glee.

Lenore, pleased at the effect, waited.

Finally, mopping his eyes and gasping, he managed

to ask, "And where, Duchess, had you hidden the cause of this farce—the baby?"

"On the lovers' staircase."

"On the *what?*"

"That is what I call the stairs from my bedroom to the ballroom, used by your grandmother for her rendezvous."

The duke sobered. "What stairs?"

Lenore described Charles's discovery of the secret door and the steps to the ballroom, then added, "I had a worry persuading Maria to stay there, but given a candle, she consented to let me close the sliding door. Thank heaven you and Alfred stayed only a few minutes in my room; I quaked that the baby might cry."

The duke thought back to Lenore's telling him of the ballroom. "Why was I not told of the staircase?"

"I—I just didn't." Lenore's head lowered. "I'm sorry."

The duke studied his duchess. "Go to bed, Lenore."

"No, I want to hear about Alfred and—"

"Tomorrow, but now—bed."

"But, Myles—"

His voice was stern. "Lenore, the threads of tonight's events are tangled. By morning I will have secured my thoughts and made my decisions."

Lenore sprang up. "Do not put yourself in a worry in decisions on my account, Your Grace. Good night." She left and slammed the door. "Lenore!" The duke started to follow, then paused and decided, Tomorrow. . . . He poured a brandy and for the first time in months, he seated himself and pondered. His expression was austere, as at times he shook his head; once or twice he smiled. Finally he stood and gazed at the barely glowing embers in the hearth. After stirring the ashes until they flared, rekindling the log into a blaze, he stood the poker in its place, then laughingly said aloud, "Good night, Lenore."

61

Rising early, the duke sent a message to Doctor Sylvester, inviting him to breakfast in the library.

Entering, the doctor paused inside the door. The duke rose and made a deep bow. "Doctor, with my apologies. I match my tribute to your talent—Mrs. Siddons is indeed bereft not to have such a leading man."

The doctor returned the bow.

"Doctor, I'd have laid a monkey that you were drunk as a drum."

"Hoy—by experience faking bosky came easy, but the snoring—cursed difficult. My antics were a disgrace; my regrets, sir."

"You performed at the behest of the duchess, did you not?"

"Well, er—"

"No tattle, Doctor, she has already informed me. An ingenious ploy, and successful—even your mighty snores—most convincing."

The doctor smiled. "Quite so—I snored myself to sleep—didn't wake until dawn."

To the doctor's surprise the duke chuckled. "Last

night was a hubble-bubble. Do you know why you were called upon to give your raree-show?"

"Not entirely. The duchess had no time to explain—however, if Her Grace wished a drunken tutor," the doctor said, laughing, "why question such logic?"

Again the duke chuckled. "Come, I will recite the whole of it, but breakfast first."

Over coffee the doctor listened to the duke's story without interruption, but when he heard of Sir Alfred's role in the affair, he growled, "Your Grace, Sir Alfred is your enemy made dangerous by his hatred of you."

"Jealousy, Doctor," the duke amended.

"Jealousy—a dire emotion engendered by your very existence and fed by your every act—no matter how trivial or inevitable—that you breathe infuriates him —do not take his threats lightly, Your Grace," the doctor urged darkly.

"Thank you, but you may be easy on that score; I have a plan to protect myself. My night, unlike yours, included little snoring." The duke smiled. "I twisted many thoughts aright."

Encouraged by the duke's smile, the doctor said in a less serious tone, "Then, sir, may I perhaps introduce one you may not have considered?" The duke nodded. "Your need of me revolved around Madame Grassini; now the birth is over, Heath is soon off to Oxford, and Charles—do you not wish to employ a younger tutor for him?"

"Do you wish to leave, Doctor?"

"No, it is merely—"

"Are you content in our household?"

The doctor smiled. "Very, Your Grace."

"And should we remove to Asherwood?"

"Asherwood sounds charming; Heath and Charles

have spoken of the palace and village frequently; the duchess also speaks of its beauty and the people, especially of Mrs. Thomas and the vicar."

"Ha! The vicar—a havey-cavey fellow who will beat you at chess and piquet, and probably get you leg-shackled to some female before you're unpacked."

"Famous!" The doctor laughed.

The duke became serious. "Doctor, if you so choose you will be welcome permanently in our household, and should the vicar succeed in his wily plays, a home will be your wedding gift."

"Your Grace!" The doctor, stunned by the duke's largess, could speak no further.

"Retain your thanks, sir; Charles needs a tutor and the village a doctor—Doctor Sagout is aging. For now go visit the boys—they must wonder why they can not return, but until Madame Grassini leaves . . ." The duke shrugged.

The doctor stood. "Your Grace, my gratitude is beyond bounds."

As the doctor opened the door Fenwick stood poised to knock.

"What is it, Fenwick?" called the duke.

"Mr. Pettibone is here to see you, sir."

"Have him come in."

The doctor and Mr. Pettibone shook hands and the doctor left.

The duke said, "You're prompt, Pettibone; have you the papers we need?"

"Yes, Your Grace."

"Good!" The two men settled down to work.

62

When Maria left tea and toast by the bedside, Lenore feigned sleep. She did not desire to talk, but wanted to pursue the tangles in her mind. One thread, she confessed, she alone had snarled—Madame Grassini was not Myles's ladylove. That knot untangled, she quickly wove what to her was golden floss into a comforter. He doesn't love her, he doesn't love her, clicked her heart.

But he did attempt to deceive me—I was not to know of her presence—why?—Didn't he trust me? Am I such a prattlebox? Did he assume I would chatter to Lady Vaga, Lady Jersey—even Mamère—that he had given refuge to Madame Grassini? Why did he surround her with so much cosseting? She was a past love giving birth to his by-blow . . . ridiculous! Myles would have married her . . . besides, he was in Asherwood asking me to be his duchess, to go to London and help fulfill his obligation. She was his obligation! Lenore's mind raced. The other night when he proclaimed to be free, he meant Madame Grassini was safely arrived to give birth to her baby—safe from whom?—from what? What enemies could an opera singer have? Who would be in a taking if she had ten by-blows?—I would have, had it been Myles's—

Ninnyhammer . . . ! But of course it is the father of her baby who signifies . . . but who . . . ? another opera singer, an artist, a writer? No, none would have called on Myles. But someone did—it would have to be a man of importance to—Oh, dear God, what had Maria said . . . ? A man threatening to expose His Grace as a French agent—and the marquis once said of Madame Grassini—she was worshipped by all of France—even the emperor is at her feet—Bonaparte! Bonaparte's by-blow!

Lenore lay back on her pillows, and gazing at the ceiling, tried to fit the pieces together.

But why would Myles turn his life upside down—even wed—at the request of an enemy of England—Bonaparte? Lenore gasped. Alfred could have ruined Myles—one whisper of the truth—Lenore winced. Is it treason? To help protect a woman and her baby—no matter who the father—No! And if so, I'm also guilty—I hid the child. Dear God, what if Alfred had found the child—what would he have done—or did he only want to expose Myles? Lenore shuddered. I must see Madame Grassini and discover her plays for the future. Lenore dressed hurriedly and ran to the guest room.

She found Madame Grassini standing before her long mirror, singing scales. When she finished, Lenore applauded.

"Don't, Lenore, I'm singing flat; I need a piano—have you one?"

"Only the square one on the drawing room balcony."

"Impossible! I'll ask Myles for a harpsichord."

"How are you this morning, Madame Grassini?"

"*Mon Dieu!* After our charade last night, can you not call me Josephina? I sing—therefore I'm fine."

"Josephina, then." Lenore smiled. "You suffer no ill from our adventure?"

"*Oui*, dire pain in my sides from laughing; you should have seen the doctor—the seducer *terrible*—maudlin, clutching, toppling in wine. Molière himself would have wept with joy to cast such an actor." Madame Grassini reeled a bit in imitation. "Then this morning—the stern, the worried—Oh, the contrast." She drew her face into set lines.

"Molière would enjoy you also, Josephina; how is the baby?"

"See for yourself." The singer began her scales again.

"May I pick her up?" asked Lenore, bending over the crib.

"Pick her up, take her to your room, anything—just let me sing, please."

Lenore cuddled the quiet baby, and sitting down, rocked the infant to sleep.

With a final trill the opera singer frowned, then sitting on the bed, said, "My voice is in dreadful condition—it will take months." She sighed. "*Alors*, now we can coze, if you like."

"Josephina, your baby's lovely; have you named her?"

"No."

"But you must—she should be baptized and—"

"Myles can tend to the details—"

"Josephina, don't you have any wishes about the baby?"

"Only *la nourrice*, so I can return to France and the opera—Myles has made all plays for its care."

"Josephina!"

"He has already found a fine school where they take infants."

"I can scarcely believe you would—"

"Lenore, don't frown—you must understand—only a few are blessed with *la voix*—I am so favored—I must sing—besides, the child can never be introduced to France—ever!"

"I understand, but to give up—"

"You do? About France? How did you learn? Did Myles speak of the great one?"

"No, Myles has told me nothing—on the night of the masquerade I thought you to be his ladylove."

"*Mon Dieu!*"

"I know better now, but," Lenore felt constrained to ask, "are you his past love?"

"Myles? *La . . . !* Never! The Rake of Europe has only one love—*vino—oui,* he always appeared with a Paphian on each arm, but only to keep him from falling on his face." Madame Grassini laughed.

Lenore rose and put the sleeping baby in its crib, then went to the bedside. "Josephina, what obligation did Myles owe the great one?"

"*Je ne sais pas.* When I consulted the great one about the baby, he comforted me, and said the Duke of Asherwood would care for me and the baby— *Tiens.*" She shrugged.

Lenore sighed. "I must go now, Josephina; I've thought about you and the great one, and I will keep your secret."

"I am indifferent as to the secret, but I suppose . . ." She shrugged. "Please, before you leave, hand me the music on the table—I must study."

63

Sir Alfred Lanier, partaking of his favorite meal—the eggs and sirloin prepared perfectly, the coffee the proper strength, *The Gazette* full of encouraging news—was content. The events of the night before, though not forgotten, were relegated to—What is done is finished.

On the drive home from the duke's house his anger and frustration had melted as he relished his initial success in frightening the duke and the revelation that the supposed perfect household harbored a drunken tutor. The *ton* would delight in that morsel of on-dit. Even meeting Madame Grassini, if she could be persuaded to accept Martha's invitation, would add luster to the Laniers.

Before retiring Sir Alfred felt relief that no baby had been discovered, for what he'd do with an infant—Martha's reaction to his appearance in the middle of the night might have been, at best, hazardous.

Naturally disappointment must ensue—his French friends—Josephine—even himself; but weighed against the accompanying pother and uncertain rewards . . . besides, he thought, I am an Englishman.

In bed he reviewed the evening once more; satisfied, he concluded his ruination of Myles Asherwood could wait.

Sir Alfred had slept well and now greeted the marquis, who always timed his entrance into the breakfast room late enough to permit his host and hostess time to read their newspapers.

"Good morning, Pierre." Lady Martha laid aside her reading.

The marquis bowed, then installed himself in his accustomed chair. "Lady Martha your radiance rivals the sun."

"Alfred," crooned the lady, "you should emulate the marquis; he starts each day with a welcome pleasantry."

"A French knack, my love," Sir Alfred said genially. "I, alas, can only start the day with an English 'Good morning.' Dull, I grant, but today I have news that may match Pierre's airy insouciance."

"Hoy! What?" Lady Martha scoffed.

"Madame Grassini is a guest of the Duke and Duchess of Asherwood."

"What?" exclaimed Lady Martha.

"How do you know?" asked the marquis.

"I met her last night; she is a friend of Lenore's."

"Impossible; Lenore could not be acquainted with an opera singer." Martha dismissed the possibility.

"Is she *enceinte?*" asked the marquis with a slight leer.

"No," averred Sir Alfred, "Pierre, I think you were out there; she appeared quite slender for an opera singer."

"Then the baby's born," proclaimed the marquis.

"What are you two chattering about?" Lady Martha was impatient.

"Only gossip, Martha—Pierre heard some French on-dit that Madame Grassini expected a child."

"Nonsense, she's not married." Lady Martha's tone was positive.

The men ignored the irrelevancy.

"My authority was sound, Alfred. I was most certain."

"Well, you missed your tip, that's all." Sir Alfred, now convinced there was no child, spoke disparagingly. "Martha, we must give a ball; Madame Grassini will accept—she all but promised last night."

"I've just given a ball—I don't—"

"Martha!" her husband spoke meaningfully.

"But, Alfred—"

"Martha!"

"Oh, all right." Lady Martha rose. "I don't see how . . . besides, why the fuss over a French opera singer? How did she get to England anyway? All right, Alfred —you needn't glare." She swirled out of the room.

The marquis said quickly, "Lady Martha's question is to the needle, Alfred; how did Grassini run the embargo? Only with high permission could she cross from France."

"Well, she did—how does not interest me."

"And only for the gravest cause would she be—Alfred, she did have a child, and in England. . . . When did Grassini arrive?"

"I have no idea," Sir Alfred answered. "She and Lenore spoke of driving in the park yesterday."

"Hmmm, a flimflam—Alfred—the masquerade—she arrived the night of the masquerade—a superb setting to smuggle her into the house."

"Speculation, Pierre." Though Sir Alfred sensed truth in the marquis's words. "Explain to me how she could cross the Channel, rattle to London—was it two or three nights ago?—have a baby, and come downstairs last night when I met her?"

"She couldn't, but she did."

"Fiddle-faddle—there's no baby! You can ask the duke; he comes here shortly."

"Nodcock—if Myles concealed the baby in the first place, he is hardly going to admit to its presence today."

"No," Sir Alfred, now of two minds, added. "We could trick him into some revelation."

"How?" the marquis demanded. "Myles is no Johnny Raw."

"I could say Martha's planning a ball for Saturday night in honor of Madame Grassini," Alfred said, then added lamely, "with you as her escort."

"Absurd—Myles would plead another engagement but you do have a raveling of an idea—I will insist on calling on my compatriot and—"

"Are you acquainted with her?"

"No, but Myles will introduce me, then I will pay her court, feign a tendre, and insist she ride, dance and—"

Sir Alfred, weary of the whole affair, welcomed the announcement by the footman that the Duke of Asherwood and Mr. Pettibone waited in the morning room.

"Show them into the book room and bring refreshments," Sir Alfred ordered, then, after the man left, asked the marquis, "Are you of the mind to pursue this?"

"Yes! To deflate Napoleon—*quel bonheur!*"

When the duke saw the marquis enter with Sir Alfred, he acknowledged to himself a new threat.

Sir Alfred did not offer to shake hands. "Well, Myles, you said eleven and the clock strikes the hour."

"Yes, Alfred; Pierre, you have met Mr. Pettibone, I believe."

"Indeed, yes," said the marquis with a half bow. "We passed often on the wharves—I seeking news from France, and you, sir?"

Mr. Pettibone responded, "Unlike you, I sought word of an overdue ship."

"Has it arrived?" asked the marquis.

"Yes, finally it was able to run your embargo." Mr. Pettibone's tone was dry.

"How fortunate—its cargo, sir, if I may be so bold?"

"Pure gold, sir."

The arrival of refreshments brought Sir Alfred out of his trance. "Gentlemen, please sit down. Do you wish brandy—Myles, Mr. Pettibone?"

"No, thank you—nothing," said the duke.

"Nor I." Mr. Pettibone sat next to the duke on the sofa.

"A brandy, please, Alfred," the marquis said, remaining standing. "I wish to drink to the health of the duke's guest—Madame Grassini."

The duke gave a faint smile. "Thank you, Pierre; she will accept your graciousness happily. Have you met her?—charming—why don't you call; she would welcome a compatriot."

Sir Alfred choked on his brandy.

"I will, Myles; I've admired her from afar—now to come face to face at last would be edifying."

"She is a natural beauty, Pierre," the duke said.

"I do not dispute you, Myles; it is her health that stirs my curiosity."

"Health?" The duke shook his head. "You bewilder me, Pierre; she is more Lenore's friend than mine—but of her robustness—you should hear her practice scales. . . . Unless I am deceived, she is very strong."

"*Très bien,* then she may permit me to escort her to Lady Martha's ball, to be given shortly."

"A ball, Alfred? You and Martha just gave a ball."

"Well—er—Martha—when Martha heard Madame Grassini was in London, she insisted we give another ball immediately."

"I see." The duke's voice was low. "It sounds very pleasant. Of course, we all would attend with pleasure, except Lady Martha's hopes will be dashed—and yours also, Pierre."

"Why?" asked Sir Alfred and the marquis together.

"I would choose not to say my say before the marquis, but as he has lost his air of flippery, I will. Last night, Alfred, you came to my home and threatened me with a pistol, making demands which I met—to search my home. To your disappointment you found no baby—your plot to present the infant as Josephine's child was sunk."

"My God." The marquis whirled on Sir Alfred. "Was that your play?—Josephine's child? Myles, I swear I knew naught of this madness—I confess to the desire to embarrass the scourge of Europe, but this . . . !"

"I believe you, Pierre—your guilt lies in putting the idea into Alfred's head—however, the plot does not signify—even a baby discovered—the plot would have failed. Your real intent, Alfred, in this dido, however, does signify—dreams of power and favor were only veils conjured to convince yourself of the importance of carrying out your plays; stripped away, the naked spur was your hatred of me, inflamed by the jealousy that has existed since we were in leading strings."

"Myles, I—"

"Quiet, sir! I need not list the beads of my malfeasances you finger each day—a long strand indeed; and your hatred I cannot—dare not—tolerate."

"Myles, I—" Sir Alfred flushed.

"Nor will I endure living with such jealousy near me. Therefore, beginning today, you, Alfred, are to develop a passion to leave England."

"Leave England?" Sir Alfred whispered.

"Your desire to go to America overwhelms—"

"America?" The word was barely audible.

"And you leave in two sennights—Give him the papers, Mr. Pettibone."

"No!" shouted Sir Alfred when the solicitor extended a packet to His Lordship.

"Take them, Alfred," the duke ordered.

"No! I'll not leave England—America!" Sir Alfred shrilled hysterically. "We are about to go to war with that country—I'll not go."

The duke studied the shaken man and said calmly, "America frightens you—all right then, Scotland—you have a home and properties there. Mr. Pettibone, give Sir Alfred the other packet."

Sir Alfred became defiant. "I go nowhere; you can't make me. London is my home and—"

"Alfred," the duke said coldly, "should you stay, your life will suffer a sea change—your holdings will diminish—your clubs will welcome you increasingly less—later even the *ton* will find you de trop. . . ."

"You can't—I'd proclaim your cruelty," Alfred shrilled.

". . . Whereas in Scotland you can live the life of a laird—rich, respected, perhaps, in time, liked."

"My interests and my fortune are here!"

"Precisely the reason I brought Mr. Pettibone. Listen carefully, Alfred; you are to sell me your properties in Asherwood; Mr. Pettibone will help you dispose of your London holdings at a generous profit; then, if you wish, he will assist you to reinvest your monies in Scotland."

Sir Alfred made as if to leap from his chair. "Damn you, Myles, I should have shot you last night!"

"Come, Alfred, Scotland is better than the gallows." The duke's voice was not unkind.

Sir Alfred slumped in his chair. "Martha will hate Scotland—and me."

"Not of necessity; as a girl, Martha lived in the country and will run affairs in Scotland handily— London has never suited her—she will sweeten."

The marquis, stunned by the words he had heard, asked, "Myles, what of me?"

Turning to the marquis, the duke said, "Pierre, you are a French fripple—amusing at times. You are also a two-faced hypocrite. You can flirt with Lady Jersey; be gallant to the duchess; pose as a good companion to me, and at the same time tattle our conversations each night to Alfred; and use him to pry yourself into polite society. You are a coxcomb and a gossip, and you know it!"

The marquis flushed. "Very well. You shall never be embarrassed by my presence again; I leave for Germany as soon as possible."

The marquis wheeled and left.

"Hmmm, a trace of character," said the duke.

"Myles," said Sir Alfred, "am I never to see England again?"

"You may visit England whenever you choose— London, Asherwood, Oxford when Leon is there, anywhere—provided I'm not in residence."

Sir Alfred suddenly stared at the duke in disbelief. "Do you hate me, Myles?"

"No." The duke retrieved his hat and gloves. "Pettibone, stay and advise His Lordship. Heed Pettibone, Alfred, he will serve you well—good morning." The duke bowed.

Sir Alfred, who could never have explained his action, struggled to his feet and bowed to a closed door.

64

Leaving Madame Grassini, Lenore, torn in her thoughts, walked slowly along the hall to her room. Could I abandon to others the care of my baby? No! But how can I judge; I don't have *la voix*—maybe if I—at least Josephina doesn't wobble in her plans.

Lenore sighed. If I am to go to Asherwood, I must dress and depart at once—if not, then—Oh, why hasn't Myles sent for me—Stop it—What he says about last night has no—this is my decision, yesterday I'd have fled, but today? Lenore picked up her ticket, scanned it, then tearing up her letter to the duke, tossed both into the fire, thinking, I must hear Myles's wherefores.

Maria knocked and entered. "Your Grace, Madame Lanier wishes you to have nuncheon with her."

"I'll be there in a minute, Maria; thank you." Lenore went to the mirror and, fixing her hair, said to herself, "Being a duchess is a dashed smoky thing at times."

As she walked into Madame Lanier's room Lenore

said, "Good morning, Mamère—I'm charmed to see you."

"Good morning, Lenore; come sit near me."

Once seated, Lenore wondered if Mamère would ever speak. Finally the old lady said, "Lenore, do you love me?"

"Mamère, a silly question, surely."

"Well, then, do you know I love you?"

"I'd bet a flimsy on it."

"Then—" The old lady's face crumbled.

"What is it, Mamère?"

"Don't want to tell you." The old lady tossed her head.

"All right, dear."

"But I have to."

"Pray, do, then."

"No! I'm not going to."

"Pray, don't then." Lenore laughed.

"Don't laugh, missy," snapped the old lady.

"I can't help myself—this is an idiotic conversation— you love me and I love you, so speak out."

"It's Lucy."

"Lady Vaga? Has she offended you?"

"No."

"What then?"

"Old vacant left Lucy very well to pass—rich—the first buds are almost on the trees; but I ain't going to do it. She'd have married again if old vacant hadn't left her so shod and hosed."

Lenore, slightly bewildered, said, "I've always thought a large honeyfall attractive to gentlemen."

"Oh, she had chances, but vowed she'd turn old vacant's fortune over to no man on earth."

"Is there no heir?"

"No, only girls; Lucy had eight—all wed and scattered—certainly the sap is rising in the trees."

Lenore blinked. "What have trees to say to anything about Lady Vaga?"

"You'll be going to Asherwood."

"Oh, now I see; Lady Vaga wants you to stay with her while we are in Asherwood."

"No, she wants me to *live* with her, but I ain't—Bunky and you've been too good to me."

Lenore smiled. "But the buds will soon be on the trees."

"You want to be rid of me?" growled Mamère.

"Looby, no; I want you to do as your heart inclines you."

"That's schoolgirl prattle."

"Then let's talk with the sense of ancients. Lady Vaga, lonely, and with plenty of blunt, desires her bosom bow—you—to come and keep her company—don't interrupt—you, not a whit unhappy while in London, dread the thought of removing to Asherwood."

"Yes."

"You're also in a coil because Bunky and I have been like a son and daughter, and you'd cut off your thumb before hurting either of us—yet Lady Vaga tempts you."

The old lady nodded and began to cry.

"Well, Madame Lanier," Lenore said sternly, "the last thing either the duke or I could endure would be a wet goose flooding Asherwood."

"You mean"—Mamère hesitated—"you wouldn't be unhappy if I—"

"Oh, no, I didn't say that—I expect to be most unhappy—we will miss you sadly."

"Well then . . ."

"But when I am miserable, I'll think of you having cozes with Lady Vaga, and parties with your friends, and I'll be restored to high gig."

"You won't—"

"I won't, and neither will Myles—so dry your tears and inform me of your plans."

"Well, Lucy truly wants me—intends to redo a room for me on the first floor. She's located and hired Daisy, and invited Lady Wilna Gravefield—Celeste Hackingham's mother—and a Mrs. Cravencroft, a lady from Bath, so we can always have a whist game . . ." Mamère's story, punctuated with "are you sures" continued through the meal.

Back in her own room Lenore cried—she'd miss Mamère and her sharp tongue. It suddenly struck her that the household was dwindling—Mamère to go, Heath soon back in Oxford, Charles to enter Eton not far hence—leaving just Myles and herself. Dear God, his need for me is over; he can go to Asherwood and resume his life. No matter what David said about boredom, Myles enjoyed being a recluse. I must give him his freedom—or at least a choice. She threw herself on the bed and sobbed. Later, her sobs diminished, she fell asleep.

"Your Grace, Your Grace," Maria whispered.

Lenore sat up, startled. "The baby? What?"

"His Grace wants you to drive him to visit Master Heath and Master Charles."

Lenore leaped from the bed. "Maria, get my gray velvet and my cape." Dressing as fast as she could, she ran downstairs. The duke, his hand on the banister, watched her descent.

"Oh, Myles, I can scarcely wait to see the boys."

As they drove Lenore nervously chatted about her

hopes of finding the boys in good spirits and how glad she'd be upon their return home.

Disappointment awaited them; the Featherheaths had taken the boys to Oxford to see the quarters Heath and George might share.

Driving away from the Featherheaths, the duke asked if there were somewhere Lenore would like to go.

"No, I do have news for you, but perhaps you would like to tell me about the impossible Alfred first."

"No, later. I want your news first. But before you begin, shall we return to the battlefield?"

"The battlefield?"

"The park where you tamed the *ton*."

"Let's; I should enjoy seeing the park. I only had side glances during our skirmishes." Lenore smiled.

Once in the park, the duke said, "Now your news— not bad word, I hope."

"Bittersweet, I'd say—Lady Vaga has invited Mamère to live with her, and Mamère, after much worry and reassurance of our lack of displeasure, accepted."

"Hoo! So the two vixens desire to share a den." He paused, then said, "You will miss the old lady, Lenore, and so will I; she *did* liven our household." He chuckled. "No more boggards toddling on the stairs—Lenore, don't look so sad."

"I shouldn't; Mamère cossetted, happy, and the two vixens, as you call them, will chatter at the same time, neither listening, both content. Lady Vaga has asked Lady Wilna, Celeste Hackingham's mother, to join them, and also a lady from Bath to complete a whist four. Now please tell me about Alfred."

"A sorry tale." The duke's recital held Lenore silent during the rest of the drive. Once home, the duke handed the reins to Henderson and assisted Lenore

from the carriage. Entering the house, Lenore sai
"Myles, I have a thousand questions."

"I can well imagine. The doctor undoubtedly wi
have questions also; at dinner then?"

"Yes—I'm impatient, but I can wait." Lenore wei
up the stairs and to Madame Grassini's room; her ligl
knock unanswered, she peered in—the singer w
asleep. She went to the crib and gazed at the bab
who lay awake and content. Lenore studied the qui
infant a time. Back in her own rooms, she bathed ar
dressed, and an hour later tapped on the libra
door.

"Come in, my dear." The duke smiled. "The doct
and I have been discussing Josephina's swift reco
ery of strength."

"Good evening, Doctor," said Lenore.

"Your Grace." The doctor bowed. "The duke h
been explaining your theory of less bed rest for ne
mothers. If Madame Grassini is offered as proof,
must succumb to your judgment—it's worthy of study

"Based on observations at the Penn, Doctor."

The doctor addressed Lenore. "Your Grace, I d
sire to thank you."

"For being open-eyed at the Penn?" Leno
laughed.

"I want to thank you for your concurrence in th
duke's asking me to become a permanent member
your household—even at Asherwood."

Lenore, surprised, gave a flicker of a glance to H
Grace, but merely said, "I'm glad you accepted, Do
tor—ah, Fenwick—dinner? Good."

While Abel served the davenport chicken, Leno
asked, "Did Alfred truly pose a threat, Myles?"

"Yes, my dear; until you and Josephina entered,
feared for my life."

The doctor spoke. "The man is mad, but my true puzzlement is Empress Josephine—why would she lend herself to such a plot?"

"Josephine would run any course to win back Napoleon," the duke replied.

Lenore shook her head. "But even had the plan succeeded, Alfred couldn't be certain of either favor or reward."

"That was not his major aim—Alfred's heart was bent on dreams of my disgrace—or demise. Reason enough for banishing him to Scotland—I wish no sword of Damocles."

"May he not make a try on your life before he leaves?" asked the doctor.

"I doubt it—he is not so addled as to prefer the gallows to Scotland."

"Poor Mamère, she will lament his absence, though he pays her only slight attention," Lenore said.

"Alfred may visit her whenever I'm not in London."

"I hope he will." Lenore sighed.

The talk turned to the bustle of events upstairs—"the night of Alfred's outrage" as Lenore titled it. As they drank their coffee Lenore suggested, "Gentlemen, let us pay a visit to Madame Grassini; her version of the night may cast a different color on the whole affair."

Madame Grassini, bored, welcomed the three and soon insisted the duke and the doctor reenact *la séduction* for Lenore's amusement. The doctor happily took the part of Alfred, Fenwick, and himself.

Lenore finally called, "Enough, I can endure no more; if you hey-go-mads had performed in such exaggeration, Alfred would have caught your bobberies in short shrift—Oh, we've wakened the baby."

Madame Grassini sighed. "No, Lenore, it's her feeding time."

Lenore picked up the crying infant and laid her in her mother's arms. The men bowed their good-nights. Lenore stayed until the baby's fussing stopped, then promised to send Mrs. Clough, and bade Josephina sleep well.

In the hall the duke stood leaning on the balustrade.

"Where is the doctor?" asked Lenore.

"He made his adieus; he is late for an appointment with Pettibone."

"Oh." Lenore started for the stairs.

"Wait, Lenore, please. The secret staircase is the only unknown piece of the puzzle in my mind. Would you show it to me?"

"Of course; come along." She led the way, and once in the bedroom, lit extra candles. "See, Myles, how cleverly the node is carved in the marble—quite unnoticed unless one looks for it."

The duke examined the node, then opened the sliding wall; holding a candle, he mounted the steps and at Lenore's instructions from below slid open the ballroom door. Peering into the vast room, he asked Lenore to close the lower door. "I want to sense what Maria must have felt." He closed off the ballroom. In a few minutes the duke opened the lower door. "Whew, she was brave. The stairway is ingenious; I wonder who built it?"

Blowing out his candle, he looked around Lenore's room. "Other than the night of 'Alfred's outrage' "— he smiled at Lenore—"I do not remember ever being in this room." He walked to the bookcase and studied the titles.

Lenore seated herself on a sofa by the fireplace.

"Lenore, your selection of books is that of a scholar."
he duke turned toward her.

"Many of them were my father's."

"But you've read them?"

"Quite a number."

The duke, scanning the desk, picked up the book
ense and Sensibility—he frowned and moved to sit
y the fireplace on the couch opposite Lenore. "I've
eard those words before . . . sense and sensibility . . .
es! Pierre said of you, 'A lady of sense and sensibil-
y.'" He glanced through the pages.

Lenore reddened slightly. "What a rum touch he is
-he swore he'd never tell you."

"Tell me what?" asked the duke.

"That it was he who took me to Tollands, where I
ound Newton's *Principia*. Then he presented me with
he novel—I would have told you, but you teased me
bout having a cicisbeo, and I couldn't."

"Don't fluster, it doesn't signify." He laid the book
n the table beside him. "Lenore, I have something
want you to read." He withdrew from his pocket a
arge envelope. "I hope this will make many of my
ctions understandable to you; God knows they have
ppeared muddled enough." He handed her the en-
elope.

Glancing at the large script, "Duke of Asherwood,"
Lenore withdrew the sheets and noted the signature.
From Napoleon?" she asked. The duke nodded.
lowly she read.

My dear Duke,
    The long silence between us must now be
broken. My friend, I require your good services
pledged when we parted.

Parfaitement! Word reaches me that you liv
the life of a recluse—a *monastère*—I do not.

As the world knows, the Empress Marie-Louis
is to bestow upon me a child—an heir, I pray
but, not noted, I am also to be so favored b
Madame Josephina Grassini—*Donc,* my reque
for aid.

Consent will obligate you to do as I now sug
gest *en total!*

As dear Josephina's time draws near, a shi
will transport her to London, where you, i
residence, will receive and care for her—a docto
already installed in your household.

The baby—boy or girl—to be placed in
school of your choosing; support will be forth
coming.

Secrecy is of the greatest import, my frien
I press upon you.

Josephina's debarkation arranged to be unr
marked; her arrival at your home shrouded by
large gathering—*peut-être* a masquerade attende
by many of the *ton.*

And now, Myles, *peut-être le plus difficile*—yo
must wed!

No, I do not run mad. France is a cauldron . .
my enemies will attempt to build great fires. B
trayed, you *sans* a spouse, would add logs to the
flames—therefore it is imperative—if you are t
carry out my request—that you marry.

I can see you cringe, dear Duke, a magnificen
scowl furrowing your handsome brow—but I a
unmoved. There must be a duchess in residenc
in London to protect all in this concernment—
mais, oui—especially yourself, *mon ami!* Th

events cannot be under the auspices of the "Rake of Europe"—*Non!*—an abigail's whisper, a footman's wink, could drive you from England forever.

A duchess in place safeguards not only you, but everyone; she will lend respectability in the eyes of your household, even though—I stress—even though the lady must never learn of the affair— her innocence itself is a shield.

Myles, I turn to you as an old friend, and I lay this heavy burden, for you are the only man in England in whom I have total trust.

In deepest gratitude,

Lenore read to the end and folded the letter. "So it was his request you keep me in the dark concerning the plays?" The duke nodded. "Myles, this *does* explain many oddities of the affair, but it does not reveal why Napoleon could exact such a promise from you."

"He saved my life." The duke related his rescue at the hands of Napoleon, then laughed. "A Gothic tale indeed."

"A tragic one—thank God you lived." Lenore handed the duke the letter.

Studying Napoleon's words a moment, the duke finally spoke. "Old friend, my obligation is almost paid; I undertook it willingly, but I do not want it learned by my sons or their sons." He tossed the letter into the fire.

Lenore and His Grace watched the pages—that had so changed both their lives—turn brown at the edges, then burst into flame.

"Amen." The duke smiled at Lenore.

"I'm glad for you, Myles; but would you never have informed me of Josephina's presence yourself?"

The duke paused, then said, "Your question distresses me, Lenore"—he frowned—"because the answer is no; I had hoped to shelter her, and later whisk her and her baby away without your knowledge. Put it all in the past."

"And I was never to learn?"

"No."

"I can understand your reticence before Josephina's arrival, but once the obligation met . . . ?"

"I would have kept the secret. So, in a way, I must be grateful to Alfred that it fell out other gates." The duke smiled.

"Without Alfred you might have been surprised."

"What?" the duke exclaimed.

"The day after the masquerade I purchased a ticket for Asherwood, and would be there tonight—"

"Good God, why?"

"I assumed Josephina to be your ladylove."

"How could you? You were unaware she was in the house."

"Not so; I saw—"

"The devil you say—I ordered all doors closed and—"

"I had gone upstairs to change my costume and was about to descend. From the top of the stairs I saw your embrace at the door, and tenderness as you led her to the guest room."

"Dammit, no living soul was to catch a glimpse of

osephina as she entered—I'll clean out my house-
old."

"Nonsense, the blame is not theirs; besides, Alfred
id me of my notions."

The duke shook his head. "What a coil; thank God
's almost over. Then—"

"Yes, then . . . Myles, I've had long thoughts today—
nly two of import."

"Only two?" The duke smiled at her.

"Yes. The first—as you say—your debt is almost paid;
osephina is restless. She longs to return to France
nd leave as soon as possible—don't interrupt, please—
Mamère goes shortly to Lady Vaga's, and Heath is
on off to Oxford. Charles?" She shrugged. "You are
sed to a young boy in your household—the only im-
ediment to the resumption of your life at Asherwood
—me. Therefore it is only fair I offer you your
reedom, and I do."

The duke's expression was one of bafflement. He was
lent as he stared at Lenore. "Good God," he said
uietly, "do you want a divorce?"

"Oh!—well, I hadn't—It didn't—" She stopped.

"Well, madam?"

"I just thought I'd go away—"

"Indeed! Where?"

"Well . . . maybe to Lady Vaga's or . . . I planned
consult Rachel and David."

The duke gazed at her for a moment, then growled,
Lenore, your magnificent consideration for my well-
eing overwhelms me—pray, let me be privy to the
cond of your thoughts."

"Josephina's baby. Myles, you can't send the baby
a school, no matter how highly recommended—she's
o tiny. You must take her into your household—the
loughs and Maria—"

"What happens to the infant is no responsibility of mine, Lenore, nor of yours. Napoleon has long since decreed the child's future—"

"Has he cared enough to give the child a name?"

"No, but he has set aside monies to secure her comfort, and a large dowry awaits her."

"Rich, but nameless—poor baby." Lenore shook her head.

"At Josephina's behest she is to be named after my mother—Ann Boughall."

"Indeed. Then further reason for you to wish her under your care."

"Lenore, Napoleon made his plans and neither you nor I have a say." The duke's tone was chilly.

"Nonsense! He should far prefer you to bring up the child—"

"If he asked, I would refuse."

"How can you be so hard of heart? Please reconsider—"

The duke sprang up to stand at the mantel. "Lenore, the answer is *no!*"

Lenore rose, whirled to the door, and threw it open. "You have spoken, Your Grace—I bid you good night."

The duke stood still, then, in a terrible voice ordered, "Shut the door!"

Startled by his tone, Lenore looked at his angry face, closed the door, and leaned against it, her hand clutching the doorknob behind her.

The duke said in a low tone, "Listen carefully, Lenore! I will not bring up Napoleon's baby because I want daughters of our own."

For an instant Lenore stood rooted, frozen, then suddenly, angered, she stepped away from the door and, her voice hard, said, "I am Lenore Lanier

Duchess of Asherwood . . . whom you wed under duress . . . your every desire rebelling . . . and now—within months—you propose children!"

"With all my heart." The duke's eyes softened.

"Sir, you presume!"

"No, Lenore, I love you."

Lenore gave a short laugh. "You cannot—"

"I can do no other—nor wish to."

"Ridiculous! Most times we meet we are at dagger drawing."

"What do quarrels have to say to anything about love?"

"Stop it, Myles." Lenore stamped her foot. "You don't love me!"

"I don't?" asked His Grace in a surprised tone.

"No, you just have a sentimental whim—your household runs easily, your sons have regard for me—perhaps a baby in the house rouses nostalgia—"

The duke snorted in amusement. "My love, you are a nodcock!"

"I don't see—"

"Precisely, you don't see—a nodcock."

"There's no need to call me names."

"Forgive me, for of course you can't see what's not been visible." He smiled. "Lenore, would you wish to sit down and let me describe the downfall of a Dour Duke? Will you do this for me?"

Lenore hesitated, then, her gaze never leaving his face, seated herself on the sofa. The duke sat across from her—an expression in his eyes that made her blood race.

The duke's tone was gentle and bemused. "Lenore, should there be awards for a heart's blindness, I should surely win—the blue hair ribbon."

A tiny smile touched Lenore's lips, but she made no response.

"Once, long ago, Mamère asked why I had snapped myself shut like an oyster."

"An odd comparison, surely."

"Nevertheless one I concede apt—I was an oyster, one shell pride, the other self-pity—tightly clamped—until Heath's fall forced upon me an irritant—which was you. In the days that followed, I was rolled around like an oyster shaken loose from its bed—Napoleon's demands, Charles's arrival—by Jupiter, I was whirled from surprise to bafflement." He laughed, "Consider, madam, the Dour Duke buckled to a female who wished, for a wedding gift, a village festival!"

Lenore reddened slightly, but said nothing.

"Then to London—hoy! Here things *did* come tumbling about." He gave a short laugh. "The marbles in the stairway niches"—the duke shook his head—"finessed into accepting Wiggles—enlisted in a war on the *ton*, and finally out and out bullocked into violating rooms sacred to my ancestors!"

"Have you forgotten the introduction of Mamère into your household?" Lenore asked coolly.

"Deuce take it—I had." He stared into her eyes. "Well, a man in love can't remember everything."

"Of course."

The duke began his story. "Lenore, the oyster was adrift, loose in a strange sea, and abraded by the chaos around it, the shell of self-pity wore thin—memories, counted each day at Asherwood like miser's gold pieces, were swept into oblivion; however, still thick, still strong—the shell of my pride." He rose and moved to stand again at the mantel. "My dearest, are you aware that I consider myself a man of intellect?"

"Why shouldn't you—you are."

"But, little nodcock, like a horse, intellect must be exercised, and in the swirl of happenings I neglected its paces."

"I don't believe that, Myles."

"Oh, it's true. Although you occupied my thoughts continually, until Alfred threatened and you saved my—by the by, in China there's a custom that if a man *or female* saves another's life, he *or she* is responsible for the one rescued for ever and ever." The duke grinned. "Very civilized but, my darling, I digress. After Alfred left and you, in a flame, announced I was not to put myself in a worry on your account, I belatedly did what months ago David advised me to do—attempt to fathom why you charm others, but irk me."

Lenore shrugged. "Easily explained—I cross you."

"Madam, you do." He bowed. "However, that night I gave heed to the cause of our brangles—"

"How drearisome it must have been for you. . . ."

"Oh, no, the word is abrasive." The duke reseated himself on the couch. "Now, I was not such a fool as not to recognize 'you have brains in the attic' as Pierre once told me, but never having dealt with females of wit, you confused me."

"Hoy, if I had been truly needle-witted, I'd have been meek, silent, and never ventured to naysay you."

"Fustian, love, you couldn't help yourself—you're you!"

Lenore caught her breath and for the first time smiled. "I am!"

"Praise be! But I didn't rest my laurels on that one

conclusion." He laughed. "My reasoning was frisky that night and galloped from this quarrel to that—a steeplechase indeed. The course almost run, though I balked, I had to concede that from our every breeze ensued good—don't clutter in, dear—and in the small hours I hurdled the truth. You, my beloved, always use your sense and sensibility for others' benefit—for my villagers; Mamère and her boggards; Heath, Charles, and their varmint troop—others—but most of all for me." The duke quirked an eyebrow. "Often in unexpected ways, but to exquisite satisfaction—an effort to admit, but true."

"Myles, you come on too strong, I—"

"Madam, do not enter caveat with me; long hours and deep ponderings were spent in the abrasion of my pride, but at dawn I was able to peer into my heart, and there lay my irritant—my grain of sand—a pearl!"

Lenore burst into tears.

The duke leaped to her side and gathered her in his arms. "Don't cry, my precious—it was so joyous!"

"I can't help it," Lenore sobbed on his shoulder, "I've loved you for such a long time."

"You have?!" The duke held her tighter.

"Yes, and your ridiculous comparison heals my spirit! Please give me your handkerchief."

He handed her his handkerchief. "I don't know why you loved me," he said simply.

"Does it matter?" asked Lenore, turning her soft eyes to his.

"Oh, my dearest heart," murmured His Grace as he kissed her.

Minutes later, Lenore, her head tucked on His Grace's shoulder, said, "Myles, I've loved you since the day you cheated at piquet."

"Since then? Damme, I never twigged—why didn't you tell me?"

"Myles, that's the silliest question you've ever asked."

"I know—it's just I'm addled with love."

"Stupid," crooned Lenore.

After a time the duke mused, "Since I cheated at piquet—but that was at Willowood, long ago."

"Did you never wonder why I agreed to wed you?"

"No, David had told me you were a lady of marked good sense."

"Hoo, my lofty one; for your present enlightenment, I would never have married any man unless I loved him."

"And you've had a tendre for me since that day I cheated," the duke said comfortably.

"Yes, Your Grace."

"Madam, do you realize what a Herculean labor it was?"

"To cheat? Nonsense—anyone can—"

"Not such a player as yourself—you caught me out, even though for useful tips I'd turned to my vicar."

"David? Why he—Oh, Lord." Lenore sat straight and faced the duke.

"What, my sweet?" drawled His Grace.

"Oh, Myles, I'm afraid I'm going to cost you a long price."

"Ummm?" asked the duke lazily as he ran his finger along her cheek.

"Myles, I've done a dreadful thing—it will cost you a fortune."

"What now, love—a London fair?"

"Don't be hey-go-mad, this is serious."

"Tell me, little Lenore." His Grace gave a tiny tug to a curl temptingly near him.

"Myles, I made a deep wager."

"My gaming duchess." The duke sighed. "Ah, well, what and with whom?"

"David."

"My ramshackle vicar? What high stakes could he wager?"

Lenore twisted the duke's handkerchief. "Oh, I made it so lightly—maybe he did too—other gates—oh, my!" She frowned. "Maybe I can pay it out of my allowance—you're so generous—and Billy's not yet twelve."

Retrieving his handkerchief and kissing her fingertips, the duke said, "You are confusing me."

"If I had a grain of sense—"

"Madam, my patience runs thin."

"It was so absurd—David was comforting me about your lack of love and said that though he wasn't a betting man—"

"An obvious bouncer," injected the duke.

"—he would bet that before our first wedding anniversary, you would have a tendre for me."

"By God, David's a clever cove."

"But I lost the wager, Myles." Lenore's voice had a hint of a wail.

"Bless the Lord! What stakes, my flippery gamester?"

"Well"—Lenore hesitated—"well—" then with a rush, said, "That all his sons be sent to Oxford; and Myles, he has four, and Rachel's expecting again!"

The duke stared at her for an instant, then shouted his laughter.

Lenore, distressed, asked, "Myles, you aren't furious—"

He sobered instantly. "Yes, madam, I am furious."

"Oh, I don't blame you—it was—"

"Yes, little court card, I'm enraged that my plans for David's sons were forerun in a wager."

"Oh, dear." Not grasping his meaning, Lenore asked, "What plans?"

"Each son that Rachel and David produce so regularly is entered on my list of boys bound for Oxford."

"Oh, Myles." Lenore threw her arms around his neck—the delighted duke knew exactly what to do.

Later His Grace said, "Of course, madam, you must pay a forfeit for your furious flinging of my blunt."

"Certainly, dearest piper—what terrible estreat?"

" 'Estreat?' " He sighed. "Well, if I would be buckled to an educated female—your estreat, my lady, is that you must adopt the Chinese way of life—responsibility for me forever."

"Oh, an onus indeed, but hold your reins, sir—I have a query for you—did I dream your presence, or did you enter my room the night I was so ill, and hold my hand until I fell asleep?"

"Good God, that dire night! Your hand like warm swansdown—I quaked—I prayed—and I cried. And still—my damn pride—"

"Oh, Myles, my dearest." Lenore clung to him for an instant. "But for you I would have died." Then drawing back, she laughed. "So, Your Grace, you too must accept the Chinese custom."

After a most civilized and charming exchange of vows, Lenore sighed. "You know, the nicest thing about being the Duchess of Asherwood—is that I am."

The duke held his breath as he let the meaning of her words engulf him; then he sprang to his feet, extended his hands, drew her into the circle of his arms, and, gazing down into her eyes, asked, "Lenore?"

"Oh, Myles," Lenore whispered, "do you think—
is this—are we—should—"

"Madam, hold your tongue—you've been my duchess
long enough—now—will you be my wife?"

"Oh, yes, Myles," said Lenore.

The passionate sequel to
the scorching novel of
fierce pride and forbidden love

THE PROUD HUNTER

by Marianne Harvey

Author of *The Dark Horseman*
and *The Wild One*

Trefyn Connor —he demanded all that was his—and
more—with the arrogance of a man who fought to
win . . . with the passion of a man who meant to pos-
sess his enemy's daughter and make her pay the
price!

Juliet Trevarvas—the beautiful daughter of The Dark
Horseman. She would make Trefyn come to her. She
would taunt him, shock him, claim him body and soul
before she would surrender to THE PROUD HUNTER.

A Dell Book $3.25   (17098-2)

THE WILD ONE

by
MARIANNE HARVEY
bestselling author of *The Dark Horseman*
and *The Proud Hunter*

Proud, beautiful Judith—raised by her stern grandmother on the savage Cornish coast—boldly abandoned herself to one man and sought solace in the arms of another. But only one man could tame her, could match her fiery spirit, could fulfill the passionate promise of rapturous, timeless love.

A Dell Book $2.95   (19207-2)

At your local bookstore or use this handy coupon for ordering:

AN OCCULT NOVEL OF UNSURPASSED TERROR

EFFIGIES

BY William K. Wells

Holland County was an oasis of peace and beauty . . .

    until beautiful Nicole Bannister got a horrible package that triggered a nightmare,

    until little Leslie Bannister's invisible playmate vanished and Elvida took her place,

    until Estelle Dixon's Ouija board spelled out the message: I AM COMING—SOON.

A menacing pall settled over the gracious houses and rank decay took hold of the lush woodlands. Hell had come to Holland County —to stay.

A Dell Book $2.95   (12245-7)

Dell Bestsellers

- [ ] **RANDOM WINDS** by Belva Plain \$3.50 (17158-X)
- [ ] **MEN IN LOVE** by Nancy Friday \$3.50 (15404-9)
- [ ] **JAILBIRD** by Kurt Vonnegut \$3.25 (15447-2)
- [ ] **LOVE: Poems** by Danielle Steel \$2.50 (15377-8)
- [ ] **SHOGUN** by James Clavell \$3.50 (17800-2)
- [ ] **WILL** by G. Gordon Liddy \$3.50 (09666-9)
- [ ] **THE ESTABLISHMENT** by Howard Fast.........\$3.25 (12296-1)
- [ ] **LIGHT OF LOVE** by Barbara Cartland \$2.50 (15402-2)
- [ ] **SERPENTINE** by Thomas Thompson \$3.50 (17611-5)
- [ ] **MY MOTHER/MY SELF** by Nancy Friday \$3.25 (15663-7)
- [ ] **EVERGREEN** by Belva Plain \$3.50 (13278-9)
- [ ] **THE WINDSOR STORY**
  by J. Bryan III & Charles J.V. Murphy \$3.75 (19346-X)
- [ ] **THE PROUD HUNTER** by Marianne Harvey ..\$3.25 (17098-2)
- [ ] **HIT ME WITH A RAINBOW**
  by James Kirkwood \$3.25 (13622-9)
- [ ] **MIDNIGHT MOVIES** by David Kaufelt \$2.75 (15728-5)
- [ ] **THE DEBRIEFING** by Robert Litell \$2.75 (01873-5)
- [ ] **SHAMAN'S DAUGHTER** by Nan Salerno
  & Rosamond Vanderburgh \$3.25 (17863-0)
- [ ] **WOMAN OF TEXAS** by R.T. Stevens \$2.95 (19555-1)
- [ ] **DEVIL'S LOVE** by Lane Harris \$2.95 (11915-4)
